Aren't We Sisters?

PATRICIA FERGUSON

PENGUIN BOOKS

For Richard, Tom and Roly, again

PENGUIN BOOKS

Published by the Penguin Group
Penguin Books Ltd, 80 Strand, London WC2R ORL, England
Penguin Group (USA) Inc., 375 Hudson Street, New York, New York 10014, USA
Penguin Group (Canada), 90 Eglinton Avenue East, Suite 700, Toronto, Ontario,
Canada M4P 2Y3 (a division of Pearson Penguin Canada Inc.)
Penguin Ireland, 25 St Stephen's Green, Dublin 2, Ireland (a division of Penguin Books Ltd)
Penguin Group (Australia), 707 Collins Street, Melbourne, Victoria 3008, Australia
(a division of Pearson Australia Group Pty Ltd)
Penguin Books India Pvt Ltd, 11 Community Centre, Panchsheel Park, New Delhi – 110 017, India
Penguin Group (NZ), 67 Apollo Drive, Rosedale, Auckland 0632, New Zealand
(a division of Pearson New Zealand Ltd)
Penguin Books (South Africa) (Pty) Ltd, Block D, Rosebank Office Park,
181 Jan Smuts Avenue, Parktown North, Gauteng 2193, South Africa

Penguin Books Ltd, Registered Offices: 80 Strand, London WC2R ORL, England

www.penguin.com

First published 2014
001

Set in 12.5/14.75pt Garamond MT Std
Typeset by Jouve (UK), Milton Keynes
Printed in Great Britain by Clays Ltd, St Ives plc

ISBN: 978-0-241-96647-1

www.greenpenguin.co.uk

Lettie

Lettie Quick believed in what she was doing as other women believed in the Trinity: she was spreading a faith. To this end she had suffered. She had worked for even lower wages than she earned at present, had in the early days fought her way to work through placard-wielding mobs shouting *murderer, whore*, and found shards of glass in her hair one evening, from a half-brick flung through the clinic window.

When Dr Stopes had come up with her travelling-caravan idea, Lettie had instantly volunteered. A mobile clinic, drawing up week by week in a different town or village, spreading the precious knowledge all across the country! It was another masterstroke, to Lettie; in those days she had adored the Madam. But it soon turned out that no one wanted to climb in or out of a van so clearly marked. And if it wasn't clearly marked, how would anyone know what the van was supposed to be for? Hardly a soul had turned up anywhere but even so on a trip to Bradford someone had managed to set the bloody thing on fire, and not before time, thought Lettie by then, but the Madam had been distraught.

'It is stark madness,' she had cried. 'Why must our culture deny the existence and purity of marital passion?'

It was best, Lettie had found, not to smile when the Madam said things like that, though the idea of pure marital passion down some dank gunnel in Poplar was enough, some of the girls said, to make a cat laugh.

Still, the idea of travel had stuck, for Lettie. Why not set up officially, then, with discreet Council support: get things moving, train up the locals, and move on to pastures new! If most current practice was still essentially home-made – the plug of beeswax, the wad of waxed paper, cotton wool smeared with vaseline and dipped in boracic powder – essentially home-made, and ineffective, or wholly reliant on the willingness and cooperation of Men – if the whole country lay in such utter darkness, what was more important than personally spreading the light?

'So, have you been using anything already, Mrs Tucker?'

'Well – yes, but . . . not very . . . you know, not very nice –'

Which meant do-it-yourself. Something sticky out of the larder, something perilously hard to get fully out again, something that stained the sheets or hurt you or made your husband look sick.

'Well, ah, he's been using one of them, you know, them French things – and sometimes he just ain't got one, or it's been in his wallet so long that –'

Which meant the sheath.

'We'll find out what suits you best – so it's up to you. It's you gets pregnant, not him.'

Usually Lettie begins with the cervical cap. She takes out the first little box, all clean and new.

'Here. Ever seen one of these before?'

The cap is folded into soft clean white muslin prettily tied (one of the Madam's ideas, of course) with a bit of blue ribbon; as the Madam also suggested, she has chosen for her example the very smallest size. She unties the bow, unwraps it, and sets it, mushroomy, delicate-looking, in her own clean palm.

'See it's like a little bell? Bit thicker round the top – see?' She turns the thing over, so that its inner ridge may be inspected. 'It's very soft.' She squeezes it, demonstrating bendy resilience, and smiles a little. 'Not that bad, really, is it?'

If Lettie had her way, the way of her faith, the cervical cap would be as familiar a shape as the socks on any husband's feet, and displayed in shop windows like sweeties for all to admire and choose – if Lettie had her way the cap would not be made only in witless pink imitation of skin tone but in a rainbow of colours and choices, pretty stripes, pink and white dots, gold stars, why not?

As it is she waits, while the wretched woman sitting in the client's chair beside her thinks about whether the ordinary pale example on display can in any way be said to be anything but revolting, while she wonders whether she could ever bear to touch one, let alone pick it up and put it – oh God, and how on earth it's supposed to – oh Lord, and while she remembers with strengthening despair just why it is that she is here in the first place.

'Here. Take it, go on. That's right. Just a little bit of rubber. But reliable. That's No More Worry, that is, that little thing. That's almost all you need, right there. See?'

Giving them time, that's the main thing, time to relax a little, to understand that Lettie is giving them permission to think and talk in detail about things usually kept secret, or hidden behind those baffling vaguenesses, health, efficiency, purity, and racial strength. Time to realize that above everything else Sister Quick is *on their side*. She's not just an expert here; she's been a customer herself. This is where the wedding ring on her left hand is such a help. A little unprofessional, certainly, but she is serving the faith. Her voice very low: 'Of course I'm a widow now, but this is what I used to use myself. Bit difficult at first, but you get the knack ever so fast. And – it's *discreet*.'

Which further enables her to say something hardly anyone ever dares to ask about; perhaps because it simply doesn't occur to them there and then. But Lettie prefers to get this particular reassurance in early, just in case: not every husband knows all his wife's concerns. Not every husband shares them.

'What I mean is, your husband won't' (voice lowered even further) 'ever *feel* it. Far as he's concerned' (pause for emphasis, so that all implications will eventually sink in) 'there's nothing there at all. See?'

That's the first few hurdles over. But the next are much higher: the examination. The half-undressing in a strange place, in front of the waiting hard high table-like bed, its cold oilcloth draped with a slippery sheet, and the electric light suggestively mounted on a wall bracket beside it.

'All set?'

Lettie enters from the outer office, or in less salubrious places from behind the folding screen, with her apron on and her hands freshly washed. She proceeds as quietly as possible. She has lain on such hard high beds herself, and fully understands the horripilating power of the squeaking trolley wheel, the padded chink of steel instruments being set out in preparation on a covered tray, and the snap of rubber gloves.

'I'm going to be slow and gentle, you say if it hurts, alright?'

First-timers should always be thoroughly checked. That was one of the Madam's maxims. There are all sorts of things to look out for.

'Now, just bend your knees up, ankles together. That's it, keep your ankles like that, and just let your knees fall apart. Perfect. Touch of cold water now. Sorry –'

Entertaining, thinks Lettie sometimes, how much everyone varies down there. You never know what to expect. Meek little mousey-haired creatures take off their drawers and there's Blackbeard the Pirate, springy and magnificent; redheads faded brown with the years may still be brilliantly pale orange in private; some glamorous blondes turned out not to match themselves at all. There are the crisply gilded, the neatly tufted, the matted, the gnarled, the almost bald; none of it particularly related, it seems, to hair anywhere else: a hidden array of localized personality. Or as if each woman were following not so much a pattern of humanity as a rough guide.

Nor is there any particular standard for the inner lips. It all makes what Lettie is really looking for just a little harder to spot: the distortions of trauma and poor healing, scar tissue, disease, infection, prolapse.

Then the speculum. She holds it in her hands to warm it. The light is on, properly angled, so that she can nudge it into perfection with her elbow. She dips the thing in her bowl of warm water, carefully parts the labia with one hand, introduces the shining steel with the other.

5

Sideways it slips in easily enough. It's turning it right-way round that's uncomfortable, and opening up the long beak of its curved distending blades that hurts, forcing potential passage into actuality.

'Nearly there, ever so still now, that's right –'

Lettie directs the light, and stoops to look through. The walls of the revealed tunnel gleam reddish in the lamplight, pressing softly inwards on either side of the long steel beaky jaws. There is variety here too, of breadth and length, reflecting the bony structures underneath, the widely varying shapes of pelvic brim, cavity, and outlet. She measures, calculates. The neck of the womb, that little circular nub of flesh, hangs centrally right at the back, its little mouth slightly open as if meekly pouting, for this, of course, is a cervix that has already opened wide to let a baby through, usually more than once, more than twice: for the law requires that officially Nurse Quick may deal only with the married.

'Perfect,' says Lettie this time, and she withdraws the speculum and switches off the light and gives the poor thing a moment to recover while she herself decides which type, which size of cervical cap to go for: always the Madam's preference if she can – the Madam was very down on diaphragms.

She holds out the right-sized cap, never as small and neat of course as the one first on show, but the correct multiparous size.

'See, you just put a bit of the jelly inside. And you squeeze it together, like this. And you pop it in. You could try it with one foot up on a chair. Or crouching. But you let go of it – and it just sort of *jumps* into place. On to the neck of the womb – it's working by suction, see? That's why you have to get the right size fitted.'

Sometimes they're game, even eager, to try straight away there and then; sometimes they need a little persuasion. 'You see,' Lettie must explain, 'if you just take it home to try, you won't have had any experience of taking it out again. And that can be the hardest part at first. I just need to know you've done it the once, see?'

Often the poor soul can't manage any of it. Can't get the thing in at all. Can't get it out again.

'Just a fingertip. And then gently pull sideways. Loosens the suction. No?'

But perhaps until this afternoon, until this very hour, the patient had no prior knowledge or personal acquaintanceship with her own insides at all. She has borne three children but if told what an orifice was and pressed to say how many of them there are between her legs, she would have said Two. All these years she's assumed without thinking about it at all or wanting to that she pees out of the same place her husband has sexual relations with; naturally enough, since this is the arrangement he so evidently has himself.

But newly in the know or not, the patient still has to get over putting her own fingers there, and of all the information Lettie's clients tend to have had at their disposal already, this is the most widespread: Don't touch yourself down there at all, because it's not just immodest and dirty, it's *wrong*.

'How you getting on?' calls Nurse Quick from the outer office, or from behind the folding screen, while the patient in the exam room struggles to commit dirtiness and wrong in private.

'I just check, make sure the fit's right? . . . Oh yes. That's right – perfect!'

Or if the thing is still impossible, if the cervix is too far away, too far back at the end of a vagina rather longer than usual, there are the Madam's despised diaphragms to try. Less discreet, perhaps, these wedges across the passage, not so much closing the door as obstructing it; Lettie has a variety, simple coin-shapes of curved amber rubber, which must fit with a fine exactitude to work, and the newer thin membranous kind with springy circumferential metal rings, which must be compressed before insertion, and which naturally at first tend to slip through the fingers when well jellied and ping themselves right across the room. Lettie only smiles if the patient does.

'Never mind. Happens to everyone. Try again –'

And eventually, sooner, later, the woman has what she came for. She has control, sovereignty. She can put the thing in, or not; it's all up to her. Control means freedom. No need to specify what from.

'Best to set up a routine,' says Lettie finally, when the patient has straightened her hemline and stockings, put her hat and gloves back on, checked herself in the mirror Lettie has caused for that purpose to be hung near the door. 'Every night at the same time, even if you don't usually have relations. Just in case. Makes it harder to forget. Because one thing's for sure: no matter what you use, no matter how good it is, it won't stop you getting pregnant if you leave it in the box.'

There is not a detail of the entire interview that Lettie, virtuoso of contraception, has not consciously thought about, rehearsed, carefully adjusted. It is as kind,

8

sympathetic, and practical as she can make it. I really am the best, Lettie thinks to herself quite often, with a little sigh of satisfaction, as she writes up her notes, or tidies her office after a long, full afternoon.

Three comforting thoughts: Only contraception can save the world. I am spreading the word. I'm the absolute best.

Surely this extreme professional virtue more than balances out any private personal lapses? So Lettie thinks. The lapses are mainly on the side of right in any case, she believes.

```
A client finds herself in difficulties, and has
asked for discreet assistance . . .
A sincere client of more than ample
means . . .
A distinguished client in urgent need of
privacy . . .
```

Such letters, typed, unsigned, arrive at Lettie's office, wherever that might be, at widely spaced and irregular intervals, but very much to her eventual financial advantage. There are risks involved, of course. But in a while, only a year or two more, perhaps, the special bank account will reach the right sum.

Security, that's all she's asking for. I'm not greedy, Lettie reminds herself, slipping the wedding ring back in her pocket, buttoning up the drab gabardine raincoat, setting the hard felt hat firmly central on her head. I'm not greedy.

Well, not very.

Norah

After her mother died Norah Thornby had a bad few months. She was very troubled, for example, by a bag of potatoes in the scullery cupboard. She had bought too many, and soon they were sprouting little white pointed shoots.

'Ought to use those up,' Norah had thought to herself, but the little shoots seemed somehow touching in their hopefulness; she decided to have bread and butter instead. But after that she kept forgetting them, and went on opening the scullery cupboard and being shocked, by shoots that had quickly grown longer and longer into something more like waggling spindly arms, topped here and there with tiny pallid leaflets.

Presently she could not close the cupboard door at all, for fear of trapping the shoots, and severing the little imploring leafletty fingers. Norah had dealt with the situation by avoiding the scullery altogether, and washing her smalls in the kitchen.

She forgot a great many other things too, committee meetings, library books, choir practice, and dental appointments. It seemed to take her much longer than before to get through her normal working day at the estate agency; she muddled files, put the wrong letters in addressed envelopes, left a folder of private papers on a bus. Once she found herself walking down the lane heading towards the coast road, out to Wooton, and completely unable to remember why. She was carrying her briefcase, but when she opened it for clues had to sit down for a moment on the grass verge, weak with unease; the bag contained only her embroidery, and while it was bad enough thinking that someone had inexplicably broken into her home to fool about with her belongings, it was rather worse when common sense prevailed.

Was it perhaps her time of life? She had read somewhere of perfectly normal women suddenly developing all sorts of peculiarities as middle age approached, going off their heads, in fact. Women without men, without children, were especially prone, it seemed, like dogs that hadn't been allowed to have puppies.

Now and then Norah felt an intense shame at not being married. Everyone sneered at spinsters, and who could blame them? What had you been born for, if not to marry and have children? But sometimes she was able to push past this steady weight in her mind. You were born to live, that was all. You were born to do your best. And one might take a certain pride, she could sometimes tell herself, in turning away from the whole unimaginable business.

Literally unimaginable for Norah, who had been raised in complete ignorance of anything sexual, and had gathered only patchy information since. She had the basics: male anatomy was not a complete mystery to her, and she knew that the man's penis somehow stiffened, and that this stiffness enabled him to insert it in some way into the woman. But this struck her as not just frighteningly crude and unpleasant, involving as it did those body parts more usually concerned with the frank dirtiness of excretion, but inherently unlikely – how could anyone want to try something so bizarre?

There were questions Norah hardly dared frame to herself, though not knowing the answers occasionally bothered her. How long, for instance, did the insertion have to go on for? Perhaps it was brief. Birds took no time at all, she had often seen a cockerel leap on to a hen and off again without the female having so much as looked up from her grain. But it seemed likely that human beings took longer. There was so much fuss about the process after all. A woman's honour, and so on; that was important; there had to be more to it than mere birdlike leapings.

But her vague mental picture of sexual engagement was essentially avian, a silent congress with both parties needing to keep fairly still once in the correct position: rather as Norah herself had once, for several uncomfortable minutes, beneath the dentist's drill.

And surely it must hurt. Not that she had ever discussed it with anyone, but it was obvious to her that insertion must hurt the woman. Clearly it didn't hurt men; she was aware that on the contrary the process was something they were particularly keen on. Women of course didn't feel like that, but put up with it. A woman had to allow insertion if she wanted children. It was the price married women had to pay.

But worst of all was the spine-chilling notion, gathered from various sources during her wartime experience as a VAD, that once the insertion process was underway it was dangerous, in fact impossible, to stop it. A man could not, it seemed, alter his course. Once a woman had agreed, and let him start, or at any rate reach a certain point (whatever that might be, another blank) she had to go through with it, because the man had no choice, he was physically unable to desist. As if he had just jumped off a high place, he couldn't change his mind: he must fall. How terrifying it would be, thought Norah, to be helplessly alone with a man who had abandoned his normal everyday self and let the unstoppable animal process take him over! Of slightly less but still considerable horror was the idea of clothes, the impossible embarrassment of taking off one's drawers in front of someone else, and the someone else a *man*!

Sometimes, as she half considered these ideas, a certain quick slithery sensation lightly darted through Norah's insides, a sort of deep shiver she associated with fear, and generally took as a signal that it was time to jump sensibly out of bed, or concentrate properly on her sewing, or pick up her book again, or at any rate firmly to think about something else.

Perhaps it was a little galling, to be so ignorant, when so many completely uneducated people obviously knew all there was to know. But what they knew was shameful, after all. Everything that Norah didn't know helped to keep her pure, and purity was valuable in itself. In some way she did not understand, but had implicit faith in, virginity had grace. Part of the consolation of religion, for Norah, was the respect it seemed to accord to purity and virginity. She was not quite aware of this, though, and thought she went to church every week from conventional religious conviction, and because she liked the hymns, especially at Evensong.

Though in fact what she felt at St George's, even at the most perfect Evensong, was nowhere near as intense, as uplifting, as lasting, as the wonderfully complete release from being Norah Thornby that she achieved, also once a week, in the smoky shifting darkness of the Picture Palace, or recently, even better, the Silkhampton Rialto.

Norah's mother had simply not noticed cinema, any more than she had known the whereabouts of the local gymnasium or the nearest four-ale bar. Such things had not concerned her. But every Thursday, while she had attended the last of her remaining charitable committees, Norah had made her choice, paid over her one and tuppence, and departed this life for an entire blissful Palace or Rialto evening.

It was almost enough to keep her going until the following week, especially if it was helped along by the *Film Lover's Weekly*, which in those days of relative plenty had arrived by post every Monday direct from London, in a discreet plain brown wrapper, to be read in greedy secret and then hidden in the suitcase beneath the bed: pages of photographs of stills from coming delights, interspersed with beautiful studio portraits of wonderfully perfect young women and clear-eyed young men, all wearing lovely new clothes, the women often holding bouquets or kittens; there were also brief articles beneath each photograph, about the actor's earlier films or stage background and future plans. The young men sometimes held pipes, and smiled into the camera, showing their perfect teeth, their smooth faces glistening with health; the young women often confessed to a desire to travel the world, or learn how to fly an aeroplane; they had often decided to further their careers by moving to America, or sometimes adored being back on the London stage, where they felt so delightfully at home.

The *Film Lover's Weekly* was like nothing Norah had ever read before. It was so optimistic, for one thing, its pages crackling with the powerful energy of Hollywood itself. It seemed to promise a complete world of choice and beauty, and of a strange complex excitement, as if the stories in the films Norah saw at the Palace or the Rialto had somehow had a lasting effect on the actors who played in them; as if anyone, even Norah, might share that excitement, taste it just a little on the tongue. It was the closest Norah could get to the haven of cinema at home.

Of course she had cancelled the subscription straight away, as soon as she had understood that every single penny counted, when Mamma's small pension had died with her, and still rather missed those fresh new Monday-morning arrivals; though of course these days she was able to go to the pictures almost any night she chose, albeit in the cheapest seats right at the back; would (and had) rather go to bed hungry than miss a programme change.

But how was she to live? That was the question that had roughly slapped her awake night after night. She was four years older than the century; in September she would be thirty-six. The last few years had sapped her, she thought, they had aged her, they had made her catch up with Mamma. They had been two querulous old ladies together, saving up for little treats, arguing over the merits of new embroidery stitches, petulant if the tea tray was brought in late.

In better times Norah might have sub-let her old home, and moved somewhere smaller. But she knew perfectly well from her work that houses like this one, so old-fashioned when it came to heating and bathroom, full of heavyweight Victorian furniture and dreary with faded wallpaper and threadbare carpet, would never find a tenant. Not even for the summer, this far from the sea.

At night sometimes, Norah pictured herself in her bed in the second-floor back, as if the house were a doll's house; she saw all of it, the rooms full of varying furniture, all in scale, matching, all of it carefully chosen to look as much like a real house as possible. Herself the only occupant, not really cosy in bed but a lifeless simulacrum, a stiff little dolly, part of the furnishings that went with the house.

Five floors of doll's house: at once home, refuge, and inescapable cage.

Interlude

It was her perfection, he said. Her secret beauty. He just wanted to keep a record, a proof. It would be entirely private, of course, it would be something just the two of them knew about and shared.

Him? Well, yes, of course, if she wanted him to.

Laughing: 'I'll wear whatever you wear. Promise.'

A winter afternoon, the curtains drawn against the chill, nice little fire glowing in the grate. The camera ready on its tripod.

'What, now?'

'Yes. Now.'

'Well – how, then? I feel a bit, you know –'

'Don't worry. I'll direct you. You look, oh, wonderful . . .'

He touches her. He stands behind her, his fingertips lightly caressing her nipples.

'Just here. And bend over a little. Lean on the table. That's right. Little more. Oh, lovely. Can you look over your shoulder at me? Yes. And smile. Hello, darling.'

flash

'Bend a little further. Oh God.'

flash

'Can you turn round now? And –'

He gestures, cupping his hands round his own naked chest.

'Yes, but look right up, up at the ceiling while you – yes. Oh, yes.'

flash

'Mmm – oh, come here, that's enough, that's quite enough of that, quick, you, you –'

That was how it started. Both of them naked, and laughing, in it together, literally in it together sometimes. He could do that, rig the camera somehow so that it flashed only when he had joined her. He couldn't get enough of her then, nor she of him.

Once when she was having a cup of tea in the café he had passed by outside, and seen her. He had come in, saluting one or two other familiar faces, and briefly sat down at her corner table, his manner abstracted and professional as he looked through his bag for a particular envelope.

'Ah, here it is. Thought these might be of some interest to you, Sister.'

She had slit the envelope open with a clean butter knife, assuming of course it was something official; opened it there and then in the Little Owl Tearooms, tables nearby crowded with locals, and what seemed to be dozens of photographs had slipped out on to the starched white tablecloth, large glossy black-and-white images: she sat naked with her knees apart, she wore nothing but high heels and bent right over, she knelt, offering her breasts.

'What do you think?'

Covering them fast with her napkin, breathing hard.

'Good, aren't they!'

His face unreadable.

'Just a joke,' he said afterwards. God, what was she

getting in such a state about? No one had seen anyway. He thought it was wild, so many nice old ladies sipping their tea, and all the while in a corner these marvellously undeniably pornographic –

'– Porn*ograph*ic?'

'Well yes, that's what it means: arousing. Literally arousing photographs. See them and *rouse*.' Nuzzling her neck by then, so that her insides dissolved with happiness, happy body winning out over uneasy mind. Uneasy mind making all sorts of clever excuses for him, coming up with arguments on his account. He made none of them himself.

At night sometimes as she lay in her bed she pictured the two of them in the Little Owl Tearooms that day. He in his sober grey suit, she in tweed and her spectacles, with her hat on straight, and her secret body displayed all over the table in front of her.

Sometimes she thought about Marion, whom she had arranged to meet in the Little Owl Tearooms that afternoon, and who had been delayed by a patient. But suppose she'd come after all! Suppose Marion had, say, just gone to the Ladies or something as he came in, and arrived back at the table as she was slitting open the envelope! Sometimes, imagining this, she let a photograph fall, and made her friend bob down for it, pick it up, and turn it over, while she and he waited, their eyes on each other, for Marion to understand what it was she was seeing.

She began to long for him to run the risk again.

Lettie

She was restless; a year anywhere was long enough. And she was certainly very bored with David. What had she ever seen in him? That was a question Lettie had often asked herself over the years, about various types, and usually the only answer was a shrug.

That autumn evening was all David's idea, and she didn't fancy it; felt far more like going somewhere lively, bit of dancing, maybe. Art galleries not her cup of tea, thanks.

No, no, she didn't understand, he said. It wasn't an art gallery at all, it was some sort of travelling exhibition, all for charity – ex-servicemen – and of course they would go on anywhere she wanted to afterwards, please, darling Lettie – I said I'd go, d'you see. And it's in the West End –

Oh alright then, she said.

At least West End meant The Coat. A Vionnet. Her latest acquisition, and not something you could put on for any-old-where. Though sometimes Lettie liked to wear it at home with nothing on underneath, as if it were a dressing gown. This meant that it had certain swoony associations for David, who might thus be tiresome later on. But there, Life is full of trouble, thought Lettie idly in the taxi, stroking her discreetly splendid cuffs.

There was a waiter holding a tray just inside the hall door; she caught his eye as she helped herself to a glass of something. 'Thanks, mate,' she said to him, for the fun of seeing his face change.

The place was hung not with proper painted pictures, she saw, but with old photographs framed as if they were art, and all about them thronged the sipping chattering moneyed, men in cashmere, women in fur.

'Thought I'd lost you!' said David later. And so he had.

Some of the photographs were ancient, women in crinolines, city streets full of horses, all fairly dispiriting until she came to one labelled *The Square, Silkhampton*, and gave a little gasp aloud of pleasure and surprise.

The Square, Silkhampton, was crammed with market stalls, and people with antique clothes and faces, and cheeses as big as cartwheels.

Perhaps Mum had known those stalls, walked about on those cobbles, maybe admired those very cheeses. Perhaps if the camera had veered off a bit to one side, it would have caught Rosie Quick aged eighteen, sitting on a wall or something in her ankle-length skirts and her whopping Edwardian hat, waiting out her time far from home.

Seduced and deserted, that was the phrase often applied to girls like Rosie; not that Dad had entirely deserted her, at the time, Lettie remembered. Though on balance, she thought, leaning in for a closer look at *The Square, Silkhampton*, it might have been better for everyone if he had.

Lettie had known about Silkhampton all her life, but until that evening she had hardly thought of it as real. It had been a special half-imaginary place where Mum had been young and pretty and hopeful, where she herself had been born, and where for a happy month or so, before they went back home again, it had been just the two of them, safe together all those years ago, Rose and Violet.

'Two flowers, you and me!'

Lettie could find no name attached to the photograph, just the initials PPS in white handwritten letters in the bottom right-hand corner. Presently she realized there was a whole wall of others: PPS really seemed to have gone in for historic market towns, crammed stalls in Truro, stony-faced women in huge boots cleaning fish in Penzance, idlers leaning in doorways in Launceston, scruffy children now and then caught eyeing the camera, all of them a pre-war world ago.

And not only in Cornwall: here was PPS doing London. The East End, look at that, two of Roman Road market! Lettie bent to look closer at the lank-haired women in shawls, the dirty children sitting in gutters.

And then.

Then her heart seemed to stop altogether.

After a while someone touched her arm. It was David. 'Bit of a crush,' he said. 'Ready to go?'

She said: 'Wait.'

The photograph was called *July 1914*. It showed a park in summer, bunting overhead, the edge of a bandstand to one side with a hazy suggestion of trumpets just visible; and throngs of young people standing – they were listening to the music, thought Lettie, the girls holding lacy parasols, the men in boaters, children in the foreground. In the bottom right-hand corner was written, in the same white handwritten capitals, small but perfectly clear, PYNCHEON PHOTOGRAPHIC STUDIOS, SILKHAMPTON.

July 1914. Dear God. Who would ever have guessed

that? PPS. From Silkhampton, where she and Mum had once been two flowers together.

'Lettie? Are you alright?'

'Yes – no – can you buy me this one? Please.'

'What? Oh, well, of course I'd love to, darling, but – it's not for sale.'

'Ask them.'

'It's just not that sort of show, I'm afraid.'

'Who does it all belong to then?'

'Well – some collector or another. I could find out for you – which one is it anyway, this one?' Stooping to look at it dispassionately, as if it were ordinary. 'Really? Why?'

None of your business, she thought.

'Might be able to get hold of a copy, I suppose,' he said, peering at it again. She wanted to push him violently away from it. Then she had the idea. After all, she was ready for pastures new anyway. Restless, looking for change. Hadn't fate just sent her a ruddy great sign?

'No, forget it. Never mind,' she said. She slipped her arm through David's, sumptuous fur-trimmed wool through decent tweed, and spoke as lightly as usual: 'Let's go, shall we?'

A week or so considering, and then she had written several letters, and made one or two appointments. If not Silkhampton itself then perhaps somewhere else nearby in the countryside; a bit of greenery might be a pleasant change.

But hardly a fortnight had passed before she had a letter from the local Borough Council, written in the usual circumspect code, inviting her to attend an interview there the following month, and soon she was cheerfully handing in her notice, packing her things, sending off one or two parcels, and finally giving David the mitten.

'I'll send you my address when I know it,' she told him, during their last evening together, trying to cheer him up. It was always best, she thought, to part friends. Just in case.

Norah

Alice Pyncheon dropped round, with a proposal. 'Saw Aunt Daphne yesterday. You know.'

'Yes?' Norah said, guardedly.

'Well, she's looking for lodgings, somewhere really central, she said. And I thought of you.'

'Me? Oh Lord, Alice – you didn't say anything, did you?'

'Steady on, it's not for her, you perfect idiot. Gosh, you are actually ashen-faced. At the very thought. I may take this personally.'

'Sorry, Alice, but –'

'Oh come, I was teasing; I wouldn't want her either, frankly, and she's my aunt, not yours. She's just so frightfully *capable*, isn't she.'

Once, as a young Ward Sister, The Hon. Daphne Redwood had the privilege of taking tea with Florence Nightingale herself, in the stuffy little front office of St Thomas'. Miss Nightingale had been in her mid seventies then, a shrunken old lady tucked into a plush high-seated wheelchair set carefully near the fire, her white hair almost hidden beneath her old-fashioned lacy bonnet. But when you saw her eyes, said Miss Redwood, you saw the very girl: dark still, and merry.

Miss Redwood's own eyes were of the palest blue-grey, and invariably serious behind her spectacles, though she certainly seemed to have taken on her share of Miss Nightingale's steelier qualities.

'She was marvellous on the committee,' said Norah now, 'you know, for the statue; Mother always says –' She broke off, remembering again.

Alice pretended not to notice. 'Now – I didn't actually say anything, of course I didn't, not without asking you first. But think about it – mightn't you take a lodger?'

'I hadn't considered it,' said Norah weakly, after a pause.

'Well, darling, *do* so!' said Alice. 'All this space. Empty rooms. Wouldn't it actually be rather jolly, having someone else about the place? And paying rent!'

Norah looked away. She had not fully confided in Alice, of course, for anything you told Alice would be passed on to Freddie, who was so unpredictable. She had allowed Alice to understand that circumstances were a little trying. Though in fact desperate would have been nearer the mark. Already a roof-repair bill loomed unpayable.

'Well – who, then?'

'A person,' said Alice grandly, 'recently appointed by the Borough. You know, the committee Aunt Daphne bosses around – anyway, she made them appoint this woman, and she's the one who needs somewhere to live, very soon – for at least six months, anyway. What d'you think?'

'But – oh, Alice, how could I – the house isn't nice enough, I mean, there isn't that good a boiler, you know, we're always running out of hot water.'

'She might not be too particular,' said Alice. 'Oh, but I don't suppose you'd *want* someone who wasn't too particular, would you? I wouldn't.'

Norah laughed.

'No, no, really I meant, imagine *Freddie* with someone who wasn't too particular! I wouldn't mind a bit for myself. Talking of whom – I should be off; I've left him on his own all afternoon, poor darling.'

'Quickly, then – tell me about this woman.'

'Well – I don't know much. A single working person, you know – not a gentlewoman.'

'Oh. Well, I work, Alice – am I a gentlewoman?'

'Near as makes no difference, my dear.'

'Thank you,' said Norah.

'She's – well, running some sort of ghastly female clinic. One of Aunt Daphne's bees-in-the-bonnet sort of thing, you know,' said Alice vaguely, and got up, gathering her scattered impedimenta, scarf, gloves, cardigan, three library books and a string shopping bag bulging with tins. 'May I tell Aunt that I might know somewhere, then? Otherwise – you know what she's like – she'll find somewhere else double-quick.'

'So – I'm sorry, Alice, I don't quite understand – is she a nurse then, this woman?'

'A midwife, I think – I wanted to keep this from you, but apparently she is and I quote – Aunt Daphne, I mean – "a very good type of person, hard-working, used to roughing it, and absolutely above reproach".'

'Oh,' said Norah.

'I *know*, sounds simply frightful, doesn't she! But remember – it's only for a while. And it's decent money, Norah. Now I really must go, or Freddie will have one of his turns, and we don't want that, do we? No indeed . . .'

'Alice? Well – yes. Alright then, let Miss Redwood know. That I say yes. And thank you.'

'Oh topping,' said Alice.

After that various letters had set in train an inexorable process.

The night before the stranger arrived Norah, who had slept a little better in the intervening weeks, partly due to the physical labour involved in doing all her own spring-cleaning – for there was nothing, she had discovered, like taking a lodger to make you see quite how frowzy certain corners of your home were, how dirty its curtains, how dusty its carpets, and in particular how crazy it was to let potatoes grow into spindly plant-life in your scullery cupboard – Norah had still wondered, at bedtime, whether it was actually worth going to bed at all, when she felt so acutely nervous.

The coming Person had slowly assumed a certain solidity in her mind, at once as vague and vivid as a dream. It was never the woman's face that Norah envisaged, but her heft, a large mealy softness spread into armchairs. Certainly the Person wrote a cramped childish hand on cheap lined paper; very much not a gentlewoman, if you cared about that sort of thing, which, Norah told herself, she did not, but all the same it was hard to see how having such a possibly *very* common guest at dinner night after night (used to roughing it!) was going to be tolerable.

Cooking: that was a huge worry in itself. In later years Norah had learnt how to open tins of corned beef and slice the contents very thinly; she could cope with eggs, slice and butter bread, grate carrots, and boil potatoes.

28

She could do several on the whole disappointing things with mince. 'Plain English Cookery will suffice,' Miss Redwood had said, in her grand, careless way, but perhaps she had not meant quite as Plain as all that.

In any case the Borough Council had already paid a decent deposit on the Person's behalf, and Norah had paid for the roof tiles. There was certainly no going back. Norah spent the wretched night she had expected, and left for the office feeling heavy with dread. She only worked a half-day on Wednesdays, but the hours were still hard to get through, and when Miss Pilbeam spoke coldly to her about some missing carbon paper, it was all Norah could do not to cry. She couldn't face lunch, but came straight home.

The market was still in full noisy swing, the air thick with the smell of frying onions, and as if things weren't bad enough, thought Norah bitterly, it was one of those weeks when the three dingy semi-beggars showed up, with accordion, violin, and comb-and-paper, their card on the pavement reading EX-SERVICEMEN, their several crutches propped nearby against a lamp post.

She let herself in to 'Tea for Two', rendered as if for a funeral, sat limply down at the foot of the stairs and put her head in her hands. It was all too cruelly clear to her now, when it was far too late, that she had allowed herself once more to be ruled by timidity. Despite all she had vowed in the first days after Mamma's death, she had feebly agreed to the first escape plan someone else had come up with. Had she even *tried* to assert herself? No. No, she had not. She had laid herself down and let Alice and her beastly aunt walk all over her, and so was now stuck for months on end with some vulgar professional baby-fancier, who would knit bootees every evening and noisily suck bonbons, and simper non-stop about Little Ones!

'Oh God!' groaned Norah aloud; and then there was a loud rap on the door. She jumped up. The Person in person! Could she pretend to be out? Could she actually run away, just leave by the back door?

No. No, she could not. Come along, Norah, she thought to herself. No getting out of it now. She reached out, and opened the door.

She would remember her fears, her pounding heart and trembling knees for the rest of her life. Perhaps she had been right all along, she sometimes thought. She remembered Miss Redwood's description too, of the very good type of person, hard-working, used to roughing it, and absolutely above reproach.

She had repeated it to Lettie herself once.

'Spot on,' Lettie had said deadpan, and after a moment they had both burst out laughing.

After the War Mamma had been much put about by servant trouble. Cooks inflated bills, kitchen maids broke quantities of china and threw cutlery out with the peelings – or more likely pawned it – and chambermaids knocked figurines off mantelpieces with broom handles. Singly they had stomach aches, bad legs, spots, moods, and endless sniffles – most unpleasant when one was being served at table. Together they ate food for an army, squabbled, ganged up on one another, had occasional comprehensive servants'-hall rows involving shrieking, name-calling, and once actual fisticuffs, and worst of all had what Mrs Thornby called 'followers'.

Followers hung about in the area outside the kitchen door in the morning, wasting the time – paid for by Mrs Thornby, of course – of kitchen maid or cook, by engaging them in empty-headed chatter. Followers were largely deliverymen of some kind or another, intent in any case on giving Mrs Thornby short change. They connived with the thieving footmen and laundry maids, all of them certain, it seemed to Mrs Thornby, that she was simply made of money. They thought her so filthy rich that a few shillings here and there quietly shifted from her pocket to theirs would neither show nor matter, if indeed she so much as noticed the loss; or even worse they claimed (and Mrs Thornby often pictured them laughingly doing so, in dark and grimy public bars) that such quiet shifting would not technically count as stealing, as they were all of them pretending to believe in the pernicious Bolshevik nonsense spouted by the various organs of the socialist gutter press.

Followers above all of course were out to corrupt the morals of silly girls too weak-minded to see where their own real interests lay, which were in truth to go on respectably working, rather than giggling and flaunting their very few or indeed completely non-existent physical charms; not that even the most disconcerting levels of personal plainness seemed to put followers off entirely, as Mrs Thornby, cunningly selecting the most unprepossessing specimen on offer from the Register, had more than once been disgusted and baffled to see.

'Mary is in my moral charge,' Mrs Thornby once crossly

explained to her husband, when he had one morning expressed the idea that some half-trained kitchen chit of seventeen, neither very bright nor entirely clean, might be allowed to choose her own friends for her afternoon out: 'I cannot encourage lewd behaviour in my own home.'

In some ways the collapse of her fortunes in 1923, on Mr Thornby's death – the discovery that the large double-fronted department store bearing his name, so imposingly part of the square for so many years, was not merely failing but already mortgaged – simplified things. Bit by bit Mrs Thornby retreated, from the upstairs drawing room, from the morning room; even from certain entrenched moral positions of her own, to do with the possibility of paid work for any woman with the least claim to gentility.

There was still the old parlourmaid Janet, of course, grown so very elderly that one simply could not let her go, despite her inadequacies; with help from Norah she could still manage meals and washing-up, though she made such a fuss about clearing the grates. One particularly bitter winter all three of them, Mrs Thornby, Norah, and Janet, had been forced every evening to sit together like equals in the kitchen, by then the only room in the house that was habitable; a circumstance Mrs Thornby found bearable only in the knowledge that Janet herself felt its shame, and so would not reveal it to her cronies, should she have any. But Janet had died before that winter was out. Of course there was no question of replacing her, and so Mrs Thornby's servant problems were finally at an end.

'It can't be that difficult,' she told Norah. 'We shall manage perfectly well between us: we are hardly helpless females.'

Norah made no reply to this. After a great deal of joint and private letter-writing and string-pulling she had at last secured what Mrs Thornby in public called *salaried employment*, in private *your beastly little job*. It was part-time but still undoubtedly better than nothing at all, and at the offices of Bagnold and Pender, Surveyors and Estate Agents.

'When I think what that miserable George Pender owed your father!' cried Mrs Thornby, but Norah suspected that the debt had long since shifted the other way about, and that Mr Pender, for all his pernickety ways, had simply been kind to the daughter of his old friend.

Domestic chores, said Mrs Thornby, would simply be shared between them. 'If I set the table and so on, you can start the cooking as soon as you come home!'

Norah had found her work hard at first. Typewriting machines had come on a great deal since her last experience of them, and the other girls in the office, both younger than she was, typed far more quickly and accurately than she could, and the head secretary, Miss Pilbeam, was often sarcastic. Should Norah misfile a document, which happened rather often during her first weeks, Miss Pilbeam liked to point out how seldom little Annie here, or Mrs Placket, had ever made such stupid mistakes, despite missing out on the expensive education that had been lavished on Miss Thornby, along no doubt with childhood ponies, kid gloves, velvet frocks and so on, while the others grinned and snorted.

Though Mrs Placket herself was decent enough to mutter 'Don't you mind 'er' in Norah's ear as she passed one morning; and later, when Miss Pilbeam's back was turned, Annie stealthily took a paper bag from her pocket, leant across, and offered Norah a toffee.

At home Mrs Thornby did a little dusting, less sweeping, and no washing-up, as prolonged immersion in soapy water affected her hands. Eventually she arranged for a local woman to come in every afternoon to clear away the breakfast things, and the remains of Mrs Thornby's simple luncheon, and to bring in tea on a tray before going home again, just in time for Norah, home from the beastly office job.

'Oh, we just have a little woman popping in these days,' said Mrs Thornby airily, when the slowly decreasing circle of her old friends met, and the ancient subject of servant-trouble came up; and then Mrs Caterham and Mrs Bingley would nod, and tell her how very wise she was.

But now she was gone, and so was her pension. And if you would rather have starved than take in lodgers, thought Norah on the evening of Miss Quick's arrival, well, Mamma, I would not, and starving has actually been on the cards.

The trouble was that on certain subjects Mrs Thornby, though dead, was now and then no less forthright than before. She seemed especially exercised about Miss Quick.

That accent — Norah, how can you bear it!

For passed her teacup that first afternoon Miss Quick had said 'Ta' in shameless cockney (*Pert!* hissed Mrs Thornby) and, asked if she wanted more, had replied, 'Alright.' She was small and meagre-looking; shown into Mamma's room afterwards she had looked about carelessly and said, 'Smashing, ta.'

Even conscious Norah had felt a little flattened by this

apparent insouciance. Mrs Thornby had been beside herself.

The impertinence! Who does she think she is?

She thinks she is my bread and butter, Norah reminded both herself and the frothing presence of her mother. And she's right. Anyway, I might come to know her; we might be friends one day.

Oh, what rot! sneered Mrs Thornby.

'The bathroom is at the end of the corridor,' said Norah aloud. 'I'm afraid there's only enough hot water for one rather small bath every day – I thought perhaps we should have some sort of rota.'

'Okay.'

'And dinner – what time should you prefer?'

'What – you mean it's just the two of us?'

'Yes, it is. So, ah, it's up to you.'

Miss Quick, who had been looking out of the window at the square, her hands in the pockets of her cardigan, turned round. 'You go out to work, don't yer?'

How dare you! gasped Mrs Thornby, insulted; Norah answered rather stiffly: 'Well, yes, I do, as it happens.'

Miss Quick seemed not to notice the stiffness. 'Let's not bother then.'

'I beg your pardon?'

'Let's not be all . . . ceremonial. You come home, you feel like cooking, fine, leave some for me, but if you don't feel like it, don't bother. I'll sort meself out.'

There are certain standards, Mrs Thornby began, then abruptly fizzled out.

'Makes sense, dunnit?' said Miss Quick, in what felt to Norah like a sudden quiet.

She thought about not bothering after all with the dining room, and its special starched tablecloths, and the steep turn of the stairs up from the kitchen, and all the trays that had to be carted up and down them; she thought about timetables, menu plans, and the resultant endless shopping; she remembered the time she had already spent worrying over Janet's only cookbook, a scruffy late Victorian edition of Mrs Beeton full of faded prints of catering nightmares, banqueting tables laden with pyramids of messed-about vegetables and enormous joints of meat, mammoth en croute, roast saddle of mastodon.

'Egg on toast do me,' said Miss Quick, as if she were party to these thoughts. 'In the kitchen. I mean, we're just two women, ain't we? Let's keep it simple – see how it goes?' She smiled.

'Um, alright then,' said Norah, but she was too anxious to smile back. Besides, Mrs Thornby had roused herself, and was worrying about the amount of tea leaves a stranger might get through, given free run of the kitchen.

'I'll let you settle in,' she said, and took herself and her mother away into the downstairs sitting room, and tried to think.

Norah had known for years that Mrs Thornby had been a difficult employer, high-handed, censorious, suspicious, and mean; she had stopped trying to intervene long ago, since it had seemed to do no one any good. Or maybe it had just been easier. But perhaps leaving her mother unchallenged had affected her own thinking; perhaps hauteur was infectious.

She remembered creeping down to the kitchen as a child, drawn in by the smell of baking, by the warm crowded comfort of that steamy busy place, and often being given a little cake for herself, and a lovely sit on someone's aproned lap, or a go at podding the peas. On her birthday there had always been a small spiced pastry N for Norah, crusted with toasted sugar, and dotted with currants, every single year, until the end: a present from Janet, the parlourmaid.

It is true, thought Norah carefully, that I shed more tears for Janet than ever I did for Mamma.

She got up and went to the window, to draw the curtains against the darkening sky. Outside, of course, as always, was the statue, of her brother and all the other long-lost young men. The thoughts that so often occurred to her as she saw him seemed especially vivid this evening: everything would have been different, Guy, if only you had come home. Papa would not have lost heart if you had been there all bright and lightsome and full of ideas, and ready to be first the Son and then the Thornby in your turn. When you were gone he didn't care.

Mamma would have been different too. Grief killed Father, but it poisoned Mamma: slow-acting, deadly.

Poisoned me too, maybe. Turned me into something else. Not that I know what I'm like. Except that I fear it's not up to much. Help me, Guy. Help me to be reasonable if I still can. Not mad.

Then Norah sat down with her library book, and tried to read over the faint alien noises coming from overhead, footsteps lightly crossing and recrossing, the rattle of the distant window sash, as the stranger in Mamma's room made herself at home.

Lettie

Though a newcomer Sister Quick was soon unremark-able; almost unnoticeable, in fact, in her uniform overcoat and hard felt hat. Within days it was established in town that she was heavily bespectacled and near or even past thirty; within weeks, that though she had not yet attended any service at St George's, she had joined the library and the Women's Institute, and had several times visited the market on a Wednesday, where it was known that she gen-erally bought two ounces of best ham, very thinly sliced.

In short Sister Quick herself was dull, as far as gossip went; far more intriguing was the juicy item, instantly common knowledge, that she was lodging not with the other midwives, Sisters Wainwright and Nesbit – well, how could she anyway, place that size – but with Miss Norah Thornby, of the square; who'd have thought it, what would the old lady have said – why, it didn't bear thinking about – dear Lord, what a comedown there!

As the months went by though a number of other women – for Sister Quick was surely more or less invisible to any passing male – had different ideas, for they had already consulted her in her professional capacity and knew her, in some ways, for what she was. But not one of those women, her clients, publicly spoke up, at some cheerful tea table, say, or over cocktails, or after choir practice, or at the Mothers' Union:

'Oh, I went to her last week, she was so helpful . . .'

'I'm going, Tuesday . . .'

'Of course I was terribly anxious, but she was completely reassuring . . .'

No. No one said anything like that. They kept quiet. Perhaps when the coast was clear two sisters shared a whispered confidence. Or old school friends spoke in carefully modulated voices over the telephone. Slowly the word would spread.

The new Silkhampton Mothers' Clinic was above the chemist's in a respectable but nondescript side street. Anyone, of any class in life, might need to pick up a prescription, or a tin of talcum powder; anyone might wander over to inspect the more exclusive soaps and bath oils in the glass-fronted cupboard at the back of the shop, linger there until the quiet moment of her choosing, pass through the open doorway in the far corner and vanish unnoticed up the turn of the stairs.

Lettie herself had quickly found and engaged the two rooms, had them freshly painted, furnished and equipped with proper lighting and a telephone; she had conferred with three sets of medical men, and contacted almost a dozen midwives; she had ordered the usual obscure leaflets and distributed them to all the local surgeries; she had acquired supplies. (Presented with receipts for these considerable expenses, the relevant committee of the Borough Council had instantly paid up without a murmur, thus avoiding any further discussion of a topic most of them found too disgusting to think about clearly, let alone name out loud; prudishness occasionally had its uses, Lettie thought.) Finally, in just over a fortnight, the clinic had opened up for business, fully equipped, up to the minute, and as always in almost perfect secrecy, as if the whole business were still illegal.

Though as it happened one of the special unsigned typed letters had arrived in the very first week.

```
So unhelpful of you, this decamping to the
wilds of Cornwall. We have a new client.
Affluent. Similar arrangement as last time,
except needs somewhere completely private.
Can you arrange that? How are you fixed,
generally — ready to go ahead? Let me know
as soon as you can.
```

Lettie, reading this at her office desk at the end of a long afternoon, tapped her front teeth with her pen as she considered. There were drawbacks to assent, apart from the obvious one of ending up in clink.

First off, she thought, she hadn't come here to play silly buggers, but on her own account for once, to see for herself the places her mother might have known, to stand where the PPS photographer had stood. She already knew, from the telephone directory in the Post Office, that Pyncheon Photographic Studios no longer existed, but there were still a couple of living Pyncheons promisingly residential, a Mr F. W. Pyncheon, and a Miss A. F., no more than five minutes' walk away from the square itself. Had one of them once been PPS, touring photographer, chronicler of historic market towns and moody streetscapes? She had made no move to contact either of them yet, but she had visited the market more than once, aware of an emotion she was unable to identify, though it had felt like longing.

I'm busy, she thought. And I don't know the manor. Where am I supposed to put someone in urgent need of privacy?

On the way back to her digs she walked all round the square until she came to the corner with the telephone box on it, and put through a trunk call. Mrs Esme Bright, she told his secretary.

'Mrs Bright, what can I do for you?' He just loved that sort of thing, thought Lettie, without affection.

'Better if you find the place yourself,' she said. 'How much, anyway?'

He told her, and her hand tightened on the receiver; it was nearly twice as much as last time. She thought fast.

'I want sixty-forty,' she said.

'Oh, do you indeed – and why is that?'

'Take it or leave it,' said Lettie, inspecting her fingernails, all different because she bit them.

'But, darling –'

'It's more of a risk.'

'I thought we were friends.'

'You know what we are. Look. If it's sixty-forty find her a place and send her along. If not, don't.'

He hung up then, silly bastard. Up to you, mate, thought Lettie. She checked her hat in the little mirror, and pushed the heavy door open.

Other fish to fry anyway.

There was a usual pattern to Lettie's official business: first nothing-doing at all, then one or two bold pioneers, then the steady increase, though always the numbers were lower than she wanted. Until it was time to move on, and she could hand the whole going concern over to someone else. This meant ensuring as early as possible that there would be a trained and willing someone else to hand over to; usually this meant the nearest local midwives, since it was so easy for them to tack on a little contraceptive know-how.

You could never tell, though. Sister Nesbit, a small narrow woman with cropped hair just beginning to grey, had been friendly enough at the welcoming tea party laid on at the surgery, and self-confident, one of those women, Lettie had thought as they shook hands, who would have married, had she belonged to any other generation. But at the same time Lettie had spotted the tiny gold crucifix Nesbit was wearing on a chain round her neck, discreet, but probably indicative.

Overt religion generally meant refusal, Lettie had found, along with membership of any political organization of any shade whatsoever; she had lost her own already minimal faith in the efficacy of politics after a Trades Union conference a few years back, when a Durham miner's wife had stood up and begged for party support for birth control: reminded the packed hall that it was four times as dangerous for a woman to bear a child as it was for her husband to go down the mine.

After the vote Lettie had torn up her Labour card.

Sister Wainwright looked more likely, on the whole, though she'd been a bit gushing at the tea party, seemed none too bright, and her careful accent put your teeth on edge, *Oh, how naice!* Still, thought Lettie at the end of a promisingly busy afternoon several weeks after her arrival, chances were in a place like this both midwives had delivered destitute women of their fifth or sixth unwanted babies; no matter how dim or pious you were, you tended to listen more readily to the good news when you'd seen and heard enough ailing little children downstairs, while up in some comfortless bedroom you were adding to their half-starved number.

And of course Nesbit and Wainwright would know about the usual alternatives, in a place as poor as this: the helpful neighbour, the friend of a friend, the one who knew how. But who sometimes didn't know how quite well enough.

For a moment, keeping these thoughts in her mind, Lettie sat very still at her desk, holding her breath. Then the time passed, and she looked about her, remembered that one day contraception would save the world. Try them both, she decided. Nesbit and Wainwright.

At least the person in urgent need of privacy was fully organized. He'd settled, of course, for sixty-forty, as she had known he would. Half the money had already reached her special account.

'How far along?' Mrs Esme Bright placing another discreet call from the phone box in the square.

'Thirty weeks – something like that. Young and healthy, everything fine. Arriving first week of January.'

'Where, exactly?'

'Very pleased with myself about that. Place called Rose-vear House, rather grand, used to be some sort of children's home or something, but empty now – for sale apparently. Very discreet skeleton staff, used to odd guests.

About six miles away from you – but near a branch line. Really isolated!'

'What's the good of that, then?'

'I told you, she wanted complete seclusion. Society lady or something, I don't know. None of our business. Calling herself Mrs Wickham.'

'How'm I supposed to get there, miles from anywhere?'

'Well, old love, that *is* your business.'

Silly git. 'Telephone?'

'Of course. So – it's all as before. Her ladyship lets you know when. You take the parcel on the train. Same address.'

'You mean in London? Couldn't you get somewhere closer?'

'What difference does it make?'

Trust him to think a woman with a newborn was unnoticeable, thought Lettie now. To him, maybe; to most men, probably. But not to any normal woman. I'll have to go First Class, she decided, wear a veil, take a late train. A married lady going home with Baby. Still noticeable, of course; just not at all Me.

Next item on the agenda, ladies and gentlemen: The Possibility. Increasingly likely, if I'm any judge, thought Lettie, with a delicious inner flicker of excitement. The question in his eyes had been showing more and more clearly; was it time to let him see her answer? Hardly sensible, with Society Lady in the offing. On the other hand, what good had holding back ever done her?

Lettie opened the top drawer of her desk. Here she kept a small private collection of untested products, one-offs, pioneering attempts from new companies:

re-usable condoms, obsolete diaphragms, sets of little white cotton drawstring bags each containing a taped continental sponge and a small knob-ended wooden stick to insert it with. Hidden amongst them, a hand mirror.

She switched on her table lamp, took off her spectacles, and looked at her own thin, colourless face, drawing back her lips to examine the wonky front teeth that showed when she smiled. Finally she met her own eyes, which were a very pale grey; once years ago a besotted young man had told her that her eyes were silver. She had quickly forgotten him, but never this one heartfelt compliment, which had changed the way she felt about herself ever afterwards.

Reassured again, she put the hand mirror back and got up to unbutton her uniform dress. Beneath it she was wearing her nicest underwear, a gleaming close-fitting rose-pink crêpe de chine. Pity about the stockings, work-aday lisle; but anything better might be noticed. At least they were a decent fit, and didn't matter much. Her dress mattered more, and would stay hidden until – unless – it was needed. She opened the cupboard and took out her raincoat: she had hung the dress behind it, smuggled it into the office that morning folded into tissue paper in her nurse's bag. She took it out now on its special padded hanger and gave it a little shake.

The dress was of plain black jersey, and its skirt had a dancing swing, as if it had a life of its own. There were three small buttons at the neck, on a neat little placket, and the black silk label hand-sewn into the collar read *Gabrielle Chanel Paris*, embroidered in gold; it was Lettie's dearest favourite, had been so ever since she had unobtrusively removed it from the dressing room of a grateful patient the year before.

Shouldn't have left it lying about, thought Lettie, slipping it off its hanger. The grateful patient had not exactly done so, of course, but then she hadn't locked it away either. Lettie slid the dress over her head, and shook the playful skirt free. Probably hasn't even noticed it's gone, she thought, doing up the buttons. And so what if she has? Bet she's got herself a couple more by now anyway, Lettie told herself, and after fluffing up her hair a little went to look in the tall mirror by the door, trying to see herself as the Possibility might. Not that men really saw your frock; all they saw, she thought, was the broad intention behind it, the *yes* or the *no*.

Most outfits were hardly that definite, of course. But the trick, thought Lettie complacently, was to know exactly what your dress was saying, and to know whether it agreed with the rest of you. The trouble some women got into, wearing clothes that didn't back them up, that actively contradicted them! If you meant *yes* and your dress said *no*, how was a man to find his way? Different sort of trouble the other way about. Fact was, men only saw the obvious. Or only the stronger signal. A lot of women did too.

Here though, delightfully, was a dress that said *yes, almost certainly*, and was thus exactly right for this exploratory evening. Lettie owned one or two other more positive favourites, and had very recently acquired a white silk bias-cut backless evening gown that said *yes, now!* She looked forward to wearing that one day. Not in Silkhampton, of course. Not out of doors, anyway.

There she stood looking back from the tall mirror,

Lettie Quick on the way to meet her new Possibility, slender and petite, chic and silver-eyed. Or she was a heartless trollop in a stolen frock: it just depended on how you looked at things, thought Lettie, giving her reflection a complicit smirk.

Which would Dr Philip Heyward see? That was the important question.

It had been instant, noticing him.

'Nurse Quick, delighted to meet you!' Her first day, and at her knock he had swung open the door of his office – he must have been on the verge of going out, had his coat on – dropped his bag to take her hand. 'Absolutely delighted to meet you! Been waiting to meet you – someone like you, I should say – for years!' And hadn't just waited – no, he'd *lobbied* for her, he'd told her, bombarded the Council with begging letters – mind you, he'd laughed, miracles of careful wording!

She had looked up at him and made her demure reply, all covert signal: 'Health, efficiency, purity, and racial strength?'

The curve of his mouth as he answered her: 'Exactly so, my dear Miss Quick!'

Thinking of that moment now gives Lettie the most delightful feeling inside, a light quickening shift of desire. She sees again the breadth of his shoulder, the enticing male fall of his shirt front, the gallant swing of his coat.

Sees and does not see; for all her exact awareness of the power and utility of female clothing Lettie has somehow not fully noticed the corresponding power of male dress. It is partly Dr Heyward's dashing and masculine overcoat that she is in love with, and the delicious tilt of his hat brim, but there is no way yet that she can see this.

One more thing to do, she remembers: practise what you preach. Lettie opens her handbag, and the little silk drawstring purse stowed in one of the lining-pockets, and takes out her own version of her favourite device, though unlike all those used by her clients this is of the smallest, neatest nulliparous size.

It won't stop you getting pregnant if you leave it in the box, she recites in her head as she crouches down and pulls aside the rosy crêpe de chine. Warm kitten fur. Her own silky insides. The thing leaps into place from her fingertips: that's freedom right there.

Standing up thus armoured, Lettie takes her hard felt hat from the hook on the door and without looking pulls it, firmly central, on to her head, then shoulders on the raincoat. Button up, spectacles on. Loosely buckle the belt, and there: clothes that thoroughly back up her everyday intention, and flatly say *never.*

Unnoticeable Sister Quick, respectably on her way home to her digs, and shepherd's pie, and watery cocoa!

She checks her watch. Tonight there is to be one of the larger monthly meetings in the surgery, with Wainwright and Nesbit and the district nurses all present, and the relevant medical men, and several board members from the various local supporting charities, and afterwards, possibly, one or two of the gathering might well find themselves left behind earnestly discussing – thrashing out – some question, possibly of supply, while the others heedlessly one by one take their leave . . .

Time to go, thinks Lettie, and her heartbeat is glorious, almost sickeningly excited, greedily alive.

Rae

Rae counted: there was Mrs Givens, one; there was the delivery boy from the bakery, half-frozen to his bicycle, two; there was Nameless Gardener, rheumy-eyed, three; sometimes, briefly, there was Minnie from the village, clearly not all there but doing The Rough; and now and then there was the postman, generally bringing someone else's letters. Human contacts: five.

Nameless Gardener, biblical in wooden-Noah jutting white chin-fringe, was not only Nameless, but had other similar lacks, thought Rae, watching him now and then out of the library window. He was often Motionless, for example, especially in the kitchen garden, and in over a week so far had returned no greeting: Speechless.

There was also a grey kitchen cat with yellow eyes. The cat had its own special chair at the table, and when on her first afternoon Rae had visited Mrs Givens there it had glared at her with the most extraordinarily hostile intensity. She had tried not to look back but every time she turned her head there it was again, rigid with outrage.

''E ain't a bit friendly,' Mrs Givens had said at last.

Rae had had a good go at this herself later on, in front of her dressing-table mirror. The West Country accent was easy enough, child's play; the placing more difficult, as Mrs Givens seemed to speak right from the back of her throat, with a certain coaxing quality to the sound. And the various strands of meaning in her tone had been hard to reproduce too, as they were so slight: amusement, approval, and a cautious hint that despite Tabby's intransigence Mrs Givens herself was prepared to prove at least moderately friendly, should circumstances permit.

''E ain't a bit friendly,' said Rae to her mirror again, this time absolutely spot on; realizing as she did so that for once there really wasn't anyone to amuse. To show off to.

'And your hair's too dark,' she added accusingly, in her own voice. Leaving the unsatisfactory image behind, she got up and went to her bedroom window.

'An isolated house, beside a lake,' the helpful if unsigned letter had read. Presumably from the presiding doctor, who was apparently based in London. And in fact, thought Rae, it was more like an isolated lake with a house. She stared out at the great ruffled sheet of water, steel-grey, murky, fringed at its distant far shore with a yellowed ruin of bulrushes, just the sort of place you despairingly waded into at dead of night; though of course this was partly due to *Tell Her Now*, with dear old Antony Wayward.

Seven whole years ago now, marvelled Rae, resting her forehead on the cold glass of the window. All that fuss about the lighting. Paid off though, you'd've sworn it was a moonlit night. Antony bellowing, 'Head back, arms back, face *up*, you're saying goodbye to the *stars*!', his voice actually breaking a little, the old softie. But he'd been right enough; Rae had seen the whole film herself once in Piccadilly, at a full-house matinee, and women all round her had sobbed aloud.

At the far end a Regency someone had built a little

bridge of prettily arching wrought iron, in order to make the lake look even bigger than it was, a bridge over nothing.

'Mostly shut up, apparently,' the typed unsigned letter had continued, 'but with long-established service in situ, and everything as private as you could possibly wish.' Once, when she thought Mrs Givens was out, Rae had crept about trying doorknobs. Both rooms on either side of her own were locked, and so were all the rooms on the next floor up, apart from a narrow side room where a blue-and-white floral lavatory stood throne-like on a plinth of creaking mahogany.

The staircase above the third floor was uncarpeted and worn, and every step squeaked. At the top was another narrower corridor, with several more locked doors. But at the very end the last dented brass doorknob had loosely turned in her hand.

No carpet here, just floorboards, a narrow iron bedstead with a ticking mattress covered in a sheet of calico, and a plain pine chest of drawers: a maid's room. A lower servant, perhaps the under kitchen maid, thought Rae. From the little attic window she could see the horizon, grey and distant. On top of the chest of drawers there was a set of stains, rings within rings, marking years of wet jugs. The room was very cold. No fireplace at all.

On the way down she had met Mrs Givens coming up.

'I'm trespassing,' Rae had said at once. 'Sorry: I'm nosy.'

'Not much to see,' Mrs Givens had returned, almost easily. 'Shall you take your tea in the library again, ma'am?'

Rae had seized on the library, had stood on the threshold on being shown round and, despite the exhaustion of travel, gasped aloud with pleasure and greed. Along with the sack-like dresses and the selection of nasty adjustable underwear, she had brought an entire suitcase full of stuff to read, together with stacks of notebooks and her sleek new typewriter. But here was a whole real library just for her, shelf after packed shelf floor to ceiling on three entire walls! It had taken her some time to understand that most of the books were about the same age as the house, perhaps even a job lot: that the matching leather covers and gold lettering and spines with stout horizontal welts were largely decor.

They were beautiful, and smelt delicious, of dry cleanly decay, sweet and peppery, or flowery as daffodils. But impossible to read, memoirs of titled dullards, accounts of battles in wars she had never heard of; some had complex pictures faced with a protective rustle of ancient tissue, woodcut illustrations mainly as indecipherable as the texts, like one busy mystery of digging labourers, wheelbarrows, bonfires, and mud-pie-making which had suddenly resolved itself into clarity:

'They're making bricks!' Rae had cried aloud, triumphantly, and then heard herself, exclaiming to no one.

On a shelf beside the nicest armchair, handled into crumbly suede, she had found *Lovell's Complete Bestiary*. The engravings on its thick and speckled pages were straightforward to begin with, squirrels holding acorns and hares leaping in March madness; but then *Lovell* set off for foreign parts, and seemed less and less sure of itself.

The picture labelled 'Hippotomos', for example, had looked alright at first, big broad familiar head on great barrel of body, and short thick legs. But Lovell's hippo-potamus sported fur like a mole's, a hippo in velvet. Another shaggy spaniel-headed beast with a curved back and enormous feet like furry hobnail boots was merely 'An Animal of the Bear Species', while the mysterious pig-like 'Babyronessa' would hardly have been able to see where it was going, thought Rae, not with tusks that curved right up and practically speared its own eyeballs.

But here was a 'Camelopard', kitten-fur spotted like a leopard's, sturdy camel-like body, long curving neck as graceful as a swan's, demure little sideways smile. No real giraffe could be half so charming, thought Rae, and under-stood at last that none of these unfamiliar animals had been drawn from life. They had been lists of attributes, imagined and guessed at. That was how they had done things in those days.

These days too, thought Rae, looking up. Hadn't she taken her lover's words and a selection of his deeds and turned them into her own construction of him? He was another imagined animal, she thought, that had never really lived, and was suddenly engulfed by one of her bad moments.

These were not thought, she told herself, when it had begun to pass, and she was herself again, but feeling; you *felt* the choices you had made, and *felt* that there was now no other way out, that it was far too late to change your mind. You could only wait out a bad moment; but when it was over you just had to remind yourself what you still stood to gain: your entire future. Possibilities.

And remember that you were doing the best you could. You weren't beaten, you weren't *finished*. You had merely withdrawn for a while, to safety, here, at Nowhere with Lake, and you were just going to wait here a few vital weeks more until your problem had solved itself. Then, thank God, others – others you had paid, professional experienced others – would take over and you could set about forgetting the whole ghastly business.

Norah

Asked – as of course she would be, many, many times, for a good while afterwards – why she had decided to go for so long a walk so very early on such an unpromising morning, Norah could only go on repeating herself, though every time, she felt, the answers sounded less convincing.

No, there had been no particular reason. She had just woken up before dawn, and suddenly decided that whatever the weather she was going to walk all the way to Wooton, right along the shore, maybe even as far as Trewortha, with a picnic – well, with a sandwich – there and back before lunch. Yes, nearly seven miles, depending of course on the tides. No, she hadn't checked them. Had just set out in her stoutest shoes. Had *just gone*.

It was all perfectly true; the lie, Norah thought, lay in all she was leaving out.

For weeks now she had been arguing with herself, her thoughts going round and round, scolding herself: it was nonsense to feel that Miss Quick had somehow pervaded the whole house. It was idiotic to carry on being agitated by the sound of Mamma's bedroom window being gently opened, by the intimate scrape of the top drawer of the dressing table. It was certainly none of her business why Miss Quick left the house so early and came back so late, why she so often dined elsewhere, received no post, and made so many telephone calls from the phone box in the square.

And it was specially absurd to feel almost cheated when Miss Quick constantly did nothing for Norah to complain about, nothing she must carefully refrain from noticing, nothing she might nobly keep quiet about; sometimes, Norah thought, it was as if she had actually been looking forward to discreetly loathing the splayed toothbrush in the bathroom, the ragged towel, the intimate items left in soak or sagging on the dryer above the stove. But so far Miss Quick had not left so much as the lightest sprinkle of talcum on the bath mat!

With the ham sandwich wrapped in greaseproof paper in the pocket of her overcoat she had quietly closed the front door behind her and felt that at last she could breathe. The market people were setting up already, in the near-light.

I mean, we're just two women, ain't we? Let's keep it simple – see how it goes?

Norah thought often of those words, hearing them over and over again in her head, spoken so lightly. No one else she knew would say anything so direct.

But I misconstrued it, she thought, because after all I have been so very lonely since Mamma died. Miss Quick was just being businesslike, not suggesting the possibility of friendship. It was absurd to feel slighted. Hurt, even.

She walked briskly along the square, past the few open shops – wonderful morning smell of course from the baker, Mrs Bettins already behind the counter; passing, she caught a glimpse of Mr Gilder himself at the ovens at the back, loading the high trolley with another tray of loaves. Presently, trying not to look at all, she passed the boarded-up windows of what had once been Thornby & Son's, afterwards an inferior menswear shop, currently empty again, then turned into the dim warren of lanes towards the old rope factory, and out at last into the fields that would eventually take her to the edge of everything, to the clifftop and the sea.

I'll be alright when I see the sea, thought Norah, as she tramped along the footpath, luckily fairly dry underfoot, the mud stiffened with cold. It was fretting indoors that made one lose all sense of proportion, made one feel one simply could not bear any more –

Any more *what*, though? I have absolutely nothing to complain about, Norah reminded herself again, as she climbed over the gate and into the next field, which was so misty that she could not see the far end of it.

Something stirred in Norah's memory then, and she remembered the surprising appearance of Joe Gilder at Wooton, in the sad days of the auctions there. It had been one of Norah's earliest tasks for Bagnold and Pender, helping to oversee the final end of that great household. She had been there every day for weeks, helping to itemize, to pack away, to sort for private sale or auction, had in fact several times walked it, when there was no bus at the right time or available lift, along this very path, summer then, of course, years back . . . and twice on the way she had caught up with Joe Gilder, limping along with his stick making for Wooton too, and slowed her pace to his for a while, to speak to him.

'And are you coming to the sale, Joe?'

No, he had said, or rather *nay*, you'd think he'd left the

North yesterday, the way he still talked, nay, he'd a mind to see the old place again while he could, and of course then she had remembered that he had been a patient there, when it was a hospital, during the War.

'Oh, and you met – your wife there, didn't you –?'

He had shot her a look then, of surprise. Aye, he had said, he'd met his Grace there. Or perhaps, she thought, he had met grace. Both.

Strange she did not feel particularly shy of him, maybe because he was a newcomer, even though he was so good-looking; very nearly as handsome in his way, Norah had more than once noticed, as the delightful young men pictured in the *Film Lover's Weekly*, though of course none of them ever stood behind shop counters or wore flat caps. As it was, Norah was able to remark, almost lightly, that perhaps he did not know that she had been at school with the long-dead Grace Gilder, once Grace Dimond, oh, so long ago; had once helped her to make a daisy chain.

Then she'd had his whole attention.

What else? What else could she remember?

So little, she found, that she could tell him. A dress, a very pretty little blue coat. Gracie had always looked so nice. I was nearly ten, when she was just five; we all adored her, we used to walk home with her at dinner time, we used to hold her hand . . .

She remembered the awkwardness, that in those days Mamma's charity work had largely concerned midwifery, and saving the local poor from the dirty and untrained likes of Grace's adoptive mother Violet; she remembered Mrs Dimond's brief hard stare from the doorway at herself on the pavement, her enemy's child. But that was hardly the sort of thing Mr Gilder wanted.

I loved Grace so. But then we all did. We used to argue about whose turn it was to hold her hand. We made such a little pet of her.

She had no term for the delicacy of feeling which held her back from mentioning this.

'She could run very fast,' Norah had said instead. 'The Redwoods held a sort of children's garden party at Wooton one summer – I'd left the school by then but I was there because – well, because I'm a sort of relation, cousin of a cousin sort of thing, you know – it was to celebrate the Coronation, so it must have been what, 1911, with lots of games and races and so on, and Grace won all the time, all these little red rosettes . . .'

But he'd known about that, it turned out. She'd told him – Grace had told him – on account of something she'd seen there that day, at Wooton. Some young chap had taken her inside the Hall, someone who lived there –

'At the Hall?'

'Aye, one a the family, what was his name . . . ?'

'Was it Billy – Billy Redwood? He was the younger son, I know he was there. I think Henry was away.' Both of them long dead, of course, their names on the plinth below the stone soldier in the square.

But Mr Gilder was not listening. 'Any road, he takes her into the ballroom . . . I were there meself once, in the War – when it were a hospital, you know – you can see the sea! Anyway this lad, this Billy Redwood as lived there, he shows her this picture ont' wall, and it's a lady in olden times, with a little dark lad by her – like her, you know. Like Grace. D'you know the one?'

'Billy showed Grace a picture?'

'Aye, it were hanging in the ballroom, them days. One a the portraits. Grand lady all in blue, and this little dark lad in the background, like, you know, long time ago. Gracie – she were only a little lass – she thought the grand lady had adopted him, see. Tickled pink, she were, to think she's not the first. Of course he hadn't been adopted, poor little tyke. Servant, he were. Mascot sort of thing. But they knew his name alright, it were Barty Small – that's where Grace got our lad's name from. The little dark lad like her in the picture. D'you know the one, miss?'

The grand lady in blue was an eighteenth-century Redwood, Norah thought; but she had not been able to guess which picture he meant. But then I would have looked only at the lady, she thought. I might not have noticed a little Barty Small in the background. At least she knew that all the pictures in the sale were then hung in the long gallery upstairs, and had shown him up there later on, and they had looked at all of them together. But there was no eighteenth-century lady in blue, and no little dark boy anywhere.

'Apparently the family portraits all went to the London house – I could find out for you, if you like.'

But he had only smiled, and shaken his head, and she had thought once more what a fine-looking man he was, considering.

Barty hardly more than a baby then. Extraordinary to think he was getting on for fourteen now, the age his mother had been when she worked behind the counter at Ticknell's Woolshop. How had that happened?

The mist was as thick as ever as she neared the cliff edge, which was disappointing; she had been counting on the great wide view of the sea to soothe her, and now there was nothing but cloud. Still, she knew that sometimes mist cleared as quickly as it arrived, and climbed carefully down the old zigzag rocky path to reach the tossed sand at the bottom.

It was low tide, and the sea was very calm, the quiet little waves turning softly a hundred yards away. The mist appeared to be gathered in a circle all around her, enclosing her, moving when she did, letting her see only several yards of the beach at a time. She walked out on to the clean flat sand, passing rock pools, stepping over seaweed. She took some deep breaths, and turned to walk on, enclosed in her circle. Her shoes made no sound at all on the firm damp sand. She thought again of Grace Dimond, aged five. How desperately I wanted to look after her then, to amuse her, to be the one she liked best!

It came to her suddenly, out of nowhere, that thinking about the lost friendship with Grace was in part another way of thinking about the frustratingly distant Miss Quick.

Could it be that I have a bit of a *pash* on her?

Pashes had been fashionable at Norah's boarding school. Many of the girls at one time or another had fallen into a fit of adoration for another usually older girl; sometimes several at once all admired the same one, so that the two or three most charming girls in the sixth form might have something approaching teams of adorers, all expressing their feelings by following the beloved about on the off-chance of being allowed to do her some small favour, peeping at her en masse from behind pillars, vying with one another to write her poetry, and copying her hairstyle if humanly possible.

And at bedtime the night before Miss Quick had flung open the front door in a swirl of cold air just as Norah in her dressing gown was coming up the stairs from the kitchen with her cocoa. Miss Quick had her usual raincoat and hat on, but there was something different about her, something Norah could not at first identify.

'Good evening, my goodness, such long hours, Sister Quick!'

'I like to be busy,' said Miss Quick, unbuttoning her coat, and though her voice was perfectly friendly it was somehow clear there was to be no further exchange.

'Goodnight, then,' said Norah, and then saw that for once Miss Quick was not wearing her heavy spectacles, and that her eyes were a startling, an almost luminous, pale grey.

Norah had blushed. Did one in fact have girlish feelings, a bit of a pash, for one's lodger? If so one must take care to keep them hidden. No peeping through banisters, no yearning verses . . . she laughed to herself at the thought.

I was right to come out, she thought; it's working, I feel better already. And I have the lovely beach and this strange beautiful mist all to myself, and soon – when I feel like it – I will sit upon the perfect rock of my choosing, and jolly well eat my sandwich.

The mist was thinning anyway, she realized. All around her the enclosing circle was enlarging itself, fading. To her right now she could see the glittering grey sea all the way to the long straight line of the horizon, though that was still rather vague; to her left the sloping fall of the cliffs, and the range of bays beyond them slowly darkening into existence in the growing sunshine.

She walked on happily for a few more minutes, and presently noticed something brownish fluttering amid the rocks far ahead of her at the base of the cliff. A bird, perhaps? Was a bird somehow caught there, flapping its wings, but unable to fly away? Some other injured creature? She walked a little faster, just in case. Soon she could see more of it, see how large it was, that it couldn't be a bird, as it was far too big; in fact it looked more like a pale roll of carpet, wrapped in something that had come loose, fluttering in the rising breeze. An old roll of carpet thrown over the clifftop – honestly, people these days –

She walked further, closer and closer, until – no. It wasn't carpet, she could see that now. Not a roll of anything. Now the pale thing lying ahead of her on the rocks had a fragile forked look.

Norah stopped abruptly, stood still for a little while. She heard the long low surge of the sea turning, a little closer now the tide was beginning to run in. The thing on the rocks was a shop-window dummy. The mannequin of a woman; the fluttering was from something it had been wearing, still entangled.

Now that was very strange, thought Norah. This was some sort of very cruel prank. But she would just make sure. Obviously it was a mannequin, but she must be certain, when it looked so very broken, though, at the same time, so very real.

Courage, she told herself, and walked right up to the rocks, chest-high, on which it lay.

She recognized the skirt first, the brown velveteen. Then she knew. The body lay on its front, but the back of the poor draggled head was also instantly familiar, the blonde permanent wave, the long white neck. It had been the back of her best blouse Norah had seen, untucked, and fluttering in the rising breeze.

Norah bent, and after a moment's hesitation reached out to touch the back of the hanging left hand. It was icy. The sleeve was rolled back, and about the slender wrist the tiny gold watch, Sister Wainwright's pride and joy, and as Norah happened to know, a very new possession, was still going, still telling anyone able to look at it the right time, which was ten past eight.

But Dolly Wainwright was broken all over, thought Norah. She straightened up and looked up at the clifftop high above her: from up there, all the way up there, dear God! And tried to close her mind to instant thoughts of the very edge, to standing there summoning the strength to take that last endless step –

She turned and took in the long wide stretch of the beach, fully clear now, not a soul about but herself. There was the long trail of her own footprints reaching back and back into invisibility. Here was the body lying on the rocks.

Oh, Dolly, poor Dolly, what have you done to yourself?

Her heart began suddenly to race, dizzyingly, as if directing herself to the corpse had been too much for it. She was cold, too, shivering now, despite the sunshine. She turned, and began to run back along the sand the way she had come, haltingly at first, and then faster, until she was running flat out, her hat in her hand, panting hard, gasping as she hauled herself as fast as she dared back up the cliff path, and as at last she neared the first outlying houses she began to shout, to call urgently aloud for help, help: as if there could be any.

Rae

Early one morning Rae, venturing out before breakfast for a breath of air, missed her footing on the gravel and fell, knocking her elbow against the path's tiled edging. For a moment she was too shocked to do anything other than lie still. She smelt the earth so unusually close at hand. The fine blue sky hurt her eyes, so she closed them again. Presently footsteps came crunching by.

'Madam? Mrs Wickham, are you alright?'

'My foot turned,' said Rae, after a pause.

'Here, take my hand,' said Mrs Givens. 'Just sit up for now. That's right, slow-like. Does it hurt?'

'I don't think so.'

'Nice and slow, then, that's the way.'

Mrs Givens put her arm round Rae's shoulders, and helped haul her upright.

'Doing grand,' she said, as they made slowly round the house and into the kitchen.

'Here. You just sit for now, I've got the kettle on.' It was blessedly warm. Rae remembered the cat. 'E ain't a bit friendly, she thought, but there was no sign of him.

'Thank you *so* much,' said Rae. 'You've been so kind.'

Mrs Givens had her tray nearly ready, Rae saw, clean white tray cloth, silver, a little bunch of snowdrops in a tiny blue vase. And a willow-pattern plate with a battered metal cover on it; beneath it, she thought, would be flabby swags of bacon and a flat wet egg in a welter of grease.

'Oh I – don't think I –' Rae began, finally understanding how ill she felt. Her stomach kept taking her by surprise these days, so moody and prone to making scenes, a prima donna of a stomach. Now what? she thought at it unkindly.

'I'll put a bit of sugar in your tea, if you don't mind. Set you up, like.'

Rae looked away, to concentrate on what her stomach was doing. Impossible to ignore it now. But its signals were so hard to understand. She waited a moment more, still uncertain, then stood up abruptly, casting round in despair, where, where could she, the door was so far away, the sink, oh God –

'Sorry, I'm so sorry –' The effort of retching made her feel dizzy. She sank down at the table again, resting her head in her trembling hands.

'Don't you fret,' said Mrs Givens, briefly running the tap, and apparently more in amusement than anything else. 'Weren't nothing much to come up, were there? You got to eat,' she went on. 'You're one of those has to eat all the time. Then you'll feel better. Hope you don't mind my asking, but when you due?'

I don't know what you're talking about, Rae thought to herself, just to see what it might sound like, which was clearly no good at all.

'March,' she said.

'Your first?'

'Yes.'

'And Mr Wickham –'

67

'Abroad,' said Rae, 'with the Foreign Office.' Should she need the respectability of family, Rae had Mr Wickham's only brother ready, farming in Southern Rhodesia, and a bed-bound great-aunt of her own; both these entirely imaginary people thus usefully hard to visit, rely on, or identify; but Mrs Givens asked no more.

'Will you try your breakfast now, ma'am, if you're comfy here, like?'

Comfy here, like, thought Rae, trying to keep note of words and tone, instantly seeing herself repeating them exactly, to amuse her friends; though at the same time her heart had melted with pleasure.

'Might not stay down,' she said aloud.

'Try anyway,' said Mrs Givens. 'I'll take a cup with you, ma'am, if I may.'

Rae looked at her as she set out more blue-and-white china. It occurred to her that Mrs Givens was actually a real-life version of a fairly familiar supporting character: the housekeeper of the old empty house in the middle of nowhere. White hair, in a complicated and, thought Rae, surprisingly stylish knot at the nape of her neck; faded blue eyes, rather protuberant; face so worn it was hard to itemize, everything drooped and sad-looking when she wasn't talking or smiling, but a good colour.

In fact perfect Central Casting housekeeper-of-old-empty-house, thought Rae, except that the costume was all wrong. Hollywood would surely have gone for floor-length Mrs Tiggy-Winkle; celluloid servants were always Victorian. Mrs Givens wasn't even aproned, was almost chic in a white blouse with a shawl collar, a light-green boiled-wool cardigan, and a green-brown tweed skirt, well cut if very old indeed. Shoes flat brown lace-ups, lisle stockings. And not a bad figure either, elegantly narrow at the hip, especially considering her age, which must, thought Rae, be at least sixty or seventy, or something. And her back so straight, and the way she holds herself, very grande dame; she could even have played the lady of the house, rather than the housekeeper.

But look what happens when she sits down, Rae told herself, taking her usual automatic mental notes: it's in the way she leans forward, and there's something in the way she tilts her head to listen that says *service*. What is it, exactly? Keep looking: catch it. And anyway no real lady would ever have hands like that, so hard and thick, hands that have really worked.

The bacon was crisp and salty and delicious. I'm *starving*, thought Rae, happily applying herself. The egg looked almost edible too, perhaps she would risk it.

'Where d'you come from, Mrs Givens? Have you always lived here?'

'Born and bred, over Silkhampton way.' She poured tea, passed over the cup.

'D'you have family nearby, then?'

'Near enough,' said Mrs Givens pleasantly, but it was clear to Rae that she was to ask no further personal questions, which was only fair, she thought, remembering the as yet uncalled-for bed-bound great-aunt. There was a sudden thud from outside. Was it Minnie, lumbering up from the village, poor thing?

Mrs Givens rose. 'Excuse me, ma'am, that'll be the bread: he's late today,' and she went to the kitchen door and opened it, letting in a great draught of cold air along with, Rae saw with some alarm, Human Contact Number Two in person, the bread delivery boy, carrying a large bloomer loaf wrapped in tissue paper underneath each arm. How old was he, eleven, twelve? He won't know me, she told herself: calm down. Nothing she could do about it now anyway –

'Come in and have a warm,' said Mrs Givens, taking the bread. 'This here's Mrs Wickham, Barty – don't just stand there, where's your manners?' Reprovingly she pulled his cap off. 'Say How Do.'

Rae's smile felt tight. 'Hello, Barty.'

The boy had turned bright scarlet and dropped his head, rigid all over, as if the sight of her had turned him to stone.

'What's the matter with you?' Mrs Givens put out a hand, and ruffled his dark curly hair. 'Dad alright, is he?'

Barty nodded, and briefly looking up shot Rae a glance of mingled disbelief and avidity.

Her heart gave a thump of fright, but almost at the same instant she realized that she had seen him before; not just idly watched him once or twice from the morning-room window as he wobbled off back down the drive on his heavy delivery bicycle, no; she had met those beautiful longing eyes before, and recently, surely?

'Still two sugars, my lovely?'

She remembered: on the interminable journey from the Southampton dockside, in the very nice Daimler she had simply had to organize for herself, what with one thing and another, towards dawn they had stopped, at a little town – well, Silkhampton, presumably – so that the driver could ask directions to this House and its Lake.

They had pulled up in a cobbled square, where people were already setting up stalls and unloading carts. She had been half asleep, waking only when the engine stopped. She had let up the little blinds on the windows, wiped away some of the condensation with her handkerchief, and looked out, with the dazed acuity of the spent traveller, at the shadowy figures carrying baskets of apples and oranges, big heavy bolts of material, and trays of what might have been cheese. Against the paling sky she could see that the statue in the middle of the square was decked about with faded rained-on poppy wreaths, a sight melancholy enough to turn her back to the pavement, where light from the one or two opened shops was streaming over the flags.

The Daimler rocked as the driver, a heavy-set fellow, got back in, and started up the engine; it was then that she saw the skinny child quite close at hand on the pavement outside the steamed-up bakery, standing very still with a broom in his hands, admiring the car. But then she caught his eye, and realized that he could see through the window: it wasn't the Daimler he was gazing at so helplessly, so ardently, but herself, in her furs, inside. Not with recognition though, she decided, remembering: there had been no sharpness in that open-mouthed gaze.

He was arrestingly pretty himself, in a dark Italian sort of way, very delicate-looking; and he had just looked so sweet, she thought, that despite everything she had put up her manicured hand as the car slid away, let her eyes meet his once more, and blown him a little smoochy kiss.

Oops, thought Rae now.

*

71

When he had gone she immediately forgot all about him, but later on, when she was getting ready for bed, he prompted a Bad Moment.

She'd known all the time that she was annoying some very important people, disappearing like this, despite the studio contract she had signed: that was fine, that was Rae against the Bosses, Rae against being told what to do by anyone else. What had not occurred to her, though, was the possibility of Rae against Rae, ignorance against experience.

Ignorance had told her that you just swelled up where the baby was, not all over, you just swelled in the middle until it popped out somehow (no not thinking about that) and then afterwards there you were, back to normal.

But despite her constant nausea, her thighs had thickened, her breasts were heavier. She had assumed that she could pretty well cancel out the whole getting-knocked-up business; she'd imagined forgetting all of it as fast as she could, and she'd forgotten far worse things, she told herself, oh, you could dismiss anything in your past if you really put your mind to it. But suppose you couldn't erase it from your face, your body?

All her life men, boys – Barties of all ages – had gazed ardently at Rae, courted her, striven for her attention, done her favours, tried to please her. How was she to bear it if they stopped? How was she to live?

Bad Moment.

When she could breathe again she climbed into the bed, where Mrs Givens, definitely something of a treasure, had earlier put two hot-water bottles wrapped in flannel, and lay down, propped against the pillows.

Pointless worrying, she reminded herself. Get through this bit first. The secret bit.

It was a pleasant-enough room to hide out in, walls papered with leaves and ribbons faded greyish-beige, old-fashioned well-polished mahogany furniture, and floor-length curtains of deep-red velvet, bleached into soft stripes; amusingly reminiscent, in fact, of the bedroom in *The Spectre of Sowerby Hall*, in which Rae herself, nicely double-exposed, had played a long-dead girl in a portrait, who every night nipped out of her ornate picture frame to shimmer about in corridors.

It was always cold, though; despite the heavy curtains, the two enormous windows were very draughty, and tonight, as so often, she'd had to go to bed by candlelight.

'You can't trust th'electric,' Mrs Givens had said when she had first arrived, and so it had proved. The supply was intermittent, the wiring antique; there was no point fussing. Though the suddenness of the darkness, Rae had found, was always a shock. Whatever you were doing, reading, having another go at the indecipherable knitting pattern, trying to write letters, you forgot straight away that the light was unreliable, that it could be instantaneously withdrawn. Often it felt capricious, personal, as if the higher electric power had waited on purpose for her to be in the middle of painting her fingernails, or picking up a dropped stitch.

But the first time she had to take a candle up the stairs to bed with her had been full of emotion. There was already a powerful nostalgia in the feel of the worn brass holder, the quality of its little light, but as she lay beside it waiting for sleep she smelt the melting wax and the faint sweetness of its smoke, and at once the clear idea of her mother came to her, a murmuration of skirts, the faintest possible creaking of seams as she bent over the bed to say goodnight, the warm softness of her blouse.

For an instant Rae had simply rejoiced; she had few such memories. But then she had remembered again why she was here, and what she was doing. What would Mother have thought of her now? That had been a very Bad Moment.

But she was getting quite used to candlelight now, she thought. She rested her hands on the eiderdown, on the strange new mound of her belly. Weeks and weeks to go yet of growing and swelling, how big was it going to get? Rae had no idea. The latest typed letter had instructed her to make the important telephone call when the pains were five minutes apart, but *what* pains? How much was it going to hurt?

She sighed, and put out a hand to douse the candle. As she did so the right-hand door of the wardrobe at the foot of the bed shifted all by itself and uttered a small sound, as if clearing its throat. The pale glimmer of her own reflection in the glossy dark wood shifted and vanished: slowly, silently, the door swung itself wide open. Within it lay an entirely lightless dark.

For a long instant Rae sat frozen, engulfed in fear; but presently the instant passed. The door had opened but no one had come through it; nothing else had happened. She drew a quivering breath, and in a fairly successful attempt at the commanding sneer she had used years before to such onstage effect as that heartless beauty Lady

Hermione Pringle in *Satan's Lord* demanded, 'Well, are you coming in, or aren't you?'

Nothing did.

Faulty hinge, failing catch; unless the entire spirit world had just been sent packing by Lady Hermione, whose haughty smirk had come in handy elsewhere more than once. Still in character, Rae stepped out of bed, marched across the carpet, and pushed the wardrobe door shut again.

Stay closed? She shivered a little, waiting. But the wardrobe made no further sound or move. She backed towards the bed and climbed carefully back into it. There was the pallor of her own face in the shining mahogany, a faint gleam at the foot of the bed.

Absurd, the childish terror, she thought. As if reality wasn't bad enough! She blew out the candle.

Lady Hermione had been such fun to play; but there's no half-comic stereotype, no dramatic tradition, no history at all, thought Rae, for the part I'm playing now. Hardly so much as a rumour. Who knew of anyone else preparing to give birth secretly, the better to pretend not to have given birth at all? No doubt it had been done before, over and over again. But the whole point, of course, was that it had been done in secret.

So many things it was best not to think about. Lucky these days she was always so shatteringly tired.

And of course I was a restless spirit myself once, she remembered, half smiling to herself in the darkness, I was *The Spectre of Sowerby Hall*, set in a real old house rather like this one, where was it now, somewhere out near Purley, wasn't it? All those long corridors. And mirrors where

I had no reflection, because of, what was it called, so clever, double something . . .

Already she was drifting deliciously, images in her head disconnecting themselves, flowing together.

She was standing beside the lake now, by the bulrushes. She looked across the water, trying to work out which of the windows were hers. Where were the deep-red faded curtains? She would walk right to the far end of the lake, her dream-self thought, and cross the little pretend bridge to nowhere, but as she set off she realized how close to the edge she was, how slippery the flattened grass beside the freezing gunmetal water. As she tried to step away it seemed to her that there was swift heaving movement in the water. Weeds stirred, the surface rippled and murmured. Something in the water knew she was there. It had been waiting for her. It knew her name. Rae's throat was closed with terror. She could make no sound, tried no struggle, as she passed with terrible slowness into the water's icy embrace.

Gasping, Rae awoke, to a panting indefinite terrifying pause. Secret, hiding, she remembered, at last. House with Lake. Bad dream.

And no light, ah – she scrabbled in the dark at the bedside table, and presently managed to strike a match, and re-light the candle. It was some time before she felt calm enough to look about her; then she saw that at the foot of the bed lay only blank darkness; for the wardrobe door had once again opened all by itself.

Barty

First the buns; the smell would always catch them, his dad said, especially on the colder mornings. Open the doors of the shop, and the toasted caramel of freshly baked, lightly glazed currant buns would fill the whole square.

That was just before seven, for the shop was perfectly placed to catch those on their way to the station for the early trains, as well as close to the bus stops. So one of Barty's first tasks was to slip single buns into paper bags and pile them up ready for the rush. Often he sold more than two dozen while in the back of the shop his dad and Mrs Bettins hauled the great hot trays of loaves from the ovens and slid them on to a high multi-tiered trolley on wheels. When all its shelves were full they coaxed this between them into the front shop, perfuming the air now with the smell of new bread, even better than the buns, Barty thought: earthy, deeper, the warm smell of plenty.

Sometimes Dad greeted him:

'Alright, lad?'

On other days, forcing the emptied trolley back into the kitchen for a refill, he might shoot Barty a brief ferocious glance, as if daring him to speak, though as it happened Barty spoke very little anyway.

This was one of the many things that Barty had so far not noticed about himself, though he was aware that he felt a great deal; however, he knew also that he often had

77

no idea what it was that he was actually feeling. Sometimes he could recognize that it was too complicated to be one thing at a time. Though there was often no easy way to unravel the complication into separate strands, and no guarantee if he did that strands thus separated would be any more identifiable than the fully knotted article.

When the loaves were cool enough it was Barty's job to stack them on top of each other on the shelves behind the counter: the tins large and small, the crusty cottage loaves. He liked the bloomers best, their warm thick brown crusts scattered with poppy seeds, their inner damp resilience.

Once when he was five he had stolen a particularly fine one, wrapping it in paper and hiding it all day behind one of the roll baskets, telling himself that he was keeping it back for a customer. He had felt a certain discomfort when someone popped in just before closing time:

'Haven't got any bread left, have you, by any chance?'

Dad cashing up right beside him.

'No, sir, sorry.'

Barty had felt himself go red. He was not sure why he had hidden the loaf. He had not pictured eating it at all; just seen himself in private, looking at it joyfully, and fingering the sharp dark ridges of its top crust and its lighter smoother sides.

But shortly afterwards Dad had bent to retrieve and shake out all the roll baskets, which Barty had somehow forgotten was a nightly occurrence.

'What's this then? Eh? What's this?'

Barty had stood looking at the crumb-strewn floor in silence, his ears very hot.

'I just wanted to look at it,' he had said at last.

'You what?'

Though in fact this was not quite true; Barty had wanted also to embrace the loaf, to lie down in his bed with his arms round it, breathing in its perfume.

'Sorry, Dad.'

There was a silence, but after it his father sighed, then sounded altogether different, not angry at all.

'You weren't – *hungry*, were yer?'

In this way Barty glimpsed the fact that he was a puzzle and a worry to his father. He felt rather impressed with himself, though anxious too.

But that had been long ago, when he had lived with his Nannas, both of them, in the two rooms in Market Buildings, Nanna Vi, Nanna Bea, and Barty; Dad visiting. Of course, none of that had seemed at all odd at the time. He had never once grasped at Sunday school that while many other children there also had two grandmothers, they all had two different ones, whereas he had two exactly the same.

One of his earliest memories was sitting on the padded top of the kindling box while his Nannas put on a special show for him.

'You sit still now, Barty my lovely,' one of them would say, and then they would sit one on either side of the table and pretend to be one old lady looking at herself in a mirror, smiling and preening and combing out her thick white hair. He could tell the game was meant to be entertaining, and so it was; but there was often something frightening about it, and he had always carefully hidden from them how glad he had felt when they stopped – nearly always at the same time – and turned to him for applause. But mainly he had clapped with relief that Mirrors was over.

He had realized only recently why he had never quite trusted any mirror himself, why even his passing reflection in a shop window made him a little uncomfortable: a small part of his mind seemed to be worried that one day the image would do something different by itself, turn sideways or yawn or wink, the way Nanna Bea or Nanna Vi occasionally did when they were playing. The game was always abruptly over when that happened, and if it had happened too soon one of the Nannas would be angry with the other one, and argumentative, as if something had been spoiled.

The Nannas had moved away when he started at the Bishop Road School, and gone to live with just one another, in the great empty house far away with the sheet of lake beside it, though when he came to stay for holidays he never went near the water; everyone at school knew the stories.

The house was huge, with places to run up and down in all day if it rained, and banisters to slide down, and one big room full of books. Nanna Bea had taught him to read there, from their favourite, the book of animals with all pictures in it, and he had helped Nanna Vi in the enormous walled kitchen garden, feeding the chickens and collecting the eggs for her, and in the evenings they would sit by the fire and he would read aloud to them while they sewed and knitted, a waistcoat for his dad, socks for himself. He read them *Treasure Island* and *Kidnapped*, he read them *Alice in Wonderland*, though then he'd had to keep stopping for laughing too much to speak.

He was better than the pictures, the Nannas had told

him, and he had believed them, because he was only eight, he thought now.

It had been dreadful at first, to think of a Nanna being all alone. He was nearly eleven when it happened, big enough to ask his dad if he could deliver the bread there, once, perhaps twice a week.

Dad had been puzzled at first. 'Ain't there a baker in Porthkerris?'

There was; Barty had looked at the floor. He was unable to explain the idea to himself either.

'What about your schoolwork?'

Barty had answered this with a look, which said: how am I doing at school, Dad? For both of them knew that the headmaster Mr Vowles was very struck with Barty. Very pleased indeed, Mr Gilder, quite an exceptional lad, reading so advanced, writing so fluent, a positively remarkable essay here on the local rock pools, Mr Gilder, and always top in mathematics too – we really think young Barty here should go in for the grammar school examination!

'Twelve miles round trip, to Rosevear,' his dad had said.

To which Barty had shrugged.

Sometimes Dad had moods. There were one or two people he wouldn't serve in the shop, Barty had noticed. Now and then on a Sunday morning he would be very pale and sick-looking, and smell sourly of old beer, and start on about the French and what bastards they all were, every man-jack of them; and then it was best to keep out of his way.

'He's missing your mother,' Nanna Bea had told Barty once, and he had looked away, for he had lately discovered that he had killed his mother just by being born. He knew it hadn't really been his fault, he hadn't meant to; how could he? But the fact of the killing was connected in his own mind with the fervour with which he took in everything Miss Tracy told him, carefully memorizing tables of numbers, names of shapes, of animals, dates of kings and queens and battles, tidying sentences into planned paragraphs. Besides, all his cleverness came from Grace in the first place; everyone was always very clear about that, and pleased, as if he had done something right by taking after her, when surely it had no more been his choice than killing her when he was born. Once he'd tried protesting:

'Couldn't I take after you and all, Dad?'

But his father, deadpan as usual, had shaken his head: son, what claim to intelligence, or even common sense, could be made by a bloke who'd volunteered to go to France and get half his bum shot away? Then he had pulled Barty's cap down over his eyes, and gone off whistling.

That was his dad all over, Barty thought. He knew his father lacked something. One evening just before he started school, before the Nannas moved away, Dad had smelt of old beer on a weekday, and stood outside the back door at Market Buildings shouting and banging on the door, and it had all been about himself, Barty; as if there were any question that he belonged to all three of them, that all three of them belonged to him.

'Whose son is he, that's what I'd like to know!'

It had been the first and so far more or less the only lengthy time that Barty had heard his father being serious; nearly everything was a sort of joke to him, almost every exchange an opportunity to take the mickey, which made it hard to judge how much real notice his father took of anything.

The bread delivery to Rosevear, for instance. He'd been managing it twice weekly for close on three years now, and had been beginning to worry what Nanna would do when he started at the grammar school in September. But then he had forgotten all about that, started wondering instead whether there was any way of pulling the wool over his dad's eyes and making out that he needed to go more often; ever since that day in the kitchen when he had finally seen daft Minnie's Beautiful Lady for himself the temptation to get the bike out and ride there every single day for another chance to see her had occupied him almost to the exclusion of everything else, even aeroplanes.

Such a jolt it had been, understanding that Minnie's Lady and his own were one and the same; that the celestial vision in the dim luxury of the swankiest car in the world, who had caught his eye and blown him a real lipsticked kiss as he stood there gazing in disbelief, this being of impossible glamour and perfection, was living now just a few miles away in Rosevear House, with his very own Nanna!

It was the most exciting thing that had ever happened to him, knowing about the Lady, knowing that she was a secret. One day, he thought, he would manage to speak to her. They would talk of interesting grown-up things. She would look at him as if he were a man, she would see that he was one. And no matter how much he wanted to know he wouldn't ask her what she was doing at Rosevear, or why she was pretending to be called Mrs Wickham, or why – oh, most of all – why she had decided to dye her beautiful golden hair as dark as his own.

Rae

All the next morning, sitting at her typewriter in the library, or trying to read, she found herself considering the wardrobe door and the slow shift of her own pallid image as it opened.

It had taken her some time to make herself get up and close it once more, and then she had not slept again until it began to grow light. The real trouble, thought Rae, her fingers paused again on the typewriter keys, is the nightmare. I had a very nasty dream – obviously to do with wading into the water in *Tell Her Now*, and in the way of nasty dreams I can't quite shake it off, and because it coincided with – or was brought on by – that beastly wardrobe door, I've got the two things connected.

She could find something to wedge the wardrobe door shut. Folded paper would probably do. Perhaps she could deal with the lake – with the nightmare version of the lake – by simply going for a proper look at the real thing. Suppose she went out after lunch, say, and stood exactly where she had stood in her nightmare? Everything would look so different in daylight.

The afternoon was grey but still. Outside, the chilly air had a fresh hint of spring to it, and there were one or two primroses in bloom in the big flowerpot beside the front door. Instead of walking up the gravel drive to the gate-posts, as usual, she turned right and went past the library windows, glancing in at the shrouded shape of the type-writer waiting for her there, and further on, past rooms she had not entered, past the chained and locked front door, past more rooms with their blinds pulled right down, until she turned the corner and came to a broad paved passage.

Ahead the garden, a dripping tangle of neglect, brambles waist high, beds full of collapsed and blackened weeds. The only possible path led away to the left, to a large kitchen garden, also partly in ruin. The walls were high, and the great wooden doors at the far end were padlocked, but there was a small wrought-iron gate in the right-hand corner, which proved close up to be merely leaning in place. It was light enough to lift. She shifted it to one side, and went through.

Now at last she could see the glint of water through the fringe of rushes. I could walk all the way round it, Rae thought, and her heart began to beat faster. She went closer, walking with some difficulty through the wet uneven grass. Here there were one or two trees leaning into the water, it was the very end of the lake that she could not see from her window.

Closer still the ground was marshy, awkward to negotiate in her thin shoes, but concentrating hard she worked her way past the end of the lake before allowing herself to stop and take in the full view of the house across the water.

The back of the house was a great deal more dilapidated than the front. Some of the windows were actually boarded up, and there were great discoloured patches on the walls where the render had fallen off. Strange how many of the upper windows seemed to be barred, like windows in a prison, but that was surely a trick of the light from here. And she could see all round the lake, an opalescent grey, and very still. The top half of the house was reflected in it, the tiled roof, the crooked chimneys, the two upper storeys. There was her own window, the red curtains lined with cream, above in the air, and below, quivering in the water.

It was very quiet.

It looks haunted, she thought. But how could it not, to anyone familiar with the works of M. R. James, Edgar Allan Poe, Dickens, Conan Doyle? Once you'd read them they stayed put, dormant, apparently forgotten, until you checked into the wrong hotel, or suddenly noticed on the way up to bed that you were alone in the house. Films too, perhaps; maybe a simple-minded few were even now being kept awake at night because of *The Spectre of Sowerby Hall*.

She remembered one of her friends – Dodie, wasn't it? – saying that the whole barking-mad Victorian obsession with ghost stories had really all been down to gaslight, so intense but so small-scale, casting a bright circle of light and deep flickering shadows everywhere else; down to gaslight and of course laudanum, because they were all such frightful dope-fiends, those eminent Victorians, Dodie had shouted cheerfully over the racket the others were all making, in the Savoy wasn't it, or the dear old Café de Paris?

Rae walked forward, with some difficulty, her shoes squelching in the sodden ground. Was this the place? Near enough. There ahead was the little arching bridge to nowhere. On a sudden impulse she bent and put her hand in the water. It was fiery with cold. She straightened and waited for a little while, her hands in her pockets, watching the quiet water.

There was no supernatural menace here, she told herself, no nightmarish foreboding: it was just a lonely stretch of water beside a neglected and almost abandoned house. There was something sad about it, of course. But that was all. It looked haunted not because of ghosts, she thought, but because of ghost stories: tales told to make someone an honest living, helped along by gaslight and laudanum.

She turned to walk back the way she had come, trod sideways on to a boggy patch which gave way unexpectedly beneath her, lost her balance, and not believing what was happening, still thinking quite clearly *this is not real this is not happening*, paddled wildly with her arms in the air for a long doomed moment, and then fell backwards full length into the water.

Unlike the bad dream, everything did not stop right there. The water was freezing but about six inches deep, with at least a foot of very soft mud beneath it, that rose in stinking clouds as Rae thrashed about trying to get a footing, hauled herself upright, slipped over again with a splash, and finally crawled out coughing and blackened and spattered with duckweed, half crying with shock, half laughing; this shallow mudbath was hardly the stuff of nightmares.

For a moment she knelt on the bank, panting and cursing, helpless with giggles: it was impossible not to visualize what had happened, her own grave mooning about being all Emily Brontë, the sudden slapstick scrabble, the big muddy splash. But now her legs were shaking, it was hard to stand up, her teeth were chattering, and her hair was streaming muddy water in her eyes. Her coat was too heavy; after a short struggle she managed to wrench it off, and dragging it behind her squelched away in her ruined shoes, reaching the house at last in a rush of high spirits, shivering violently, her ribs aching with laughter.

'Mrs Givens! Quick, where are you!'

She had an overwhelming desire to talk about what had happened to her. Shuddering in the dark doorway she threw down the coat, pulled off her shoes and the filthy rags of her stockings, hauled the clinging dress over her head and added it to the sodden pile, and barefoot in her bodice and petticoat tried to run along the passage to the kitchen. Her great belly bounced uncomfortably; she had forgotten all about that, she realized. The stone floor was like ice. She looked back, and saw that she had left a snaking trail of droplets.

Mrs Givens appeared round the corner, and stopped dead with a great inward gasp.

'Sorry,' said Rae at once, 'I just –' She broke off; Mrs Givens was still staring at her as if horror-struck. Was it that bad? 'I fell in,' she finished, and to her own surprise began to cry.

'Dear Lord!' said Mrs Givens, shaking her head, and then she was suddenly herself again, opening a nearby cupboard and pulling out a pile of white towels, throwing one round Rae's shoulder, and drawing her down the passage into sudden lovely warmth, a little room Rae had never seen before, with a rug to stand on in front of the range.

'Quickly, ma'am, every stitch, or you'll catch your death.'

The bodice was impossible, wet. She had to let Mrs Givens unbutton it, her own fingers were too stiff to manage the buttons. The massive elastic brassiere, the clinging wet drawers, everything dark with filth.

'I'm getting everything all muddy, I'm so sorry –' Now Rae could hardly speak for shaking.

'Don't you fret now,' said Mrs Givens, setting a kettle on the spirit stove on the other side of the hearth. 'You sit here, ma'am, that's it. Won't be a minute.'

She disappeared, and presently Rae could hear the thundering of nearby bath taps turned on full. Shivering still in her towel, she looked about her. It was a small room, very plain and neat, with a tall ceiling and a window too high to see out of, a small battered armchair beneath it, covered with a blanket made of knitted squares. On the little table was a spotless white cloth. There were no pictures, just a few books on a shelf on the wall, a long mirror on a stand, and two small framed photographs on the mantelpiece.

Mrs Givens came back, accompanied by a little swirl of steam.

'Won't be long, ma'am.'

The kettle was boiling. It was very soothing to watch her going about tea-making, taking down a teapot from a cupboard, warming it, measuring out the tea, setting out china.

'I'm so sorry I startled you,' Rae said.

Mrs Givens smiled. Extraordinary, the sheer number of wrinkles all creasing together! The deeply hooded eyes still blue.

'I dint know you, ma'am, straight off. Dint know what to think!' She went to check the bath's progress.

Rae rose a little unsteadily, and picked up the smaller of the two photographs for a closer look. It was an ancient tin-framed oval of fading sepia, a Victorian girl in a little tilted straw hat, and a dress as closely fitted as upholstery, the skirt a festoon of swags and bows, the narrow bodice tucked and pleated and tightly encasing a bosom forced into one plump curve like a pigeon's. You felt breathless just looking at it, Rae thought. The face was lively and beautiful though; and the smile had hardly changed at all.

Mrs Givens came back ('All ready, ma'am') and began to pour the tea.

Rae held out the photograph. 'This is you, isn't it!'

'Sunday best.'

'Look at your tiny little waist!'

'Boned stays, ma'am, tight as they would go. You drink it while it's hot, now.'

'I love the hat. You looked so pretty. Oh, tea . . . oh . . . that's wonderful. Thank you so much, Mrs Givens.'

Meeting her eyes as she stood there, one hand still on the tea cosy, Rae suddenly remembered Miss Venables, her headmistress at school, a woman of superb presence who never once needed to raise her voice, who could silence the crowded hall at dinner time merely by entering it, and reduce the boldest member of the sixth form to abject tears in minutes. Natural authority, she thought: it was a mystery, a trick, perhaps, of experience or acting skill.

'Ma'am – was you just walking, at the lake?'

Rae hesitated. She could hardly say she had visited the lake because of a dream, especially one about falling into it. Not when she'd really gone and fallen into it, she thought, and suddenly she was on the verge of giggles again. She pulled herself together.

'I thought I'd walk over that little bridge-thing. But it was so boggy.'

'The edge ain't safe, ma'am. And you fell before.'

'Did I? So I did . . . clumsy of me.'

'Alright otherwise – no headache, ma'am – no spots before your eyes?'

Rae shook her head, smiling. I won't mention it: it's too silly, she told herself, and then found herself quickly saying it anyway: 'Just the most dreadful nightmares!' Adding what sounded even to her own ears like a faked and nervous laugh.

'''Tis common, ma'am, when you're expecting.'

'Is it? Really?'

'You being so near your time, the baby's dreaming his own dreams now. Along of your own – makes 'em all too strong! So my old mother used to say.'

'Did she? D'you think that's true? What would an unborn baby dream about?'

'Well now, ma'am, none of us can remember that. How about getting into that hot bath, now, you alright to stand up? Nice and slow, now.'

Her head swam a little as she stood up, trying to gather the towel more securely about her shoulders. 'Just a sec.'

Steadying herself against the mantelpiece she noticed the second photograph, and for a moment wondered if she was giddy again: 'Oh! What's this?'

For what she had taken to be a recent and rather uninteresting picture of two women seemed, close up, to be a photograph of two Mrs Givenses. It was a trick, thought Rae in confusion, a double exposure, like her own transparent image in *The Spectre of Sowerby Hall*. There was a line of glittering sea behind the two figures, and a glimpse of wall; Mrs Givens, unsmiling, stood arm-in-arm with herself, in two long severely tailored black coats, two plain hats pulled well down, two drooping muffs, and four black gloves.

'Me and my sister,' said Mrs Givens. 'We was the Kitto twins, long since.'

'Oh, of course –'

'Like as two peas we were.'

'Is she –'

'Dead these three years, ma'am.'

'I'm sorry.'

'Grand funeral she had: four black horses, crowds, shops closed and all sorts, you'd a thought she was royalty. Steady, ma'am? Here, take my arm.'

'I'm absolutely fine, now, thanks.'

'Straight to bed after your bath, ma'am, if you'll take my advice. I'll bring you your supper on a tray.'

That room again, thought Rae, with a pang; and soon it would be dark. But as Mrs Givens opened the bathroom door in a great gout of steam there was a faint buzzing click from somewhere unidentifiable, as if from the air all around them, and all the electric lights in the passage came brightly on at once.

'Oh glory!' said Rae joyously, and she reached over and gave Mrs Givens a kiss.

Lettie

You'd think The Body on the Beach was the most exciting thing that had ever happened in the world the way people went on and on about it. It was all over the papers too, *Local Woman Finds Body*.

Women she had never spoken to before had stopped Lettie in the street with fulsome enquiries as to poor dear Miss Thornby's state of mind, dozens had turned up daily at the house with flowers as if to a sickbed, three different policemen had shown up, one in plain clothes; he had given Lettie a nasty jolt. She feared policemen at the best of times, especially the sort with careers to make.

Some had expressed direct condolence. 'No, I barely knew her,' she had said several times now to various sympathetic faces. 'We worked in – different areas.'

Things had just begun to die down a bit when the inquest whipped them all up again. Two journalists had banged on the door, and a photographer had lain in wait outside the church hall. *Mysterious Aspects to the Case of the Body on the Beach*, shouted the local papers. Lettie had kept well clear of the inquest, of course, but it was impossible to avoid the findings, since few in Silkhampton seemed able for the moment to talk – albeit in lowered tones – about anything else.

To start with, Miss Wainwright's chemise had been found to be on inside out. There were those who thought this perfectly understandable. Why shouldn't a woman accidentally put a vest-like item on inside out, especially when dressing in the dark? Others claimed that poor Dolly had not so much been dressed as dressed *up*. Who would put her undies on back to front beneath her nicest blouse? Someone getting dressed in a hurry, perhaps. Or someone getting dressed *again* . . . Miss Wainwright, who'd a thought it?

Me, thought Lettie scornfully, though she did not say so. I'd've thought it. Why shouldn't the poor sod have had a private life?

Then there were the traces of Veronal. A largish dose, it was thought, a whole grain, but taken some considerable time before death. What did that mean? No one could say.

Tragedy of the Body on the Beach. Why on earth had Miss Wainwright, certainly dressed a little haphazardly, perhaps groggy from her sleeping draught, perhaps not, it was impossible to tell, made her way to a well-known beauty spot in the middle of the night? The implication that she had gone to meet someone there was obvious. Had she merely slipped somehow, and fallen? There were no witnesses and no signs of a struggle, but had whoever it was she met there pushed her over and done her in? Had Dolly Wainwright made enemies?

Of course not, said Sister Nesbit briskly, at the inquest. Such notions were absurd. No, she knew nothing of any affair of the heart. Yes, she and the deceased had been colleagues for many years. They had always been on good terms; amicable, but not foolish. No, she had not had any contact at all with Miss Wainwright on the day of her death; their shared workload had meant they rarely saw one another more than twice a week.

No, the deceased had said nothing to indicate distress of mind. She had been planning a summer holiday with her mother, had written to a boarding house in Ilfracombe with suggested dates; Miss Nesbit knew this because Miss Wainwright had asked her to drop the letter in the post for her. Yes; that had been the day before she died. No; she had not read the envelope. She had merely done as she had been asked.

Most of the other questions raised at the inquest turned out to be similarly unanswerable. Though practically everyone in town, at the clinic, in the market, met in passing, was eager to have a go, Lettie thought. Many seemed satisfied, or even rather pleased, that Dolly Wainwright, an apparently respectable working woman of close on forty, with no family but a widowed old mother, had secretly been seeing a married man, and messing about with drugs; under these circumstances it was hardly surprising that she had sickened and despaired, and finally taken the only decent way out.

'It just seems so unlike her, that's all,' said Miss Thornby unhappily, hanging about on the stairs the evening after the verdict.

Lettie's experience of landladies was extensive; she was not inclined to give any of them the benefit of any doubt whatsoever. But she had to admit that after the first shock Miss Thornby had been rather impressively matter-of-fact about her discovery, and had clearly neither enjoyed nor encouraged her own instant celebrity. In a similar position, Lettie found herself thinking, the Madam would have gone berserk, opining and running off articles and striking poses and making sure her face was all over the papers.

Perhaps for a toff Miss Thornby was not such a bad sort, thought Lettie, if you could overlook the accent and the inherited-property-owning, which you had to admit were hardly her own fault. And the fact that she frequently went in for the single vilest hairdo known to woman, the coiled-plaits-cum-earphones arrangement, which was. And as for her clothes – this was before one or two other things had gone wrong as well, when Lettie was still feeling comparatively light-hearted – her clothes just made you want to cry.

Aloud, her hand still on the bedroom-door handle, Lettie had asked her, 'You think it was an accident, then?'

'Yes. I do. Much more like her. Some sort of dreadful mistake, poor thing.' She sighed, turned away, ending the discussion.

Next morning another unsigned letter for Esme Bright had arrived. Lettie had telephoned London as soon as she could.

'She having a nervous breakdown or what?'

'Mrs Wickham needs a little reassurance, Esme. The place is obviously getting on her nerves, that's all.'

'You booked it, miles from bloody anywhere.'

'So who went to the back of beyond in the first place?'

'It's too risky. How'm I supposed to get there and back without being seen? I'll phone her.'

'Not good enough.'

And later that day Lettie had by chance run into Sister Nesbit on the High Street. Nesbit was pale with strain;

presumably her workload had doubled since Sister Wainwright's death, though the Council, if it was like every other Council Lettie had ever come across, would be in no hurry to step in with a replacement.

'How's it going?'

Nesbit shrugged, grimaced. 'Oh, you know.'

Not really, thought Lettie, looking at Nesbit's drawn face. Amicable, but not foolish, she had said at the inquest. But still she must miss her old colleague.

'If you need a bit of help,' said Lettie now, 'I could cover for you now and then. If you want me to.' It was safe enough to offer, she thought, and sure enough Nesbit's eyes widened with alarm:

'Gosh, that's frightfully kind of you!' she said. 'Of course patients always prefer someone they know – familiar face and all that, but still, thanks awfully – and if I'm ever, ha ha, you know, trying to be in *three* places at once –'

Lettie nodded. 'But I suppose you can't ah, manage what we were talking about, remember? The Mothers' Clinic?' For Nesbit, despite the little crucifix, had come across straight away, and agreed to learn the tenets of Lettie's own faith. Every child a wanted child, oh yes. An end to illegal abortion, yes please. Every woman in charge of her own destiny, absolutely, Nesbit had said, rolling herself a rather surprising cigarette. Contraception would save the world? Well, something had to, said Nesbit, coolly breathing out smoke.

'Sorry,' said Nesbit now. 'Simply no can do at the moment. You see how it is. Completely snowed under! In fact, I simply must dash right now – goodbye, Miss Quick!'

She bumped the bicycle into the street, swung herself into the saddle, and pedalled busily away.

Lettie sighed, watching her; selfless dedication always got her down.

Nesbit was clearly one of those for whom each child-birth was a jealously guarded pleasure; for not so much as an extra penny she would happily work day and night – was in fact already doing so – rather than lose out on a single delivery. Whenever she left the house she would always leave a note on her door as to exactly where she was to be found; Nesbit would have her own particular place at the end of a pew at the back of the church, so that she could always slip away when needed, and her own special seat at the Rialto, so that the usherette could always find her. Nesbit probably hadn't had any real off-duty time for years.

All very fine and noble in its way, thought Lettie as she set off for home. But carryings-on like that really spoilt things for us less fine non-noble types, who felt that training and professional expertise and long hard hours ought at least to mean enough money to bloody well live on.

And if Nesbit wasn't going to step into the clinic when Lettie was ready to move on, who would?

She was still feeling moody when she met up with Philip Heyward later, and he'd got on her nerves, and said one or two things she wasn't prepared to put up with, and she'd lost her temper and walked out in high door-slamming style, only to find him – and it was hard to comprehend just what he thought he was doing, a family man with his career to think of, let alone hers – standing on the door-step of her lodgings, having leapt presumably into his car and raced her there, all apologies and heart-rending flowery nonsense, and insistent enough for her to walk him along the street to the darker places off the square, where there were usefully deep shop doorways; anything to calm him down and shut him up.

It was the last thing she needed, frankly, what with all the scandalized gossip and policemen and reporters, and Nesbit crying off about the clinic, not to mention Her Ladyship going bonkers in the countryside; she'd phoned him next day, told him to behave himself or get lost, then after several attempts got through to Rosevear House and briskly spoken to Mrs Wickham herself, agreed to a personal visit, date to be arranged in the usual way, though not without giving it to her straight about who was running what degree of risk; and decided what with one thing and another to lay low for a while.

Shorter office hours, less likelihood of publicly running into Philip. She would dine in, and go to bed early.

Virtues which were, strangely enough, soon unexpectedly rewarded. Remembering Miss Thornby's more or less standing invitation to tea, and thinking with a shrug *well why not*, she had one afternoon knocked on the ground-floor sitting-room door at the right time:

'Oh, Miss Quick!' cried Miss Thornby, apparently delighted, the way nobs so often seemed, thought Lettie, when in fact they could hardly wait to wash the hand you'd just shaken, 'How very nice of you to join us!' and she was ushered in to find someone else there already, another plain toothy female a lot like Miss Thornby in generally disheartening appearance.

'Alice, my tenant, Miss Lettie Quick; Miss Quick, this is my dear cousin, Alice Pyncheon.'

Just like that! No awkward letters to write and rewrite or replies to wait for or dread, no complicated plan of campaign: a real live Pyncheon, presumably Miss A. F. herself, beaming at her from the armchair by the fire.

Miss Pyncheon wore an assortment of ancient knit-wear, a very long bias-cut silk scarf in the style that had looked dashing more than a decade earlier, and round steel-framed spectacles. She held out her bony fingers: 'How do you do?'

'Hello there!'

Miss Pyncheon, Lettie could tell, was of an even higher order of classiness than Miss Thornby. It was partly in the way she held herself, but mostly in her emphatic fluty voice:

'How are you settling in, Miss Quick – though of course present circumstances are *most* unfortunate, *most* unusual –'

'Very well, thanks,' she said.

Then there was some fussing about teacups and sponge cake. There was no hurry, Lettie told herself. Wait for an opening.

'And how *are* the local infants – measuring up as they should? *Bouncing* nicely?'

Perhaps Miss Pyncheon did not intend to sound quite so patronizing. Perhaps she thought she was being straightforwardly friendly to her cousin's lowly paying guest. I want her on my side, Lettie warned herself, and so carefully kept the only natural response, a low-key off-hand *Look just fuck off will you?* out of her eyes.

'Up to a point,' she said.

Miss Thornby said: 'Miss Quick doesn't actually work

with babies – do you, Miss Quick – it's more, well, family planning, isn't it?'

So word was out. Though it had not yet reached Miss Pyncheon, it seemed.

'Family what?' she asked teasingly, but clearly understood as she spoke. 'Oh. I see,' she added in a different tone, and blushed. There was a pause, and then:

'Alice has invited us to a lovely party,' said Miss Thornby brightly.

Strike me pink, thought Lettie. She knew she was supposed to say something on the lines of *Oh how very kind*, but often even now such formulations were simply beyond her. Luckily before she could try for one Miss Pyncheon herself weighed in: 'Oh, ah, only a *sort* of party, really – though I do hope you will be able to come, Miss Quick. My brother and I should be *delighted* to welcome you to our little show.'

Brother, thought Lettie. Mr F. W. Pyncheon. Aloud she asked: 'Little show?'

'Alice and Freddie own the Picture Palace,' said Miss Thornby. 'Perhaps you don't know it? It's next to St George's –'

'– Used to be the tithe barn,' Miss Pyncheon broke in.

'I think it was the very first cinema in the county, wasn't it, Alice?'

'Among the earliest, certainly. So clever of Freddie. My brother was simply mad about cameras from quite a small child, Miss Quick.'

'Oh really?' said Lettie nicely.

'It was his hobby,' said Miss Thornby.

'And then of course his profession,' said Miss Pyncheon. 'Portraits. Most artistic views.'

Pyncheon Photographic Studios, thought Lettie. 'And then he opened the cinema?' she said.

'We both did,' said Miss Pyncheon, 'it was a joint venture. Which reminds me, so is our little ah *entertainment*. Very small, very quiet – you are *sure* next week's not too soon, Norah, considering . . . the circumstances?'

'Quite sure,' said Miss Thornby firmly.

'Next Wednesday, then! Do say you can come, Miss Quick!'

Would Philip Heyward show up too, though? Did he move in the Pyncheon circle? Almost certainly not, Lettie told herself.

'I expect you know that the Picture Palace is no more, alas – but – the plan is, we're going to open it all up – for one night only! – and show one or two of the dear old silent favourites. Some light refreshments, perhaps a little sherry – and Freddie on the piano, Norah, just like the old days!'

'Oh, lovely!' said Miss Thornby.

Oh Gawd, thought Lettie. But still. It would be a small enough price to pay, she thought.

'Smashing,' she said.

Rae

That night as she was getting undressed for bed the wardrobe door swung itself open again. But the electric light was on, and while her heart jumped she was much less frightened than before.

You are broken hinges, thought Rae, you're a failing catch, though at the same time she was aware of the Dickensian echoes, of Scrooge telling Marley's ghost he was indigestion, a bit of toasted cheese. It's not the uncanny that's frightening, she reminded herself. It's all those stories about the uncanny. It's other people's imaginings, sprung from gaslight and too much laudanum, and made up in the first place to get a decent sale. It's pot-boilers. It's *The Spectre of Sowerby Hall*, for heaven's sake.

Still, for a tense moment she waited, in case now, on what she at the same time perceived to be the romantically correct third occasion, the message from the supernatural world might finally emerge.

But there was nothing. She breathed out: just an old wardrobe door hanging open. Even so, Rae decided, firm measures were definitely needed. She pulled the leather briefcase out from under the bedside table. Typescripts, half a dozen of them, none worth the paper they were written on, she thought, but every one of them stapled into a stout green cardboard folder. *The Last Dance*: that would do.

She laid the folder on the bed and with some difficulty tore a broad strip from the front cover, *The Last Dan*, then concertina'd it – no, too thick. She shortened it, refolded it, held it in place between wardrobe door and inner edge, and forced the door shut.

There. She finished undressing, slipped her nightdress on and picked up her book, but as she climbed into bed the baby shifted itself so violently that she gasped aloud. She had been feeling it move for months, of course, but just in mild flicks and nudges. Whereas this – she spread out her hands on the great rounded surge of her stomach – this had felt more like someone grumpily heaving themselves over in bed. Someone who couldn't get to sleep was thrashing about inside her. What's the matter, baby?

Most of the time Rae was able to close her mind to the enormity of what she was doing. She was going to *wait for her problem to solve itself*. She was going to *hand the brat over*. Others – paid professional experienced others – would take over and then she was going to forget the whole ghastly business as quickly as possible. Bad Moments had broken through now and then, of course, but largely she had managed to keep herself safe from tenderness; it broke over her now, in a great wave of desolation.

After a while she heard herself crying and stopped. She got out of the tumbled bed and remade it, practical sensible Rae, bucking herself up. She poured some of the water in her bedside carafe into the washbowl and splashed her face, her puffy eyes. Back in bed she resolutely turned out the lamp and lay down. Made my bed, she told herself: lying in it.

Won't sleep, of course, she thought, but presently she

was drinking gins with Dodie and the others, and when Mrs Givens came in and told them they couldn't trust th'electric everyone laughed at her accent, and Rae was ashamed. A long time passed, but soon she knew that it was time to go and stand beside the water.

This was the best place. The slope was shallow here, you could just walk right in easily among the floating leaves. The House was watching her from all its windows, some of them blinded. I don't want to, thought Rae, but there was no escaping the bitter enclosing water, because everyone wanted her to do it. The wide cold crowd all around her, they were waiting for her to do it, willing her to do it. She had no choice, she had to walk into the burning chill of the water that was already cramping her feet with cold, dragging heavily at her nightdress, pulling her in deeper and deeper –

She woke. A second more of sobbing horror; then the realization, blissful so quickly, she thought, that it almost made you feel nightmares were worth it. For a few moments more she lay quietly luxuriating in the unreality of fear. Strange how so powerful a nightmare had already nearly vanished. She was almost sure it had been something to do with the lake again; not surprising, really, considering what had happened earlier. She still had a sense that the dream had been familiar in some other way, that she had possibly dreamt it before.

Then it occurred to her that thank God, the electricity was on. Sighing, she sat up and found the switch, and at once the room leapt into brightness. It was dazzling though, so it was a few seconds before she saw that once again the wardrobe door was standing open.

There was the cardboard wedge, fallen out on to the floor. That was not possible.

And beside it lay a small white huddled shape. It was cloth, she saw.

It took all her courage to force herself out of bed to look at the crumpled shape more closely. Then she saw that it was her own spare nightdress, from the top drawer of the three inside the wardrobe. Slowly she bent and touched it, then took it chill into her hand, and straightened up to shake out the heavy folds. It was somehow no surprise at all to find that the nightdress was dripping wet.

Norah

A week after the inquest, it was rumoured that Sister Nesbit had come across a forgotten or well-hidden letter written by Miss Wainwright herself, unluckily addressed to one named only as *Dearest*, indicative of the utmost personal wretchedness, and begging for another chance, a final meeting, or one last embrace: details varied.

Miss Nesbit, frankly appealed to in person at the sewing circle (for old Mrs Ticknell was fearless), had lowered her head. Yes, she said, there had been such a letter, the merest scrap of a draft, passed immediately to the police; the subject was most painful; she would prefer not to talk about it, please.

All the confirmation anyone needed. By then of course gossipy attention included Miss Nesbit as well. She had shared a house with Miss Wainwright for years. How was it possible for her to have guessed nothing? She must have known Miss Wainwright's sordid secret; it had been her moral duty to speak up, and she had not done so. Perhaps she had such secrets of her own, who could tell? She was, after all, that bit younger than Miss Wainwright, and no less attractive to the opposite sex, though of course – if you were being strictly honest – that wasn't saying a great deal.

On the other hand, Miss Wainwright had clearly been a practised deceiver, ready to take full advantage of the innocent trustfulness of others. You hated to speak ill of the dead, but who would have suspected Dolly Wainwright of such slyness, such sustained and ingenious duplicity! Because as well as looking so prim and butter-wouldn't-melt, she'd always seemed – if you were being strictly honest – a bit on the gormless side.

'I wouldn't a thought she had the gumption,' said Mrs Bettins, sly across the counter at the bakery as she served one of her cronies, and Norah, standing two customers back, and catching only this line, knew instantly who they were discussing, and that it was a reference not to Miss Wainwright's act of self-murder, but to her sexual misconduct.

Everywhere Norah went these days she was no longer Miss Thornby, of the square, whose private life, social position and prospects were at once entirely familiar and deeply uninteresting; she was the Local Woman who had found The Body on the Beach.

She turned and walked out of the shop, though on the pavement she paused and looked at her watch before hurrying away, as if she had suddenly remembered some urgent appointment. It was not until she was nearly home again, with only half of the shopping she had set out for, that she realized that the discussion in the bakery had at least in part been aimed at her, in the hope of provoking some interesting reaction. And in her footling way she had given it to them; it had been another version of the Test, she thought; and once again she had not seen it.

The notion of the Test had come to Norah at school, and begun as a small but successful joke. They had been ploughing through an interminable series of booklets entitled *Great Women Through the Ages*, featuring saints, queens, explorers, poetesses, reformers, and other famous powerful women whose lives nevertheless had seemed always to involve terrible suffering of one kind or another, beneath which a lesser woman would have cracked.

'Oh crumbs that's me!' Norah had suddenly groaned aloud into the silence of prep one evening, 'I *am* the lesser woman!' and all about her had burst out laughing. It had been her finest social moment at school.

But afterwards the idea returned to her often, weighing more and more heavily. The lesser woman, she decided, was lesser not merely, or even largely, because she cracked beneath suffering, but because in any testing crisis she either failed to notice what was happening right under her nose, or noticed, dithered, and did nothing. Whereas Great Women noticed, understood, and acted: Great Women knew a Test when they saw one.

'Why don't you just go?' Guy had asked her in the first year of the war, when their parents had refused her permission to volunteer as a nurse. 'Just get on the train with me tomorrow, I'll bung you the fare.'

Norah's clearest Test: during the sleepless night that followed she had at least recognized that. Next day she had gone meekly to the station with Mamma and Daddy to see Guy off again, but as soon as the train was moving she had at last made her mind up and nodded, and Guy had understood, ducked instantly back from the window, opened the train door, grabbed her hand – she was almost running by then – and yanked hard as she leapt to join him. On board the train to London, with nothing but her handbag! Part of her elation then was in knowing that she had at last done something worthy of a Great Woman.

She had managed to enrol herself on a course that same afternoon, and then seen the smaller Test before her as well, the brief trip back to Silkhampton to face both parents alone before her training began. Passed that one too.

It was pleasant to remember such triumphs now and then, since failure was far more frequent.

Not long ago in the crowded greengrocer's, waiting to give Mamma's order, Norah had stood behind a short young woman in a headscarf buying potatoes, and who had then bought one banana, and taken her time finding the correct money. Norah had grown rather impatient, the shop was draughty, her own shopping bag too heavy. She wondered whether the young woman would be insulted if she simply dug out her own purse and handed over the tuppence herself. While she hesitated the young woman murmured softly to the grocer that she was very sorry, she didn't have enough after all; then she handed back the banana, and turned to leave, and Norah saw that the headscarf had misled her, and that she was not a short young woman at all, but a child, and very pale and thin.

For half a second more Norah had struggled with the idea of stopping the girl leaving, of buying her the banana, and with the impossibilities of thus drawing attention to herself, of letting the child know her poverty had been overheard and witnessed, of subjecting her to public charity.

Only some time afterwards, trudging home full of

generalized regret, had Norah recognized the Test pure and simple. Over and over again, that evening, the next day, she had replayed the scene, with herself quickly finding the tuppence and silently handing it over without fuss. What upset her most was the thought that she had been given the opportunity not merely to buy the poor girl a small treat, but to give her something far more significant: a demonstration of the occasional unforced kindness of others. She had been given that opportunity, and she had not seen it; she had failed the Test, and merely confirmed the essential indifference of the world.

It had been right to walk out of the bakery when that beastly Mrs Bettins said what she said, Norah told herself, as she opened the front door, but wrong to pretend there had been another reason. Looking at her watch had been a failure of nerve, a further hidden Test she had not seen in time.

She went down to the kitchen and dumped her half-empty shopping bag on the kitchen table, remembering the heads turning as she opened the bakery door, the quality of the sudden silence, and Mrs Bettins' open grin.

It was because of Miss Quick as well, she thought.

Mrs Placket at work had first passed on the information, just after the inquest. She and Annie had been frankly thrilled by their own proximity to the Local Woman, and even august Mr Pender had several times singled Norah out for some small office task more usually undertaken by Miss Pilbeam, merely in order, it seemed, to grill her for details. Miss Pilbeam herself refused to make or to countenance in her presence any reference whatsoever to Norah's sudden notoriety or to its cause; perhaps it was the effort involved in maintaining this fine indifference that made her so extraordinarily bad-tempered. ('Er's fair to burstin',' whispered Annie, grinning behind her hand.)

So the office was already a tense and self-conscious place, even more prone than normal to heavy silences, faked insouciance, and the quick exchange of meaningful glances. But:

'Was it true?' Mrs Placket had murmured one morning while Miss Pilbeam was safely closeted with Mr Pender. Was it true that Miss Thornby's lodger was (here Mrs Placket lowered her already lowered voice still further, so that Norah had to lean over to catch her words) doing the *Family Planning*?

Luckily Miss Pilbeam flung open the inner-office door at this point so that Norah was spared trying to make an instant answer. She had blushed, of course; perhaps all the reply Mrs Placket needed.

'Her didn't have a clue!' She imagined Mrs Placket passing this on, to someone else also richly amused. Or disgusted.

Miss Thornby of the square, the notorious Local Woman, sharing a roof with someone involved in *Family Planning*! No wonder Mrs Bettins had been unable to contain herself.

No new loaf, then. But one had to eat something. And tomorrow as well. In the larder: the dry remains of Sunday's small roasting joint of beef, on the very edge of edibility; a sad heel of cheddar, four potatoes, half an onion, two elderly carrots, and a paper bag containing three large but leathery mushrooms. What would Janet have done?

For once this familiar question quickly had an answer: toasted cheese for this evening, and everything else cut up, mixed together and cooked a bit, and then put in a pie, Norah thought. That was what Janet would have done, and it would have been perfectly lovely. Well then! She checked the flour bin. Yes, more than enough. And lard. And marge.

She dragged the scales, in their sticky coating of mysterious household grease, on to the kitchen table, washed her hands, carefully measured everything out, the way Janet had shown her all those years before, and began. She had always rather enjoyed rubbing fat into flour. Though of course it gave you lots of time to think.

Family Planning. Birth Control. This was the other phrase sometimes used to describe Miss Quick's employment and if anything, thought Norah, giving the bowl a little shake, it was somehow even more indecent. What would Mamma have said?

At once she was smiling down at her floury fingers: Norah had at first been very troubled by the thought of what Mrs Thornby would have said about Miss Quick's profession, because every time she formulated this usually lowering idea she had found that she was laughing. The first time she had imagined Mamma's expression on being introduced to Silkhampton's own *Birth Control* practitioner she had had to sit down, positively overcome. It was unseemly and inexplicable, as well as meanly disloyal, but still Mrs Thornby's notional pop-eyed spleen went on being funny, and for a while Norah consciously had to be careful not to think in public about what Mamma would have said, for fear of suddenly laughing out loud in the street, or at work.

Though her real difficulty, she thought, was her own maidenly ignorance. Norah knew broadly what *Family Planning* meant, but she had absolutely no idea what it involved in detail, and most fervently did not want to.

Mixture like breadcrumbs, or near enough. Norah ran the cold tap into a cup, and cautiously added water; careful now. Not too much. Blunt knife first: then one kneading hand, the way Janet used to do it. There. She wrung out the tea towel and draped it over the bowl, folding the corners neatly; all her cookery methods were an unconscious homage to Janet, whose personality still lingered sweetly for Norah in the ancient cake tins, the enamel pie plate, the very rolling pin she had laid out ready.

Half an hour for the pastry to gather itself, said Janet cosily in Norah's head. Kettle on? Yes, please.

One might have certain standards, but one must not be narrow-minded, Norah told herself as she scalded the pot. Miss Quick was honestly employed doing something not to be spoken of, and impossible to contemplate, but which would nevertheless stop the poor from having children they were unable to keep.

Norah had heard much disapproving talk over the years about the fecundity of the undeserving poor; had read more than once that people of the coarser kind, unintelligent, feckless, too lazy to earn an honest living, were nevertheless multiplying at a rate that far outstripped their gentler countrymen; that unless they were somehow prevented from doing so, the whole racial stock of the nation would be weakened. *Family Planning*, one might say, was actually patriotic, in the best post-war sense, not about dying for your country, but about making it a better, cleaner, healthier place.

Though Miss Quick herself, it had turned out, seemed to have very different ideas. Last week at one of their increasingly lengthy chats in passing on the stairs Norah had raised the modern patriotism idea, and she had sounded positively indignant.

'You what?'

Of course the awful thing, Norah had instantly remembered, was that she had no real idea what they were talking about, and knew that whatever else she said might reveal the extent of her ignorance, and Miss Quick would be aghast, or amused, or contemptuous. Or all those things.

'Isn't it?' she faltered. 'Am I wrong?'

'*I* don't know,' said Miss Quick. 'I don't care about all that rubbish.'

'Oh. I thought it was the – the bigger picture.'

'Don't give a stuff about that either.' Less sharp though.

'May I ask – what you do, ah, give a stuff about, then?' asked Norah, her heart beating fast.

'Putting women in charge,' said Miss Quick.

'Oh. You mean –'

'Not of the world,' Miss Quick broke in, suddenly intense, 'not the country, or the government. I just want to put women in charge of themselves. That's all.'

It was dismal for Norah to reflect that she had absolutely no idea how Miss Quick's work might help to put women in charge of themselves, admirable though this undoubtedly sounded.

'All women?' she hazarded.

'Rich and poor,' said Miss Quick. 'I'm not fighting the class war.'

'You don't give a stuff about that,' said Norah.

It was the first time she had heard Miss Quick laugh.

Such progress had certainly helped mitigate the discomforts of being the Local Woman, thought Norah, as she sipped her tea. Though what a pity Miss Quick had chosen to come to tea that day, when Alice was there!

'Miss Quick doesn't actually work with babies – do you, Miss Quick – it's more, well, family planning, isn't it?' uttered so lightly, as if such shocking words fell from her lips every day! An unspeakable phrase; yet Norah herself had spoken it, and merely to crush poor Alice.

Though it had hardly been the first time she had needed to shut Alice up; faced with anyone who was not, as she herself would put it, quite *quite*, Alice had always had a deplorable tendency to put one in mind of Mamma interviewing an unpromising new scullery maid. Norah had rather dreaded Alice meeting Miss Quick, and on those grounds alone, she told herself, should have been more prepared.

It's because the phrase is so much on my mind, she told herself. *Family Planning*. It's bound to spring to mind in an emergency. But then of course I simply panicked. Very awkward, telling her about the party like that; and jolly sporting of Alice to pretend so valiantly that she had meant to invite Miss Quick all along.

But now I will have to explain about Freddie, thought Norah. And the Picture Palace itself will be so grim at this time of year, freezing, damp, the seats all showing what two decades of hard wear had done to them. And the film, oh Lord. Well, how could one expect poor Freddie to understand how much things had come on since his day? Or Alice, for that matter?

Still, this thought reminded her once more that today was Thursday, programme change at the Rialto; Norah had been encouraging herself with this happy circumstance all day, in between all the other more oppressive thoughts. The blessed relief of the darkness, and of not being herself for a while. And the newsreel was always safely national, not local.

But much later, after half the sad cheese and the very end of the loaf – the other better slice and the rest of the cheddar left carefully between two plates for her tenant, the pie cooling in the meat safe (it had turned out very nicely, at least as far as looks went) – the door opened as she was buttoning her coat in the hallway, and Miss Quick herself bounced in. For once she seemed disposed to chat.

'You off out?'

The habit of instant truth was impossible to resist. 'Just taking myself to the pictures.'

'Woss on?'

'I don't know – it's got Dracula in it though. Bela Lugosi, you know.'

'Mind if I come?'

Even at the time Norah was struck with admiration. She knew she could never have formed such words herself, let alone make them sound so genuinely casual. Mind if I come? Impossible! She knew she would always have waited to be asked. And if I was waiting for someone like *me* to do the asking, thought Norah, I'd never go at all, because the someone like me wouldn't be able to ask either. How simple some things looked, from the outside! Despite all this she gladly answered straight away:

'Oh – not at all! Please do!'

Rae

She woke, and for a moment had no idea where she was. She was lying in a high narrow bed, well tucked in, warm, lavender-scented. There was a little bunch of primroses on the bedside table beside her. Was this Mrs Givens' own bedroom?

Then she remembered everything all at once, the wedge of cardboard, the sodden nightdress. And herself running, despite the great jouncing belly, holding it with one hand as she staggered along the corridor and ran crying down the stairs.

Small far-away Mrs Givens in her nightdress and shawl, throwing open a door at the end of the downstairs passage, running towards her.

'What is it, my lovely?'

Then there was a curious gap, and an odd memory of sitting down, leaning her head against something hard. Rae worked her hand free of the tightly tucked-in bedclothes and felt her temple. A bump: tender.

She had been lying down for a while, she remembered, on the stone flags of the passage. Her fingertips vividly recalled their icy hardness. She remembered feeling quite relaxed there on the floor, not worried about anything. No, nothing more would come back. Presumably she had recovered enough from her faint to walk here, to Mrs Givens' own bedroom. To get into this bed.

Rae sat up and looked about her. Unfamiliar curtains, cotton striped green, moved a little in the draught from the window, but the light about them looked sunny. Rae slid out of bed, with some difficulty as the bedstead was so high, and slipping the black shawl, left on the back of a chair, round her shoulders, went to look out. This was the front of the house, at the far side, view of the weedy path curving out of sight.

I can't stay here. Not a day longer. Oh, what shall I do?

She turned, and looked about her at the room. Small mirror over the fireplace, no, don't look into it, wait until you feel strong enough. A sewing basket with knitting in it. Two more photographs in metal frames on the small mantelpiece. More oddities perhaps, she thought, remembering those in the sitting room, and bent to look: a school photograph of Edwardian children, dark, under-exposed perhaps, and dated 1911; poor things, just the wrong age, she thought automatically, half the boys dead no doubt; the other a young couple – the rather beautiful consumptive-looking young man was Mrs Givens' son, presumably. Another spoilt picture, though, a real botched job, the girl on his arm so badly lit you'd almost think she was a black, thought Rae.

She was still puzzling over it when there was a knock at the door, and Minnie came in, smiling broadly over a heavily laden tray, and bringing with her a heartening smell of buttered toast.

Minnie from the village, who came some mornings to help out with The Rough, Rae remembered: Human Contact Number Four. But those light-hearted days seemed long ago now.

'Morning, ma'am,' said Minnie, banging the tray down on the little table. 'You feeling better? You want your breakfast now? 'Tis mumbled eggs!'

Rae smiled with pleasure. She had heard Minnie speak only rarely, for her working hours were sporadic and she tended in any case to stay out of sight in the enormous Victorian laundry room, where Rae had glimpsed her once or twice, ponderously turning the dolly in a pan of steaming water.

It wasn't just her accent, thought Rae; it was the way she seemed to revel in every word, charging each one with potent domestic significance.

'You Feeling Better? You Want Your Breakfast Now? 'Tis Mumbled Eggs!'

Rae sat down on the bed, feeling instantly more cheerful; not exactly ready for anything, but more herself, she thought.

'Hello, Minnie, yes I am, how very kind of you, thank you so much.'

"Er says, as you're to stay in bed for now.'

And it was the *w* sounds, thought Rae. So cosy. They went on such a long time. For Nowwww.

'Is this Mrs Givens' bedroom, Minnie?'

"Tis 'er own bed! I come here sometimes,' she added proudly. 'When I were a little maid. Ma says to me, she says, Minnie my lamb, you come right in here for a cuddle, and so I did.'

This was a little puzzling, but Rae's attention for the moment was elsewhere. 'Is there tea in that pot?'

'Bless me, I forgot! 'Er says, I am slow,' said Minnie, carefully pouring out, 'but I am thorough.'

'So – you were working here when you were a little girl?' Odd!

Minnie laughed. 'Why no, I was here, ma'am! In th'ome.'

Th'ome?

'With all the other childer, ma'am.'

'What children?'

Minnie drew back looking anxious, and Rae understood she had spoken sharply.

'I'm sorry, Minnie, I just didn't know, you see. About the other children,' she added. What are we talking about?

'We done lessons and all sorts, I was learned the washing. Us had our beds. Et our dinners. Done our play. Skipping. Ma was our ma. See?'

Rae put the knife and fork down. The scrambled eggs were suddenly no longer edible. She was remembering the strange number of barred windows she had seemed to see at the back of the house. That had been no trick of the light at all, she realized. The windows really were barred. Not to imprison anyone, but to keep small children safe. House with Lake had its secrets after all, and this was one of them.

'You sure you're alright, ma'am? Shall I go and get 'er for you?'

'No, I'm fine, thank you, Minnie. I'm absolutely fine.'

Where was Mrs Givens, anyway? Rae thought of her earliest impressions of her, the real-life version of that fairly familiar supporting character, the housekeeper of an old empty house in the middle of nowhere. A supporting character in a ghost story, of course, she thought now. But what else was she? Ma to all those other children. *Us had our beds.* An orphanage.

That superb natural authority – yes, I thought of experience, the trick of it; I remembered Miss Venables from school. So. It seemed that Mrs Givens, whilst of course real enough, genuinely a housekeeper efficiently keeping a house, was at the same time acting the part. No wonder I thought of Central Casting, Rae thought. She's a natural.

At the door Minnie turned. 'You're to stay in bed for now, 'er said. You got a do what she says.'

Rae smiled. 'Have I?'

Minnie tiptoed back in again, and looked about her, a parody of furtiveness. ''Er were proper vexed,' she said in almost a whisper, 'on account of the Lake. We ain't allowed to play by there. Ain't safe, that Lake.'

'No,' said Rae, 'it certainly isn't.'

Minnie dropped her voice even further. 'You know. On account of. The woman in it.' Then quickly clapped one enormous hand over her mouth. 'I weren't supposed to say! And I forgot!'

'Oh, that doesn't matter,' said Rae, and was surprised and pleased by how calm and friendly she sounded. 'I knew all about her anyway.'

'Did you see 'er?' Minnie asked. 'I ain't never seen 'er,' she added conversationally; she was evidently very easy to deceive. 'Plenty have, mind. A-standing in the reeds with 'er ankles in the water!'

'Minnie,' said Mrs Givens sternly from the doorway. 'You know I won't have that kind of talk. You're upsetting Mrs Wickham, you bad girl.'

Minnie now a parody of anguish. She caught up the bottom edge of her apron, and held it bunched in both hands over her moon-face, so that only her appalled eyes showed. 'Oh Lord!' she cried through it. 'I'm sorry!'

'Come straight back, I said to you, didn't I, and now look – I've had to come and fetch you!'

'I forgot,' said Minnie sadly.

'Off you go now,' said Mrs Givens, still rather harshly. Minnie dropped her apron and fled.

For a long moment Rae and Mrs Givens met one another's eyes.

'I think we need to talk. About some things,' said Rae at last.

Mrs Givens folded her arms, her gaze unflinching. When she spoke her tone was all Miss Venables, and Rae felt herself quail a little already.

'Indeed we do, ma'am,' she said.

Norah

The square was looking its best, Norah saw happily as she opened the front door, the whole generous space freshly swept, and the varied and rather beautiful Georgian buildings enclosing it all glowing pinkish-gold in the last of the sunshine. The shops were still open, a few striped blinds still down, their windows lit.

They set off, skirting the square. It was the first time they had gone anywhere together, the first time they had walked along side by side. Pleasant thoughts, for Norah, though she knew they would of course be seen, and remarked upon. Coarsely, by some. At least it was dusk.

It was striking how small Miss Quick was, Norah thought. You didn't notice so much normally. But she hardly reaches my shoulder. I feel rather huge beside her. Well, of course I *am* rather huge. Perhaps we look like Laurel and Hardy, her so small and thin, me such a thumper. *Such a stalwart thumper of a girl!* sighed Mrs Thornby, turning away from Norah's image in the mirror, long ago.

They rounded the corner, and at last Norah came up with something she was prepared to say aloud: 'D'you go to the cinema often, Miss Quick?'

'Not really,' said Miss Quick. Norah took a moment to recover, then tried again:

'This is my favourite street,' she said. 'I've always loved the name. But it's awfully pretty, don't you think?'

Silver Street was ancient, and the houses and shop-fronts were all different, some with bow windows and stone steps, others with covered entrances deep inside their double windows like tiny arcades. The jeweller's, the little plush trays emptied now. The arcade next to it lit and crammed with ready-made shoes, the sweetshop a bow window full of gleaming jars.

Miss Quick stopped at Modes de Madame, where both arcade windows were stuffed from top to bottom with headless female torsos in blouses of every imaginable shape and colour, rayon, silk, lawn, plain, embroidered, striped, and flowery.

'I like that one,' said Miss Quick.

'Very nice,' said Norah, peering in too, and managing not to gasp aloud at the price tags each wore like a little paper brooch on one shoulder.

'And that one. The blue. What about you?'

Two weeks' wages, thought Norah. 'They're all very nice,' she said. This was not a game she had ever played before, and she was uncertain of the rules. Nearly all her own clothes had been made for her: planned beforehand, discussed in detail with Miss Harlesden, Mamma's own dressmaker, who had always done her best to conceal Norah's large unwieldy frame in cleverly constructed outfits she referred to as 'costumes', like today's suit of brown tweed, mid-calf skirt and matching coat, which fell just below the knee.

Such clothes wore well; the brown tweed had been made nearly ten years earlier, with little reference to fashions then current, in order that (as Miss Harlesden had explained at the time) it would never seem out-of-date. Finished seams, stout linings: with any luck her clothes would last for ever, thought Norah. Would have to do so, in fact, she remembered.

'Perhaps that one,' she said, pointing into the crowded window of Modes de Madame. 'The green one, with the long sleeves. Or the grey? What d'you think?'

'Don't be stingy,' said Miss Quick, 'get both.'

Norah smiled uncertainly. They walked on, past the chemist's window full of shapely bottles of mystery coloured fluids, past the beery breath of the pub and the Little Owl Tearooms on the corner, Norah understanding with a little pang of pity that of course someone like Miss Quick would never have known the luxury of clothes expressly tailored to fit her. Her coat for example, though perfectly respectable, was (Norah could not help noticing) not only well-worn but rather too large for her.

It occurred to her suddenly that the reason the coat did not fit properly was because it had actually been made for someone else; that Miss Quick, unable to purchase even ready-to-wear items, must needs resort to the cast-off, the second-hand.

Someone else's old clothes. Often Norah helped to sort jumble for the church fete or the WI, and the stink in the church hall afterwards, of so much mingled human staleness, had always transferred itself to her hands, on to her own clothes, for a while.

She remembered too the several days she had spent clearing out Mamma's wardrobe. Miss Harlesden herself had come, red-eyed, to help sort and bundle everything up, the wool skirts and fitted jackets and simple blouses; all to be given, as Mrs Thornby had directed from her deathbed, to one of her charities.

Miss Harlesden had urged Norah now and then to keep some especially valuable item, the pre-war beaded velvet evening cloak, the silver fox-fur stole. 'What about this, then, Miss Thornby?' Or lightly worn day dress: 'Could alter it for you easy, Miss Thornby.'

And Norah had looked again at some wizened garment full of her mother, and tried not to shudder. The thought of wearing anything Mamma had held against her own skin was terrible to her, she had been surprised by the strength of her revulsion. It had been all she could do to touch the things as Miss Harlesden had hauled them from the wardrobe.

'Hello there,' said a jovial voice. It was Dr Heyward, one hand politely lifted to the brim of his hat, Mrs Heyward on his arm, very *soignée* as usual in furs and a hat of sleekly tucked and feathered velvet, perched sideways on her head as if ready to take flight all by itself.

Dr Heyward booming: 'So you do actually stop working now and then, Sister Quick?'

His wife smiled stiffly, and said, 'How lovely to see you out and about again, Miss Thornby! Miss Quick.' She gave the second-hand gabardine a glance she did not trouble to hide, and Norah remembered that early in her marriage young Mrs Heyward had several times made Mamma friendly overtures, quite as if they were social equals; Mrs Thornby had very much enjoyed letting her know otherwise. *Ghastly woman*, she said to Norah now.

It was pleasant, reflected Norah as they walked on, to agree now and then with one's Mamma.

'I didn't know you worked for him,' she said, after a pause.

'I don't. I work on my own.'

Norah glanced down at her. 'Actually, I've never really taken to him,' she said. She knew of course that it was wrong, absurd of her to blame him for the death in childbirth of her old schoolfellow Grace Gilder. Heaven knew he had done his best; no one could have done more. Even Grace's adopted mother, Mrs Dimond, who had attended so many childbeds herself in the days when such untutored care was legal, had said not a word against him, though she'd said so many about poor Grace's midwives, Sister Goodrich, and, ah – of course, poor Dolly Wainwright – that there had been talk at one time of slander, and the threat of a court case.

'There's just something about him,' Norah finished hopefully. But Miss Quick only said: 'You see her hat?'

'I was concentrating on the fur,' said Norah, 'but I did happen to notice it. She always looks like that.'

'You know her?'

'Not well, really. She's not out and about that much. Well, three small children, I think. Look – St George's. Begun in 1143. Or thereabouts. Have you seen the memorial brasses yet?'

Miss Quick looked blank.

'They're very distinguished. If you like memorial brasses. And over here: the Picture Palace.'

They stopped for a moment, Norah leaning against the railings. 'You can see it used to be a barn, the tithe barn, actually. The Roundheads kept pigs in it for reasons best known to themselves. And horses in the church. Then nothing happened for years and years, until a particularly louche vicar with pots of money made it into a theatre, and put on private performances. Caused a great deal of talk apparently. Though I fear it was just his sisters singing operetta, that sort of thing. Then it was the church hall for another hundred years or so. Alice did the Sunday school there, for simply ages. You know: Alice, my cousin.'

'Pyncheon,' said Miss Quick. They walked on, past the remains of what had clearly once been a small billboard set up on one side of the arched doorway.

Oh gosh, I still haven't told her about Freddie, Norah thought, as they turned the corner. I must, of course. Soon. But not tonight though. 'Freddie was so determined,' she said aloud. 'Their mother was simply *horrified*, the kinematograph was *so* disreputable. But they did frightfully well – the place used to be packed, people coming for miles. Of course, this was during the War, before the Rialto. Then everyone went there instead. I used to feel so guilty about it, but there's no comparison really, freezing in winter, and the music was always just Freddie on the piano. We cross here. Then this way. Not that he isn't awfully good, even now. But of course they're not wired for sound. And the Rialto's all – well, here we are. You can see for yourself.'

It occurred to her that never before had she arrived at the Rialto quite so openly; in fact she had always preferred the winter months, when she could sneak into the cinema under cover of darkness. And she had generally been alone before, for of all Norah's friends only Alice had any time for such lowbrow entertainment, and she, of course, felt obliged to avoid the very street the Rialto stood in.

There was no queue, so they paused for a moment in front of the poster, which featured Bela Lugosi's head in huge menacing silhouette, the glaring eyes just visible, and a very small frightened-looking blonde in a nightdress.

Oh *yum*, thought Norah. 'What d'you think?' she asked, then had a moment's dread. Why had she not thought of this before? 'I, ah, prefer to sit at the back, myself,' she said.

Miss Quick shot her a tiny look, then said, though amicably enough, 'I'd never pay more than eightpence,' and pushed open one of the heavy glass doors. The familiar rich intoxicating cinema-smell of chocolate, face powder, and tobacco smoke slipped warmly out to greet them.

Rae

'Where are we going? Not to the Lake, surely!'

Mrs Givens snorted. 'It's just a lake, ma'am. We'll take the other path.'

A weak sun shone as Rae followed Mrs Givens through a series of corridors, down a creaky wooden spiral staircase and finally through a door Mrs Givens carefully locked again behind them, leading out into a big cobbled yard.

'This is where they used to play,' said Mrs Givens over her shoulder.

Rae tried not to visualize them. But a ball would bounce well against those walls, she thought. The cobbles were smooth enough to skip on. 'You were the housekeeper? The matron? Why did it close?'

'Lease ran out. Had to find another place. Not up to me, ma'am. Through here, now.' She took a single great iron key from the pocket of her overcoat, and opened the tall gate. 'See? This is the easy way.'

'I went the long way round,' said Rae.

'You shoulda asked me, ma'am.'

'Would you have let me come this way?'

'Why not? You ain't a child.'

'So what Minnie said –'

'Minnie will always be a child, ma'am.'

'Yes. I can see that.'

'So she won't never come this close. On account of her blessed woman in the water.'

They had arrived at the little arched bridge at the end of the lake. On one side, the water; on the other, reeds, blending into the soft marsh grass. Up close the delicate pretty wrought-iron bridge looked very battered, its white paint peeling and stained green with algae.

'Is it safe?'

For answer Mrs Givens walked on to it, and stopped in the middle with her arms folded, waiting for Rae to join her. 'No ghosts here, ma'am. No ghosts anywhere. Just folk imagining things. Scaring themselves. Or scaring children, make 'em behave. Keep 'em safe.'

'I didn't make it up, you know. About the wardrobe door and everything.'

'I'm sure you didn't, ma'am.'

'Well, please don't tell me it's just a broken hinge or something.'

'Course it is. And floorboards.'

'What?'

'Place so damp, see, I bin lighting fires in there these past few weeks. Dried the boards too, and they do shrink, ma'am, and move when you walk on 'em.'

'Oh really. And the cardboard wedge – you saw that, didn't you – I *forced* it shut. And. The nightdress. It was just *there*, when I woke up! All wet – when I woke from my umpteenth bloody nightmare about this, this horrible lake!'

'Don't you upset yourself, ma'am –'

'How d'you explain the nightdress, then? If it wasn't – *her*? Something from the water, I don't know – she's in there though, isn't she – what happened? Tell me!'

'I've known this place all my life,' said Mrs Givens coolly, 'and I ain't never seen a ghost, or heard one, nor nothing else, on account of, there ain't any.'

'You thought I was her though, didn't you! When I fell in that time, all wet in my petticoat, you were frightened – you thought I was her!'

'I've heard the stories, ma'am, course I have; I won't deny you give me a turn just for a second. But ghosts do *not* exist, ma'am, they do not, and if you really want to know who went and dropped your nightie on the floor all soaking wet I'll tell you: it was *you*.'

'But – no, I didn't, I swear!'

'You did it yourself, ma'am.'

'How can you say that – d'you think I'm mad? Or – or lying – what?'

'No, ma'am,' said Mrs Givens. 'Ain't you never heard of sleepwalking?'

'What?'

'I think you sleepwalked.'

'Well, you think wrong then,' cried Rae, turning to stamp away. 'That's absolutely – I mean, I've never –' She broke off.

'Never what, ma'am?'

Rae felt suddenly a little breathless. She turned back. 'Well, I was a – it was years ago. Years. Not since –'

'Since when?'

'Since I was a little girl.'

'You walked in your sleep, ma'am?'

'Well, I – they said I did. Yes.'

'Let's go over here, there's the seat, look,' said Mrs Givens, and they crossed the bridge and walked on a little, to a semicircle of bushes run wild, once a rose arbour sheltering another piece of delicate wrought ironwork, a bench to match the bridge in peeling paintwork and greenery. Mrs Givens gave it a wipe with her handkerchief, and they sat down facing the back of the house across the still water.

'There, not too damp. And if you don't mind me asking, ma'am, what else was happening that time, when you did the sleepwalking? That *first* time, I should say.'

Rae felt in her pockets for a handkerchief. She seemed to be feeling too many emotions at once for any to dominate and help her make sense of things. How could she have forgotten that terrible time, she wondered? And yet she had. She had never spoken of it since, and without any effort on her part it had disappeared as if it had never been. There was a sort of wonder about remembering it now, as of discovery.

'It was, well . . . it was just after my mother died. I was ten. And I had to go away to school. And I apparently – did this sleepwalking. A bit.'

'What did you do, do you remember?'

Rae shook her head. She had just one picture of herself, somehow exactly as she was now and at the same time a little girl with her hair in two plaits, standing bewildered at the bottom of a staircase, or in an unfamiliar kitchen, as if her sleeping body had been looking for something. Someone.

'Well, 'tis no matter,' said Mrs Givens. 'Except that you're doing it now.'

'Oh, but surely –' Rae began again to deny it. But as she spoke she remembered her hot draggled bed, and how she had got out of it to wash her face; she remembered pouring water from her carafe into the washbowl, to splash her swollen eyes. The chill of the water, her hands in the bowl.

Oh God it was me, she thought. Of course it was. I was the ghost. I was *The Spectre of Rosevear House*, I haunted myself. Strange thought: anyone watching me would surely have thought they were seeing the real thing, rising in my nightgown, going to the wardrobe, opening it, taking out my nightdress and setting it in the bowl. Was I washing it, in my sleep? As if I was trying to make something soiled clean again. But I would all the multitudinous seas incarnadine.

Ghosts in stories were never pregnant, though. Were they? Rae could not remember one.

'Shall I tell you for why, ma'am?' said Mrs Givens.

Rae looked at her, a little startled; for a moment she had forgotten where she was. Straight away though it seemed imperative not to hear any more, talk any more, give away any more.

'No. No, thank you. I think I'll go back now, Mrs Givens. I'm feeling rather tired.'

'Not yet.' The hooded eyes so hard! 'Why are you here, ma'am? Why are you staying in this house all alone?'

'You know why – I simply wanted privacy, that's all.'

'You ain't being private. You're being secret.'

Without thinking about it Rae took refuge in class, summoned her old standby the haughty Lady Hermione Pringle: 'I *beg* your pardon?'

'I know it ain't none of my business. But I can't let you do it. Not with you sleepwalking and all.'

'Thank you, Mrs Givens,' said Lady Hermione superbly, standing up, 'that will be all.' Mrs Givens made no move to restrain her, but stood up too, followed her.

'You shouldn't have forgotten him, ma'am,' she said.

Lady Hermione spoke over her shoulder: 'I haven't the *least* idea what you're talking about.'

They came to the gate that led into the courtyard. Mrs Givens darted in front of it, the great key ready in her hand. 'Mr Wickham, ma'am. Remember *him*?' She shoved the gate open.

'My husband is away,' said Lady Hermione crisply, as she swept through. 'He is in the diplomatic service.'

'No he ain't,' cried Mrs Givens, banging the gate shut behind them. 'Because you know what? You ain't said a word about him all this time. Not his likes, his dislikes. His little *ways*. Not a word. Mr Wickham, ma'am. Your husband. You forgot him.'

There was a pause.

'Ah,' said Rae, putting her hands in her pockets. 'I suppose that was a bit careless.'

'You slipped up there, ma'am. But he don't exist,' Mrs Givens went on. 'Do he? You ain't got a husband at all.'

'Ah, well, there you are wrong, Mrs Sherlock bloody Givens,' said Rae, 'because it would be absolutely fine – well, perhaps not absolutely fine, but not so completely impossible, if I didn't have a husband. The difficulty – if you must know – is that I *have*.'

'Oh.'

There: that foxed her, thought Rae in small triumph. She hadn't expected *that*. 'He's a rotter and a swine and we are in the apparently endless process of divorcing, as it happens, but unfortunately at the moment he is still all legally mine. And I am his. And he'd love it, he'd simply *love* it, if I had a child that can't be his! He would make sure everyone knew. And that would be it. I'd be finished. You think I can work, d'you think anyone will employ me, ever again, with a bastard in tow? I *can't* have a baby right now. I just can't.'

'And the . . . real father, is he –'

'Oh, he buggered off,' said Rae brutally, and saw Mrs Givens flinch. 'Now open the door, for God's sake. Please.'

Mrs Givens' hands gave Rae a pang, so gnarled, so old. But when the door was shut behind them she began again: 'You got money though! Paying a fortune to stay here – you got a bob or two! And you don't want to do it. Sleepwalking, nightmares – because you don't want to do it, not in your heart –'

'You don't know anything about my heart.'

'This is worse than you being a little girl, and your own ma dying. This is worse than that. What you're doing. Believe me, ma'am.'

'I'm going to pack now,' said Rae. 'I'm leaving.' She began to hurry along the corridor, hardly knowing where she was going. It was difficult to walk fast so encumbered; she put her hand over the great swollen front of herself, and through her coat felt the baby kick its little self against her palm, felt it both inside her and out.

'Find some other line a work, ma'am, why don't you?' Mrs Givens, horrid old incubus, jabbering at her shoulder.

'Leave me alone.'

They came to a large entrance hall at the front of the house; the flags had given way to worn black and white marble, and the grand opening curve of the mahogany staircase. Sunlight gleamed through the complicated tracery of the windows over the cobwebbed and padlocked double doors. Where on earth did these stairs go to? The thick coiled banister was dusty beneath Rae's palm.

'Wait, ma'am, please!'

'This has got nothing, *nothing* to do with you! Just go away! Leave me alone!' Rae began to haul herself upwards.

'No, ma'am, listen!' cried Mrs Givens at the bottom. 'I had a – friend once. She done it, years back. She didn't have no job, no money, no husband, she done it for the best.'

Rae stopped, turned. It was clear to her, from Mrs Givens' anguished voice, exactly who the friend had been. For a moment they looked at one another in silence. Then Mrs Givens swallowed, and went on more calmly:

'But what – this friend a mine dint know was – that babby, she couldn't have no more. She give up her only one, ma'am. Her only treasure. And she never got him back.'

This was too much.

'Oh, God.' Rae sank down on the stair above her.

'What other folk think – it ain't as important as all that. It ain't important enough. See?'

Rae put her hands to her hair, thinking; then came to a decision. It was not exactly all her own to make, of course, but – too bad. If there was anyone in the world that you could trust with this, she thought, it was Mrs Givens. And it would be *such* a relief to tell her.

'Listen,' she said. 'You're right: I'm being secret, not private. You're right about nearly everything. But I'm not going to give up the baby. I'm not doing that at all. Or not exactly.'

'How d'you mean?'

'There's a plan,' said Rae.

Lettie

Word was spreading now; some days the clinic was almost full. Which was lucky, Lettie thought. Because Philip Heyward was beginning to get on her nerves. Every time she picked up the office telephone she knew it might be him, and often it was, four, five times a day. Notes too, full of kisses and declarations. Of course it had been rather thrilling at first. But for her the glorious excitement of the early days was already wearing off. He had a way of smirking that she kept noticing now. He kept saying things that made her wonder if he was a bit thick.

'That's the kind of chap I am!' he said, fairly often, about quite boring things like what sort of motor car he liked best, and why, or about golf, the dullest game for dullards in the world, Lettie thought. She didn't like the stuff he put on his hair, and when he changed it she didn't like the new stuff either. I don't like his hair, she thought, and heard her own inner voice, sullen, childish. Unappeasable.

'I say. Thought I'd take a few pictures of you. D'you mind?'

'How d'you mean?'

'Well, you know – like this.'

'You must be joking!'

No, no, he'd said, he was completely serious: it was because of her perfection, her secret beauty. He just wanted to keep a record of it, a proof. It would be entirely private, of course, it would be something just the two of them knew about and shared –

'No.'

'Oh, say yes, do – it would be artistic – it's a hobby of mine, you see, photography, in my own small way. You're so lovely, you see. Wouldn't you like to keep just a little of that loveliness for ever?'

'I said no.'

'It would be fun – I'd undress too, if you like.'

'You can stand on your head for all I care. Ask me one more time I'm off, alright?'

'Lettie – you don't mean that!'

He kept saying things like that, she'd noticed. Telling her what she meant. Telling her she was wrong. When of course he didn't know her at all.

An early admirer had once shown Lettie his pornography collection, photographs set neatly in an album like family portraits, only instead of aunts in their Sunday best, and wedding groups, this was full of postcards of naked women, sometimes with men, wearing ropes of pearls, or feathers, or other stuff meant to signify abandoned luxury. The admirer had thought to titillate:

'Look, sweetie! Ever seen anything like this?' He had turned the pages for her, nasty old letch. She said nothing.

'What about this one! Eh? Eh?'

In almost every one the woman had looked into the camera's eye, and thus into those of whoever saw the photograph. What men there were, no matter how their bodies were displayed or entwined, looked elsewhere, as if unaware of the camera, caught up in what they were doing, holding, embracing.

All you had to do, thought Lettie, was imagine those parts of the scene the camera left out: the rest of the ordinary slummy back room, one corner disguised maybe with a borrowed rug and a length of curtaining, but elsewhere the sagging bed, the bare floor, the dirty windows painted shut; the cameraman in his braces with a roll-up in one hand; the cheesy smell of the socks the man had thrown in a corner, and of yesterday's cabbage from the floor below; a crying baby nearby; children playing outside. Maybe the baby was this woman's; perhaps when the shutter clicked and the man whose name she did not know released her she had hurried over to where it lay wrapped in its blanket in front of the fire, and soothed it with a little feed.

After a bit Lettie had just got out of bed and started dressing. Old Letch had been another one eager to tell her what she thought. 'Sweetie, I thought better of you – don't be so prudish – the human body is a thing of beauty!'

It was in the women's gaze, she had worked out later on the tram home. That look, almost always directly at the camera and the potential customers beyond it, was somehow the opposite of real life, where a direct look might be a challenge. Here it signalled only submission. I am content to be displayed, said each bought smile; look all you please, I meet your eyes because I am available. The whore's invitation, captured in black and white: some of the saddest pictures Lettie had ever seen.

'I'm sorry,' Philip had said. 'I'll never mention it again. Taking your picture, I mean. Say you forgive me. It's only because I'm so mad about you. Wanting to see you all the time. You do know that, don't you? Absolutely crazy about you. That's the kind of chap I am.'

The trouble was she just couldn't summon the right response any more; was already suspecting herself of pretending. It was all over bar what was presumably going to be a great deal of shouting, thought Lettie rather uneasily, sitting in her office at the end of another busy day. He'd already shown himself capable of a stupid recklessness; it might be safer to string him along, until it was time to do a bunk. But that was never fun.

She was roused by a knock at the door: today's last client. 'Hello, come in. Take a seat.'

This was a familiar face; after a second or two Lettie recognized the woman from behind the counter at the bakery in the square. Out of the clean buttoned pinafore and starched cap she wore at work she made a sadly shabby, even blousy appearance, in her ancient overcoat and splayed old shoes. Her sagging face was very pale, with a waxen sheen; and she was panting still, from the climb up the one flight of stairs.

Lettie was on the alert immediately. 'What can I do for you, Mrs . . . ?'

'Bettins, ma'am. Lily Bettins. You seen my sister. Rosie Hancock. I was hoping you might . . . see me right.'

'I take a few details?'

She was thirty-two; had six living children, between four and thirteen, and three dead; husband a labourer, ma'am, casual-like.

Husband aware and consenting, wrote Lettie, as she always did; for some things, she had privately decided, really should go without asking.

'So, have you been using anything already, Mrs Bettins?'

'Not really, no, ma'am.'

'It's Nurse. Well now – have you ever seen one of these before?'

Confronted with her first cervical cap, Mrs Bettins flushed and sniggered. Lettie smiled too: 'I know – it don't look much.'

'What am I supposed to do with that?'

'I'm coming to that. It's a knack, using it. Not difficult.'

Mrs Bettins nodded, and Lettie noticed the sweat pearling her upper lip.

'Don't be frightened. Take it, that's right. See how soft it is? It's a sort of door, that you can shut, to stop your husband's seed getting in.'

Her forehead too. Ah.

'Now you just lean forward for me, Mrs Bettins, right down . . . head between your knees, that's it, you just stay like that for a little while. Good. Here, sip of water. You were feeling dizzy, and now you're better. Alright?'

'Oh my Lord.'

'You well enough to go on? Or d'you want to come back tomorrow?'

'Better, ma'am.' Her hand shook as she held the glass to her lips.

'I'd like to have a little look at you now, if you're sure. Look – through here. You just take your things off, lower half, you know – ring the little bell when you're ready. There's a sheet to cover yourself with. Okay?'

As Mrs Bettins shuffled off into the inner room the telephone rang.

'Darling?'

'I'm with a patient.'

'Tonight, though?'

'No, I told you. I'm busy tonight.'

'Call me back. I'll be waiting. Goodbye, my own one.'

Berk. Lettie banged the telephone down. She buttoned her apron on, washed her hands, and forgot him as soon as the bell rang.

Half-naked Mrs Bettins could be smelt from the doorway, the familiar compound of fresh and aged sweat, but with something else more disturbing, a breath of gin, a hint of sweetish fleshy decay. Her stomach was slack and heavy, clawed with silver stretch marks, and clammy to the touch.

'Firstly – I'm just going to check your temperature, if you don't mind. Under your tongue, there. Don't talk now, please, until I take it out again. Lie right back, just relax, that's right.'

Gently Lettie pressed the soft flesh. Yes: the fundus well above the pubic bone.

'Let me take that now. Good.'

Feverish. Obviously.

'Any pains anywhere? Any discharge?'

Mrs Bettins briefly closed her eyes, as if too spent to answer. Looking down at her Lettie could see her heartbeat, a quick bouncing flutter of the taut cotton over her bosom.

Lettie pulled up the stool from the bottom of the examination couch, and sat down.

'Why have you come here?' she asked. 'What did you want me to do?'

There was a pause. Mrs Bettins put up her arm, drew her sleeve beneath her nose, blotted her eyes. 'Help me.'

'You're about five months along. There really isn't anything anyone can do about that.'

'I ain't *felt* nothing,' said Mrs Bettins, her voice aggrieved.

'Don't matter,' said Lettie. 'It's still against the law.'

'I can't have another. I can't.'

'What have you tried so far?'

The faintest shrug.

'You went to someone?'

There would always be someone, in Lettie's experience. Even in a little place like this.

'I have a look? Best I should.' She got up, pushed the trolley into place, went to wash her hands again and put on her gloves. 'Just bend your knees up, ankles together. That's it, keep your ankles like that, and just let your knees fall apart. Perfect. Touch of cold water now –'

Damp mousey-grey fuzz about the private parts.

It was worse than she had feared. Pushing the wall-light into better position with one elbow she was sure without needing the speculum at all. She reached one gloved hand down, parted the labia, slid in one finger, touched – something sharply alien, wedged in the vagina. Oh God.

Mrs Bettins gave a little groan.

'What's this?'

Mrs Bettins shook her head feebly. 'I dunno. She said it would a come away by now. But nothing. Just this pain. I got such a pain, ma'am.'

'When? When did she do it?'

'Last week. I dunno. Week before.'

It was all the way through the cervix. Presumably.

'Can you – make it work?'

'No. No one can do that.'

Whining: 'My sister said you'd help me.'

'She got me wrong then. I don't do this stuff. No one should: it's dangerous. To you, I mean. I'm going to take this out now. Ready?'

Sterile forceps, very slow. Slow as possible. A slight shift; then it was free. Withdrawn, a long sodden sharp-ended sliver of bark that dinged softly when she dropped it into the kidney dish. Slippery elm, remembered Lettie, trying to breathe slowly. One of the old methods; patchily effective. Though more often inserted in powdered form, to swell with absorbed moisture, and sheer off the developing membranes.

'Is it done? Will I miss now?'

'I don't know. Maybe.'

'Oh, can't you make sure? Please!'

'You need to see a doctor now. This evening. I'll write you a note for him.'

Mrs Bettins sat up. 'You could give me something.'

Lettie shook her head. 'No. It's not safe.'

'Bin alright before,' said Mrs Bettins sulkily.

'You were lucky before.'

'Safer'n having a baby, though, en it! Three times I done it. My sister more. Ain't nothing wrong with her, nor me neither.'

'You want to watch your mouth,' said Lettie coldly. 'Get dressed.'

'Wait!' The whining voice again; she knew she had said too much. 'You won't go to the police – will you?'

'No – not if you come back here afterwards. Okay?'

Sitting at her desk writing the note Lettie was overcome for a moment with a familiar sense of hopelessness. On the one hand there were so many like Miss Thornby, too lady-like to say the words Family Planning without a blush of shame, and on the other thousands like Lily Bettins, still needlessly Planning Families with yet another criminal abortion carried out by the friend of a friend, by someone's old mother, by the neighbour who'd done you the good turn last time and the time before that. Or worse, perhaps, done by the paid stranger up the flight of stairs. The older methods of birth control.

Mrs Bettins appeared fully dressed and hangdog now in the doorway, the worn coat clutched tight. She had a ghastly pallor. Still frightened.

'Here's the letter,' said Lettie, sliding it into an envelope, though she knew the chances of Mrs Bettins taking it to any doctor were vanishingly small. 'Try to get some rest, and drink plenty of boiled water. Just tell me one thing.' Lettie stood up. 'This woman who did it for you – was it the same one? The one you usually go to?'

'Don't know her name,' said Mrs Bettins instantly.

'Did I ask her name? Was it the same one?'

Mrs Bettins took the letter, squashed it into the pocket of her coat. Finally, not meeting Lettie's eyes, she said: 'No. Her took bad. Ain't been to this 'un before.'

'Don't recommend her then.'

She looked up at that, with something like a grin.

'Tell people to come here,' said Lettie. 'Tell everyone you know. Alright?'

'Ma'am,' said Mrs Bettins, bobbing her head.

'Nurse,' said Lettie, but she had already gone.

Rae

'How d'you mean, a plan?' Mrs Givens folded her arms.

Rae hesitated. 'It isn't just a plan. It's a conspiracy. A crime, in fact.'

'What crime?'

Rae came back down the stairs. 'Nothing that bad – we're just lying under oath, that sort of thing. Me and someone else, two other people.'

'What, friends of yourn?'

'Can we go to the kitchen now, have a sit down? They're not friends,' said Rae, as they turned and began to walk slowly back the way they had come, 'I'm paying them. You were right about money, I've made a fair amount one way and another. I'm spending it. The point is, in the end: I keep the baby.'

'How?'

'At first: I pretend it's not mine. Someone else pretends it's theirs. False papers. Then – when I'm divorced, when I'm free again, a while later, maybe months – I adopt her. Or him.'

'So – you're, you're going to adopt your own child?' Mrs Givens stood still, her hand to her breast.

'Yes, that's it!'

'Adopt your own child, dear Lord!'

'It's the only way, you see. To keep my good name as well.'

'Ah.'

'Yes, so I have to be secret – that's the main thing really.' Rae looked at her uncertainly as they walked on. 'Well. What d'you think? Would you – go to the police, about a thing like that?'

'What would I say to 'em? You ain't done nothing yet.'

'I'm going to, though.'

At that moment a nearby door suddenly opened in the passage, and Minnie's big round face appeared, a smear of soot on one cheek.

'Missis, did you – oh my!' She broke off when she saw Rae, and looked away, grinning.

'Minnie,' said Mrs Givens pleasantly, 'would you make a nice big pot of tea, please, for Mrs – Mrs Wickham here. A real proper tray, like this morning. That cake too.'

'With a tray cloth, and all?'

'Yes. For my sitting room. You do that for me, Minnie, like a good girl?'

'After I done the grates?'

'No, you leave those for now. Tea first, that's it. She *would* bring you your breakfast, ma'am,' said Mrs Givens, as Minnie stumped away ahead of them and disappeared round the corner, 'she begged and she pleaded.'

'Did she? Why?'

'Desperate to see you up close, ma'am. You being the Beautiful Lady. That's what she calls you,' said Mrs Givens. 'Here we are,' she added, and she opened her sitting-room door.

Going in, Rae jumped a little to see the yellow-eyed grey cat in the armchair below the high window, cleaning itself. When it caught sight of her it stopped instantly, and glared at her with the same outrage as before, though it looked much less menacing with one back paw in the air.

'I wondered where he'd gone. Is he – missing an ear?'

'Seen him go for a dog once,' said Mrs Givens, busy with the fire. 'Jumped on his back, all claws.'

Rae looked about her, aware that already she felt different, lighter. Stare all you please, foolish beast, she thought at the cat, then affectionately greeted the pictures on the mantelpiece, the twin Mrs Givenses grimly arm in arm, the youthful vision in her frilly bonnet: Hello again, you three.

Presently the door banged, and Minnie appeared, her mouth open in a huge coy smile, the tray this time laden with full teapot in a blue knitted cosy, a milk jug, and a battered enamel cake tin.

'How kind of you, thank you,' said Rae, and Minnie blushed scarlet with pleasure.

''Tis fruitcake,' she said.

'My favourite!'

'She do talk, ma'am', said Mrs Givens, when she had gone. 'I don't doubt the whole village knows you're here, being the Beautiful Lady. Or Mrs Wickham. That matter?'

'I don't see how.'

'One thing bothers me about this scheme a yourn.' Mrs Givens opened the cake tin, releasing the warm toasted smell, and took up the knife. 'You say, the midwife comes, fills out all these lying forms –'

'Inaccurate forms,' Rae said.

'Lying forms. As is against the law,' said Mrs Givens. 'Here. Take the big bit, go on.'

'Thanks –'

'Then she takes the baby away with her. Who to? Where?'

'Well – I don't actually know. It's protection, you see.'

Mrs Givens poured the tea. 'So, she takes the baby away to a place you don't know, to a person you don't know, and then you leave the country –'

'– I go back to America, yes –'

'– and swan about, like –'

'– I get divorced, that's the main thing. As well as the swanning. Which is also important, I've got to be seen out and about not being pregnant.'

'So when you've done the divorcing and the swanning –'

'– and got my picture in the gossip columns a few times, given the odd interview coming over ever so spiritual –' Rae put her hands together as if in prayer, heaved a sigh, and in a swooping high pitch said: 'Oh how I long to make just a tiny difference to this cruel hard world! D'you know, I've been wondering if even though I am alas and alack only a single girl once more I might be able to give a loving home to some poor little orphan from the Old Country! It's so much a question of timing, you see,' she went on, in her normal voice. 'I really don't see why it shouldn't work. Smashing cake by the way.' She took another big bite. 'Mmm.'

'It's a mad idea, ma'am.'

'I know. But it's a mad world. Which was the one thing? That bothered you?'

'It all bothers me, ma'am. As it would anyone in their right mind.'

Rae looked at her. 'Well – I mean, do *say*. I've sort of

brought you into all this now, haven't I. So – you have every right, if you see what I mean.'

'No, ma'am,' said Mrs Givens, after a tiny pause. 'Maybe another time. There's something else I'd like to know.'

'Anything.'

'If you don't mind my asking, ma'am. I don't like to call you by a falsehood. If you ain't Mrs Wickham – who are you?'

Rae laughed. 'Well – you can choose. I've got so many names, you see. There's my married name – I've got two of those. My stage name. Which is slightly different from my pen name. Most of them are made up anyway. I mean for a start, you simply cannot have a career on the stage with a name like *Gundry*. Which is my real real name. My own maiden name, I mean.'

'Gundry – 'tis a good Cornish name,' said Mrs Givens, pleased.

'Oh I know. My father was born in Truro. Yes, please,' Rae added, as Mrs Givens held up the teapot.

'So – you changed it?'

'I had to. I had an agent, you see. D'you know about agents? They find you the work, because they know everyone who counts, that sort of thing. Anyway mine insisted, about the name. And – eventually – we came up with – well, with me. You might have heard of me: I'm Rae Grainger.'

There was a pause.

'Rae Grainger,' Rae repeated, less emphatically. 'Ring any bells?'

'I'm sorry, ma'am.'

'I was in *Her Best Friend*. And *The Milliner*, I was the

assistant. You must have seen that one, everybody did. Everybody in the entire country went to see it at least twice, I happen to know.'

'I don't go to the films, ma'am, not for this many a year.'

'Well I was on the stage too, you know. The West End. Rep.'

Mrs Givens shook her head.

'Oh well. I suppose I had been less . . . active that way recently. Screenwriting, that's the thing. That I've been doing. Lately.'

'But you said you married, ma'am?'

'In haste. Repented et cetera. But as I said. Still legal. So in some circles I am in fact Mrs Rod Lacey, though frankly I'd rather you didn't go for that one. Rod Lacey. No? Tends to play the baddie's second-in-command, gets killed just before the end of the second reel – oh Lord, not him either – well, I must say, this is all jolly bad for morale,' said Rae cheerfully. 'Would it be too frightfully greedy of me to have another . . . mm, thanks. The worst name though –' she laughed – 'I was *so* mortified when Rod told me what *his* real name was. Such a come-down: makes me Mrs Ernest O'Malley, which would hardly impress. This was just before we got married. But then of course I had to come clean about being Ruth Gundry – we both simply *fell about*. Oh. What is it?'

'That your own name then? Ruth? As your mother called you?'

'Yes. Parents came over all biblical: Ruth Mary Gundry, that's me. Are you alright?'

'My sister's daughter. My niece. She was Ruth, too.'

'Was?'

'Died long ago, ma'am.'

'Oh, I'm sorry. Let me pour you another cup.'

'Ruth.'

'No one's called me that for years. You could, if you want to. I'd quite like it, actually. Especially if it stops you ma'aming me all the time. You do rather overdo it.'

Mrs Givens smiled, her own rare oddly playful smile. 'I know,' she said.

Lettie

She went the long way round, and quietly slipped a note through Nesbit's letter box; Mrs Bettins would surely not risk the doctor, but she might let Sister Nesbit in.

Less likely to bump into Heyward this way too. He'd called again while she was tidying up. Oh, he was a pain in the arse. She turned into Silver Street to look in the windows on the way home.

Why had she gone for him in the first place? Every time she reached this stage she never could remember. But he'd seemed so vital, so aware, at first. Setting up a successful Mothers' Clinic always depended so much on the local medical men; they had to be actively involved, not just vaguely in favour – no point trying otherwise. And he had swung open the office door, so gallantly: 'Nurse Quick, delighted to meet you!' But his dashing overcoat had no power to move her now. It's still true, she thought: the longest I've ever liked anyone was the Madam. Lettie paused to look idly into the chemist's windows. Five years I loved her. Of course I wasn't getting into bed with her. No wonder it took me so long.

She walked on to Modes de Madame, and stopped again. Cardigans today, twin sets and a very nice little fitted jacket-type one in creamy yellow. She remembered the Queen's Hall that time.

I was just eighteen, she thought.

The nurses' home had been sent the usual free tickets, and Lettie and a couple of other girls had gone along hoping for something musical, with maybe a free cup of tea thrown in, you never knew your luck. The other two had decided against it, seeing the poster outside, and went to the pictures instead, and for the first hour Lettie had deeply regretted not going with them. There had been some music, but only on the organ, and when that finally stopped some old geezer got up on the podium and jawed on and on about the Navy, how he only wanted A1 types, not enfeebled wastrels.

I could have been watching Harold Lloyd, Lettie had thought at him, crossly, but soon grew too bored for anger and almost nodded off, as the hall was warm and she had worked an early shift. And there was still no sign of tea.

Finally, after a lengthy pause, she was announced. Dr Stopes.

Dr Marie Stopes was the author of a famously dirty book; to some she was a murderess, a harlot, and the arch despoiler and corrupter of England's youth. About flaming time, Lettie had thought, sitting up hopefully.

A young woman who looked barely older than Lettie herself stepped lightly to the centre of the stage. She was tall and slender and pretty, with a mass of dark hair piled about her head, Edwardian style, but it suited her and went well with the cut of her pale grey suit and the low-cut pink shawl-collared blouse she wore with it. She had the loveliest little high-heeled button boots, grey kid. She stood there in silence, waiting for the hall to quieten.

When she spoke her voice was thrilling, vibrant, at once confiding and resolute: 'Ladies, gentlemen, why have I gathered round me this great multitude? How glad I am that you have responded to my call!' And her large dark eyes for a moment seemed to look deep into Lettie's own.

'Tonight we consciously and publicly step into the first days of a great new era of human evolution!' cried Dr Stopes. 'We will bring forth an entirely new type of human creature, stepping into a future so beautiful, so full of the real joy of self-expression and understanding, that we here today may look upon our grandchildren and think almost that the gods have descended to walk upon the earth!'

Lettie, come in the base hope of hearing something rude, had stayed to worship, for it soon turned out, under all the eloquence, that the Madam thought that married couples should have as many children as they wanted, and no more; and that the famous dirtiness lay in explaining how.

Five years, thought Lettie now, as she passed the sweetshop.

Even now it was best not thought about. But unavoidable, this evening: her own paid stranger, her own abortionist, waiting for her at the top of the stairs.

It had been summer. The place was in Holloway, down a little side alley near a church. She had the address off by heart. Though exactly as she had been told, there was a flyblown postcard in the window, handwritten, reading STOPES MOTHERS' CLINIC.

The ground floor was a small tobacconist's shop with dirty windows. The doorbell pinged when she went in. A wizened little man behind the counter moved his eyebrows.

'Morning.'

It was the sort of place where you could buy one cigarette. The floor was wooden boards, worn almost furry at the threshold.

'Ah, I've come for, the ah . . .'

The man jerked his head to one side, and Lettie saw the door at the far end.

'Up there?'

''E's in,' he returned. He watched her pass him. Lettie felt herself stiffen; his gaze had a sudden charge to it. Even he, drab starveling penned in his gimcrack shop all day, felt he had the right to a knowing stare once he knew where she was going.

The stairs were narrow, worn brown paint, and turned like a corkscrew up three storeys, all smelling dingily of damp and tobacco, damp banister knobbly with paint, tacky to the touch. A child was wailing behind one of the closed doors on the second. The right door was at the top, marked with another handwritten postcard. Lettie knocked.

'Come in.'

What, who, had she been expecting?

He was rather big, moon-faced, eyes a little protuberant, heavy white bags beneath them. He wore an old black suit, the jacket tight, but as if it had fitted him once. The desk in front of him held nothing but an ashtray. He stood up as she came in, and held out his hand.

'Good morning, Mrs er –' The skin of his face was stiff-looking and very dry; you could see scurfiness on his cheeks where shaving had made it drier still.

'Mrs Swift,' said Lettie.

'And I am Gerald Spencer. How can I help you, Mrs Swift? Do, please, sit down.'

'Thank you. A friend of mine – well, I heard that you might be able to help me. In a very private matter.'

'Yes?'

Lettie glanced all about her in a further surge of fright. There was little to suggest that her information had been correct. No visible equipment, no cupboard looking medical, not even a smell of disinfectant, just the same general damp and tobacco with added smokiness: whatever else he was doing up here, Gerald Spencer was clearly enjoying the occasional cigar.

Wasn't he going to help her out at all? Or was this part of his ploy?

'I'm afraid I'm in a great deal of trouble, Mr Spencer.' There.

'I see. And is your husband aware of your difficulties?'

'It would be best,' said Lettie carefully, 'if he didn't find out at all. If possible.'

She swallowed.

There was a pause. Mr Spencer looked at his empty desk. There were crumbs on it, Lettie saw. Had he sat here nibbling biscuits?

'There is a price,' he said. He looked up. 'How far along are you?'

Oh Lord, the right place after all! 'I think nearly three months,' said Lettie. 'No more.'

'Then there really shouldn't be any difficulty. We can proceed straight away, if you, ah, have the funds. Is that convenient, my dear Mrs Swift?'

'What, now?'

'Yes. Now. Do you have the funds? I take payment beforehand.'

'Of course, Doctor.'

Why *of course*, why *doctor*? The words just fell out of her mouth. But if he heard what she had called him he did not correct her.

'I'll need you to take off a few things, if you please,' he said, 'as I will need to examine you. It may be possible to release you from your difficulties very easily.'

She held out the envelope she had brought with her. He took it, looked inside at the three notes, 'Good, good,' and slid it into the drawer of his desk. 'We must go into the other room. Will you come this way, Mrs Swift?'

He stood back, letting her pass before him into the little side room. There was no door.

Inside there was a screen, two panels papered in faded brownish flowers. Against one wall stood a narrow bed like a table, hip-high with no foot- or headrail, a small plain wooden kitchen chair beside it. Against the other there was just room for a desk and an ordinary marble-topped washstand. At the window hung a scrap of greyish net.

He unfolded the screen, blocking the doorway. 'Call me, please, when you are ready.'

Lettie sat down on the chair, trembling violently. The bed was raised on bricks, she saw, rough red bricks from a building site, one for each leg. She was dreadfully aware of him, a man and a stranger, between her and the door and the stairs and escape. Every warning voice she had ever heard or scoffed at seemed to be vibrating inside her,

Don't Talk To Strangers, Don't Trust, Don't Allow, Don't Risk!

This wouldn't do. She was here now, wasn't she? Got this far. Had to go through with it.

She stood up, and put her handbag on the floor. She bent and fumbled under her petticoat, pulled down her drawers, stuffed them in the bag. How much did she need to take off anyway? Wasn't this enough? Shoes, though. She undid the little buckles and stepped out of them.

The bed had a sheet over it, a pillow at one end. She climbed up, shivering. She felt all wrong with no drawers on. There was nothing to cover herself with. The sheet looked passably clean but when she leant to sniff at the pillow she caught the strawberry tang of someone else's greasy head.

'Ready,' she called, and her voice trembled.

He had taken off his jacket. His shirt sleeves were rolled up, showing big hairy forearms. He pulled the chair up and sat down beside her.

'We're quite sure we understand one another here,' he said, in a way that made this almost a question.

Lettie nodded. But he said: 'You must trust me, you know, if you want this business done with.'

'Yes. Yes I do.'

'Good. Good.' He looked at her face, into her eyes, for the first time. She could not hold his gaze, flinching sideways almost straight away. So that it was even more of a shock when he put a hand on her breast, and worked his fingers on it, squeezing a little.

'Breasts tender?' he said.

Again she nodded. Speech was beyond her. Her mouth so suddenly so dry that her tongue seemed stuck, stiff.

He moved his fingers again, examination, caress. Then abruptly left her, and went to the washstand, where he splashed noisily, washing his hands. She dared a look; saw the tattoo on his left forearm, a blue blurry anchor.

'Now then,' he said, and he put out a foot and pushed the chair over to the desk. It scraped across the floorboards. 'You must do everything I say, d'you see? Or the whole business won't work.'

He went to the desk, and lowered its lid, making a narrow side table. He took a little bottle from a shelf inside. 'I'm going to give you some pills to take home with you. Herbal, perfectly safe. Here.' He took her hand, and folded it round the bottle. His was slightly damp still, cold from the water. 'Important you take every last one – three times a day with meals, if you please.'

He stood beside her. His eyes were an unreadable light grey. 'But first I must make some small adjustments here. Understand? What I use is perfectly safe; but it still needs to go in the right place, d'you follow?'

Lettie tried. She wanted to say, 'What do you use?' A reasonable question. Her tongue refused. Her whole body seemed in revolt. It lay there. It shook but it did as he asked. It raised its knees, it laid the soles of its feet together, it let the knees fall apart, wide apart, that's right, that's just dandy, my dear. It let him lay his ungloved hand on her bush, while his eyes met hers. It made no sign.

What do you use.

What do you use.

What do you use.

164

He answered as if she had spoken: 'Slippery elm,' he said. 'Heard of it? No? Just a little concoction of bark. No harm done. Old ways are the best ways, Mrs er, Swift.' As he said this he put up his left hand and with thumb and forefinger parted her down there, and slipped the cold thick middle finger of his right inside her. His head bent, looking at what he was doing. She could see the parting in his hair, the little grooves where the comb had pushed through the oiled brown, specks of dandruff here and there. He pushed his finger in harder, higher. A moment; then he took it out again, and held it briefly to his nose. 'All seems healthy enough.'

Lettie's insides seemed to be full of noise. It was hard to hear him over it.

'Shall we proceed? You agree? You must trust me, Mrs Swift. There are one or two stages that must be gone through. Or the whole thing just don't work, d'you see?'

Perhaps, she thought later, it was the tiny slip of grammar that freed her. The careless cockney jauntiness of it. *The whole thing just don't work.* Suddenly her body was her own again, lying still and shocked but somehow no longer inert on this, this table-on-bricks, in this crummy smelly room over a nasty little tobacconist's, was the man mad, trust him? Trust *you*? My arse!

But still she watched. Her heartbeat still fast, but not faint now, stronger all the time with some unidentifiable but wildly growing emotion, a great inner rising. He had turned to his desk again, to take out something else, the bark presumably, another jar anyway, and then dear God! something wrapped in a handkerchief, unfolding, yes, craning her neck she could just see it, the long curved metal probe, a flash of metal in the dusty light, setting it by him ready on the desk lid, but half rising now, undoing ah it was true then it was all true undoing the buttons of his own fly, reaching inside to free himself, turning now, on his feet, letting her see the big red prick, stiffly poking out of his trousers, funny angle, half-mast practically –

'Now then, the first stage –'

Oh but his face, when she swung herself sideways and leapt in transcendent rage to her feet! Stunned didn't cover it. What a colour! Mouth open, stupid, he looked so stupid!

'I've changed my mind,' shouted Lettie, and as he made a move towards her, perhaps in mere surprise, she flung out her right arm without thought and hit him, her closed fist hard against the small sprung curl of his ear.

He fell away clutching at his head, his thing still hanging purplish, and she lunged for her bag, scooped up her shoes in the same hand, pushed the screen aside and ran, bumping *crash* into his empty desk in the outer room, hurling herself at the door and through and down and down in her stocking feet as if he were pounding full of murder behind her. But as she burst through the shop and out into the street she knew he would still be standing there, one hand on his ringing ear, the other perhaps wandering down to his disappointment, and still, still not suspecting anything, the miserable dopey bastard, wouldn't she just see him right!

Breathless on the pavement, where passers-by were passing by as if nothing had happened; she bent to brush some of the grit from the soles of her poor feet, stockings done for, her shoes oh, lovely underfoot, and despite her trembling legs she began to want to laugh, seeing his moonstruck face and his open mouth and his sagging prick looking out of his trousers. It was an effort to control herself as she reached the corner, turned it, and saw the glorious sight of the Madam and a large and rosy-cheeked young police constable; she clutching him firmly by the arm as if he had already tried to make off.

'Here she is now! My dear! What happened?'

Lettie ran forward, and was for an unforgettable moment held close in the Madam's perfumed cashmere arms.

'Well?'

A little dizzy now. Nowhere near laughter all of a sudden. She nodded.

'Hah!' The Madam in triumph, turning to the policeman, all superb flaring nostrils and head held high: 'And will you act now, constable, or must I report you to your commanding officer?'

Lettie saw him blush beneath his helmet. He's just a boy, she thought, and no match for the Madam, but then who would be?

'Wait,' she said quickly. 'He sold me these,' and she opened her hand to show him the little bottle of pills. 'He's on the top floor,' she added, and then at once he was off, striding back the way she had come, and very likely quite keen, it occurred to her, to get a bit of his own back. She hoped so.

'Good girl,' said the Madam, with her usual cool smile. 'This will teach him to desecrate my name. And now I really must go. I shall want a written report, mind – shall we say tomorrow morning? You had better stay here until our good but I must say rather unfortunately *slow* member of the constabulary reappears; best to ever so discreetly check he has the right man, don't you think – *à bientôt* then, my dear! A job well done. Taxi!'

And she was gone.

Left me there on my own, thought Lettie now, turning the corner into North Street. Shaking like a leaf. Not enough bus fare. Had to walk all the way home. And I'd've told you then, if you'd asked. What else he was up to. Victims who came to him, and paid him. Who climbed the stairs to the waiting stranger.

But for you none of that mattered enough, did it? He'd just taken your name in vain. That was all you were interested in. So you didn't ask at all.

And after that, when the others complained about you: I listened.

Slippery elm, though. Took you right back. Made you feel low, thought Lettie, with a sigh. Perhaps she would bag the bath again tonight; lucky Miss Thornby was such a pushover. She slid her key into the lock, then jumped back startled when the door instantly swung open, as if by itself.

Miss Thornby held it, her hat on, wearing the awful brown tweedy coat-thing. She was smiling happily: 'Miss Quick! What perfect timing!'

Oh, no! Instantly Lettie remembered: cousin Alice, the Picture Palace, the grisly silent film-show party. It was tonight. And Freddie, Pyncheon Photographic Studios in unmissable person. She pulled herself together.

'I'll just drop my bag off,' she said cheerfully.

At the Picture Palace

But as soon as they set off, she remembered. Oh my goodness!

'There's something I should have told you before,' Norah said. 'I'm sorry. For some reason – well, I kept putting it off, I suppose. I must tell you about Freddie, my cousin. He was badly injured in the war: well, he's blind.'

'Oh.'

'Yes. It's particularly cruel, isn't it – for someone so very drawn to, well, to the visual. An artist, really. And of course the cinema – well, you can imagine. Oh dear – are you alright, Miss Quick?'

They were passing the bus stop, and Norah took Miss Quick's arm.

'Let's sit here for a moment. That's it. Have you – forgive me, have you eaten? I often feel a little dizzy myself if, you know –'

Miss Quick, who had leant forward over her lap, now straightened up and drew a long breath. She was still alarmingly pale, Norah thought. 'I'm so sorry,' she said, 'I shouldn't have rushed you off like that. It really doesn't matter if we're late. Or if we don't go at all. Let's go back home now. And have tea.'

'No, it's alright. I'm – not hungry anyway. Just felt a bit . . .' Miss Quick stood up. 'Fine now.'

Norah rose too. 'Are you quite sure, Miss Quick?'

'Lettie.'

Norah's heart gave a great thump of joy. 'Norah,' she said, blushing. *Just two women, ain't we? Let's keep it simple – see how it goes?* It had been a Test all along, she thought; and despite everything she seemed to have passed it. 'You're sure you're well enough?' she asked. 'I don't mind giving the whole thing a miss, you know. If you'd rather.'

'No, I'd rather go,' said Lettie. 'You were saying: about – your cousin.'

'Ah yes. Poor Freddie.'

'Was it gas?'

'No. A head wound. The blast damaged something inside his eyes, the, ah –'

'The retina?'

'Yes, that's it. At first they thought they might be able to save a little sight. He had dozens of operations at Moorfields, poor chap, in London, you know. He had to sit in the dark all day, staying very still. Sideways, leaning on a pillow. Hours at a time – it was torture, almost.'

'But it didn't work.'

'It did for a little while, a year or two. Alice used to read to him. Sit by the window with a crack of the blind open, reading to him, trying to take his mind off things. Well, you can imagine. He was such a large part of the Picture Palace, before, before it happened. Not just managing – he used to play the piano there, you see, and he was marvellous. He somehow – he made the funny ones funnier, he made dramas more, more –'

'– dramatic?'

'Heart-stopping,' said Norah seriously. 'And of course if it was sad – well, it was almost unbearable, he was so brilliant. Oh, Freddie in his heyday was an absolute *star*! So. This evening. Well, it will be – a little odd, perhaps. You see I had to warn you about it. Sorry – I should have told you earlier.'

They walked on in silence for a while, then Lettie spoke: 'Didn't you say he would be playing the piano? Tonight?'

'He shall. He can do that, as well as before. If not better. Alice helps him.'

'Helps him to play the piano?'

'You'll see,' said Norah, and then they were there.

Lettie's heart hammered as they walked down the short stone-flagged path, and she had to be careful to take slow quiet breaths. Didn't want to go all dizzy again. It was all down to Mrs Bettins and her slippery elm, she thought.

Of course there had never been any chance that Freddie Pyncheon would recognize her, not after so many years, and she wouldn't know him from Adam either. It was being so forcibly reminded, she thought, about who she once had been, that open loving heart, so innocent, so idiotic. So easily gulled and robbed. Freddie Pyncheon had looked upon that self. He had asked her: 'Can I take your picture?'

For a long moment she had been right back there with him in the past, her two hands on the handle. All of it still to happen.

Then a gentle voice had broken through, have you had enough to eat, I'm so sorry, let's go home again, and Lettie had taken hold of the voice and its kindness, and drawn herself back along it into the present, and there was Norah.

The Picture Palace door stood ajar.

The anteroom smelt musty, as if it had been shut up a long time. Swags of cobweb in the corners had blackened, and the walls near the high arched ceiling were leprous with loosening plaster. A kiosk near the entrance stood empty. Framed photographs hung here and there on the walls above the panelling, dim with dust. Dim with dust, but still decipherable. A glance at each one was enough.

Lettie made for a closed door in one corner with *WC* painted on it, in antique font.

'Won't be a sec.'

Inside, the door bolted, she sat down in a dank smell of bleach and took some slow breaths. No hurry, she thought. You can take your time. Calm down. You can give this some thought. Presently she felt strong enough to pull the clanking chain and go out again.

Norah was waiting at the entrance, where an ancient velvet curtain had been looped back.

'Are you sure you're alright?'

'Fine now,' said Lettie, and followed her into the darker space of the cinema. A few lights were on, bare bulbs dangling from the ceiling on wires through hooks in the crossbeams; so the place really was a barn, Lettie thought, looking up at the great wooden arches dark with age. They walked down the central aisle, and as they passed Lettie saw that many of the seats had grinning splits in them, the hessian beneath showing through like decay, or deeper tears emitting frizzled grey swags of horsehair. The air smelt of years of tobacco smoke, the yellow smell Lettie associated with pubs, with a further admix of something ecclesiastical, a generic smell of ancient buildings, stone dust, beeswax. It felt like a church, Lettie thought. A church with padded seats instead of pews, for a different kind of worship altogether.

A scattering of figures stood or sat at the front, near the stage in the semi-darkness. There was a low buzzing of voices raised in mild party chatter. One of the figures turned as they approached, and became Alice Pyncheon.

'Norah, darling! I'm so pleased you could come, and Miss Quick, welcome!' Alice was in a terrible state of nerves, Norah saw, and immediately felt anxious herself – was Freddie in one of his moods? She had no wish to expose Lettie to that sort of thing. Especially when she had felt unwell so recently.

With her eyes she asked Alice the question. *Yes*, said Alice's answering look. But it also clearly read *Thank God You're Here*, so there was nothing for it, Norah decided, but to sit down and hope for the best.

'May we sit at the front?' she asked.

'Of course, if you want to – though –'

'Are you happy here, Lettie? Or shall we go back a bit?'

'There will be a little sherry,' said Alice, in a low voice, 'afterwards. *I* thought,' she added, in even lower tones, 'best before, but Freddie – oh, excuse me, back in a moment –' Someone had called her; she scurried off.

Now her eyes were growing used to the darkness Norah could make out who else had turned up, all the usual familiar faces, she thought, as she waved at one or two. 'Hello, Jane!' she called. 'Mrs Brotherwood, how are you!'

They sat down, unbuttoning their coats, though it was too cold to take them off.

'I'm with her,' Lettie whispered. 'I think better before.'

Norah turned. 'Me too,' she whispered back, and at this delightful intimacy was seized for a moment with a happiness so profound that she could not stop smiling.

After a pause she had to ask. 'Where is he, then?' Lettie whispered.

'Who, Freddie?'

'He is coming, isn't he?'

'Of course. It's all *for* him, really.'

'What d'you mean?'

But before Norah could make any answer Alice came to stand before the front row, and waved her hands in a gesture that asked for quiet. Her small round spectacles flashed now and then, catching the light as she turned to address her audience.

'Thank you all so much for coming to our little soirée; it's such a treat to open up the dear old place again. And what a pity Mrs Hatt is unable to join us after all this evening, because I know that this *smashing* little film is one of her particular favourites – indeed, one of Wayward Brothers' finer productions, reflecting our true English sensibility, *such* a treat – which some of you may remember. It stars Hetty Harper –' someone sitting behind Lettie uttered a little squeak of pleased excitement – 'and it was directed in 1924 by the simply marvellous Bertram Wayward.'

None of these names meant anything to Lettie. But then, she reflected, how many British films were worth seeing anyway?

'Freddie?' said Alice, turning a little. 'Ready to begin?'

Lettie leant forward, realizing for the first time that someone was sitting alone in the darkness at the far right of the stage, at the upright piano there: Freddie Pyncheon, in real and personal darkness, needing no light to play by. This thought gave her a dreadful shifting inside, as of fear. She could make out the shape of his head, little else. He sat at a slight angle to her. His arms perhaps folded as he waited. Something odd about his ears turned as she looked harder into the frames of glasses.

He had given Alice some sort of signal, it seemed, for she turned again to the audience and said breathlessly: 'Ladies and gentlemen – thank you – and now, accompanied on the pianoforte by of course my dear brother Mr Frederick Pyncheon – we present *Aren't We Sisters?* Ready, Mr Trefusis? Lights in just one moment, please!'

She hurried to one side, and pulled on a rope, so that the heavyweight velvet curtains swept slowly apart, revealing the screen suspended on the stage, waved assent at someone standing by the light switch, and in sudden complete darkness made her way back and sat down; not in one of the seats, Lettie noticed, but right beside Freddie at the piano, as if they were going to play a duet.

Freddie began to play. It was not a tune Lettie recognized. It was light, a waltz, though rather sombre somehow, and after a few premonitory flashes and whirring numbers the screen settled, and glowed into slightly unfocussed sepia-tinged life.

Wayward Brothers present

Aren't We Sisters?

At the piano, Alice put her lips to her brother's ear. *House*, she muttered, and Lettie, lifting her eyes to the screen, saw the grand country house by night, a row of tall windows casting their brightness on to the smooth tended lawns outside, saw the twinkling lamps hung between the rose beds, while Freddie played something cheerful and summery, and . . .

Dance, said Alice, and instantly the music was fast jazz, and a crowd of young people were wildly swinging one another about to its rhythms, among them the beautiful Hetty Harper herself in the arms of a tall glossy young man, until *cake*, said Alice, and as the scene took in people singing round a table with little glasses in their hands the jazz softened and slowed and became a complicated version of 'Happy Birthday', and Lettie understood that Alice and Freddie really were playing a sort of duet; that she was being his eyes.

One, two, three . . . On screen now the glittering young people, in the styles of nearly ten years before, were waltzing in perfect time to Freddie's present music. There was something disconcerting in it somehow, Lettie thought; the story made so long ago but recorded, lasting; the transient music happening now.

The two of them must have practised, Lettie thought, and imagined the rows of unlit empty seats while Alice and Freddie slowly took a film apart frame by frame, counting, and timing, and learning it by heart.

On screen Hetty – though the character she was playing had of course a name, this hardly mattered, thought Norah, as Hetty Harper had always played the same person, blithe, affectionate, gently born, and fearless – took her admirer's hand, and ran lightly with him on to the dance floor to join the other revellers.

Norah felt almost feverish: everything about the film was dated and feeble, especially to one accustomed to the violent excitements of Hollywood and the Rialto, but at the same time she was possessed with a familiar longing. Oh, Hetty Harper, so beautiful, so graceful, oh, to be like her, to *be* her!

Alice counting, so that Freddie's music danced in time. Poor Alice not exactly sotto voce, thought Norah. Had such a carrying voice; though of course few people knew that poor Freddie was just that little bit deaf as well.

AFTER THE PARTY read a caption repeated by Alice, the grand stately home now gloriously sunlit. Lettie sniffed; why were British films always about sodding toffs? At least Hollywood went in for stuff about ordinary people, the sort who actually *went* to the flicks in the first place.

The camera dwelt lovingly on various noble facades (*conservatory*, said Alice) until Hetty appeared again at the top of the immense flight of stone steps at the front door, in a loose daytime frock that had been particularly chic in 1923 or thereabouts, followed by *her sister*, said Alice, and the music altered, took on something faintly sinister.

Strange how even their expressions were dated, thought Lettie, their gestures, the way they held themselves. Who would guess there were fashions in the way you moved your hands? Hetty Harper laughing, pulling on a very sad little straw cloche – there was nothing more frumpy, Lettie knew, than the fashions of the previous decade – as the two girls climbed excitedly into a waiting *car*, said Alice, evidently from their expressions meant to look all sleek and exciting but really, thought Lettie, near laughter, a right old jalopy these days, and driven by a sleek-haired beetle-browed broadly smiling young *man*, murmured Alice, and the music told everyone to beware what lay ahead.

But the young people on screen, for all they had danced in time to Freddie's music at their party, seemed not to hear him any more, and took no notice. **OFF FOR A RIDE** read the caption and muttered Alice, and the sisters were borne away waving through the stone gateway and out on to winding moorland roads at suddenly reckless (*speed*, whispered Alice, as Freddie's fingers raced wildly up and down the keyboard), while Hetty's (*sister*) in the front passenger seat produced a (*hip flask*) from her handbag, swigged from it, and passed it to the driver though in the road round a bend or two several little (*children*) toddled innocently about near their picturesque thatched cottage, which the camera also dwelt on at wobbly and tedious length, thought Lettie, but (*back*) with the car Beetle-brow, to a fury of minor chords, swigged with one hand and twirled the steering wheel with the other, the younger sister laughing wildly, Hetty begging him to slow down until (*one two THREE*) the picture went dark.

Norah spoke aloud: 'Oh, no!'

AFTER THE CRASH read the caption, and said Alice, followed on screen by a long shot, which to Lettie at least felt very long indeed, of the outside of a tall turreted building, where a sign went on and on reading HOSPITAL. Get on with it, thought Lettie, mutinously shifting about in her seat, which was lumpy as well as hard.

On the screen Hetty Harper's sister sat alone beside Hetty's hospital bed, thoroughly miming remorse and despair while Freddie's music sobbed in sympathy, and Hetty lay still in a snowy and becoming head bandage, set about with stray curls.

After that the sister rather faded from the story, fleeing in hopeless shame while Hetty herself (**THE CRIPPLE** read the caption, and Alice) was heartlessly spurned by her young man, and emoted in a bath chair until at length she learnt patience and the value of good works, and how to walk with a crutch (**'LEAN ON ME'** said the new and handsome young vicar, and Alice) and at last the meaning of true love, holding her engagement party in the humble thatched cottage where luckily enough the little children seemed to have escaped all injury ('Thank goodness,' murmured Norah), while the sister, by now apparently married to Beetle-brow and not of the party, peered in through a window and wept, though later she was seen writing a letter from **THE ABODE OF DESPAIR**, just able to quickly hand the note out of the window to a passing cloth-capped urchin before the drunken Beetle-brow lurched in and swept all the crockery off the table with his forearm.

Going for her, muttered Alice, so that Freddie's hands stalked the keyboard as Beetle-brow made a rush at his wife, grabbed her throat, and swung her to the floor.

Lettie had stopped feeling the disjuncture between old story and new music, they had become one. She had forgotten how uncomfortable her seat was, and how hungry she was, she had even forgotten Frederick Pyncheon, and why she had come. She had stopped being herself at all, completely caught up in the story, watching the wretched sister's struggle for life, her hands tearing uselessly at her husband's great paws clamped about her throat.

Now Lettie did not consciously hear the music that was keeping time with her pounding heart, though it immensely deepened what felt like real horror. She did not notice Freddie's right hand fluttering higher and higher up the keyboard, giving despairing sound to the victim's heels as they scrabbled for purchase on the floor, or register the abrupt fall in pitch as the dying woman's eyes fluttered closed, nor the slowing minor chords, in graceful falling cadence, as she settled still and limp at last in the murderer's arms.

One, two, three! murmured Alice into the soft dying music, and no one heard her but Freddie.

The murderer stepped back, appalled, wild-eyed, his

hands tugging at his hair, and then everyone watching him started in their seats, seemed really to hear, as he did, the doom-laden rush of footsteps outside, the sudden *crash-bang* as the door flew open and Hetty, still clutching the tell-all note in one hand, burst into the room with her fiancé and a policeman. In despair – with a cry of bestial horror the audience heard – the murderer flung himself out of the window, chased by the two men so that Hetty was **ALONE WITH HER SISTER**. *Stop*, murmured Alice, and Freddie put his hands in his lap.

In a silence full of heartbeat Hetty threw her crutch aside and cast herself down beside her sister's body and embraced her, drawing back to shake her a little by the shoulders, calling her name again and again, and weeping, weeping.

Norah felt a quiver of pain all around her heart. She no longer envied Hetty her grace and beauty, no longer noticed them, except that they served somehow to make her grief more unendurable to watch. She saw the tender arch of Hetty's body, and her own eyes filled.

Like everyone else she did not notice when Alice tapped Freddie's hand, or hear the music quietly beginning again, faint, heart-broken; though it set her tears flowing.

Then the sister's eyelids fluttered, her head turned. She was alive.

Again only Alice heard the music, tremulous with Hetty's incredulous joy, fervent as she flung her arms about her sister, rocked her lovingly. Until the sister caught sight of the crutch, wrenched herself from Hetty's arms and turned away, hiding her face in the crook of her arm, the other stretched out behind her, palm towards Hetty in shame and renunciation.

Now, whispered Alice, and Freddie played a fragment of Bach, restrained, sorrowful, as on the screen Hetty resolutely stepped in front of her sister, took both her hands in hers, and spoke her final words of forgiveness and love: **AREN'T WE SISTERS?**

Yes, yes, and for always, cried the music in passionate answer as the women at last embraced; and Norah heard her own half-smothered gasp, and awoke to the real world, her face wet with tears.

Beside her Lettie too became dazedly aware of where she was, the hard seat, the chilly hall, how hungry and tired she was, the task ahead. The man at the piano. Stealthily, trying not to sniff, she wiped her cheeks dry with her fingertips, first one hand, then the other. She was aware too of the near approach of the old almost overpowering grief and resolutely turned herself away from it, forcing herself not to give in to it.

Since for a long time she had seen this manoeuvre as a kind of cowardice, she suddenly had no other course but to pretend to herself that she had really been crying only about the film. Just look at you, she sneered at herself unkindly: just look at you snivelling over this old rubbish, you ought to be ashamed of yourself!

The screen cleared suddenly, became an empty rectangle of hard white light. Someone switched the hall lights back on, and Freddie and Alice both stood up and turned round, Alice blinking in the glare, Freddie's eyes, Lettie saw, hidden behind dark glasses. He was not quite as tall as his sister. His face was flushed, glowing; his shoulders moved as if he had been running. It came into her mind that the whole evening had been designed not for the nostalgic pleasure of the audience, but for the more specialized delights of the performer. For Freddie.

'Oh, Alice, that was simply wonderful!' said Norah, standing up too and raising her voice. 'Thank you so much, perfect choice, *what* a story, and thank *you*, Freddie, playing so beautifully, I think a well-deserved round of applause, marvellous!'

Everyone clapped as hard as they could; the thin pattering echoed for a while high up amid the ancient smoke-blackened beams, circled there briefly, and died away.

Lettie

At least Philip wasn't there. She'd forgotten all about him until the lights went on, then had a moment's anxiety just in case. But nearly everyone there was ancient, even older than Alice, several old buffers looking vaguely military, a dozen or so elderly ladies in various stages of decay.

And Freddie, of course. The beard was a surprise, she hadn't noticed it at all in the darkness. It was neatly trimmed into a small point; easier than shaving, Lettie thought. Thin haggard face. The glasses she had seen earlier were dark, like sunglasses. Why would he need those, she wondered.

'Come and meet him,' said Norah, and they made their way through various chattering groups to join the little circle of elderly admirers all about him.

'Lettie, this is my dear cousin Freddie; Freddie – Miss Quick.'

'Ah, hello.' *Hellow*. His voice was as flutingly upper-echelon as his sister's, and almost as feminine in register. 'Alice has told me all about you.' He held out his hand.

Lettie dared his face, that could not return the gaze, and understood that she would not have known him. It had been too long ago.

'Miss Quick is my lodger, Freddie,' said Norah.

'How awfully jolly,' said Freddie. Despite the tinted glasses it was possible to see that the irises of his sightless eyes were in constant movement, jittering about in his head as if looking urgently for the light, or for a way out; as if his eyes were still appalled, after all these years, by the darkness they found themselves in. Could he actually feel them moving? It is a war wound, she reminded herself.

'You played ever so well,' she managed.

'Thank you,' he said. *Thenk yaw.* Even now that languid bleating tone gave her a qualm, she thought. An accent like that was a weapon; though mainly its power lay in your response to it. You could let it make you feel awkward and mysteriously ashamed of yourself. Or you could resist.

'Where did you get the film from?' she asked.

'We have a small collection,' said Freddie.

'Actually it's a *vast* collection,' said Norah, 'the crypt here is *stacked* with celluloid. The entire British film industry lies beneath our feet.' She sounded rather like him now, Lettie noticed, as if the emphatic flutiness was catching. 'We cried simply *buckets*, you know, Freddie.'

He smiled, showing big yellow teeth. 'Awfully jolly making people laugh,' he said, 'but seriously *delightful* to make them cry.' One or two old ladies standing nearby simpered at this, *Oh he was dreadful!*, and fluttered their hands.

'You mean you listen out for us all sobbing away?' said Norah, mock-indignant.

'Not exactly. But there's something different in the silence, perhaps. One can *feel* rapt attention, you know – it's nothing mystical: people merely stop fidgeting. And possibly breathe differently, there's a certain –'

'Sherry, anyone?' Alice pushed forward with a tray full

of tiny glasses, each bearing a small amount of something brown.

Freddie's face stiffened.

'Oh, lovely!' said Norah, and she put a glass into Freddie's hand.

'Have one yourself, Norah, do. And Miss Quick?'

'What *is* this stuff, Alice?' Freddie's tone was pleasant, conversational. But it was clear that there was something dangerous in it. Alice's eyes bulged with unease, and she gave an uncertain laugh.

'Well, it's sherry, darling,' she said.

'Delicious,' put in Norah.

'Alice, this is cooking sherry,' said Freddie loudly, and with an unselfconscious sharpness, as if they were alone.

'Oh no, Freddie, I assure you –'

'You think I don't know cooking sherry when I'm given it?'

There was a moment's bursting silence, then Norah said brightly: 'Lettie, do come and meet Mrs Porlock!'

Lettie followed her back down the aisle past the various clusters of dithery old folk towards the entrance, where they stood for a moment, and briefly met one another's eyes.

'Blimey,' said Lettie, inclined to laugh; there was something enlivening about bad behaviour, rather like those days at school when the teacher was picking on someone, enthralling fun so long as it wasn't you.

'Perfectly decent sherry,' said Norah. She looked wretched, so Lettie reined herself in.

'Let's go home,' she said suddenly.

'What, now?'

'Why not? Film's over; he's an arse; let's go.'

Norah uttered a snort of startled laughter. 'But –'

'See you outside in five minutes.' Lettie knocked the rest of her drink back, and felt all the better for it. She gave Norah the empty glass. 'Say goodbye for me – tell her I loved it. Okay?'

Going to try for it right now, she told herself, as Norah turned back. She had seen her very own special picture straight off, soon as they got here. As if it had called out to her. Pity about the toilet; made it far more likely there would be someone else in the anteroom, or even a queue.

But when she pushed back the velvet curtain and went through there was no one there at all. Norah would surely take several minutes to say her polite farewells, so this might well be her best or even only chance: one must take resolute action *now*, as the Madam would have said.

Quickly Lettie stepped into the kiosk, unhooked one of the photographs hanging there, a street-view of the Picture Palace itself decked with long-ago bunting, and carried it across the room. Here she took down another picture, tucked it under one arm and hung the kiosk one up in its place. Then she stepped smartly into the lavatory and locked herself in. Ten seconds maximum, she thought: done it.

It was possible no one would notice the pale rectangular gap on the wall in the kiosk; but if they did, she thought, they would assume it was the photograph of the Picture Palace hung with bunting that had gone missing, not the one in her hands. She gave the grimy glass a wipe with the forearm of her coat and took another quick look at it. Yes: it was the one, alright. *July 1914.* The one she had come

187

all this way for. Waiting for her all the time, right there on the wall, no need for begging letters or complicated plans.

She could not examine it properly yet. But it was hers now, and soon she would be able to look at it as long as she liked, whenever she liked. Or put it away and never look at it at all. She had the choice.

Lettie opened her coat; the everyday gabardine was not, in fact, altogether respectable inside, for she had fitted it out several years before with a large hidden inside pocket, neatly and strongly stitched into place just below the waist. The photograph fitted in nicely. She buttoned up, buckled the belt. No sign, she knew, of the stolen goods.

Not stolen, she told herself. Not really. Taken back.

She unbolted the door, and looked out, but her luck still held, there was no one about. She took her hidden treasure outside, to wait for Norah.

Rae

The next morning – and after her first decent night's sleep for months, she thought – she had awoken to find a swerving line of little reddish blisters as if handwritten right across her swollen stomach, like some primitive decoration, a tattoo perhaps. Standing shivering in front of the mirror in the bathroom Rae tried to convince herself that the blisters were normal. Perhaps every pregnant woman came out in horrible little sores like this. Perhaps some had them far worse. How could you tell?

But the blisters hurt, they seemed to prickle and burn. She would wait and see, she told herself. Perhaps they would just go away, as mysteriously as they had arrived. She got back into bed, and lay quietly, caressing them with her fingertips through the cotton of her nightdress, touching their pattern as if they were Braille, she thought, and might mean something. A script written while she slept, on her own skin.

Should she get someone to read it?

Mrs Givens, perhaps? She was uneasy, she realized, at the thought of Mrs Givens. Rae despised self-consciousness; saw it as a form of indulgence useful to one's rivals, one's enemies. But it was hard to picture seeing Mrs Givens for the first time this morning and being brightly insouciant. She imagined it, tried a little rehearsal. *Why, good morning, Mrs –*

Oh. I suppose I can still call her Mrs Givens? I don't

mind what she calls me; but we didn't go into what I'm meant to call *her*. Not that I'd want to use her Christian name anyway. I wouldn't dare. Especially when she's being all Miss Venables at me.

Her hand crept once more to the line of blisters, which had presented themselves to her again like a series of tiny electric shocks. You can't trust th'electric, she remembered, then jumped when Mrs Givens herself rapped on the door, and came in with a loaded breakfast tray, her manner just as usual, though her opening words were rather different:

'How you this morning, my lovely?'

'Oh, very well, thank you –'

'Sweet dreams?'

'None at all, but –'

She was tidying back the curtains. 'Something wrong?'

Rae sat up in the bed. 'D'you – d'you *know* anything about, well, about having babies and so on?' Rae had imagined this coming out idly, but the pitch was too high, she thought.

'Why do you ask?'

'Well – because, I don't, you see. Not a thing!' Laughingly, that was easier: 'I'm just *wondering*, that's all. Whether there's anything I ought to be doing, or not doing, you know, that sort of thing.'

Frightened, Rae realized: I sound frightened, because I am. I don't know what will happen to me. I don't know how the baby will get out. And there is something writing on my skin.

The blisters stung, they burnt, as if a little flame were flickering to and fro there. Rae decided: quickly she shifted the tray sideways on to the bedside table, and folded back the bedclothes.

'Look,' she said, pulling up the nightdress. 'Will you – can you have a look at this, please. Is this – d'you think this is normal?'

Mrs Givens took a pair of spectacles from the pocket of her apron. 'Lie back, then.'

Miss Venables again, thought Rae: that sudden authority of tone. She did as she was told, and Mrs Givens sat down on the edge of the bed, and for a moment looked searchingly into Rae's face.

'Pull the nightie right up, will you? That's it. Ah. This what's bothering you?' Then she asked no further permission, just put out her worn old hands and touched, no, thought Rae, she *felt*. She set the hard edge of her left hand just below Rae's breasts, and pushed it down a little, as if feeling for something, and at the same time she pressed all about the swollen stomach with the flat of her other hand. She peered closely at the swirling line of blisters, but she was careful, Rae saw with another spasm of fear, not to touch them. What was she doing?

''Tis well-grown; a fine child. Here's his back, see?' She pressed again with the palm of that hard right hand. 'Here's his little head; let's hope he turns hisself about before too long.'

'What do you mean?'

'He's a-set to coming out feet-first at present; better t'other way about.'

'Is it? And the – well, these. Does everyone get them?'

'How d'you – oh, I see – bless me, no. That ain't the baby – that's shingles, that is. Does it pain you?'

'A little. Not much. It does sort of prickle. As if I keep running into a cactus. *What* did you say it was? Is it bad?'

'Shingles – can be bad enough, for old folk.'

'Am I old folk?'

'What d'you think?'

'I feel about a hundred.'

'You'll be right enough. It'll hurt a bit, then go away again all by itself; honest, it ain't nothing to worry about.' She drew the bedclothes back and tucked them in.

So the prickling blisters were *shingling*, Rae thought. They were shingling all over her stomach. How disgusting shingles sounded, medieval somehow, a downtrodden-peasant disease; or something horses got. 'Shouldn't I – get it treated, or something?'

'There ain't no treatment,' said Mrs Givens. 'It won't harm you, nor the baby. It'll just go away by itself. Now, I must get on – you still want to help me sort those cupboards later on? See what we find?'

'Yes, I do – but – how d'you know about – you know, what the baby's doing, what way it's facing and so on?' said Rae.

'My mother. She knew all there was to know; delivered half the neighbourhood. Delivered herself: me and my sister.'

'Did she really? How? What did she do?'

'Bless me, I nearly forgot,' said Mrs Givens, and she put her hand into the pocket of her apron, and took out an envelope. 'Letter come for you. Mrs Wickham,' she added, as Rae took it. Then in a different voice: 'You eat your breakfast now, Ruth my lovely, or that egg'll be downright rubber.'

When she had gone Rae opened the envelope with her

192

butter knife, and read the letter, one hand still caressing the italic script of blisters on her stomach, as if her fingertips might yet discover some hidden message there. The letter was clear enough. It was typed on very thin paper, and without preamble informed her that Esme Bright would visit on the following day between three and four in the afternoon.

There was no signature, only a typed postscript, which read: *Burn this*.

The cupboard was on the third floor, several deep wide shelves stacked with cardboard boxes and bundles of cloth tied about with string. A short set of stepladders had been set up ready, and several large wooden packing cases stood empty beside it, with a great sack of soft shredded card, two pairs of scissors, piles of old newspapers, and a stack of luggage labels held together with a rubber band.

'So we're . . . emptying it?' Rae asked hesitantly.

'Don't belong to no one,' said Mrs Givens, briskly answering the unasked question. 'Rubbish, see, left behind long since. Should a bin got rid of years back.'

'But some of it might be nice?'

Mrs Givens shrugged. 'Some of it might sell. Had a look before, years ago. Put it all back again. My sister –' She broke off.

'Your twin sister,' Rae prompted, after a pause.

'She liked to keep it by her.'

'Oh. You mean she used to live here too?'

'No – well, yes, she did, for a while, that's true . . . anyway. It can't stay here no longer. You still want to help?'

I'd do anything, thought Rae, what with these shingles shingling at me, anything practical, help Minnie with the laundry, dig the garden with old Nameless Gardener, pull carrots. Anything, so long as it wears me out and stops me thinking.

'Yes, please!' she said.

'You're to stop, mind, the minute you starts feeling worn.'

Worrn, thought Rae, cheering up. 'Who says, anyway?' she asked, as Mrs Givens, going very slowly and carefully holding on to the handle, ascended the stepladder and peered into the dark recesses of the top shelf.

'Who says what?' Mrs Givens' voice was muffled.

'Who says it can't stay here any longer?'

Mrs Givens turned. 'Th'state agent. Bagnold and Pender, over to Silkhampton. Got the place up for sale.'

'Oh. Who would buy it though?'

'No one so far,' said Mrs Givens. 'No one wants to buy it; no one wants the lease. Here. You take this? It ain't heavy.' She passed down a narrow bolt of velvet, with something hard and ribbed inside it.

'What on earth is it?'

'Take a look. That's your job.'

'Ooh goodie, is it?' Rae laid the bundle on the floor, and unwrapped it. Within the folds, she found, she thought instantly, something more truly like a ghost than anything she had so far seen in the house or its lake: the frail remains of a parasol, folded, its delicate wooden struts barely held together in a sheer webbing of ancient fabric; silk, she thought, touching its papery fragility. A lace trim. An inset band of filigree. It had been beautiful once. The handle set into an ivory holder was carved with a pattern of tiny acanthus leaves.

'Look! Isn't it lovely!'

The sunlight of long-ago summers, thought Rae. She got up and as slowly as she could pushed the struts up into place, opening the parasol for the first time, she thought, in about a hundred years. When had people stopped carrying them? Had Mother had one once? The fragmented silk hung down between the struts, the filigree floating free. The struts were fine as bird bones; two were broken, one missing altogether. The ghost of a butterfly, she thought.

'Mrs Givens – what are we to do with it?'

'Put it on the fire.'

'Oh I couldn't!'

'Keep it then.'

But I can't do that either, thought Rae. Ah, was the whole cupboard like this?

'Can you take these, now?'

Another wrapped pile, then another, round, dense. Rae set them both on the floor and waited while Mrs Givens climbed slowly down again before kneeling to open the first.

'Goodness!'

It was china, three or four plates of blue and white porcelain, and very fine, she thought, densely painted with patterned edges and pictures of flowers and trees with long waving branches. All of it was chipped and cracked though.

'You're not throwing this away, are you? It's so lovely.'

'Dealer might take it.'

'Oh, look at this one!' Rae held up the largest plate; it had at some presumably remote time been broken in half, but then very carefully put back together again with what seemed to be metal staples, like four big flat stitches on the back.

'How did they do that?' said Rae. 'How can it not show at all from the front?'

Mrs Givens took it, turned it to the light to see the delicately drawn pagoda beside a pond, the three little golden fishes leaping out of the water.

'Going to so much trouble,' said Rae. 'I actually like it more than if it was perfect – don't you?'

'Keep it, if you like it,' said Mrs Givens, passing it back.

'Really?'

A broken plate, riveted carefully into the semblance of perfection: an item altogether too heavy with symbolism, thought Rae. The shingle blisters prickled as if passing on a message: still here. She set the plate down on the floor beside her.

There was a great deal more. Some she thought she recognized:

'Isn't this Sèvres?'

None of it was perfect.

'This here's Bristol ware,' said Mrs Givens, holding up a particularly glittering chipped floral teacup. Its saucer was missing. Some was packed away for a junk dealer Mrs Givens knew, from Exeter; choicer pieces went into a smaller box, to be given away. The biggest pile was for the rag-and-bone man.

It was pleasant work. Besides china there were various curiosities: a set of narrow metal items Rae eventually decided were adjustable ice skates, a wide-bladed smooth-handled implement Mrs Givens said had to do with the separation of cream from milk, a great number of wrought-iron hooks, two brass warming pans, three tall brass jugs, all greenish and dented, a set of badminton rackets with the strings all gone, and a large and beautiful shallow box of softly gleaming cherrywood, faintly lettered in gold, *StJ CH*.

'What's in here – it's a display case, isn't it?'

'Oh, nothing, just seashells, dealer might take the box – what's that old thing doing there? That's for the furnace.' Pointing at the teddy bear.

Rae picked it up, turned its balding plush head. 'It's a good one. Honestly, let the dealer see it.'

'Dirty old thing it is,' said Mrs Givens, but she let Rae pack it in with the china.

It was a pity, Rae thought, as this companionable morning wore on, that she would soon have to spoil things; but she couldn't put it off much longer. How difficult could Mrs Givens be, after all? Various possible answers to this particular question kept making her delay again.

After an hour or more, towards eleven, she forced herself to speak out. 'Mrs Givens,' she said carefully as she balanced a jigsaw puzzle of St Paul's Cathedral on the furnace-pile – the box was labelled *Two Bits Missing from Dome* in handwritten sepia, and after some discussion they had decided to take the label's word for it – 'you know that letter I had this morning?'

'Yes?'

'Well, it was from her. The ah, midwife. The one who's going to, you know, help me.'

'Oh yes?' Mrs Givens' voice was muffled, from deep inside the top shelf. Rae waited.

'She's coming here. Tomorrow, to see me,' she added at last.

'What? Is she, indeed?' said Mrs Givens sharply, turning round. ''Cause *I* got folk coming then.'

'Really? Oh dear, when?'

'Ten, thereabouts.'

'Well – she won't be here before three. Sorry – I mean, she hasn't given me much notice – d'you think it'll be alright?'

'Suppose so,' said Mrs Givens grudgingly. She turned back to the cupboard, and with a deep sweep of one arm caught hold of something at the back ('Got you!' very muffled) and turned, her face flushed, holding out a parcel the size of a shoebox. 'There, that's the last of it! That shelf anyway.'

Rae reached up and took it from her outstretched hand. 'You don't mind, do you?' she asked. 'About her coming?'

'Nothing to do with me,' said Mrs Givens, climbing back down the stepladder. She wiped her dusty hands on her apron. 'If you consort with criminals.'

'Oh, don't be like that, please.'

Mrs Givens folded her arms. 'Suppose you'll be wanting tea for her.'

'If you wouldn't mind,' said Rae meekly. There was a pause.

'Want some now?'

'Ooh yes please,' said Rae. 'I'll just do this one first, shall I?' She seized the scissors, snipped through the string and unfolded the brown paper, worn soft with age. An ordinary box, with a fitted lid. She set it down on top of the packing case and took off the lid: inside, the usual layer of torn sheeting, then lots of white tissue, crumpled into packing. Gently she pulled it free, and discovered a very small cylindrical coffee cup in blue and white bone china, painted with a blue bird like a sort of peacock. Beside it, also carefully wrapped, another.

'Look, these are perfect! Aren't they beautiful! There's two saucers – and look at the coffee pot, lovely – no lid though. What d'you think – dealer pile?' The china was so fine that it was almost transparent; she could see the bird from the inside.

Mrs Givens, who had been gathering newspapers together, let her bundle drop and came closer. 'Let me see.'

Rae passed her the little cup.

Mrs Givens was very still for a second. 'Ah, Ruth,' she said.

'What?' said Rae, looking up; there had been something slightly odd about her voice, she thought, though she looked alright.

'I meant – t'other Ruth,' said Mrs Givens.

'Oh, the one who died?'

Mrs Givens nodded. 'Just a little girl, she were. Near on four. She liked that blue bird; so I give her one a the cups to keep for her own. 'Twas the last thing she held. In this life.'

'Oh no! And you mean – one of these?'

'No – we kept that apart special; but it broke long ago.'

'Oh, Mrs Givens!' Rather to her own surprise Rae's eyes had filled. It was a touching story enough; but I wouldn't have cried over it before, she thought. I wouldn't have felt it, the way I do now.

Though at the same time she understood that she was mentally filing the whole story away, as a perfect Hollywood detail. Ashamedly, she blinked the tears away before they felt false.

''Tis just a bit of old china,' said Mrs Givens, passing her the cup back. 'Put it back again, will you, Ruthie?'

Rae sniffed. 'And – what do you want me to do with it?'

Mrs Givens sighed. 'Think I'll have to keep it. For now.'

Norah

Outside the tithe barn the air was darkening blue and pleasantly still.

'I'm starving,' said Lettie. 'Can we go back by the chippie?'

'I'm sorry – what did you say?'

'Fish and chip shop. On North Road – don't say you ain't tried it.'

'Alright. I won't,' said Norah. Though in fact she had eaten chips before, and out of newspaper, she remembered: during the War, when everything had been different in that chaotic wartime way. Some of that had felt like freedom, she told her mother's instant scorn.

A fish and chip shop – pray, why not a four-ale bar? But somehow this evening Mrs Thornby lacked her usual vigour. They turned right past the churchyard, and took the short cut through the Rope Walk, turned a corner and met the deep savoury familiar smell.

'Oh God,' said Lettie, quickening her pace.

The chip shop was powerfully lit, deliciously warm. They entered, blinking in the strong light, snuffing the hot aromatic air, just as the only other customer, a burly workman in a flat cap with a packet under one arm, was leaving.

'Cod and chips twice please,' said Lettie, without preamble, resting her palms on the warm wooden counter top. 'Salt. And vinegar. Got any gherkins? Want a gherkin, Norah?'

'No one'll see you,' she said, when they were back outside. 'Who cares anyway?' Her packet of fish and chips was not wrapped, so that she could eat it with her fingers on the way home. 'Tastes best that way, honest!'

But Norah had known the name of the woman behind the counter, caught her eye as she was shovelling chips on to clean white paper, and knew that Sally Hissop – as was, at any rate – knew her own. And that of course she was the Local Woman too. 'Good evening, Sally,' she had said.

'Miss Thornby,' Sally had replied, as if cordially; and Mrs Thornby, detecting irony in her glance, had perked up and raised the possibility of lower-class sniggering as soon as Norah's back was turned.

All the same, the streets were poorly lit, and the smell of Lettie's chips was simply unendurable, Norah thought. Perhaps Mrs Thornby found it so as well, for exposed to it she slipped away altogether; when they were safely round the corner Norah stopped, pulled off her gloves, stuffed them into her coat pockets, and unwrapped her hot newspaper parcel. In the dim light steam arose; the hot chips glittered crustily with salt.

'Oh, bliss!' said Norah. They walked slowly now, both of them steadily eating, breaking off manageable pieces of the crisp batter, crunchy on the outside, milkily yielding within. The fish inside was almost too hot to touch, gleaming, succulent. It warmed you all through. It was the most delicious food she had eaten for years, thought Norah, as they neared Silver Street.

'I'm sorry about this evening,' she said, as they reached the darkened Little Owl Tearooms on the corner.

'How d'you mean?'

'Well – it was all a bit – peculiar. Wasn't it?'

Lettie shrugged. 'The film was okay. Sort of.'

'I'm not sure it would have worked at all, without Freddie. It was so slow.'

'Can't remember him playing at all,' said Lettie, folding up what remained of her supper and wiping her hands on the outer newspaper.

'No, nor can I really. That's part of his artistry, I think. That you stop hearing him.'

Lettie's glance somehow plainly said what she thought of Freddie.

'Are you – are you someone's sister?' Norah dared, as they passed the muffled swell of talk and piano-bashing from the pub.

Lettie shook her head. 'Not for a long time.'

'Me neither.'

'Thornby G. W.,' said Lettie, to Norah's surprise. 'Was it him?'

Yes, Norah agreed, that was him, her dear brother Guy, who was and was not the statue in the square. She noticed she had eaten everything, the whole packet of fish and chips, and screwed the heavily greasy papers into a ball; and then without thinking about it at all she began to tell Lettie a story she had never told anyone before, had tried her best to forget: the story of her family's trip to France, early in 1920. Began and then went on and on, as if unable to stop herself:

'It was all my idea,' she said. 'And all because of something I'd seen in a magazine, a reproduction of a picture. I've never forgotten it. I can see it now. It was called *So, It Was Here, Then?* The picture, I mean.

'It's in France, there's a few people in the background, looking French, you know, and some French-looking ruins. But mainly it's this English couple, very well-dressed, oldish, arm-in-arm. And they're standing near a big car in a field, muddy, with all bits of hedge and tree trunks, broken, snapped off, you know, the way they all were in those days. And there's a young woman with them, obviously their daughter, very pretty, and d'you know I can still see *exactly* what she was wearing, this soft-looking coat with a big shawl collar, very loose and long, and a sort of draped hat, you know the date because of her clothes, it's absolutely 1919.

'And the three of them, the old couple and the girl, they're talking to a soldier, a British officer. He looks tired. They all do, they all look sad and quiet, but sort of peaceful. As if they've found what they were looking for, and done everything they can. It's the father talking, you see, the older man, he's saying to the young officer, "So, it was here, then?" And so you know what he's asking, you know who isn't in the picture, who's never going to be in any picture ever again.'

Norah stopped, her voice trembling. They had been standing still for a while, she realized: had somehow drawn naturally to a halt. She turned and looked into the dim arcade window of the shoe shop: *Wider Fit for Comfort!* she read.

Lettie said, 'So. You went too? To see where your brother died?'

Norah nodded. 'Idiotic – because of the picture. I thought it would – help in some way, I suppose. I talked them into it. But we weren't like that. Like the picture. Not a bit of it. The worst thing was –' She stopped, unable for a moment to speak.

'The worst thing was, my parents kept arguing with one another all the time, and complaining. About everything. Of course we didn't know how ill Daddy was – he died not so long afterwards. But nothing I could do was right. And Mother. She was just a hard little . . . nubbin, complaining *really bitterly* about the tea.

'And I'd always known Guy was their favourite. I didn't mind, he was my favourite too, but I hadn't known how little use I was to them. They really couldn't forgive me for being alive, when he was dead. I couldn't forgive myself either.'

There was a pause. They walked on, slowly, past the jeweller's, and reached Modes de Madame, where they stopped again, as if looking in at the bank of pastel twin-sets there.

'I can't help thinking,' said Norah at last, 'that in a way, our trip: it was the end of my being a daughter at all.'

Then it was as if she awoke from her trance of confession, and became aware of all that she had said. I should be ashamed, she thought at once. Yet it seemed to her that she had not so much complained and betrayed as simply told the truth after hiding it for a long time, and bearing the concealment as an extra burden.

'D'you think that's dreadful?' she asked. A silence.

'Don't always get it right, parents,' said Lettie at last, and they turned and began to skirt the square.

'Did yours?' Norah asked.

Lettie almost laughed before she shook her head. 'God, no.'

Lettie

Are you someone's sister? There was a question.

Lettie smuggled the photograph out of her coat's secret pocket while Norah was safely in the bathroom, and in her own room took her face cloth, still damp from the morning, and set about carefully cleaning the glass.

July 1914

Slowly the scene clarified. There was the bandstand, edged in iron curlicue as delicate as icing on a wedding cake, and all the young people gathering beside it, on an early evening in summer. Strange, she thought, to see something that looked so very historical, when you could remember it so well: the soft air, the smell of crushed grass, the way the little coloured lights had gleamed through the greenery.

Just in shot was the band itself, a dense wedge of blurred movement, lighter towards the top with misty suggestions of trumpets and peaked caps; to one side a perspective of diminishing lamp posts carried swagged bunting.

What were we celebrating? She hadn't known that at the time either.

The clothes, thought Lettie. Dear Lord. Antiques. Every young man in a boater, some tipped at wild angles, every girl in an almost shoulder-wide hat loaded with various blurs of tulle and flowers. They were the very last

Englishwomen, Lettie thought, to wear unselfconsciously and in daylight the long concealing skirts of all the previous ages. One carried a ruffled parasol.

Lettie crossed the room to her chest of drawers, took out a slim box, opened it, and drew out the magnifying glass. Then, sitting down beside the window, with ceremony, she at last allowed herself to look with all her closest attention at the children in the foreground.

He hadn't asked first, she remembered. She'd heard an indecipherable sound, something between click and firework, looked up from the pram handle and there he was, holding the big black box against his chest, staring at her over it, cheeky git. Then he had said it: 'Can I take your picture?' As if she could still say no.

"'Ere!" Lettie had cried indignantly.

He had turned out to be a gentleman though, able and willing to part with sixpence, just for the one picture. She remembered she had invited him to take more, hoping for another tanner; she had tried to straighten Wilf up a bit so that he looked less gormless. But Freddie – the gentleman, he'd seemed so old to her then – had just shaken his head politely enough and gone away. She had never entirely forgotten him though, nor the fact of the photograph.

Well, well. There she stood, her own child-self, eleven years old, in plain calf-length pinafore and boots, a small sharp face squinting in the late afternoon light, her hair pulled back into a ponytail at the nape of her neck and tied with a big white ribbon.

The pram.

Lettie took a deep breath.

The pram was a big-bellied stagecoach on very small wheels, and had a folding leather hood on stiff struts that caught your fingers if you weren't in the know. In the picture the hood was squashed flat as far as it would go and leant upon by the tousled middle baby Joey in his thick cardigan; in front of him sagged his younger brother Wilf, a small bald head almost submerged in flannel, while facing them on the seat hooked across the foot of the pram, sweet-faced, placid, his boots in the blankets, sat –

'Ezra,' said Lettie aloud in her room, a world away. Ezra, the eldest, the baby of babies, the king of her heart.

None of them faced the camera, of course. He'd crept up on us, Lettie thought, had Freddie Pyncheon, young photographer-about-town visiting London, crept up on us with his big black box of tricks. Or just caught sight of us and seen what he could do with us, make out of us.

And what had that been, Lettie wondered, what had he thought he was doing?

The copy in the exhibition that had started all this, brought her here, had been given a title: *July 1914*. Had Freddie done that? Or Alice? Perhaps the collector who had bought it. But one of them had seen –

'Ha!' muttered Lettie –

One of them had looked at this and seen the *bigger picture*. Not the nicely composed shot of holiday crowds flowing past the still little girl in the centre, both hands clamped round the handle of the pram, but the bigger picture, the terrible significance of the date. July 1914: Just Before.

A title you could only give this picture Afterwards, Lettie thought.

Social comment maybe. Perhaps that was the sort of thing Freddie had really been after when he clicked the shutter. Was it still clear, at this late date, that the children – herself, her brothers – were vastly poorer than the young people all about them?

Though even at the time, thought Lettie now, there were things the photograph had of course left out. She could look back in sharp memory, knew all too well how unkempt the three little boys were, sickly underfed children inexpertly cared for by another child. She knew that Joey's nose was caked with snot, twin scabs of it running down to his upper lip, that all three wore old tears streaked in the grime upon their faces.

None of this was visible, even with the magnifying glass. Nor could the camera show that the pram had been hired for the afternoon; and the image had smoothed out the dents, and wiped away the ancient gatherings of grime. The dress hidden beneath Lettie's pinafore was far too small for her, and torn under one arm; inside her boots her sockless feet were deeply ingrained with dirt. She could remember the fat black sausages of filth that had daily formed between each toe.

And the ribbon. The precious ribbon in her hair. It was the first she had ever worn, and it had fallen minutes earlier from the head of quite another little girl, walking ahead of Lettie with her Mamma; Lettie had seen it fall, and moved in sharpish to claim it.

The lovely youths and maidens walking past her and her pramful of brothers had wrinkled their noses and avoided one another's eyes as they met with so clear an example of poverty and neglect. Soon a park keeper would arrive, and remind Lettie that listening to the music cost money, and she would start the long trek home again, with the photographer's sixpence warm in her pocket, proud in her hair ribbon, to visit the chip shop well before she got home.

'It wasn't just the boys,' Lettie had told the Madam once, in the days when she had thought her understanding. 'She lost two. And she miscarried so many times I think she lost count. Well, I think she was doing something – bringing them on, you know. To be honest.'

'Oh, Lettie, how simply dreadful!'

Lettie had been a little surprised. 'Ain't always been a crime, has it? Used to be your own business, what you did. Who says it's so wrong anyhow?'

'Dear girl – everyone,' said Dr Stopes.

'Everyone who's never had to do it,' Lettie had said.

Joey. Wilf. Ezra. Her mother's survivors. Perhaps. Maybe she'd have got rid of me, if only she'd known how, thought Lettie. But you were a bit too young then, weren't you, Ma? To try one of the other ways out.

Holding the photograph to her bosom Lettie stood up and went to the window and looked out at the square below, deserted at this hour except of course for the stone soldier on his plinth. Norah's brother, she thought. She remembered the old film they had seen, *Aren't We Sisters?*, and how Freddie Pyncheon's music had made it heartbreaking. All this feeling that man's made me feel, she thought. And he has no idea, and he never will.

Am I someone's sister, Norah? I was once; but am I still?

I wish I knew.

In Bed with Dr Heyward

The death of Dolly Wainwright bothered Dr Heyward a great deal. It was bound to, he told himself sometimes, when he awoke from some fit of abstraction to realize that he had somehow once again been thinking of her. He had not slept well either, since the inquest. But one was bound to be upset, he told himself, when an old friend and long-term colleague passed away. It was only natural.

Had he actually dreamt of her just now? He stretched out in the roominess – he had the double bed all to himself for once – and remembered once more that he was after all a decent chap, an all-rounder: good at a party, good in a shipwreck.

He knew how good because of the shipwreck of the War, when he had done all in his power to save lives in more than one front-line hospital. The memory of those few years of almost non-stop exertion was often with him, useful proof of virtue.

Towards the end of the War when a field station had to be evacuated he had volunteered to be dropped by parachute behind the fracturing enemy lines. He had never been in an aeroplane in his life, never even been near one. He had sat beside the quiet monster in its hangar, waiting for the pilot to arrive, while another young officer showed him his Guardian Angel, and explained how it worked.

He could remember how damp and cold his hands had

been, that he had been forced to let the young RAF officer buckle one or two of the straps for him. When the pilot came and the monster bomber was brought roaring to thunderous life he had expected to die; he had heard how many parachutes failed to open. But all the same he had climbed up and over the wings into the beast itself, and been swung sickeningly up and into the air, and when after some indeterminate length of time the leather-helmeted head in front of him had half turned and nodded the signal, he had at once scrabbled to his feet, and leant sideways, and made himself fall right out into the endless darkening air.

It was like a dream to him sometimes, those deafening headlong moments of drop. But his hand had found the pull, and the silken ghost of his Guardian Angel had flickered up and flung itself overhead, and jerked his whole body back into sudden tranquillity. He had landed almost gently in a potato field, and even now the smell of the leaves, the sight of small white potato flowers gleaming in twilight, give him a swingeing turn, a pang at his heart.

It is the Guardian Angel he thinks of, in those uncomfortable moments after he has done something part of him recognizes as not entirely consistent with decency. The opening parachute cancels out such uncomfortable recognition, reminds him that while it's true he has a mistress, a man must be a man; having a mistress hardly counts. And that no one ever has or ever will see him strike his wife, so in all the ways that really matter he has not struck her at all.

It's certainly true that he has always been genuinely startled, as well as outraged, when she has on occasion accused him of doing so. Though of course the silly woman will go in for histrionics, flinging herself to the floor and moaning there as if genuinely hurt. When at most he's just given her a little tap. And frankly she just shouldn't be so irritating. She does it on purpose most of the time, for neurasthenic reasons of her own.

Obviously it had been a mistake to tap her that time when she was standing at the top of the stairs; if she hadn't managed to grab on to the banisters she might have really hurt herself. Not a scratch on her as it was, of course, but what an endless fuss she'd made all the same! As if it was all his fault where the wretched woman had positioned herself; she should have known better than to carry on badgering him when he had already made his displeasure clear to her. Some women just never knew when to shut up.

And Susan was a particularly tiresome specimen of the sex, he thought now. She had seemed a desirable enough prospect once, when she had been Susan-plus-fortune. But these days she was just Susan, and had been for years. All the same he should not perhaps have put his feet up like that earlier, and pushed hard at her behind until she fell out with such a thump on to the bedside rug. Satisfying at the time, of course, but undignified.

The silken Angel flickered behind his closed eyes. Sniffing like that – how was he supposed to get any sleep, with his wife making wet snorting noises like a pig all night? It was all very well for her, she could lie about all next day if she felt like it, but he had work to do in the morning.

Well, she was in the spare room now. She could snort all she pleased in there.

He laced his hands behind his head, thinking: he could always get the hell out, of course. Why not? Rhodesia, South Africa, there were still places where a man could make a fresh start. Escape was an old idea with him, but tonight for the first time it occurred to him that he need not go alone; he could take Lettie with him.

They could sail for South Africa on one of the first-class only lines. She would slip into his cabin after dark, he would lock them both inside, the ship rising and falling.

He pictured some of the things he could do there, complex things, the long pleasurable setting-up.

Her compliance.

Rae

'Still paining?'

Rae took her hand away from her stomach. 'Not really.' She leant back in the chair. Mid-morning tea had merged with lunch; they sat now at the kitchen table with half a loaf and an empty jar of potted shrimps between them.

'Tell me about your mother,' Rae said. 'How could she deliver herself, her own babies, I mean?'

'Why not? There ain't that much to it.'

'Isn't there?'

'Not when it all goes right.'

'But – she was a midwife?'

'She would never have said so. A handywoman, maybe. You heard a that before? No? She didn't have no learning but what her mother taught her. She couldn't write her own name. But there weren't nothing she dint know about childbirth.'

'People paid her?'

'Only what they could afford. She was a godly woman,' said Mrs Givens. 'I know you want to ask what she did – and I can tell you what she would a said herself: every childbed, she always did *as little as she could*. That's what she used to say. Most folk don't need much.'

'What *do* they need then?'

'They need watching. There ain't no one in charge. D'you see? The mother don't say, Right, I'm going to have this baby now. The baby don't say, Right, I'm a-going to be born. No one decides. The midwife knows that. She stands by. She watches, she don't interfere. There ain't no interfering to be done, unless something goes wrong; she just has to know when that is. That's the only judging she does. D'you see?'

'So – what can go wrong?'

'What's the point me frightening you?'

'You said the baby was upside down!'

'I seen 'em turn round the day they was born.'

'Really?'

'Once my mother turned a baby round herself. Set to coming out backside first he was, begging your pardon –'

'Granted.'

'And my mother gets the poor girl to lie down on her bed, she puts her hands upon her, and she feels where the baby is, here's his head, here's his backside, like, and she pushes up a bit with one hand, and she pushes down a bit with the other – like turning a wheel, she says, under a blanket!'

Mrs Givens moved her own hands in the air, curved about the notional baby: 'And she turns that child about, puts him right head down as he ought to be, all fine and dandy, thank you very much! The very next day, the mother goes into labour, calls for my mother – I was just a girl, I remember it as if it was yesterday, Mother goes in, and puts her hands on her, and how she starts back! Bless me, she says, if this little tyke ain't a-gone and turned his-self round again bum-first! Yes, that's what she said, right enough.'

'Oh! So then what did she do?'

'Told you – little as she could. Best-laid plans a mice and men, says my mother, he must come out as he pleases, we'll say no more about it. But when the babby finally comes into this world-a-pain, no – he's turned hisself round again, head-first smart as you please! Fooled the lot of you, he says. My mother did laugh.'

'It is best, then, the right way round,' said Rae, after a pause.

'More common, maybe. Don't you fret about it, now.' Mrs Givens stood up. 'I'll get this bit a washing-up done – you finished?' She gathered crockery and went off humming to the big stone sink before the window.

Rae looked down at the breadcrumbs on the tablecloth. The blisters prickled, and it seemed to her that all at once she understood the message of that strange italic writing on her skin. It was about powerlessness. The shingles said: there is nothing you can do. What lies ahead is inexorable.

All this time I've been afraid of the waiting, thought Rae, and I've distracted myself even from that with childish fears of darkness and second-hand shivers made up from gaslight and laudanum. Now such passing frights looked like indulgence; it seemed to her as if she had been concentrating so firmly on the waiting, and on keeping it secret, that she had somehow failed to notice that there was only one way for the waiting to end.

A starring role in a play I haven't read yet, she thought; and it's nearly curtain up.

'What's the point me frightening you?' Mrs Givens had asked, and that had sounded reasonable enough; but didn't it mean that being told what could go wrong would necessarily involve being even more horrified than if you went on knowing nothing at all? It was a sort of conspiracy, thought Rae, of women-who-knew; as if those who had done it and survived had immediately agreed that it was better not to describe any of it to those still waiting.

You would find out soon enough, went the usual argument, and again this sounded reasonable, since the event was of course inexorable. But again the implication was that when you had found out you would understand, and join the conspiracy yourself, because – presumably – whatever had happened had been so dreadful that it turned you from being your ordinary self into someone who preferred silence and lies. Like everyone else.

It seemed to Rae suddenly that everything she had ever read, every single novel, every play or film she had seen, had told her lies, the malignant lies of absolute omission. None of them had so much as mentioned her present state, or touched on what it felt like. Any baby that appeared seemed to do so as if by magic, or as if women were no more directly part of the business of producing babies than men were. All of it was just left right out, even the end bit, the labour, the birth itself. Jane Eyre had seemed like a real woman, flesh and blood and feeling, angry intelligent mind; but even she had merely set his firstborn in Mr Rochester's arms, as if with a little disclaiming shrug, oh, it was nothing. Reader, I married him – as if that was the hard part!

And this is a mystery, thought Rae, that can kill you; women in books often died in childbirth, no matter that their pregnancies hadn't featured at all, Catherine Earnshaw,

Mrs Dombey. But how, exactly? Had Emily Brontë known? Had Dickens?

I bet he didn't know, she thought. Bet he didn't have a clue. Didn't give two hoots either: Mrs Dombey's job was simply to have the baby and die, like Oliver Twist's mother. Now, says Dickens, now we can get on to the really important stuff, the proper story, the real story. Now we've got those dead mothers out of the way.

And there are no pictures, no sculptures, no Art at all. There are images everywhere of death: Jesus nailed to His cross in every parish, saints all over the place tied to stakes or shot full of arrows, ordinary sinners neatly lying on deathbeds or soldiers hacking at one another with swords in battles, and horses rearing up trampling people underfoot, and flags waving, and how many times have you seen The Death of Nelson, Kiss me Hardy, all that *detail*; departing is all very well and sad or noble or thrilling but there are no grand pictures of arrival, no Birth of Nelson, Kiss me Mother. Because birth is women opening their legs but not for sex; and that's worse than death, thought Rae, that's profane and shameful and terrifying and grotesque, so there are only ever pictures of afterwards.

If giving birth kills you, there are pictures then. Tidied up, of course, being taken up to Heaven by the angels like Princess Charlotte, the king's own daughter, quietly in bed like Mrs Dombey – but nothing detailed, just vagueness underneath the sheets, beneath the skin where the dying is quietly carrying on –

'Ruth? What is it – you alright, my lovely?'

Rae was startled: 'Oh –' She took a deep breath, let it out on a sigh. 'Sorry. I was – miles away.'

Mrs Givens gave her a look, then sat down at the table, a tea towel still over one arm. 'Tell you what,' she said, 'you go and have a little lie-down for now, and I'll have another go at that cupboard – I got a few baby things put by there, shawls and bonnets and dresses, and so on. We have a look at 'em maybe, see if there's anything you want?'

A little dress? An *outfit*, for this inchoate entirely mysterious threat to her life? You had to laugh; almost, thought Rae.

'Ruth?'

'Oh, yes, please. That sounds lovely – thank you, Mrs Givens.'

At Home with the Pyncheons

The days had attained a certain symmetry. In the mornings, after breakfast, they walked in the garden. Then Freddie went to his practice, or his gramophone, or his book; Alice to the running of the household. After lunch, a short rest; then in the afternoon walking, or in summer swimming, generally in the river, though sometimes they walked all the way along to the beach. Tea, in the sunny drawing room, or outside on the lawn; later perhaps a film, an old favourite, if there was no one coming to supper.

How all this felt, of course, depended entirely on Frederick's mood. Sometimes at night Alice thought about the day – how a diary entry about it might read something like *Rainy morning cleared by lunchtime, picnic usual place, with the Petersons, very jolly, brought cherry cake. Saw kingfisher. Petersons to Picture P, ran* The Vagabond Queen, *Freddie inspired, hot chocolate after* and sound like the nicest day anyone could possibly wish for, though in fact every part of it had been charged with despair.

She was the elder by nine years; it had seemed a miracle to Alice that the baby Freddie had so clearly returned her adoration, kicking his little legs for joy whenever she entered the nursery, lounging in a passion of contentment on her lap, and playing with her hair. Alice seldom actively remembered those days, but they had coloured dealings with her brother ever since.

She stood now in her bedroom, looking out into the garden, where Freddie was sitting well-wrapped up on the terrace, taking a breath of fresh twilit air. It was teatime, and everything was ready. She pushed the velvet curtain to one side, and held the window a little further open.

'Freddie? Alright, darling?'

He stirs, turns to face the sound of her voice. 'Hello.'

'Would you like some tea now? I can wait, if you'd rather.'

'No. I'll come in now.' He sounds calm. Tired out. Not surprising, perhaps.

Alice turns away from the window and looks at herself in the mirror of her wardrobe. She has taken off her spectacles so the reflection is pleasantly unfocussed. For a moment she stands four-square considering herself. She is wearing one of her mother's most magnificent hats, extraordinary-looking now, though she can remember the time when it was merely fashionable. It's nearly as big as a cartwheel, she thinks, with a smile. It sits at a very slight angle on her head, shading her face in the mirror, a great lacy cartwheel loaded with silken flowers sewn into a froth of gauzy drapings.

She wears a single string of pearls too, the christening gift of her aunt and godmother the Hon. Daphne Redwood, who once had tea with Florence Nightingale, and which she never removes; her shoes are of soft kid, and date from that brief period just after the War when there was money for dance shoes, and energy for dancing. They have small curved heels, and fasten with a single mother-of-pearl button each, and at the moment they are Alice's favourite possession.

Alice's reflection, naked but for these special items, looks back at her, vague with myopia. She tries to ascribe meaning to it. But the only way she can think of doing this is to give herself a title, as if she were a picture, some old painting of a goddess or mythological nymph, Aphrodite in Pearls, Danae at her Toilette, Daphne Bathing. She turns and the naked figure in the mirror turns with her, poses afresh, lifts one long slender arm. Her breasts are small and pink-nippled, her pale thighs are elegantly long. The hat is wrong, thinks Alice complacently. I am Late Medieval in shape, a Medieval beauty, white and slender, Eve ejected from the Garden of Eden; Eve alone though, Eve with never an Adam in sight.

Am I going to do it or am I not?

Sometimes Alice's courage fails her, or decency prevails, she's not sure which; maybe both, but until the very last minute she's never sure whether she really is going to go downstairs like this, or whether she's merely going to get dressed again. She is aware that the desire to stay as she is stems from something painful, but largely she does not think about what she is doing at all. It doesn't happen that often, she tells herself. And if no one knows about it but me, if no one sees me but me, can it really be said to have happened at all?

But sometimes, mysteriously, she feels she has no choice. No choice but to pick up her dress, or skirt, and carrying it in one hand slowly (magnificently, she always feels) walk downstairs. Freddie's hearing, though not perfect, is good enough; and she knows that at home her approach is usually heralded not just by the sound of tapping heels but by the soft swish of material. So she carries whatever she has discarded, just in case. Though it seems impossible that he will ever suspect.

She decides. She gathers up the plain linen skirt she wore today, raises a hand in farewell at her reflection, and picks up her spectacles, fitting them on with some difficulty round the great hat brim. Careful not to check her clear image as she passes the wardrobe, she leaves the room, closes the bedroom door behind her, her heart beating fast, and stands for a moment on the landing. Suppose Mrs Trimble has popped in from next door? Suppose Norah has dropped by on her way home from work? Both have more than once quietly let themselves in by the kitchen door, which is always open.

The deliriously exciting possibility is there, is always there. Alice pants a little as she reaches the turn of the stout Edwardian wooden staircase and begins her slow descent. The banister smooth beneath her caressing hand. The air touches her skin, as lovely as cool river water. At the bottom of the stairs is the tall mirrored hatstand; she avoids this easily.

In the drawing room Freddie is sitting by the fireplace.

'Sorry, didn't mean to keep you waiting! I was just finishing a letter.' She drops the skirt over the arm of her chair, and crosses to the table, where everything is just as she left it. She takes the cosy off the pot and touches her hand to it. Is it, in fact, just a little on the cool side? How long did she take upstairs?

She pours Freddie's tea, sugars it, and takes it to him, carrying the little side table in her other hand.

'There. Bread and butter? There's fruit loaf too.'

'Just tea. Thanks,' he adds, after a tiny pause. The pause

means something. Alice is not quite sure what, yet. It might mean *I'm sorry I was unkind*. On the other hand it might just as easily mean *There is to be a slight lull in proceedings*.

Normally, dressed, Alice might be a little flustered. It's so easy to get poor Freddie's tea wrong. Often he is upset by tea that is rather too strong or a little too weak, or has a funny stalky taste, or has surely been made before the kettle properly boiled. He is so very particular about his tea, and somehow she is hopeless at making it the way he really likes it.

Today, this afternoon, sitting in her faded chintz-covered armchair, softly lamp-lit, her bare legs crossed in a way she feels to be *lissom*, Alice can only smile.

'Bit strong,' says Freddie. But it is clear from his voice that they are to be friends again.

'Shall I put some more hot water in?'

'No. Thanks.'

Alice sips her own tea, still smiling. It is perhaps the simple power that is so delightful; the secret power of knowing that he has no idea that she is, right now, traducing and insulting him, forcing him to take unconscious part in a scene of travesty. *It jolly well serves him right*, says some small part of Alice's mind, but so softly that the rest of her cannot hear. She thinks instead of the amusing story she has ready for him.

'Saw Mrs Porlock in the High Street,' she says. 'She was wearing a new cardigan. I said how nice it was, though actually I thought it was a bit peculiar – rather a funny tow colour, and I quite wanted to touch it, to see what it felt like. Anyway she was *fright*fully pleased I mentioned it:

couldn't wait to tell me she made it herself, actually *spun* it, spun the wool, I mean, as well as knitted it. And I said, My goodness, how extraordinary, how on earth, and so on. And she said: spinning, on her spinning wheel, my dear, was simply so relaxing, and that I should take it up, simply everyone should sit about spinning all day long. Well, I am a spinster, I suppose. Oh, but you must guess, Fred. What she had spun her new cardie from. Not wool, in point of fact. Not sheep's wool anyway.'

Freddie – what a good mood he seemed to be in! – appeared to give the matter some thought. 'Ah . . . her husband's hair-combings?'

'Close. Only in fact: it was the dog's – the dog's hair-combings! From his daily *brushings*. Yes, she said, I'm wearing purest Bertie! D'you want to give him a little stroke? And of course then I really *didn't* want to, but I did. And it is actually rather wiry, and yellowish, and possibly the most revolting garment in the entire history of clothing –'

And Freddie her tormentor, her jailer, her prince of sorrows, laughs like a child.

Alice laughs with him. 'More tea, darling?'

Lettie

She had thought she was awake, sleepless, until the door opened and her stepfather came in. He looked no different despite the years, dark and fine-featured, though he was crouching; he wore a cloak of sacking over his shoulders, and crept sideways closer and closer until he could put out a hand and nudge her.

You're a dream, Lettie thought at him. Aren't you?

Then she was awake, and it was Norah touching her, Norah wrapped in a dressing gown, her hair in two plaits like a child.

'I'm so sorry, Lettie – there's someone downstairs asking for you –'

'Right,' said Lettie, struggling still to dismiss her stepfather, his sly hand. 'Who is it?'

'It's someone called Withers,' said Norah rather excitedly, 'his wife's, ah, having a baby – I didn't know you actually did that sort of – um, he says Sister Nesbit told him to come.'

Nesbit? Oh God, a delivery! She'd actually gone and done it, asked for cover! I didn't mean it, Nesbit! Jesus, I didn't *mean* it!

'I'll be two minutes,' said Lettie. Idiot, she told herself. You sodding well *volunteered*! She dressed, ran downstairs. It was nearly three in the morning.

Norah stood shivering in the hall: 'This is Mr Withers, Lettie –'

A boy, a white face, his hat twisted in his hands. 'I got a note,' he said, his words so mangled by the local dialect that Lettie would not have understood him without the clue of the letter shaking in his hand:

Dear Sister Quick

I have to go to a delivery elsewhere, and Mrs Florence Withers (g 3 p 2+1) aged 26, may be in strong labour before I can get back. Her last baby was a face presentation, RML, Dr Pascoe is aware. Thanks so much for saying you could help – I'll be back to relieve you as soon as possible. Sorry about the time and everything – do call Dr Pascoe as you think fit – so grateful, Marion Nesbit

Lettie looked up at the boy. 'Where we going?'

He nodded to Norah, who opened the door, and then they were out in the chilly darkness, Lettie half running to keep up with the young husband, who said not a word as they passed up one empty silent street and along several more until they came to a tall terrace.

''Ere,' he said, and they climbed the stone steps and entered into a faint intimate smell of cooking. 'Upstairs.'

Lettie's fingers were cold on the handle of her case, her heart beat fast. Don't want to do this. Oh, get back in good time, Nesbit, please!

The electric light was dim all the way up, so the brightness in the top floor back was almost dazzling. A wan old woman was sitting on the far side of the rumpled bed, which was empty. Where was the patient?

'Hello,' said Lettie briskly, 'I'm –'

She was interrupted by a long loud groan, apparently coming from the floor.

'Oh, get up, Florrie, do!' said the old woman, bending over and seeming to address her own feet. 'It ain't right!'

The low-level groan intensified, became louder, and presently the woman in labour rose from whatever she had been doing on the floor, a distorted face half-hidden in tangled hair, and leant forward across the bed, her weight on her forearms, and went on and on screaming all the time Lettie was taking her coat off and opening her bag.

Then the yells faded, became whimpers, and she let herself slide backwards on to the floor again; walking round the bed, Lettie saw that she was kneeling there on all fours, rocking a little, her head on her hands, while the old woman patted her shoulder.

'It come on all on a sudden, ma'am, all in 'er back!'

Not good. Lettie said: 'How long between pains?'

'No more'n a coupla minutes now!'

Worse.

'When did Sister Nesbit last see her?'

'Just gone twelve, it were, ma'am. She ain't a-doing nothing at all, she says to me, Sister Nesbit this is. I'll just nip over to Twelvetrees, she says, on account a their Julie-Anne; just you sit tight, she says to me, and I says, Twelvetrees is a deal away, I says, suppose my daughter-in-law here, suppose she takes off, like, and she says to me, Sister Nesbit, she says to me, I don't like to do it, she says, but truth to tell there is another nurse about the place, she says, and –'

'Yes, yes, yes,' said Lettie. 'Did she leave any papers, a notebook?'

'Well – this'n?' The old woman took a sheet of paper from the bedside table as the girl on the floor began to shift and groan again. Lettie squinted down the page. Two fingers at midnight. Well, things had certainly picked up.

'I need to wash my hands.'

''Tis all set. Jack! Where's that boy got to? Jack, go and put the kettle on, will you?'

Lettie had forgotten the pale boy, who had hung back behind her on the landing. She heard him galloping away downstairs now.

'This'll do,' she said.

The groans became screams again. This time the girl seemed to look directly into Lettie's eyes. But she saw nothing, Lettie thought. She was beyond noticing anything outside her own torture.

'Help me get her on the bed, will you.'

In the brief interval of quiet, they managed between them to haul the girl half upright.

'Just for a little while,' said Lettie, pushing her sideways. Her skin was fiery through her nightdress, damp.

Lettie searched for the baby's heartbeat, and after what felt like a long time found it: all well.

'Now . . . I've just got to have a quick little look – Flo, you hear me? You're nearly there, now, everything's just fine.'

But everything was not fine. Posterior lie, of course, but what was presenting itself to be born first? The cervix was almost fully dilated, but her fingertips could find none of the usual landmarks, no fontanelle, no overlapping suture lines, just a strange molten softness and blur.

Gently, gently, Lettie told herself, and in some part of her mind she opened the textbook, pictured the shape of the paragraph, and read off the lines she needed, a practice she had no name for, was not even fully aware of making. As it was she read that she must on no account forget that if the child was indeed delivering face first a rough investigating finger might poke him in the eye; that the presenting face might be so swollen as to make full diagnosis difficult; that (rare instance of textbook drollery) diagnosis of face presentation was however particularly clear when the investigating finger inadvertently entered the child's mouth, and was suckled.

Gently. There: to the right.

Ah.

Lettie withdrew her hand. She spoke softly to the old woman, whose name she still did not know: 'Go down and find your Jack. Tell him to go for Dr Pascoe.'

'She bad?'

'Tell him to go now.'

Right mentoposterior, Lettie recited to herself, as the old woman scuttled out. But there was no need to consult the memory-textbook, however, on what that meant: that the child would not deliver, unless turned with forceps.

'Going to get the doctor in,' she said loudly, encouragingly, but the girl made no reply, merely gesturing with a limp arm that said: help me on to the floor.

'No – you stay where you are for a bit.'

The door rattled as the old woman opened it, breathing hard.

'Has he gone?' Lettie asked her.

'Running. Can't you give her nothing?'

Lettie shook her head. 'The doctor'll be here soon. Can you get him some hot water?'

The old woman puffed away again.

How soon, though, Lettie asked herself. To calm herself through the renewed screams she wrote a note of what she had done so far, and listened for the baby's heartbeat again, still good, and was surprised to find when she checked her watch that barely half an hour had passed since her arrival.

'Help me!' It was the first time the girl had spoken; she wanted to get back on to the floor again, Lettie saw. She wanted to crouch on all fours like an animal.

'Christ's sake,' she said, 'stay where you are!' and the fear in her own voice made her more panicky still, so that when the girl turned her face away and started trying to roll her immense swollen unwieldy self sideways on her own Lettie grabbed her arm, and tried to hold her still by force, and shouted over the screams that she must do as she was told. Luckily the girl had gone quiet again between contractions when a distant door banged, and footsteps came hurrying up the stairs. The door opened. Dr Pascoe?

'Oh, it's you,' said Lettie gladly.

'Hello, Flo, how are you doing?' said Nesbit. 'Sister Quick,' she added, with a nod. 'Is it Face?'

Lettie nodded. 'RMP. Doctor's on his way,' she said. She felt obscurely ashamed, as if Nesbit could tell how panicked she had been. When in fact no one knew at all, she reminded herself. Everyone panicked sometimes; what mattered was how well you concealed it. 'She keeps trying to get on the floor,' she added.

Nesbit looked at her curiously. 'Well, if that's what she wants,' she said, and Lettie breathed in hard with annoyance.

'I'll leave you to it then,' she said, as Flo began her keening groan again. She picked up her bag, scanned its contents, snapped it shut. Get me out of here! As she flung on her coat, the door opened, and the old woman appeared, closely followed by –

'Good morning, Dr Heyward,' said Lettie warningly, tilting her head towards Nesbit, who would be all but invisible to him, crouched as she was on the far side of the bed with the patient. He waggled his eyebrows as if to parody someone catching on, but still his tone was heavily roguish:

'Morning, Sister Quick – yes, it's me! Thought I'd muscle in. Told the boy Pascoe to have his beauty sleep. And what have we here?' His gaze was as soppy, she thought, as if they were alone.

God he was a silly bastard, Lettie thought venomously, he was abso-bloody-lutely typical of the silly bastards she always managed to land herself with no matter how decent they all had seemed at first. She spoke formally, coolly, one professional to another.

'I'm so sorry to call you out, doctor,' she said.

Rae

On the way to her room she dropped in on the complete works of Dickens wedged along one shelf in the library, a cheap edition with covers of faded red cloth; and presently went to lie down with *Little Dorrit*. It was not difficult to find the page she was looking for. It was so near the beginning, for one thing.

And even worse than she remembered: there was anxious Mr Dorrit in the debtor's prison, and the half-drunk fellow-convict doctor, and the charwoman swigging brandy and setting traps for the swarms of prison flies that blacked the ceiling, but what I've never noticed before, thought Rae bitterly, is that they all talk to one another, and they talk to Mrs Dorrit, but she never talks back. She never says anything at all. She just lies there in complete silence doing whatever it is you do, and *three or four hours passed* and then *one little life appeared*.

That was all babies ever did, in books. They *appeared*, like white rabbits out of top hats. The doctor in the role of conjurer, perhaps, but what had he actually done? Why had Mr Dorrit pawned his rings to pay him?

And more than anything else, why did Mrs Dorrit die?

If she'd managed two babies before, and been alright, why did the third one kill her? You'd think someone would at least have *asked*, thought Rae, throwing the book aside, wide awake now, restless. She got up, and pulled the tiresome enormous dress back over her head, but found when she went to put her shoes on that they no longer seemed to fit: they were suddenly too small.

Face it: as well as shingles shingling she had big fat swollen feet. Being pregnant turns you into the Ugly Sister, she thought. Sighing, she opened the wardrobe (*Yeah, you* – she half thought at it jeeringly as she rummaged about in its lower depths: now she no longer dreaded it she was not-quite-consciously inclined to ascribe feelings of sheepishness to the wardrobe, since she had caught it out meanly and fraudulently pretending to be haunted) and at length came across her dark-green velvet evening slippers, that she could just about cram her spongy feet into, so long as she didn't tighten the ribbons.

She trailed downstairs in search of Mrs Givens. Not in the kitchen, nor the laundry room. Nor the library. Had she gone upstairs again, to the cupboard on the third floor? It took Rae what felt like a very long time to find out that there was no one on the corridor either. Mrs Givens must have gone into the village; she was alone in the house. House in the middle of nowhere, with Lake.

But she won't be long, Rae thought at the baby, as if to reassure it, and instantly felt much stronger herself. And we forgot about her funny little sitting room, she went on. We'll have a quick look there now, shall we?

It was strangely cosy, this inward conversation, as if the baby were somehow taking friendly part; not in any words, but emotionally, giving out feelings of acceptance, even tranquillity.

'Mrs Givens?'

The sitting room was empty. Rae went in and sat down

at the table, feeling worn out, as if she had walked miles. We'll just have a little rest for a moment, she thought at the baby, and seemed to feel its happy quiescence. She looked about her. There were the photographs, the three Mrs Givenses, Hello again. Sitting here she had full view of her own face in the small mirror opposite, so turned aside, and at once saw something vaguely familiar: across both arms of the little armchair sometimes occupied by the unfriendly cat lay a shallow wooden case.

Rae stared at it for a few moments before she remembered that it had come from the cupboard upstairs; it was very fine cherrywood, Mrs Givens had said, and so they had put it on the dealer pile. Why had she brought it down here all by itself? Perhaps to empty it, thought Rae. Hadn't she said it held seashells or birds' eggs, something like that? A display case?

She arose and picked it up, gave it a gentle shake, and felt movement, as of lots of little muffled things shifting inside, and her heart gave a sudden thump in her chest, as if in answer. Stories again, she thought. Part of your mind is remembering Pandora, and the box that should never have been opened. But this – *this* – is full of crumbly seashells, or someone's fossil collection. Or butterflies. This is some Victorian naturalist's butterfly haul, and you are scared to open it!

She carried it back to the table, set it down, and undid the little gold hasp. The lid was hinged, lined with padded blue silk. The box itself was divided into many small square sections, all lined with soft blue plush, worn pale here and there, each containing several odd disparate items: a delicate key, perhaps to a jewel box; one paste diamond earring; a metal thimble someone had managed somehow to squash completely flat; a slim little bone or ivory fish, rather beautiful, half the size of a woman's little finger; a bracelet of winkle shells. An acorn with a hole drilled cleanly through it.

What on earth were these things, and why were they housed like this, as if they were precious?

A thin metal medallion. Rae picked it up, and read the minute script ornately engraved on it: *John son of John Tresidder late of Jamaica 1756*. Then looked for others, found perhaps a dozen metal discs engraved with names or initials, *Mary May*, *Robert Whittaker son of James and Alicia Whittaker*, *Agnes Warne*, *JHY*, *R O'Brien*.

A faint noise made her look up: Mrs Givens was standing in the doorway, several battered cardboard boxes balanced in her arms.

'I thought you were out,' Rae said.

'Different floor: different cupboard,' said Mrs Givens. Softly she came in, set the boxes down.

'Where are all these things from?'

Mrs Givens sighed, sat down on the other chair. 'St Jerome's Hospital as was,' she said. 'Big orphanage down Exeter way, moved here lock stock and barrel.'

'And what are they?' She knew already, though. With some difficulty she met Mrs Givens' eyes, saw pity there, looked away again.

'They'm keepsakes,' said Mrs Givens, as Rae had guessed she would. 'From olden times. Hundred years back, longer. You couldn't keep your babby, you left it at St Jerome's – if you could – there weren't enough places, they had a lottery running one time, so many wanting in.

Some of 'em I dare say thought nothing of it; but some dint. Some must a reckoned things'd get better some day, and they'd get the babby back again. Only by then years might a gone by. So – this is how they'd know their own. And how they'd prove it was them as left the babby in the first place. Mother comes back, see, and she says, I'm a-come for my lad William, he'd be six year old, and his keepsake were half a silver coin, this here's t'other half.'

'You . . . did this? Kept things like this? Here?'

'Lord no, this is years back. From St Jerome's.'

'So –' Rae picked up the tiny key – 'she would have the lock it fitted.'

'Maybe. Or maybe just saying *I left a little key* would a bin enough. They dint have the writing, see.'

'So – why are they still here, then? No one came back for them?'

'Suppose not.'

'Why did they keep them? Why didn't the children take them away with them when they left, when they grew up?' She heard the shake in her voice.

'They dint tell the children there *was* anything,' said Mrs Givens. 'Stop 'em waiting, stop 'em hoping. Reckoned it was kinder, see.'

Yes, thought Rae: in the stories, in the melodramas, the poor but honest foster parents always secretly keep and cherish the golden this or jewelled that, usually proof of blue blood, that was tucked into the foundling's shawl, or fastened about the plump little wrist. But here was the real thing, and it was the very stuff of poverty, despair in each laboriously chiselled seashell, every pierced and flattened bottle top.

'And when the lease run out here, the new housekeeper, she says to me, I ain't taking that old trash. I kept it. Dunno why.'

Rae was still turning things over: one half of a carefully bisected wine cork. A fragment of white china. A painted wooden bead. A scrap of beige ribbon threaded through a card.

'I thought to keep it from you, my lovely. 'Tis hard for you.'

'Yes. It is.'

'But now you've seen it – well, I have worried – there's something I think you ain't thought about.'

'What?'

'How long's it going to take you, in America? I mean, how long before you get the babby back, make out you're adopting?'

'Well – I don't know. A few months, at least. I've got to be seen about being, you know, working. Being all carefree.'

'That's what I thought. So: you start it all off, saying you're a-going to adopt a baby and so on, all fine and dandy, someone else pretending to be the mother, ain't that right? And then you come back to England and they comes along, and they says to you, Right then, here's your babby! Well – here's the rub – how you going to know that's true?'

'What do you mean?'

'It ain't gonna look the same! Not after a few months! They don't stay the same one week to another, that age! How you gonna know?'

'Well – I have to trust them. Why would they lie to me?'

'Why would they care either way, right child or not? *You* will, though – and it's not every child looks like his mother. Nor his father come to that. I'm telling you, five years, ten; every time that child does something you don't like – and they all do – you'll be asking yourself: is he really mine? *Is he?* Maybe my own child, my daughter, my son, is still in some blessed orphanage somewhere!'

'Why are you saying this? It's just cruel – I haven't got any choice now, I can't change things!'

'You can take a leaf out a *their* book,' said Mrs Givens, with a nod at the cherrywood case. 'They done it from poverty. You from riches. You must leave a token, a keepsake.'

Rae put her hand over her eyes. I have opened the heartbreak-box, she thought, remembering Pandora. This is what it feels like when you are beaten, she thought, when you're done for. This is the worst I have ever felt, though at once she saw herself in her nightdress long ago at school, waking alone at the foot of an unfamiliar flight of stairs.

While a very small further part of her awareness, understanding that all this might well come in useful one day, was still trying to take notes.

So what keepsake, thought most of Rae, wiping her eyes with the back of her hand, would I choose to tuck beneath the pillow of my child as I abandon it, what paltry bit of trash would sum me up best so far? Used bus tickets, perhaps, or worn hairgrips, chipped buttons, an empty lipstick, the stained label from the bottle that dyed my hair back to its actual colour, a concertina'd length of green card, the ribbons from my nicest evening shoes, that will not fasten any more over these fat old feet.

'These for a start,' Mrs Givens was saying, looking livelier. 'See these – knew I'd got 'em somewhere. Take a look, go on!' Leaning aside, she grabbed up one of her battered cardboard boxes, wrenched the lid off, and pulled away the tissue paper on top.

Listlessly Rae did as she was told and took out something white. It was a very small dress, evidently not new, but well-kept, and of the softest imaginable cotton flannel, gathered from a yoke delicately embroidered with violets on either side. Violets visited by the smallest hovering silken bee. She turned it round; you did it up at the back with little white ribbons.

She looked up.

'There's six a them,' said Mrs Givens. 'And little vests to match, like, and then more a coupla sizes up.'

'It's pretty,' Rae managed at last.

'More'n that!' said Mrs Givens. 'This ain't your factory rubbish, this here's all hand-done. By – well, never you mind who done it. There ain't nothing like it anywhere else, see, and it'll last him six months. Six months, Ruth. You leaves 'em a little newborn, they gives you a strapping young feller a-sitting up taking notice; but they're both wearing these here vi'lets. See what I'm saying?'

'The clothes . . . are a token?'

Mrs Givens nodded.

'It all still depends on trust,' Rae said.

'Of course it does. And that's why I was wondering – this woman coming to see you, you know, the midwife –'

Rae roused herself. 'Oh, but I must put her off – I was all upset, you know, about the wardrobe and so on, ridiculous, but now . . . she doesn't want to come anyway. Too risky.' She had said so very coldly too, Rae remembered. 'I'd better go and call her.'

She made to rise, but Mrs Givens spoke sharply: 'No. Don't you do that. Listen: this woman, whoever she is – no, you want to make *sure* she comes. Have a good look at her, make up your mind. You want to know whether you can trust her; she ain't just looking after you when the time comes, is she, she's gonna take your child away with her. You need to look that woman in the eye, and see what you see!'

'Do I?'

'Course you do!'

There was a silence. Looking down, Rae noticed a smear of dampness on the drilled acorn in the box, understood it had been a tear. She put up a hand, wiped her cheeks again.

'Ruth,' said Mrs Givens, 'd'you want me to be there with you?'

'What?' said Rae. 'How d'you mean?'

'When she comes tomorrow. This here woman. Shall I be there too? Back you up, like?'

Rae tried to think. 'I don't know.'

'Be on your side, see. As if you had a bit a family.'

'An aunt,' Rae said.

Mrs Givens smiled. 'Better your – oh, I don't know, your old nurse, say, how about that? I wouldn't *say* nothing, just be there, see. On your side.'

Rae closed her eyes, and with an effort pictured the scene, herself in her green slippers and enormous tent of a dress in the wing chair by the fire in the library, the chilly unknown Sister sitting down opposite, all hard and bony with a steel-grey Eton crop and big front teeth.

Action! Mrs Givens came in with the tea tray, sat composedly down behind it, and said, 'Tea, Sister?'

Cut.

Then once more. Self, dress, slippers. Eton crop, teeth. Take Two: *Action!* Mrs Givens brought in the tea tray, set it down, and walked away leaving Rae alone with the teeth, closed the door behind her, click. There was no doubt about it, Rae thought, with a sudden surge of energy: Mrs Givens in was definitely better than Mrs Givens out.

'Why can't you be my auntie?' she said aloud, and without thinking about it in Mrs Givens' accent.

The effect of this was wildly beyond what she might have expected.

'How you *do* that?' cried Mrs Givens, when she could speak again.

'Do what, Auntie?' said Rae innocently, but smiling too; there was nothing quite so cheering as audience reaction, she thought.

Mrs Givens was actually blushing, her old face pink with laughter: 'Ain't you a caution!'

'Don't you go poking fun at me, Auntie. I can't 'elp the way I speak.'

'You talk like that I'll bust out laughing, then where would we be?'

Lady Hermione Pringle would probably be better anyway, thought Rae, when dealing with uppity criminal midwives. She almost laughed herself at that, despite everything.

Then remembered, saw once more the sad beautiful embroidered baby clothes with which she would one day identify her child – perhaps – and the terrible crowded case of tokens, each wretched bit of trash for a child left behind and never reclaimed.

'Thank you for offering,' said Rae formally. 'I should prefer you to be there. Will you, please?'

Mrs Givens had stopped laughing too.

'I will, Ruth,' she said.

Barty

'In hospital.'

'What's wrong with her?'

The loaded trolley was awkward to handle, especially over the threshold.

'All I know is, her youngest come round, said she were took bad in the night.'

He was ashamed later when he realized that his first thought had not been for Mrs Bettins but for himself, and the loss of today's chance to see the Lady. Now he would have to take Mrs Bettins' place behind the counter, at least until the early rush died down, and by then he would be late for school already.

Barty had a cautious regard for Mrs Bettins, and reason to be grateful. She was a grown-up, unaccountable, sharp and soft by turns, often lively and full of talk. Now and then Mr Bettins, widely held to drink most of his wages, when he had any, would occasionally drop in for a quick private word with her, and then for a while afterwards she would be very quiet, Barty had noticed. One of her children was soft in the head, had fits and couldn't go to school, but had to be looked after by a neighbour while Mrs Bettins was at work.

Still there was a certain glamour to Mrs Bettins, for Barty. Long ago, before the children and Mr Bettins, before the war, when she was a girl, she had been friends with the girl who grew up to be his own mother, Grace; not just friends, she had told him once, but *best* friends.

Of course Barty knew a great deal about his mother, that she had been beautiful and clever and charming, with a lovely singing voice and particularly gifted with her needle: every time she came wheezing into the shop and found him behind the counter old Mrs Ticknell, who had long ago employed his mother in the days of Ticknell's Woolshop, would slowly, shakily, take out one of the special handkerchiefs Grace had embroidered, and show it to him before she dabbed her watery old eyes with it, though often he saw her coming and was able to slide quickly into the back of the shop and get away before she caught him.

Grace had always done as she was told. She had swept the floors tidily and washed up without breaking anything. She had never once been late for school or idled about afterwards playing muddy games of football or scraping herself bloody and tearing decent clothing by climbing trees. She had sung in the choir at St George's every single Sunday – twice – and gone to bed at a reasonable hour with her things all ready for school the next morning, and had never leant her elbows on the table and worn holes in her jumper sleeves.

The Nannas between them had so often described the little girl Grace had been at Barty's age, whatever that was, that he had nearly come to feel he had met her, this vanished almost-sister. Of course she had always been the better child, but he had sometimes felt sorry for her even so; she was still so dead. But then the Nannas had moved away, and he had gone to live with his father all the time, and Grace had somehow stopped being a lost saintly little girl the same age as himself, and become a grown woman, and his mother.

This was partly because of the photograph. Dad's copy sat on the chest of drawers in his bedroom in the flat over the sweetshop: the two of them, his mother and father, taken in Porthkerris on their honeymoon. The Nannas had the other copy, so Barty had seen it often, had known it so well that he had stopped seeing it. But when he moved in with Dad he had noticed it again, picked it up and looked at it properly, and finally seen what it was a picture of.

'Dad.'

'Alright, lad?'

'That's her, ain't it?'

Taking it over to his dad as he sat half dozing over the paper beside the fire one evening. He had sighed, holding it in the light from the standard lamp behind his chair.

'Aye, that's 'er. And me, look at me, streak a piddle in boots.'

Barty hesitated over his next question. Though his Nannas and his father had fairly often volunteered this and that about his mother, asking any of them questions had generally come to nothing, as if the three of them had agreed beforehand that there were only certain things they were prepared to talk about. He was already sure this was one of them. But he was ten years old, he reminded himself: double figures.

'Dad. What colour was she?'

'Y'what?'

As he had expected, his father's face, soft over the photograph, had instantly stiffened in the usual way. Barty waited. This had never worked with the Nannas, but he suspected his father might be made of weaker stuff.

'Folk been saying stuff to yer, at school?'

Barty said nothing, this time because the question was too tremendous to answer. Did his father really not know?

Your ma was a darkie was very nearly the first thing anyone had said to him at school. Bill James had said it, in the playground. He had had no idea what it meant.

She's dead, he had countered.

Bill James hadn't been finished: *And you killed her*, he said.

Barty had not clearly known how he felt about this, but all the same his hand had shot out in a fist and bashed Bill James on the nose as hard as he could, and he had run away crying. Barty had very nearly cried as well, as the blow had hurt his hand a great deal.

'Next time you thump someone make sure yer thumb's outside, like this, see? And go fer his belly,' his dad had told him. Nanna Vi had argued for turning the other cheek, and Nanna Bea had said nothing at all, but given him a caramel. None of them had explained what Bill James had meant though.

He had known about killing Grace, of course. But what was a darkie? It was clear from the accusing way Bill had said it that it was something bad. He knew his mother had been good, though; everyone was pleased when they said he took after her, and sad when he seemed unlike.

'Why did he say it?'

'Because he's a silly,' said Nanna Vi, and that was the end of the discussion, though the next day in the playground after dinner time Bill James had sauntered up with his little group of mates about him, and Barty had stood there with both fists ready, his thumbs carefully arranged. But all Bill had said was,

'My ma's dead too.'

Barty knew straight away that Bill wanted him to ask him if he, Bill, had killed her, and he determined that nothing would make him. After what felt like a very long time Bill spoke again, as if off-hand:

'My kid sister killed her.' A certain tension seemed to go out of the air, and then Bill said, 'Want to play football?'

But there were other strange incidents. Barty had collected them over the years.

Miss Pyncheon, for example; when she was in one of her moods she might fling the door open when he rang with her afternoon delivery and say something like, 'Barty dear boy, how divinely Italianate you look today!'

Mr Vowles at school, generally so pleased with him of course, except when he was late for school too often, or in trouble for larking about in music, jovially ruffling his hair and saying, 'Ho ro, my nut-brown lad!' as if this were a special joke that they were sharing.

Certain sudden silences, when he went into the shop and there was a queue. He would feel himself blushing then, and it would take all his nerve to go behind the counter, and ask who was next.

The woman in the sweetshop smiling when he bought a bar of chocolate, the indecipherable nudging way she said, 'Dairy Milk, eh?'

The Doctor. They never went to Dr Heyward, for reasons that were not spoken of, they only ever went to the other one. But when he had tripped over on his way back to the grocer's with an empty lemonade bottle and cut his forearm, and needed stitching up again, Dr Pascoe had asked Nanna Vi, 'This the one, eh? Little Master Mixture?' and looked at him in a way that seemed to have the same undercurrent of meaning as the woman in the sweetshop.

'Folk been saying stuff to yer, at school?'

Barty reminded himself once more that he was in double figures, and decided to risk it, ask again.

'What colour was she?'

'Well. She was – she was brown, like.'

'So – was she a darkie?' The remembered word, carefully never examined since.

There was a long silence, then his dad said seriously, slowly, as if he were thinking it out for the first time: 'I never called her that. I never called her anything, lad.'

'This is her though. All brown.' The photograph again.

'Aye. So she was.'

'Whose daughter was she then? Nanna Vi's or Nanna Bea's?'

That was going too far, apparently. His father got up, and said that he would have to ask them, he was just nipping out for a bit, which meant the pub on the corner, and Barty was left with his central puzzle.

If his mother had been a darkie, a negro, then she always had been one: when she was the vexingly angelic little girl, when she was singing so sweetly in the church choir or working in the woolshop with Mrs Ticknell, embroidering handkerchiefs, she had been a darkie all that time. But neither Nanna had ever said so. When they were telling him over and over again what a good pretty nice little girl she had been, why had they never once said, in those same warm praising tones, Oh, and she was a lovely brown colour!

It was as if it had been something they had wanted to forget about. They hadn't exactly pretended she was the same as everyone else. But they might as well have done, he thought. And he had seen the picture and seen the picture, when he was a little boy, and despite what Bill James and one or two others had said he had somehow never noticed that she wasn't the same. Whereas now it was impossible not to see it. How had he managed it? More puzzle.

When his Nannas told him how much he took after her, how wonderfully alike he was, what were they really saying? He had looked into mirrors once or twice recently, his fingers crossed in case the image started acting for itself, and seen that whatever else he was, he wasn't very brown. It was true his hand on the school desk beside Bill's was usually darker. But every summer Bill more or less caught up with him.

Least said soonest mended, that was what his Nannas swore by. His dad was pretty good at saying least too; though when he had first taken on Mrs Bettins to help behind the counter he had told Barty exactly why.

'Knew your mother! Right good friend, she said.' He had sounded excited, Barty thought, and pleased with himself because he was doing a favour for his wife's long-ago friend. The Nannas clearly felt otherwise, not that there was any point in asking them why. A great many other local eyebrows had been raised, in fact; he had gathered soon enough that though Mrs Bettins herself had been Lily Houghton and a local girl the husband she had brought back with her from Exeter was foreign, possibly Irish, which many held only went to show how bad blood would out; for everyone knew the Houghtons had always been an idle ill-bred lot as it was.

Mrs Bettins had large dark eyes and a squashy old face, from lacking so many teeth. Told who he was on her first day she had given him so hard a stare that he had had to look away. She was distant with him for a good while, seemed to find him charmless, which was not what he was used to; but then everyone knew she had a very big family, so he decided that she was perhaps too fed up with her own children to bother about someone else's.

Presently though she seemed to get used to him. When he won the flat race at school the first thing the Nannas, very pleased, had pointed out to him was that his mother had been a fast runner too, but Mrs Bettins, leaning on the counter a day or two later, turned to him at a quiet moment as he sat on his stool near the back with his comic, and told him that once, when they were very little girls, she and his mother, tied together and brilliantly in step when all about them were falling over in heaps, had won the three-legged race.

Even just entering a three-legged race did not tie in too well with the idea of the wonderfully polite good little girl his Nannas had shown him, whatever non-colour she might have been.

Really? Three-legged?

She were a lively one, Mrs Bettins said. A right good dancer too. Bold as brass.

How? How was she bold as brass?

So then she had told him about a travelling fair that had come one year, long ago, with a steam engine and all sorts, and swing boats, and a roundabout, and a great big thing for grown-up lads to go on, a set of chairs hanging on chains on another sort of twirly machine, that turned so fast the chairs swung up and up and flew right out up high, terrifying! And his mother just a little thing, she'd paid her money and she'd climbed in and been flung round and round in circles high above everyone's heads, and she'd just loved it, she said, it was like flying.

I like flying, said Barty, when I grow up I'm going to be a pilot, what else. Tell me something else.

What sort of thing?

Was she ever naughty?

Mrs Bettins had smiled then, her ruined smile, shook her head.

'Spent all her money at the pictures.'

What? The Rialto?

'No no, this was before the Rialto, this was the Picture Palace. You remember it? The old tithe barn. Your dad never take you there?'

Now she said that he could just remember it. He had gone with his Nannas, and had trouble with a choc ice that had melted all down his sleeves.

'She loved it. She'd a gone every night if she could. Charlie Chaplin, he was her favourite.'

'Was he?'

Barty enchanted; that night had been the first sleepless one of his life. A real live girl who had dared to fly, and loved to go to the pictures! For once it seemed to him that he was not merely taking after his mother; it was that she had just been very like him. She had been darker, maybe. That was all.

The next day he had gone to see the tithe barn, to make her appear there in his mind, standing outside waiting for one of the Pyncheons to open up and let her in; that had been the start of a new idea of himself, and an extra little job, for as he stood there staring over the railings with his hands in his pockets Miss Pyncheon herself came loping round the corner, and opened the gate.

'Hello, young Barty,' she said, as she passed him, clearly not in one of her funny moods today, and he had said at once: 'Did my mum come here?'

She seemed unsurprised. 'She most certainly did! One of our regulars.'

He thought of asking what his mother had liked best; decided against it.

'Come in, if you like. I'm just opening the old place up for a while. Give it an airing.'

He had nodded, and gone in, and for the first time in his life known he was seeing a place his mother had loved.

'She always sat here, if she could,' said Miss Pyncheon lightly, and she touched a certain row, towards the back, the end seat, and when she had left him there and gone to the piano he had sat in it, and put his arms on the arm-rests, his hands where his mother's would have rested.

'Stay as long as you like,' called Miss Pyncheon, without looking up. 'Don't mind me. Just sorting a few things out.' She was sorting through folders of music, and when he had gone to tell her he was off now, and thanks, she had asked him if he fancied doing a little work for her occasionally, not much, not often, just a few things about the place that needed doing, and by a good reliable young chap like him, payment as and when. She and Freddie – Mr Pyncheon – liked to show a film now and then, one of the good old films they had acquired such a collection of – sometimes just the two of them, sometimes for a few friends, and the place always needed a teeny bit of a tidy-up beforehand, the merest flick of a duster, a sweep or two; then perhaps doors manned, curtains drawn, lights turned on and off – was he interested?

'How old? The films?'

'Well – some of them positively antique, I assure you!'

'Would I see the film too?'

'Dear child, of course, if you want to. You may find them – well, a little slow, I ought perhaps to warn you, if you are used to the Rialto, as I suspect you are.'

'I could try 'em,' said Barty.

'And slip away,' said Miss Pyncheon thoughtfully, 'if they are not to your taste. How would that be?'

Anything before 1919, he was thinking.

'When was Charlie Chaplin? When did he start?'

Did she cotton on? She was so odd you never could tell, sometimes seemed right round the twist, others straight as you liked. This time she said:

'Oh, Charlie was *very* early. Those first one-reelers practically pre-war.'

'You got any a they?'

'Dear boy,' said Miss Pyncheon with a smile, 'we have them all.'

Norah

Norah had always rather enjoyed the twice-yearly visits to Rosevear with Mr Pender, beginning with climbing into the Humber and being driven in splendour about the lanes. Of course the actual business there had its discomforts. It was Norah's job to take notes, and these often amounted to dozens of closely scribbled shorthand pages: usually a long wrangle about the faulty electricity supply and the upkeep of the outside generator preceded familiar arguments for and against re-siting the septic tanks, before the lengthy and often disheartening tour of inspection to take in further loosening plasterwork, more peeling wallpaper, jammed windows, warped doors, and finally closing with yet another discussion, with full additional notes, on the most recent developments in the boundary dispute with a neighbouring farmer, now entering its twentieth year.

Generally though these annoyances only lasted a couple of hours, and then if the weather was dry Mr Pender would ask Mrs Givens if she would care to accompany them about the gardens, for a little air, and she would graciously consent, and take his proffered arm. Then they would all set off along the gravel paths to view what was left of the gardens, returning in time for lunch, which was usually a richly decorated veal, ham and egg pie raised by Mrs Givens herself, served with salad or greens from the kitchen garden, supplied by old Givens – a cousin, Norah understood, of Mrs Givens' own long-departed Bert – and with a jug of local beer for Mr Pender, home-made lemonade for the ladies.

It was a courtly visit altogether, Norah thought. She had noticed early on that while Mr Pender treated Mrs Givens as though she were doing him a great favour by staying on at Rosevear House, Mrs Givens always behaved as though the favour was all Mr Pender's.

Though in truth it was a perfectly straightforward financial arrangement. Mrs Givens lived rent-free, keeping in decent order the house she clearly thought of as her home, whilst occasionally providing discreet temporary shelter for a series of very particular paying guests, the sort other people were legally responsible for – wealthy senile maiden ladies between nurses, well-to-do convalescent defectives – an agreed percentage of her fee payable, of course, to Bagnold and Pender.

'My dear Mrs Givens – what a pleasure it is to see you looking so well!' Bowing over her gnarled old hand, while she bobbed him a little curtsey.

'Good morning, Mr Pender. Looking hearty, sir.'

Then there was often a further ritual exchange about Mrs Givens' late twin sister Mrs Dimond, who had been held in very high regard not only by Mr Pender himself but by his long-deceased mother.

'A most remarkable woman, your sister, Mrs Givens!'

For Mrs Dimond, in her capacity as local wise woman, had attended old Mrs Pender in childbirth, and safely delivered her of her only living child, a circumstance Mr Pender himself appeared to find endlessly entertaining.

Since Norah's own mother Mrs Thornby had been directly responsible, in her charity work, for putting an end to all local amateur midwifery, this was often a little embarrassing for Norah, who knew that Mrs Dimond had been completely uneducated; privately she thought that old Mrs Pender had had a jolly lucky escape.

Perhaps that showed somehow, for Mrs Givens often turned, while Mr Pender was being courtly about her sister, and gave Norah a certain gimlet stare, disconcerting in itself, but also exactly reminiscent of the dirty look Mrs Dimond herself had always treated Norah to when she was ten years old, and helping to walk little Grace Dimond home from school.

But then during lunch Mr Pender frequently retold the story of how his mother had met his own dear father at this very house, at the last great private ball ever held here, in the high summer of 1867. The late Mrs Pender, Norah thought, seemed to have had an endless supply of anecdotes about this last private Rosevear ball, and had passed them all on to her child in every detail: the lilies, the supper table loaded with dainties, the ranked bottles of chilled champagne, the beautiful mermaid sculpted out of ice like crystal, lying full length upon the great table set up in the orangery with her tail curled among the little dishes of fruit custard and ice cream, and above all, the fleet of wooden toy boats, each masted with a burning candle, that had floated in a glittering flotilla out across the lake at midnight, to the sound of violins!

Every time he told the story of the last ball at Rosevear House Norah's heart rather melted for Mr Pender. His mother had been the newest kitchen maid, only lately promoted from the scullery; his father the second garden-er's boy, drafted in for the occasion, squeezed into the dress suit of a rather smaller footman, and required to carry trays. She had put up the trays, he had collected them, and together they had peeped in at the lilies, admired the ice mermaid, and watched – from a distance – the floating sparkle of the lighted little boats.

Usually Norah found Mr Pender's fairly frequent pub-lic references to his own lowly origins rather embarrassing, not only a kind of boasting about how far his intelligence and industry had brought him, but a demonstration, she thought, of private anxieties best kept hidden; and when he was in a particularly bad mood in the office he tended to sneer in her presence about folk born with silver spoons in their mouths, who went on and on thinking themselves a cut above, and then Miss Pilbeam would give Norah a tiny triumphant flashing glance of hatred, and Norah, despite her best efforts, would blush and look away.

But here, at Rosevear House, it was different. Here, where Mr Pender's parents had met, his pleasure in the romance of their meeting seemed only sincere and nat-ural, a proper respect for the reality of the past.

Today's visit started badly though, and then fared worse.

To begin with the Humber failed to start. Parked out-side the office it had blocked the road for nearly an hour while Mr Short from Short's Garages behind the railway station was telephoned, reasoned with, and awaited; for some time now, hanging over the opened bonnet, he had been bawling instructions to Mr Pender behind the wheel, while the engine heaved and wailed and hiccoughed, all this perfectly audible in the office itself, to Mr Bagnold's evident irritation, while Miss Pilbeam had been crosser than usual anyway, as the bun bag had failed to arrive.

Morning tea and buns at ten forty-five, that was the rule; along with a four-thirty tea and crumpets, or tea and scones in high summer. As the clock neared ten Miss Pilbeam became almost frantic, her already pale face stiff with anxiety. At ten past she came to a halt at Norah's desk. 'Miss Thornby. Go to the bakery, please, and fetch the buns.'

Norah hesitated. Outside the Humber roared to life, coughed, spluttered like the living child Mr Pender clearly rather felt it was, and fell silent again. But suppose Mr Short cured it before she was back from the bakery? Walking as fast as she could the round trip would take her nearly half an hour even if there was no queue at all. They would be late at Rosevear as it was, and if Mr Pender, the car ready at last, came in to find her absent there would be a very nasty scene. On the other hand, Miss Pilbeam was clearly spoiling for one right now.

Norah stood up. 'Certainly, Miss Pilbeam.'

'And no dawdling!'

'No, Miss Pilbeam.'

As she picked up her jacket she glanced over at Annie, who instantly put on her Miss Pilbeam face, though with her eyes crossed and her tongue hanging out. Cheered, Norah went outside, sidled past Mr Pender and Mr Short now both leaning over the Humber's oily depths, and set off.

It was certainly a relief to be out of the office, though the weather was coming on to rain, but at the bakery the queue was enormous; Norah gathered as she waited that Mrs Bettins had been taken ill (*women's troubles* were referred to, in the lowest of lowered voices) and that Joe Gilder in desperation had rushed out and taken on Bev Ashley, as used to work in the chemist's up on the North Road.

Mrs Ashley was perhaps doing her best, but all the same she was baffled by the cash register, seemed unable to remember the various prices for more than a moment, and wrapped the loaves as slowly, as tenderly, as newborn babies.

Norah glanced at her watch: half past ten. Perhaps she could run a little, on the way back; if the buns were to hand at ten forty-five at least Mr Bagnold would be stayed. But the later these dratted buns are the more trouble I shall be in, thought Norah, especially if the car is working before I get back –

'Miss Thornby?'

'Oh, I've come for the buns, please, Joe.'

He stared at her.

'Bagnold and Pender.'

'Oh, heck. Sorry, miss. I'll just check –'

Usually the buns arrived first thing, just before the post, in a large paper bag marked *B&P.* There were several such bags, unmarked, propped ready along the back wall. Joe pulled out the biggest, opened it to make sure.

'Half a dozen buns, six crumpets?'

'That's the one,' said Norah, and some demon (she later thought) prompted her to add, as he rolled the bag shut again and passed it to her over the counter, that she hoped to be setting off presently with Mr Pender to Rosevear

House, and was there any message she might pass on for him, to Mrs Givens?

No, he'd said, instantly thoughtful. But was she going by car, then? Today?

Well, yes, she'd said, not wanting to waste any time talking about the Humber and its difficulties, but as she turned to go he said, 'You – you couldn't take her bread, could yer? Bea Givens, I mean. The lad – Barty – usually takes it over, but, you know –'

St George's was striking the three-quarters as she raced through the square, down Silver Street, past the Rialto, finally giving up on carrying the great bag of bread in the crook of her arm and holding it clasped to her chest, almost running outright as she turned the final corner, and saw the Humber purring gently outside the office, Mr Pender grim beside it with his briefcase in his hand, Mr Bagnold in the doorway, Miss Pilbeam glassy-eyed behind him. It was nearly five to eleven.

Oh blast, thought Norah.

Lettie

She woke to chiming bells, and lay still for a little while longer, counting the strikes: it was eleven o' clock in the morning. But she had pinned a CLOSED TODAY sign on the clinic door, so it didn't matter. She got up slowly, stiff all over, and pulled the curtain aside a little. The square was windswept, empty; the sky grey, coming on to rain.

There have been days like this before, she reminded herself. These things happen. Try as you might things go wrong. No one's fault.

She sighed, turned away from the window, put on her dressing gown, shivering as the chill silk touched her bare shoulders, and made her way downstairs. She had always liked the basement kitchen, felt safe there. She sat down at the table as she waited for the kettle to boil.

I should have gone home. Why didn't I? I was on my way. Then somehow –

Somehow it had become impossible to leave, as if the pretence of being simply another dedicated midwife helping out in a crisis had taken on a reality of its own. Something perhaps in Sister Nesbit's eyes. Nesbit had cottoned on.

And I'd forgotten how brutal it can be, she thought. The butcher's shop vigour. At this thought Lettie held her breath; her hands went to her face, covered it. Presently she got up and made the tea, collected a teacup and saucer, took the bottle of milk from the half-full bucket of cold water in the scullery, counted out sugar, three heaped spoons.

Should she go and see them that morning? The Witherses, the boy with his hat twisted in his hands, the mother-in-law. The little children. Three of them.

She sipped. Better perhaps if Nesbit went to see them instead. They knew her, after all, and she knew them. And I have to pay a different visit today anyway, she remembered. Out in the sticks somewhere. A train to catch, then walk somewhere, for an interview of sorts. She felt tired to death just thinking about it.

And I will have to attend her: Oh Christ, let it all be normal.

Fact is, she thought, I can barely do normal either. I can't stand it. I thought I could. I thought I could make everything better. But I can't.

She set the cup down on the table, her cold hands either side of it, and helplessly closed her eyes as the draggle-haired woman from round the corner, the one everyone went to, opened her mother's bedroom door and held out the tuppence for the pram.

'Take the littluns out, go on. Don't come back till it's dark, see?'

The door closing.

Her stepfather leaning on the corner with a mate or two, smoking a cigarette, his eyes on her as she went past.

I shouldn't have come here, she thought. Silkhampton is a bad place for me. All that wondering about the photograph, years of wondering. Had it even come out? Had the stranger with the camera actually troubled to develop it? It had seemed so lucky at the time, coming upon *July 1914* by chance at the exhibition. But perhaps it had been the opposite, real bad luck just to see it. It had brought her stepfather back. It had shown her all that she had lost and could never find again.

And I can't unsee it, she thought.

Then, as if she had finally touched some deepest depth, she felt herself starting to come back up again, able to list consolations: the empty house all hers, a morning bath like a toff. She would wear something special, something strengthening. You *like* train rides, you *like* new places, she told herself. You're *earning*.

Towards that future, and the safety of a long lease on the new purpose-built mansion flat in a nice bit of London, with restaurant and central heating and uniformed lift attendants and garaging for the motorcar of her choice. Two bedrooms, three, with parquet flooring throughout. And a balcony. And views of the river.

All within her reach now. All she had to do was buck herself up, get herself going, stop being such a sap.

All the same she had to count to one, two, 'three', she said aloud, and then she stood up, and forced herself to be energetic determined ruthless Lettie Quick once more.

Norah

In the car Mr Pender was terse; it was some time before Norah gathered that she had volunteered to collect the buns, left with plenty of time, but had either dawdled or gone about business of her own in office time, or both, which simply would not do, Miss Thornby. It would not do at all.

'I'm very sorry, Mr Pender.'

The bread had annoyed him too. 'D'you imagine this is some sort of delivery service, Miss Thornby?'

'No, sir, of course not, but I thought –'

'You are not paid to think, Miss Thornby!'

Unable to come up with any non-inflammatory response to this, Norah stayed quiet. It was raining hard now and the Humber's windscreen wipers were making a pleasant rhythmic crooning sound, which she concentrated on trying to understand. *Be-lieve?* It had a slightly doubtful note, as if the wipers were tentatively asking a question. *Be-lief?*

'I so dislike being late,' said Mr Pender, changing gear as they reached the bottom of the hill, 'especially when Mrs Givens simply will not come to the telephone.'

There was another long silence, apart from the plaintive windscreen wipers. *Re-lief? Re-lieve?* But there was an *s* sound in there somewhere, Norah thought.

'She will be pleased – about the bread, I mean,' said

Mr Pender, and Norah saw that she was forgiven. 'I hope this rain clears,' he went on. 'I particularly wanted to see the boundary today. Did I tell you I have new information?'

Yes, thought Norah, yes you most certainly did. The boundary dispute had always been one of the duller bees in Mr Pender's bonnet, but recently after a great deal of badgering he had at last been granted access to all the older county court records, many of which, he had been especially delighted to discover, dated back as far as the sixteenth century.

Long years of practice with Mamma had made Norah very good at appearing tranquilly to listen. 'Oh, really?' she murmured at intervals. *Re-cieve?* asked the windscreen wipers. *De-ceive?*

The rain lessened as they turned into the rutted carriage drive. The lawns were dappled with snowdrops, and some of the marsh marigolds beside the lake were already coming into bloom. It would surely look very pretty in sunshine, Norah thought, if not exactly tended.

Mrs Givens was already outside to greet them, beneath a huge black silk Victorian golfing umbrella, large enough to shelter a whole family. She ushered them through the usual side door, propping the vast umbrella half-folded in the corridor, like a resting pterodactyl.

'My dear Mrs Givens, delighted to see you looking so well! I'm sorry we are late – unavoidably detained – but at least we come bearing gifts, do we not, Miss Thornby!'

'Good morning, sir!' Mrs Givens did her usual curtsey, gave Norah her usual cool nod. Norah handed over the heavy cotton bag.

'Barty couldn't do the deliveries today,' she said, as Mrs Givens looked inside.

'Why, Mr Pender, if you ain't brought me my bread! Reckoned we'd have to do without today – thank you, sir, thank you, Mr Pender!'

'A pleasure,' said Mr Pender.

'No deliveries today, um, Mrs Bettins unwell, apparently,' Norah said.

'That so,' said Mrs Givens, giving Norah a brief basilisk glance. She turned back to Mr Pender. 'Where would you like to start, sir?'

'Your, ah, *guest*, will not I trust be incommoded by our visit?'

'Dear me, no, sir, not a bit of it. Stays in her room mostly.'

'Another nervous case, I gather?'

'Indeed, sir,' said Mrs Givens cosily, and the visit began.

Rae

It had been an uncomfortable morning. Though the visitors had largely stayed downstairs they had trooped all over the house, and several times Rae had caught the muffled sound of their voices, a man's raised in exposition, female noises of assent, footsteps coming and going, occasional laughter. It was a little like overhearing a party, Rae thought, one I'm not invited to.

Once, hearing the man's voice apparently from outside, she pushed the curtain aside a little and peeped out. There was the tent of blue the prisoner called the sky, and there was Mrs Givens, carrying a folded umbrella almost as big as she was, standing at the edge of the lake on the far side, beside the man whose voice she had heard, carried clear across the water: stooped shoulders, decent overcoat, Homburg hat, and bald domed head, she saw, as he took it off for a moment and wiped his brow with a handkerchief. Another woman stood on his other side, carrying a notebook, wearing something tweedy and a boring hat, but for a piercing moment Rae envied her. That tweedy woman was free to stand in daylight in public, a working woman with a normal shape and a proper job and a comfortably blameless private life, respectable, even professional, oh, what would it be like to be her?

Her fingers found the shingle blisters, and reread their

bleak message. Though they were definitely a little less tender today.

'Much better,' Mrs Givens had said, approvingly, that morning.

'You think so? They still prickle.'

'Sometimes they go on hurting, years after they've gone, even.'

'Oh, thanks very much!'

'That's just old folk, mainly. Now – we see what's going on here?'

And she had carefully felt all over Rae's great abdomen, avoiding the blisters as before, though at one point she put one hand rather too deeply astride the pubic bone.

'Ow!'

'Sorry, my lovely. Just making sure. This woman coming – think she'll do this, take a proper look?'

'No idea.'

'Well, if she does, we'll have something else to go on, won't we!'

'What d'you mean?'

'Sit yourself up again, that's right. You're looking better today, you know that? You're feeling better too, ain't you, breathing better?'

'Well – it's funny you should say that, but, yes, look –' Rae demonstrated, taking a huge breath in and sighing it out again. 'Why, what is it? Is that alright?'

'It's perfect. Clever little so and so's turned himself about –'

'Oh – really?'

'And he's dropped a little, see? Lungs got more room.

Course, now he's a-squashing you down below, makes you piddle all day –'

And all night, Rae thought now.

On the other side of the water the tweedy woman suddenly looked up, and Rae stepped backwards into the shadows. It gave her a very strange feeling, to see the distant white face still turned in her direction; the tweedy woman was standing just where Rae herself had once stood, looking up at the sad old house, and thinking about ghost stories.

She's wondering if she imagined me, thought Rae. The Spectre of Rosevear House, that's me.

Norah

'Do you know how deep the lake is, Mrs Givens?'

'No, sir, I don't.'

'What about you, Miss Thornby, any idea?'

Norah thought. 'Would it be in the original plans, sir? I believe they're at the office.'

They were standing on the little bridge, looking out across the great golden rippling spread of the water.

Mr Pender smirked. 'An understandable mistake, Miss Thornby, given the age and splendour of the house. But this is not an artificial lake. No indeed. It is the genuine article.'

'But it looks so ornamental!' Norah marvelled gratefully; sincerity was such a relief after two hours of simulation.

'Indeed,' said Mr Pender. 'I must confess that until very recently I too assumed the lake was man-made; it is so very typical of the period. What is the *general* view, locally, Mrs Givens, do you know?'

'Afraid I can't say, sir.'

Mr Pender turned back to Norah: 'Mrs Givens knows, I believe, that it is bad luck even to *talk* about Rosevear Lake. Is that not so, Mrs Givens?'

'I don't hold with any a that nonsense, sir, as well you know,' said Mrs Givens shortly. There was a tiny awkward silence.

'I stand corrected, my dear Mrs Givens,' said Mr Pender at last. 'But allow me to inform you now that this body of water is at least two hundred feet deep, and is thus one of the deepest lakes in the county!'

They stood for a moment in silence, Norah shifting from foot to foot. Perhaps it was the late start, she thought, that was making this particular trip so oddly uncomfortable. And Mr Pender so full of his beastly court reports. On the other hand, Mrs Givens too seemed disinclined to observe the ritual courtesies, or at any rate to allow them their usual leisurely pace.

Well no, sir, she had said, soon after their arrival, there *weren't* no particular problems to speak of, the septic tanks was behaving, everyone knew you couldn't trust th'electric but it was no worse than usual, there was nothing new to report at all, except she'd cleared them third-floor cupboards right out; why, we could catch up on ourselves and go straight into lunch right now, Mr Pender!

More surprising still had been a moment of collusion. After lunch Mr Pender had taken various copies of his court reports from his briefcase and spread them out on the library table, to talk about their boundary implications over coffee. He had several conflicting theories to put forward and when at length the coffee was all gone Mrs Givens had begun quietly clearing away the crockery, even though he was still speaking. This in itself was startling, but when Norah stealthily half rose, and passed on her own cup and saucer, Mrs Givens' eyes briefly met her own.

The meanings in that glance made Norah turn quickly away, lest Mr Pender notice her quick involuntary smile. Aloud, after a few moments' thought, she waited until

Mr Pender stopped to draw breath and said, 'Oh, look how sunny it is, all of a sudden! Should we perhaps go and walk the boundaries now, Mr Pender, while it's fine?'

She avoided any possibility of a further glance afterwards; that would have felt like a betrayal. Still, something in Mrs Givens' new impatience was surely catching. For the first time Norah noticed that Mr Pender seemed to be incapable of walking whilst talking, and stopped every few minutes whenever a fresh aspect of the case struck him, or struck him again. Once he stopped right on the edge of the water, and stayed so long that Norah was unable to prevent herself imagining the good hearty shove that was all it would take.

It was then that her eye was drawn to a flicker of movement in the house, hardly more than an impression. The Nervous Case herself! She counted floors, trying to work out where the movement had come from. The second floor, surely?

'You know what that means, don't yer?' Annie had whispered that morning, the Humber coughing outside, Miss Pilbeam agonizing at the window over the non-appearance of the buns. 'Nervous case my foot, it's one a they old loonies – they lets 'em all out, when they're too buggered to bite. You wanna watch your step. This 'un might be spry!'

It had been a curtain, Norah worked out, half drawn on the second floor. She was left with a curious impression of grace, a slender arm, a white hand, a shadowy outline. She thought then not of Annie's superannuated lunatic but of all the other stories everyone knew about this house, especially that of the young lady who had lived there, perhaps in the days when old Mrs Pender had been scullery maid; a daughter of the house who walked out one morning and drowned herself in this very lake, and whose ghost now and then had been seen, so it was said, standing in the shallows, as if waiting.

'Miss Thornby? Are you with us?'

'Oh, Mr Pender, I'm so sorry – I was miles away!'

'Clearly!' But he was still in his good Rosevear House mood, it seemed, and presently they were on their amiable way back to the house, and the visit at last was over. After the ritual farewells, the proffering and eventual acceptance of the customary gift of a whole wrapped home-made fruitcake for Mr Pender to take home, it was nearly three as they finally drove away, Mrs Givens waving with all her old enthusiasm from the carriageway.

'I fear the passing years are beginning to weigh a little heavily on our excellent Mrs Givens,' said Mr Pender, as they drove through the open gateway and turned into the lane. 'A lack of concentration. Absent-mindedness. Lagging behind. Or tottering ahead! A pity, but I really think it may be time to begin looking out for a more . . . reliable housekeeper, perhaps a couple, with a husband who can do maintenance, that sort of thing. Make a note to look into it, will you please, Miss Thornby.'

'Yes, sir,' said Norah.

Lettie

She had the compartment to herself, so when the train was going a fair lick she took her hat off, got up, opened the window as far as it would go, and stuck her head out into the tremendous buffeting rush.

The smell of soot was invigorating, and it was wonderfully impossible to think while the wind roared in her ears and tore at her hair. She kept her eyes closed against the flying bits of grit, but presently it began to rain as well, and at last she drew back inside, flung the window back up and sat down again to consider what she was up against.

Halfway to the station she had run into Sister Nesbit pushing her bicycle along North Street.

'Sister Quick.' Nesbit looked dreadful, she thought, her eyes puffy in her greyish face. Looks the way I feel, thought Lettie, nodding back in reply.

Nesbit jerked her chin up, a tiny gesture of disdain. 'Why did you call him?' she said coldly.

'What? What d'you mean?'

Nesbit left a pause. Her voice was low, emphatic: 'We don't call Dr Heyward.'

'I didn't,' said Lettie, but Nesbit shifted the bicycle past her, and walked on without another word.

Lettie had watched her go for a moment, trying to understand. *We don't call Dr Heyward.*

It sounded like a rule. Or information, the sort

discreetly spread about the powerful, by those with no power at all. What do you do, when you suspect a doctor isn't all he should be, when he has complete authority over you, when he is in effect your superior officer? What can you do?

You don't call him.

We don't call Dr Heyward.

Oh, Nesbit, why not? Come back and tell me! What are you saying? D'you think that if it had been Dr Pascoe last night, Flo Withers would still be alive?

The draggle-haired woman everyone went to had known nothing, nothing. She had simply sat beside Lettie's mother's bed and watched her while she died. But Philip Heyward, perhaps, did otherwise. She saw the front of his theatre gown, streaming, the blood clotting on his chest. He had come instead of Pascoe, taken over the case, because she had been there. Had he been a little more cavalier than usual with those forceps, because she was there, a woman he wanted to impress? It seemed to her now that he had. And Christ he had wanted to take her photograph, all in the nude, he had tried to talk her into it; and afterwards she had still gone on seeing him!

That was when she pulled off her hat and stuck her senseless head out of the window, as if the rush of the soot-smelling wind could buffet away shame.

Norah

After a while he stopped trying. He left the bonnet up but came back round the front of the Humber, and tapped on the window. With some difficulty Norah located the handle and wound the window down a little.

'I'm afraid we may need Mr Short again,' he said. 'Miss Thornby – how far d'you think it is, back to Rosevear House?'

'About – three miles?'

He looked back the way they had come. She could see the red rim his hat had left across his forehead, which was glistening with distress, and a smear of black on one white well-kept hand.

'I'll pop back, shall I?' she said.

'If you would be so kind, Miss Thornby,' he said at once. 'Then I can continue my own small efforts here,' he added, as Norah climbed out of the Humber, and put on her gloves. 'Telephone Short and tell him where we are, that it seems to be the same problem as last time; and be so good as to notify Miss Pilbeam. There are one or two late appointments that may need rescheduling. She may be able to organize a lift, if need be. Very good; let's hope the rain keeps off!'

By all means let us do so, thought Norah, though in fact she was perfectly happy. The day was windy, but mild for February, the hedges were already whitening here and there with blackthorn blossom, the sheltered banks were dotted with primroses and between the shifting jolly clouds the sky was a pale bright blue.

She walked along congratulating herself on the whole at winning another hour or two out of the office. All the same, she was wondering. *I'll pop back*, she had said, hardly a phrase she used often; she saw that she had done so merely to spare Mr Pender's feelings. Of course he had been about to tell her to go, to instruct her to go, as he had every right, since he was her employer and this was still office time. But the red rim across his forehead, his hesitation, had somehow made her want to protect him from doing so, to protect him from having to tell a woman to walk three miles while he sat about in upholstered comfort, for it was evident he had no more clue than she did herself about putting the car's engine to rights.

How quickly he had accepted the idea of a three-mile pop, and without the slightest hint of gratitude!

Well, it's your own fault anyway, Norah pointed out to herself. Rushing in to stop an old meanie feeling a bit mean. And then being surprised when there's no answering grace – altogether ridiculous womanish behaviour. Or slavish, she thought. On the other hand, here she was alone and striding along free in the lovely flickering sunshine. Thank goodness she had been wearing her brogues.

Though still her feet were beginning to complain a little as she reached the final turn of the lane. Perhaps I've popped a shade over three miles, she thought as she turned into the gates at last, but as she made her way along the weeded gravel of the carriage drive she suddenly remembered the Nervous Case, and automatically slowed down. Perhaps the Case was being troublesome; oh, perhaps Mrs Givens' odd distraction had all been due to earlier grotesque but unimaginable difficulties with her resident lunatic! Suppose she was struggling with her right this minute, trying to get her decently dressed or prise her in or out of a bath – or suppose Mrs Givens had just let the Case out altogether, for a breath of fresh air!

Might be spry, giggled Annie, and Norah came to a halt, and looked about her. There was no sign of anyone at all, she could see nothing but dark blank windows. No Mrs Givens waiting ceremonially outside the great front door, of course.

How was she to get in? She would try the kitchen side first, she decided, and set off again, turning right as she neared the house, and knocking at the side door there. Nothing; after a few moments she knocked again, then remembered Mr Pender sitting in his car, made him glance testily at his watch. Should have come yourself then, she thought smartly at this vision, but all the same turned the doorknob, pushed the door open. Cautiously she peeped inside, saw how dark it was; but there was a reassuring smell of baking on the air, so she carried on down the stone-flagged passage. Was she, as an agent of Bagnold and Pender, trespassing or not?

I feel as if I am anyway, she thought. 'Mrs Givens – hello?' Her voice seemed to echo down the long corridor. Thoughts of the spry old lunatic possibly at large made her hesitate just a little as she passed each doorway.

But she heard no one, saw no one, until she came at last to the panelled cubbyhole towards the front hall, installed to house the telephone. It felt doubly wrong to use the telephone without asking; on the other hand it was perfectly possible that Mrs Givens had gone to the village, or even taken the Nervous Case – perhaps in a bath chair – out for a lengthy airing along the lanes.

She opened the cubbyhole door, and went inside. It was the usual comfortless Edwardian arrangement, dark, with just one small window, no chair or table, no pencil, no notepad; but she knew that the telephone, for all its antique appearance, was in working order.

'Miss Pilbeam? This is Norah –'

'Ah. Miss Thornby. Are you at Rosevear House?'

'Yes, the car –'

'Mr Pender just got back. The garage has been notified.'

'Oh – you mean he –'

'Mr Pender was able to flag down a passing motorist, who most kindly gave him a lift back to Silkhampton. You had best come back by train, Miss Thornby. I have checked the timetable: the next train is at half past six. No doubt Mrs Givens will permit you to wait there. Keep your ticket if you wish to claim expenses.'

But how much is it? thought Norah wildly. The iron teaching of her caste prevented her from asking aloud. She was almost sure there was a florin in her purse along with fourpence in coppers and a thrupenny bit, but suppose she was wrong?

'Goodbye, Miss Thornby.' The line went dead.

Slow with dread, Norah opened the cubbyhole door and in the sunlight of the hall looked in her handbag for her purse, trying not to imagine what lay ahead of her if the florin turned out to be imaginary. But oh thank goodness, no, there it was! She felt like kissing it.

She checked her watch. It was nearly half past four; at the office Annie would already have the kettle on, and crumpets toasting. Well, it had been a very nice walk on the whole, Norah reminded herself. If completely pointless. And, she told herself stoutly, I shall wait here whatever Mrs Givens says.

Then she remembered that moment of complicity, and found herself wondering whether Mrs Givens, despite the ancient past, might be prevailed upon to relent as far as a cup of tea. One needed one's tea all the more, thought Norah, when one had popped three miles for nothing.

Rae

Straight away she knew she was recognized.

'Mrs Bright,' she said, with a touch of Lady Hermione to be on the safe side. She held out her hand. 'Thank you for coming.'

'Afternoon, Mrs . . . *Wickham.*' Her touch was very chilly.

Mrs Bright was small and thready; everything about her looked mean and narrow, as if there had been barely enough of anything to make her, thought Rae, as if she'd been skimped on.

Mrs Givens stepped forward, made their guest the suggestion of a curtsey, and Mrs Bright shrugged herself out of the shapeless raincoat and nondescript hat, and handed them over, revealing a very neat beautifully fitted suit of fine dark-red wool. The she took off the heavy spectacles, shook her dark hair back into place, and flashed Rae a quick hard glance of startling silver-grey.

It was instantly clear to her that Mrs Bright was in fact a person with her own species of glamour, her own formidable style. Rae was frightened for a second, watching as Mrs Givens carefully hung the terrible old coat on a hanger, understanding that it was a sort of costume or disguise. I am employing her, she reminded herself.

'Mrs Givens – Bea – is my old nurse,' said Lady Hermione, who was exactly the sort of person who really would have had an old nurse, Rae thought. 'She knows everything.'

'Oh yes?' Mrs Bright seemed indifferent.

'Would you – like to see the place a little?' Rae asked.

'Where you going to have it, you decided?'

'Um – well – I suppose, in my room.' Rae turned to Mrs Givens, who made a tiny shrugging gesture at her. 'Would you perhaps – care to see it?'

She led Mrs Bright up the creaking wooden stairs, stopping to catch her breath on the landing; in the mirror there she saw that beside her own extensive reflection Mrs Bright was slenderness itself. She forced herself to sound relaxed, did a pretty good job:

'You don't sound local.'

'I'm from London.'

So what are we doing in Cornwall? Rae wondered, but said no more. 'It's here,' she said, opening the door. 'Will it do, d'you think?'

'Fine. You'll need something to protect the bedding. Unless you want to buy a new mattress.'

Rae's heart gave a thump. Go on, she told herself. Ask her, then. She dropped Lady Hermione. 'Why?' It came out croaky.

The silver gaze turned on her, puzzled at first. Then a faint change of tone:

'There's lots of water inside you. Cushioning the baby. Pints of it – comes out with the baby, big gush. See?'

'Oh.' Rae sat down on the edge of the bed, trying to fit the idea of a big gush in with what she already knew. Had Mrs Dorrit protected her bedding? Had Jane Eyre had a big gush? Perhaps Mr Rochester had stood her a new mattress.

'Lie down, I'll give you a quick check-up, if you like. Feeling okay? Legs a bit puffy?'

'Just my feet.'

'Nice little slippers,' said Mrs Bright surprisingly. 'They from Feldman's, Drury Lane?'

Rae stared up at her. 'Yes, that's right. Nice suit,' she added. She lay down, pulling the eiderdown across her legs. 'It's not Molyneux, is it?'

Mrs Bright raised her delicate eyebrows. 'Why isn't it?'

'Sorry.'

'It's okay,' said Mrs Bright, with a little shrug. 'It's fake Molyneux. Via this place I know round the back a Victoria station.'

'Oh. Well, it's a jolly good fit.'

'How long you had these?'

For a second Rae thought they were still talking about fashion, then understood. 'Oh – since yesterday. They just came on all of a sudden, they sort of prickle. Getting better now, actually. What d'you think they are?'

'Looks like shingles. Means you're a bit run-down.'

'They won't hurt the baby?'

'Nothing to do with it.' Mrs Bright pressed her hands over Rae's stomach. They hardly fitted the suit, Rae thought. A fake Molyneux, even second-hand, deserved at least a decent manicure.

Mrs Bright opened her bag and took out a small trumpet-shaped item fitted with rubber at its broader end, and pressed it briefly into Rae's side, her own ear tight against the other end; Rae could feel her breath.

'What are you doing?'

'Counting the baby's heartbeat,' said Mrs Bright, straightening up, the trumpet in her hand. It had left a faint red ring on Rae's stomach. 'Everything's fine.'

'Is it?' Suddenly Rae was close to tears. She sat up. 'Where will you take him? Can't you tell me?'

'It's a safe address in London. The one we've used before.'

'How many times? How many times before?'

'Look,' said Mrs Bright. 'All I meant was: it's all worked before. We keep it simple. There's just the three of us, me, the doctor, and the head of the orphanage. We got someone lined up to be the mother, sign all the forms. All you have to do is wait, and keep quiet.'

'And have the baby.'

'Yes. I'll be here. Looking after you.'

'Suppose something goes wrong? Suppose I need a doctor?'

'You won't,' said Mrs Bright. 'It's natural, see? Nearly always simple.'

'So – you do as little as possible?'

'That's about the size of it.'

'But if I do need a doctor –'

'– then I call one,' said Mrs Bright. 'You go on being Mrs Wickham – probably get away with it, you look pretty different – especially the hair. I'm not sure anyone's going to recognize you.'

'You did,' said Rae.

Lettie

That was a facer. It hadn't occurred to her that she had given herself away just like that.

'Well – fact is – I saw you in this old film,' she said. 'I think it was you, anyway, all blonde, you were the sister, got throttled.'

'Sounds like me,' said Rae Grainger. 'I always play the sister. I usually come to a sticky end as well. What was it called?'

Lettie hesitated. The title had pain in it, for reasons she was trying to avoid at the moment, what with one thing and another, she told herself. No avoiding it now, of course, and once more she saw the damp flannel clearing the grime, her eleven-year-old self looking back, a sister three times over. 'I think it was *Aren't We Sisters?*' she said at last.

'Oh, that old thing – with – don't tell me – Hetty Harper, wasn't it! Lord, I wonder what happened to her – well, nine years happened to her, I suppose,' said Rae cheerfully. 'Where on earth did you see it?'

'Privately,' said Lettie coolly. 'Somewhere local.'

Rae Grainger took the hint, and stood up. 'Well, now – d'you – need to see anything else, the kitchen, bathroom, that sort of thing?'

'Be good to know the layout,' said Lettie.

Now the landing was lit with a late-afternoon radiance reflected from the lake outside. As they made their way down the stairs Rae Grainger said: 'After *Aren't We Sisters?* I did *Tell Her Now* – drowned myself in that one. Then I got shot in *The Friday Murders*, and stabbed in *Desperation*. I was Anne Boleyn in *Good King Henry* and done for murder in *What the Butler Thought*, so presumably I was hung by the neck until et cetera. And I actually started off dead in *The Spectre of Sowerby Hall* – you have to admit, there is rather a pattern to my early career.' Her voice was full of laughter.

Lettie said: 'You survive *Aren't We Sisters?*'

'Do I? How?'

'You write a note from THE ABODE OF DESPAIR. And get rescued just in time.'

'That's fantasy for you,' said Rae, opening the kitchen door to a fine smell of baking. A wire tray full of golden scones studded with raisins stood cooling on the table, and the kettle was singing on the gas stove. No one about though. Enormous sink, Lettie noted. Hot running water, plenty of it, place this size.

'Where's the telephone?' she said.

'Miles away,' said Rae. 'I'd better show you.'

They went back along the passage and through a set of green baize doors into another finer half-panelled corridor marked with pale rectangles along the walls, where once pictures must have hung. Lettie remembered the give-away patch she herself had left at the Picture Palace. Had anyone noticed yet that one of the photographs had gone? Perhaps no one ever would, she thought.

They reached a large hall with a black and white marble floor.

'See – that little kiosky-thing.'

'Right. Does that door open?'

'I've only ever used the side one near the kitchen. Well – what do you think – is it safe here?'

'It's fine. Perfect.'

'Really? That's good. You're not – anything like what I was expecting, you know.'

'Who were you expecting?'

Rae shook her head. 'It was hard to picture anyone,' she said, 'with so little to go on. I mean, not counting myself, you are actually my very first real criminal.'

Lettie had to smile. 'You're my first film star.'

'Maybe,' said Rae. 'Might be an ex-film star soon – my contract has a morality clause, not that it needs one: talk would be enough.'

'I know.'

'How on earth did you get into this business? No, sorry – I didn't ask. Can you tell me – well – real stuff. Useful things – about having babies and so on? Please – because: I don't know anything at all.'

'I brought you a book about it.'

'No – did you really! How marvellous, how kind, thank you!'

'Everyone ought to know everything,' said Lettie. 'It ought to be the first thing they teach you at school, along with how to write your name: how people make babies. How to stop making them. That's what I think anyway.'

Rae laughed. 'Imagine the fuss!'

'Afterwards – you know, when you've had the baby – before I go, I'll tell you what to do. To make sure you never get in this sort a mess again, right?'

'Is your name really Esme?'

'No.'

'Well, anyway: thank you, Esme. I didn't know what to expect, but I didn't expect you to be kind.'

'I'm being professional,' said Lettie coolly. Inwardly she was having quite a struggle. Rae Grainger, she dimly perceived, was irresistible. But it was safer, she felt, to resist.

'We thought we'd have tea in the library,' said Rae. 'Would you like some?'

'Where is that?' The house was like a small town, Lettie thought. Imagine working here in the old days, running up and down these sodding corridors all day long!

'This way. I've often thought,' said Rae, 'that I'd need a decent pair of roller skates, if I lived here all the time. I'd have spares for visitors.'

'What about the staff?'

'Oh, they'd all have them. Condition of employment: a roller-skating clause. Of course, there'd have to be some sort of Corridor Code, for rush hour.'

'Traffic lights.'

'Might be safer,' said Rae. 'Here we are. Oh, hello, Bea. That does look nice!'

There were the scones, piled now on to a china stand; there was bread and butter, jam, a fruit cake, and beside the trolley loaded with teapot and china stood a small spirit stove with a kettle warming on it.

'By the fireside, Ruth?'

This from the old lady. Clearly local, from her speech. But we're hereabouts because of me, thought Lettie, approaching her. 'Who *are* you?' she asked, gently enough.

'This is my old nurse, remember? Mrs Givens,' Rae put in quickly.

'Ma'am,' said the old girl, bobbing a curtsey.

Lettie looked from one to the other, aware that they were lying to her. But that was their business, she decided, and accepted a cup of tea.

Rae

Tea seemed to relax Mrs Bright a little. With a well-sugared cup in her hand she leant back in the armchair and said: 'I was in a film once.'

'Really?' said Rae. 'How come – when?'

'Donkey's years ago. I played a bad girl in a nightclub.'

'Well, you can't stop there,' said Rae. 'What film was it? Have I seen it?'

'Shouldn't think so,' said Mrs Bright, 'it was about family planning.'

Rae laughed. '*What?*'

'It was the – Marie Stopes, see.'

'Oh her – did she write *Married Love*?'

'That's the one.'

How was Mrs Givens responding to this racy talk? Hard to tell, since she was sitting on her own near the window being *service*, pretending deafness while attending to the teacups. Rae turned back.

'So – Marie Stopes was in this film?' she asked.

'Oh no – she wrote it. Always up to something, trying to spread the word, books and plays and what not. She writes this film, about this girl Maisie, lives in a slum, got dozens a brothers and sisters, on account of her mum not knowing about birth control.'

'Oh dear! Were you Maisie?'

'No, I'm not an actress, I was a whatd'youcallit, an

extra – she could talk you into anything, the Madam. See, Maisie runs away, meets some bad girls on the street, and that was me. Well, there were three of us being bad girls, drinking champagne in nightclubs. WHERE APHRODITE AND BACCHUS FOXTROT TO THE MUSIC OF A NEGROID BAND, that was the caption.'

'But what happens to Maisie?'

'Oh,' said Mrs Bright, deadpan, 'she gets to understand the importance of contraception.'

Rae snorted violently into her teacup, and was instantly helpless with laughter.

'I think she jumps in the Thames at one point,' Mrs Bright went on.

'Oh stop, ow –'

'But she gets fished out –' Here Mrs Bright too was for a moment unable to continue.

'Did people . . . go and *see* this film?' asked Rae, drying her eyes.

'She swore they did. The Madam. But she never made another one.'

'And that was the end of your film career?'

'I didn't mind,' said Mrs Bright. 'It wasn't as much fun as I thought it would be.'

'True of so much,' Rae said.

They smiled at one another. Mrs Bright reached into the shabby nurse's bag on the floor beside her feet, and took out a booklet with a pale-blue paper cover.

'Here. This is the book I told you about. Keep it, for now. It's American,' she added, and held it out.

The Mechanics of Birth.

Rae took it, suddenly entirely sober. *A guide for expectant women*, read the subtitle inside. Not new, but not much-thumbed. She had a moment's sudden nostalgia for *Lovell's Complete Bestiary*, worn into suede. Other people had read *The Mechanics of Birth*, she thought, but no one had loved it. Was it, perhaps, another Pandora's box, full of information she might in fact be better off not knowing? Suppose there was some ancient wisdom in the silence and lies, in the sudden conjuring white-rabbit appearance of babies in art? Three or four hours passed, and then there was another little life. What would Dickens have written if someone had made him read *The Mechanics of Birth*?

'Thank you,' she said.

Perhaps she had looked as frightened as she suddenly felt, for after a pause Mrs Bright said: 'Everyone's different. No one looks the same on the outside, do they? Well, we're all different on the inside too. That book – it's just a guide. No one's labour is ever the same as anyone else's. But you're young and healthy, it'll all just happen anyway, whether you know what's going on or not. I think you're best off knowing. But it's up to you.'

'If it all just happens anyway, why do people need midwives?' Rae said.

'Company,' said Mrs Bright, and at the window Rae heard Mrs Givens give a little sigh. 'And listen,' Mrs Bright went on. 'This place. Bit Boris Karloff, ain't it. Bothers you.'

'Oh, yes, I'm sorry about that. Calling you and everything. That was just – me going a bit loco,' said Rae, 'imagining things, I'm fine now.'

'So – why don't you get a radio?'

'What? Here, you mean?' Rae sat up, half laughed; it

was so obvious. Why on earth hadn't she thought of it herself? Oh, dance music turned as high as the volume would go! Could any confection of gaslight and laudanum withstand the BBC Dance Orchestra?

'What an absolutely brilliant idea! Oh, but how – I can't go anywhere –'

'Cash on delivery,' said Mrs Bright. 'There must be a place in Silkhampton – you could buy it over the phone,' she said, turning to Mrs Givens.

'What, me?'

'Why not!' cried Rae. 'Oh and Bea – you can keep it, afterwards. You know, when I've gone.'

'Well –'

It was at that moment that there was a sudden brisk knock at the library door.

'Who on earth –' began Mrs Givens, struggling to rise, but as she spoke the door opened, and someone walked in; it was the tweedy woman Rae had seen across the lake, large and blooming this close up, her cheeks flushed pink and her hair all coming down on one side.

'Oh, Mrs Givens, I'm so –' she began, then interrupted herself in happy surprise: 'Hello, Lettie! What are *you* doing here?' And interrupted herself again, now in an ecstasy of wonder, her hands clapped to her face: 'Oh my! It's . . . you're Rae Grainger – oh my goodness me!'

Norah and Lettie

They boarded the train home in silence, each in a separate world.

Norah's was glowing. As the train gathered speed she consciously began going over the whole glorious episode from the beginning, trying to record each precious detail in her memory. There she was, thinking hopefully about the possibility of getting a cup of tea, trying to work out the best direction to set off in; might Mrs Givens be in the garden, perhaps?

Almost at once she had caught a faint murmur of feminine voices, conversational in tone; perhaps Mrs Givens and the Case or lunatic were getting along quite nicely after all. She had crept further down the passage trying to work out where the sounds were coming from. Could it be the library? Were they having tea in there?

Norah's heart had beat fast. Suppose Mrs Givens came out in her usual embittered-peasant mode, and accused her of trespass, and – perfectly correctly – of stealing a telephone call!

But all she heard as she neared the door was a sudden burst of laughter. Norah stopped. The laughter had not sounded like that of a lunatic, let alone a superannuated one. It had sounded normal and light-hearted, a merry girl's laugh. Was this Case too nervous to leave her room?

Unless – perhaps it wasn't Mrs Givens and the Case at all, but other completely different people! What on earth was Mrs Givens up to? She had certainly not mentioned any other guests that morning. Though of course her manner had been so different, Norah remembered. Had she been hiding something?

For a long moment Norah had stood with one hand to her mouth; it had occurred to her that all these strange circumstances might amount to a Test. What would a Great Woman do, if confronted with a faintly sinister mystery in the course of her everyday employment?

Only a lesser woman would do minor clerical work at an estate agency in the first place, suggested a small part of Norah's mind. The rest of it was seized with disgust at this craven thought, and she at once knocked, flung open the library door, and as if boldly went inside. A delicious teatime smell of baking instantly assaulted her. There was Mrs Givens, by the window, looking aghast, and there, of all people, was her own dear –

'Hello, Lettie! What are *you* doing here?'

Lettie jumping to her feet, clearly startled, saying something that was lost in the noise the chair made behind her as she pushed it back. Then Norah had seen her: sitting on the other side of the fire, gloriously perfect despite the dark curls, and unbelievably, stupefyingly real, one of that fabulous company of film stars whose careers she had once so closely followed in the *Film Lover's Weekly*, and whom she had seen so intimately near death so very recently, at the Picture Palace!

Aren't We Sisters? Yes and for always, said the echo of Freddie Pyncheon's music in Norah's head, as she stood there staring in mystified adoration, her heart flaming in her chest.

Rae Grainger's smile had been as enchantingly beautiful as ever, her coaxing gentle voice a new delight. 'Hello,' she had said. 'D'you want a cup of tea?'

That was the first thing that she said to me, thought Norah now, staring out of the train window without seeing anything. She was so nice; so pleased I'd seen all her films – thrilled I could remember them so well – nearly all the titles, something of almost every plot, and who else had starred in them; she had positively clapped her hands when Norah recalled that she had first met her husband Rod Lacey on the set of *Stepping Up*.

'Such a good actor – I saw him last week in *Danger Valley*,' said Norah, then dared: 'It must be so peculiar for you when he gets killed – rather awful, I imagine.'

'Oh, I enjoy it no end,' Rae Grainger had answered, 'especially when he plunges over a cliff, or his aeroplane bursts into flames. Poor Rod – always so careless in high places.' How they had laughed! Though at the same time Norah had felt quite near tears. That someone so glamorous should deign to joke with her!

I had tea with Rae Grainger, she thought once more, as the train rattled over the level crossing.

Somehow her thoughts kept gathering themselves into the sort of article she had read so often in the *Film Lover's Weekly*. Tea with Rae Grainger, in the Actress's Beautiful Home. My favourite room is my library, laughs the exquisite star of *The Spectre of Sowerby Hall*, who likes nothing better than burying herself completely in the depths of the English countryside.

Well, obviously there were perfectly good reasons for the burying business. No glamorous star could really afford to be seen – or photographed – in such a delicate condition. And poor Miss Grainger – Mrs Lacey, rather – had no family to speak of; every fan knew she had been orphaned as a child. It was also to do with the baby being British-born, Norah had gathered. What a shame Mr Lacey had been unable to stay with her, as planned! But of course actors, Miss Grainger had explained, simply couldn't refuse work, no matter what the effect on personal plans or family life.

Privacy is such a treasure, Miss Thornby. Every day in Hollywood one is surrounded by the forces of publicity. One submits. One must; it's part of the job, and one absolutely must not complain! But just for now. For now, Norah – may I call you Norah? Thank you – and do please call me Rae, won't you – for now I'm so happy here in this wonderful peace and quiet, with dear Mrs Givens, who has been such a Perfect Treasure, and of course my dear old friend *Lettie*, here. Oh yes, many years, haven't we – Lettie? In fact we met on a film set, a hundred years ago – well, '23, wasn't it, Lettie?

Lettie with that familiar closed look; well, I'd always known she was secretive, Norah told herself. Imagine knowing all this time that *Rae Grainger* was in hiding at Rosevear, and knowing why, and never spilling so much as a single bean!

'A film set?' Norah had asked, and then it had all come out: how Lettie and Rae, together! had both been in a film – about family planning, of all things, written by that madcap Dr Stopes – wildly melodramatic, such fun to play! They had become such friends, on set, that they had been in contact ever since, wasn't that so, Lettie?

Lettie really being rather grumpy, Norah thought, but then she so hated to talk about herself; that was one of the things Norah had noticed about her.

'And you didn't say anything, did you, Lettie, when we saw *Aren't We Sisters?*'

'Thought best not,' said Lettie, and you'd think the words were being dragged out of her by force.

'She's right, you know, Norah,' Rae had said then, seriously. 'I do hope you'll feel able to – help me. You may think I'm a big star, and so on. But I'm just an ordinary girl inside, Norah. On my own, waiting for my baby. I have my fears, as anyone would.'

Oh, the throb in her voice! Heart-breaking!

'I'm going to ask you now for a very great favour, Norah. I'm going to ask you – beg you – not to tell anyone that I'm here, or why. Not a single soul. Will you do that, Norah, please? Will you do that, for me?'

Yes, yes and for always!

Gazing still unseeingly out of the train window, Norah drew a deep breath of happiness.

Across the carriage Lettie heard the sigh, and briefly considered recrossing her legs and accidentally giving her landlady a sharp kick on the shins. But I can't be bothered, she decided, looking across at Norah's transfigured face. Who'd have thought a sensible-looking woman like her, posh as well, would be so soppy a film fan?

'It'll be fine,' Rae had murmured, while Norah was in

the lavatory just before they left for the station. 'She's not going to say anything.'

Of course Norah knowing didn't make much difference to Rae. But it's all the difference in the world to me, thought Lettie in a fury.

'How can I say now that I acted in good faith?' she had hissed back. 'She knows I know you're not Mrs Wickham!' At which Rae had instantly sniggered. But this time Lettie had not joined in. 'And what was all that about Marie Stopes?'

'Keep your hair on – it makes sense that we're old friends, doesn't it?' said Rae. 'Why else would I be down here? I mean, I *am* down here because of you.'

'And your dear old nurse just *happens* to be down here too, does she?'

'I didn't tell Norah she was my dear old nurse. I only told you that. Gosh – don't you wish you were the sort of person who had a dear old nurse, Lettie? I know I do.'

'Point is,' Lettie had said in a furious undertone, 'you didn't need to say any of it. About the film. Makes everything so much more complicated.'

'Of course. You're absolutely right. Sorry – I just got a bit carried away. Only – it hardly felt like a fib at all at the time. It's just my doomed sort of part, you see – I so often *am* Aphrodite foxtrotting with Bacchus to the music of a negroid band.'

It was hard to stay angry with someone who made you laugh, Lettie saw. It was rather a male trick, she thought. Perhaps that was what real charm was; you had the full range of all the normal womanly guiles and graces, and a fair sprinkling of the manly ones as well.

The lavatory had flushed along the corridor; moments to go.

'What about that old woman, then,' Lettie had said. 'She's a local – she just works here, doesn't she – and you've bloody gone and roped her in as well!'

'Oh, it's not like that,' Rae had said. 'Mrs Givens is my friend.'

'Who's Mrs Givens?' Lettie asked, as the train neared Silkhampton and began to slow.

'Who?' said dreamy Norah. She sat up. 'Oh, Mrs Givens – she's the housekeeper. At Rosevear. Why?'

'You know her?'

'Not really. She hates me, unfortunately.'

'Really? Why?'

Norah blew her cheeks out in a different sort of sigh. 'Ancient history – her sister used to be the local handywoman – d'you know that word?'

'Amateur midwife?'

'That's it. Learnt from their own mother. They both used to go about with her, apparently – they were twins – but only the sister – Mrs Dimond – took it up. Anyway, *my* mother worked for the Board, and – well, cut a long story short, the sister was stopped from, you know, delivering babies. And she never forgave my mother, nor me. And Mrs Givens still holds it against me, I think.'

'When was this?'

'Oh, years ago, I was a child.'

'She must be getting on a bit, then. Mrs Givens.'

'Oh yes. Still. *Rae* seems genuinely fond of her, doesn't she!' The name in italics, spoken as if sacred; I wondered

303

how long it would be, thought Lettie crossly. How long can Norah Thornby talk without mentioning Rae Grainger? Answer: one minute.

'D'you mind if I ask you something?'

'What?' said Lettie, as they crossed the footbridge at the station, passing through the cloud of smoky steam still hanging there, the train still panting at the platform.

'Marie Stopes.'

'What about her?'

'Why do you think she is a Great Woman?'

'Who said she was?'

'You did. When *Rae* said she was a nutcase. She was talking about the film and so on, then. And you said, Oh, but she was still a Great Woman.'

'Did I? Well. You know.' Lettie shrugged.

'No, no I don't. Will you tell me, please? Great women have always been dead before. I mean queens, and Boadicea, and Elizabeth Fry and George Eliot. Is she great, d'you think, really?'

It was Lettie's turn to sigh. 'She used to be. She might have been. Not now, I think. She had some great ideas once. Things I still believe in.'

'Like what?'

'Well – that everyone should know everything, for a start. About sex. Because most of us – women, I mean – we don't know much. It's not obvious, the way it is for men. So other people can tell us lies. And we believe them.'

'What d'you mean?' Norah looked away, for she knew

304

that it was very unsophisticated to blush when someone said *sex*.

'When she got married – and she wouldn't mind me saying this, she was wild people should know, she wrote about it all the time, plays and so on – she didn't know what sex was.'

'Who didn't?'

'Dr S*topes*, Pete's sake,' said Lettie. 'She was thirty-odd, and she was a doctor – not of medicine, she was some other kind of doctor, knew about plants.'

'Dr Stopes isn't a doctor?'

'She's . . . like a professor. About plants.'

'I see. And she didn't know about . . .'

'When she'd been married a few months, she went to a doctor. A proper doctor. To find out why she wasn't getting pregnant. And the doctor examines her. Finds she's a virgin. And she didn't know that was odd, see? She thought you got pregnant from kissing and cuddling. And her husband didn't do anything else. But she didn't know. See? Her mother hadn't told her a thing.'

'Goodness,' said Norah faintly. 'How . . . awful.'

'That's what got her started, really. That someone as clever as her could grow up not knowing anything about her own insides.'

'I thought she just wanted to stop people having babies.'

'To stop them having babies they don't want. Suppose every woman only had one or two – think of the difference it would make – enough food for everyone, enough work, enough houses, enough space! Listen, I'll tell you a story. I mean, really, a story. When I first went for interview, to work with her. In Poplar, this was. There's three of 'em sat behind the desk. Two old girls in nursing uniform all starchy, and the other one was her – fashion plate, furs and pearls, hat, the lot, fantastic. The nurses ask the usual training stuff, experience et cetera. Then Dr Stopes says: "Miss Quick, I should like to tell you a story, may I?" And she starts straight off, this King Arthur and his Knights of the Round Table thing.'

'What, telling you a story?'

'Yeah,' said Lettie. They crossed the road and reached the opposite pavement. 'Like this: King Arthur gets captured by this wizard. I'm going to chop your head off, says the wizard, but 'cause I'm a sport, I'll let you off if you answer this riddle, but you got to answer it in one word. Get it wrong, you're dead, see? King Arthur says okay. And the wizard says, "Tell me, in just one word: What is it that women want?"'

Norah turned, half laughing.

'"You got a year and a day to find out," says the wizard, and he disappears, puff a green smoke. So. Year and a day, King Arthur and his Knights ride all over the place asking wise men, priests, doctors, teachers, what is it – one word – that women want? They even ask one or two women.'

Norah laughed. 'Love?'

'Money,' said Lettie.

'Power.'

'Family.'

'Security.'

'Laughs,' said Lettie. They turned into Silver Street, for once ignoring the shops' lit windows. 'The answers often seem right,' she went on, 'but they're always different, and

King Arthur just doesn't know which one to go for. Then, very last day, this fat old woman jumps out of the forest. "King Arthur," she says, "I know what women want, and I'll tell you; but you got to give me a husband in exchange, and I want *him*!" and she points at Sir Gawaine, he's all young and handsome –'

'Like Rod Lacey,' said Norah.

'Just like him. Gawaine's a gent, and he reckons, here's a chance to save his king, so quick as a flash he leaps off his horse, gets down on one knee, asks the old bag to marry him. And she turns to King Arthur, and she says, "Right then, what women want, in one word, is . . ."'

'Well,' said Norah, as they turned into the square, 'what is it? What *do* we want?'

'I'm saying, that's when she stopped,' said Lettie. 'Dr Stopes, I mean, telling me the story. She leans across the desk, and she says to me, "Well, Miss Quick, what do *you* think the answer is? What is it – in a word – that women want?"'

'Goodness! What did you say?'

'Not much,' said Lettie, 'I was so fed up. I'd come all that way, no breakfast. I was broke, see. And I didn't mind the other two asking me what I knew and where I'd trained and so on. But this was messing me about. So I said: "You started telling me this story. You finish it."'

'Oh, Lettie, what did she say?'

Lettie snorted. 'Loved it.'

'You mean – because you stood up to her?'

'"Oh, spirited!" she says. That's a one-word answer alright, *spirited*. If you want to put someone in her place.'

307

There was a silence; Norah had never heard Lettie sound bitter before.

'Did she tell you what the real answer was?' she asked finally. Her eyes fell on the statue, and as always she signalled a silent greeting to it. Hello, Guy.

'Oh, yeah,' said Lettie. 'The hag says, "What women want is *sovereignty*."'

'Sovereignty?'

'That's it,' said Lettie. 'The Knights are none too sure, but Arthur reckons it's worth a try. And he says it, and the wizard howls all furious and disappears, puff a green smoke, hooray. And off they all go back to Camelot, laughing their heads off at Gawaine, 'cause he's got the fat old woman sat in front of him, on his horse. His fiancée. But he doesn't laugh. He's a real gent, see. They get married straight away, and they go to his room, and the hag says, "Give us a kiss then." And Gawaine's a gent, so he does. And crack of lightning, she turns into a beautiful blonde!'

'Like Rae.'

'Like her. "My hero!" she says. "Your kiss has saved me from the evil wizard's spell. This is my true self. But I can only be like this half the day. The other half I have to stay an old hag. So which d'you want – shall I be beautiful by day, and hag by night, or hag by day, and lovely every night?"'

'Oh dear,' said Norah; she felt the story was in danger of becoming coarse.

'But Gawaine's a gent, remember. He says, "Well, Madam, I reckon that's up to you." And crack of lightning, "Oh, my hero!" The spell's all broken now, because of what he said – she can stay lovely all the time. Because without even thinking about it he's given her what women want: sovereignty. Over herself.'

'Oh,' said Norah.

'And Dr Stopes, she says to me: "This is what our work here will be, we will grant women sovereignty, over themselves," and she jumps round the desk, and grabs me, and kisses me on both cheeks! She was like that, in those days, Dr Stopes.'

Norah slid her key into the lock. 'And did she – well, what about – you know, her not having any babies, because, well –'

'Oh, that. She had the marriage annulled. Wasn't consummated, see – had to go to court, mind.'

'What, and tell everyone? Talk about –'

'Yes,' said Lettie. 'But then she married someone else, who knew what was what, so it was all okay in the end.'

It was not until much later, when Norah was cleaning her teeth before bed, that the ideas struck her. She tried to discount them. But they kept recurring, as if they knew they had to be answered, or at any rate expressed. When she had finished in the bathroom she knocked lightly on Lettie's door, as the light still showed beneath it.

'What?'

Lettie in her nightdress, very small and pale, very tired-looking.

'Sorry,' said Norah. 'I just keep thinking, about King Arthur, and the blonde being lovely all the time. I mean, that's rather what *men* want, isn't it? I know women want to be lovely all the time, of course we do, and most of us aren't at all, are we – I mean, look at me! But d'you see what I mean? Who gets the most out of a woman being lovely all the time?'

Lettie appeared to give this some thought. 'She was being *herself* all the time,' she said at last.

'Her *lovely* self,' said Norah. 'And – Lettie, really – can it be proper sovereignty, if you have to rely on a man to give it to you?'

Lettie's eyebrows went up. 'No,' she said. 'I suppose it can't.'

'And I thought of that old film we saw,' Norah went on, 'Rae's film, you know, *Aren't We Sisters?* The title, anyway. That it's a sort of message, for men: aren't we your sisters? As opposed to – you know, your servants.'

'Your playthings.'

'Yes. Because – I think men forget. All the time. They forget that we're their sisters.'

When Lettie smiled, her front teeth showed, charmingly crooked. 'Yes. Yes, I think they do.'

Norah smiled back. 'Well. Goodnight, Lettie.'

'Night, Norah.'

Lettie closed the door. Norah stood where she was for a moment, thinking about everything that had happened to her that day.

Suppose she had listened to the craven voice inside her before the library door at Rosevear, and instead of resolutely knocking and entering, crept silently away! She would have missed everything. But she had seen the Test, and passed it, and so missed nothing. She had had tea with *Rae Grainger*. She had discovered that a real live Great Woman had been even more ignorant than she was herself. And Lettie Quick was her friend.

Norah turned at last, and passed slowly along the landing and up the stairs to bed. She wouldn't be able to sleep a wink, she thought, and that wouldn't matter a bit. She would just lie awake exulting, because it was particularly wonderful, she thought, that she was already able to recognize, so fully, that this had been the very best day of her life.

Lettie

South Africa – that was the plan, he said. He was well and truly sick of this place – this entire pathetic country – so small in every way, so narrow, so worn out and finished. Really – since the War, it was finished, hopeless. It was time to just leave the whole rotten mess behind – his marriage – a hollow sham! His cramped humdrum job, such a disappointment, so boring! His whole life was emptiness apart from her – so why not make the break, take the bold step, now, while they were both still young, with real love to guide and guard them! A fine new country, Lettie! A new world where they could be free and whole, feel the hot sun on their faces!

The Natal line was first-class only, he added, in rather a different voice. Sailings twice a month. A private cabin. Each.

Let me think about it, she said.

'What is there to think about?'

So she made up some stuff about an affectionate sister and dear little nephews and nieces; then added some other stuff about wanting to go on working, more or less just to see what he'd say.

'But you'll never *need* to work! Ever again, I'll take care of all that. I'll look after you. And – the difference between us, the, the social gap – of course it means nothing to me, never has – but out there, Lettie, it won't matter to anyone else either, these idiotic old-world prejudices mean nothing!'

So to recap, thought Lettie, I'm to give up this smashing family I've just thought up, not that you know that, but then you don't actually know a sodding thing about me, do you – I'm supposed to drop my family and my career and everything else I've aimed for all these years and bugger off to some foreign nasty place where I'd have absolutely nothing apart from what you choose to give me?

We don't call Dr Heyward, added Nesbit, in Lettie's head.

'I can't just disappear, Philip. I have commitments.'

'Break them.'

'No, I need time. I have to make arrangements.'

'Soon, though. It has to be soon.'

'It will be, I promise,' said Lettie.

Rae

Telephones, said Bea, gave her the willies. She hadn't never taken to them. Someone else's voice from far away sounding right in your earhole – and here she was being asked to *act* into one, pretending to want something she hadn't so much as thought of in all her born days!

Eventually Rae wrote her a script to read aloud.

'Is that Evans Electrical? Good afternoon, this is Mrs Givens, of Rosevear House –' though her peremptory tone, when demanding 'one a they Pye Six Valves, the latest model, mind!' had made Rae dodge away down the corridor as fast as she could, in case whoever it was down the line at Evans Electrical could hear her laughing.

'Though it hardly matters, I suppose,' she said afterwards. 'When I'm widely thought to be an elderly lunatic.'

'Not widely,' was all Bea said.

Norah

She was still considering social tactics – a simple unannounced friendly visit might be permissible, under the circumstances; an act of kindness, or even duty, like a hospital visit, perhaps with a traditional bunch of grapes in hand to underline the point, or a copy of this month's *Vogue*, if she opted out of morning buns for a week – when Mr Pender called her into his office.

'Miss Thornby – we have decided that in recognition of the fact that Rosevear has been her home in one way or another for – well, upwards of forty years, I believe – we have decided, Mr Bagnold and myself – that Mrs Givens' removal thence might be ah, sweetened by a small honorarium.'

Removal thence! Norah's mind so caught on this phrase that for a second or two she lost track of what Mr Pender was saying. But he was already talking about something else:

'– kindly entertained you during your last ah, unscheduled call, you are just that person!'

Norah hesitated, but there was nothing for it, she would have to ask. 'I'm sorry, Mr Pender – I didn't quite catch . . . ?'

Mr Pender's thin face took on its familiar patient-but-disappointed expression: 'Miss Thornby, here is the postal order. You are to take it to her, with our compliments, this afternoon. Miss Pilbeam will fund you your ticket from petty cash. Is that clear enough?'

The envelope was sealed, she saw, as she took it.

'May I ask – when she is to go, sir?' Thinking of Rae.

'It's all in the letter,' said Mr Pender, looking up at her over his glasses.

'And – Minnie?'

'Who? Oh, the half-wit. Well, that's up to Mrs Givens, I suppose.'

'But –'

'Mrs Givens has family in the area, and is well over pensionable age; her future plans are hardly our concern, Miss Thornby,' said Mr Pender, turning away.

It couldn't be really soon, Norah told herself, as she closed the office door behind her. Not after upwards of forty years. Rae needed only a month or so, perhaps. But as she went back to her desk the full implications dawned. Whatever Mr Pender called it, Mrs Givens would surely understand that along with her no doubt stingy postal order she was being given an ultimatum.

And after all those courtly visits too, Norah wanted to exclaim to someone. What about all that bowing and curtseying, and lunch, and home-made cake to take home? What about Mrs Givens' celebrated sister, Mrs Dimond, who had delivered in safety the infant Mr Pender? How could he just chuck her out like this?

Just because she'd ever so slightly hurried him, thought Norah. Because she'd turned her back on him, and picked up the coffee things before he'd finished speaking.

Still. It was certainly a cast-iron reason to visit. Norah perked up. *Vogue* and grapes as well, why not!

Rae

The fine big box arrived later that day, bristling with string and crammed with wood shavings; buried inside wrapped in flannel was the article itself, very handsome, Rae thought, in swanky reddish veneer, with the Rising Sun grille of its kind in front, and two splendid heavyweight knobs high on one side. Her fingers itched to try them.

'And look!' She waved the long brown plait of its flex. 'They did it!' Rae was particularly proud of remembering to write the plug into Mrs Givens' script. 'It's all ready to go – where shall we put it?'

There was no suitable plughole with the set on the kitchen table, so they had to wrestle it on to the floor.

'Now then. It'll take a minute or two to warm up ... and I'm not sure it's properly tuned or anything ...'

'Got a little red light on,' said Bea doubtfully, bending to look.

'Oh, that's good, that's good ... wait a minute ...'

'They got one a these at –' began Bea, but a throaty humming sound interrupted her.

'Here we go ... !' said Rae.

Very faintly, at first, barely audible over the hum, they could hear a muffled parping noise, that gathered and rose and suddenly clarified into something completely alien to Rosevear House, thought Rae in delight: of all things, a dance band, bouncing rhythm, smooth creamy brass, a faintly melancholy trombone, and then the warm sweet tenor.

'It's Al Bowlly, Lord love him!' cried Rae. 'Now – where shall we put it – isn't there another socket in here?'

But there was only the one, it turned out.

'Could we put it on a little table or something?' shouted Rae.

'How about a tea trolley? I got one a they on wheels.'

'Oh – so we can wheel it about, room to room – what an utterly brilliant idea!'

'I'm known for 'em,' said Bea demurely into the silence, as Rae switched off.

She laughed. 'Let's go and put it in the hallway – see how loud it goes!'

Trundled along the dark stone-flagged corridor on a squeaky-wheeled blackened Victorian trolley the radio set looked wonderfully incongruous, Rae thought, so sleek and modern. They arrived at the large entrance hall at the front of the house, where the flags gave way to black and white marble and the grand curve of the staircase began. Late sunshine was streaming in through the complicated tracery of the windows over the locked double doors; you could almost imagine the place might have had charm, thought Rae, in those days when you swept downstairs in a floor-length crinoline . . . oh, but was there a socket?

There was.

'Now then!' said Rae, and she smacked the plug home, switched on, and when the thing had warmed up again turned the volume knob as far as it would go. It would be like scalding a tea cloth in boiling water, she thought.

Every corner of this haunted house, basement to rafters, would soon be scoured clean with hot jazz. Take that, M. R. James! Listen in, Mr Blackwood, and sod off, Dickens!

'Lew Stone! Come on, let's Swing! – it's easy, look, nice and slow, triple step, triple step, rock step, see?'

'Oh now, Ruth, I don't think I –'

'Course you can, look, triple step, triple step, rock step, it's just like waltzing – that's it, see, I knew you could do it! Wonderful, you're a natural, no – I'm the man – start left – triple step, triple step, rock step –'

Tripping, laughing, pulling one another the wrong way, they Swung twice all round the entrance hall, in and out of the golden bars of sunlight, in time to the irresistible catch of the music.

'I ain't danced for – I don't know how long –'

'Quick, star turn, to the right, the right, ha, brilliant!'

'Not for –'

The music stopped abruptly; the electricity had cut out again.

'Not for these fifty years,' said Bea into the sudden quiet.

'Really? Why not?'

'No reason,' said Bea gently, letting go of Rae's hand. 'I must get back to my work now, Ruth, if you'll forgive me.'

'Yes, yes, of course, sorry –'

'Shall I sit this thing in the library for now?'

'Oh – I suppose so. Yes, thanks.'

'Shame we can't trust th'electric,' said Bea, and she set off with the trolley.

Rae, suddenly weary, sat slowly down on the stairs in a

patch of sunshine, listening to the retreating squeak of the wheels, until Mrs Givens turned the corner and closed a door behind her, and the sound slowly faded.

If you were a certain sort of person, she thought, you would imagine all the poor scattered spirits here noting that restoration of silence, and arising once more from their hiding places. But only if you were that sort of person. I was, once. But I've got bigger things to be frightened of now.

Lettie

Lettie had recently had a postal delivery too; a small box, well-padded with torn newspaper, had arrived not at her lodgings, of course, but at the clinic, addressed to Mrs E. Bright.

Esme had been busy; while Philip Heyward had been dozing late one afternoon the previous week she had stealthily removed his key ring from the pocket of his trousers and pressed each key one by one on to several thick slices of soft green soap, taken from her bag where she had been keeping them ready for days: ever since Flo Withers. One key, both sides; then fold the impressed slice into her handkerchief, take out another slice, and start again. Four keys in all; four slices. The difficulty would be in sending the slices without damaging the imprints; she had laid a very thin sliver of plywood between each slice, wrapped the whole thing in kapok and a couple of well-chosen bank notes, and parcelled it off to a particular acquaintance of hers half expecting none of it to work; she had never tried long-distance burglary before.

The new keys looked perfectly good, of course, but that meant nothing. And if they worked – if any of them worked – she had no idea which key opened what. It was perfectly possible that what she had here were duplicates to Philip's box of cufflinks, or to his wife's greenhouse.

One of them might actually open the filing cabinet in his office though. She had a few names to try. A discrepancy, Nesbit, that's all I can hope for. An odd pattern, maybe. Rare things happening often. Though he was probably lying to himself as much as to anyone else; there would very likely be nothing for her to find.

But I'll have a go. And then I'll get shot of him . . . just you remember this, she told herself once or twice as she got herself ready to meet him again. Next time you're tempted. Remember this, and for Pete's sake lay off.

We don't call Dr Heyward. Always now Sister Nesbit was ready with her two-penn'orth. Several times daily she whispered in Lettie's mind.

But you're not going to tell me why not, are you, Nesbit? So it's up to me to find out.

Rae

For a day or so she kept *The Mechanics of Birth* unopened beside her bed. It was the title that was the problem, she told herself. Everyone knew machines went wrong, cameras and gantries and cars and steam engines, they broke down all the time, tiny bits inside them wore out and snapped or melted or blew up, they needed constant attention and oiling and fuss. They needed skill.

Finally curiosity outgrew fear.

'You a-looking at your book, then?' Bea coming in with the breakfast tray.

'It's fascinating!' said Rae happily. 'It's all so complicated – and so *odd*! You'd think – well, I thought – the baby just came out, you know, like – oh, I don't know, like icing out of a piping bag. But it doesn't, it's more like – more like putting on a jumper that's really too small for you – you know, one with a round crew neck, and it's far too small, so – how do you put it on? Go on, show me!'

Bea looked at her. 'What's this got to do with having a baby?'

'Lots, go on, think about it, Bea, how do you squeeze on a jumper that's far too small – I mean, get it over your head –'

'Ah. Now I see. So.' Bea bent her head. 'Like this.'

'Yes!' cried Rae, fairly bouncing in the bed. 'That's just what it says, the book, I mean! You pull it over the crown of your head at the back, you bend your neck, that's the easiest way, because that's the way your head is smallest. And that's what the baby has to do, isn't it amazing! And look – there's pictures!'

Bea sat down on the bed. 'What of?'

'Well, look!'

Bea seemed reluctant. Slowly, she reached for her spectacles in her apron pocket, put them on.

'What's that supposed to be, then?'

'It's – well, science pictures are always like that, I think,' said Rae, sitting up again and taking the book herself. 'It shows you what's happening inside – see, that's meant to be her backbone. It's as if she's been chopped in half.'

'What they want to do that for?'

'Well – so we can see what's happening inside.'

'Baby ain't though, is it?' said Bea indignantly. 'How come the woman's bin chopped in half, and not the baby?'

'Well – nobody really got chopped, you know, it's just a drawing. And I suppose we don't need to know what's going on inside the baby, do we? See, it's turning. I didn't know that either, you see. That the baby turns and turns as if it's going down a really tight little helter-skelter inside you! Or as if we've got corkscrews inside. I must say,' Rae added in a different tone, 'it does all seem rather more complicated than it needs to be. I mean – why *not* just squeeze it out, like the icing out of an icing bag? Why so . . . *baroque* – don't you think?'

Bea stood up, gave her back *The Mechanics of Birth*. 'I think you'd best eat your breakfast,' she said.

Norah

But she could hardly hand over the housekeeper's eviction notice and then enjoy light-hearted social interchange with the guest. All morning she tried various possibilities over in her head. Was there any way she could see Rae first? Hand over her little offerings, briefly bask in her loveliness, and *then* go off and carry out Mr Pender's fell deed?

No. Not that I can see, thought Norah, as the train pulled into the halt at Porthkerris that afternoon. It was unlikely that she would see Rae at all; she would have to trust the grapes (black ones, with a lovely soft bloom on them) and *Vogue* to Mrs Givens, who might well, under the circumstances, feel herself at liberty to add both to the compost.

Though I suppose it may not be as bad as all that, Norah thought. At Miss Pilbeam's request she had placed the advertisement for a couple to replace Mrs Givens herself, just before setting out. But it would be several days before the weeklies came out and then there would be all the applications to read through, and shortlists to make, and interviews, and references. The whole thing could take several weeks, even months. Plenty of time for Rae to – well . . .

And with any luck time enough for Mrs Givens too. It was odd, thought Norah, the way being a little sorry for

Mrs Givens didn't in any way cancel out being frightened of her as well. She turned in through the empty gates at Rosevear, and stopped for a moment, to gather her strength for the coming ordeal. The house looked back at her, and for the first time she saw how beautiful it was, the pale symmetry, the glint and sparkle of the water just behind and to one side. The haunted house of her childhood, suddenly revealed as calm and friendly. Or was that just because someone as lovely as Rae Grainger lived there, for now?

She sighed, and set off down the weedy gravel, turning right towards the kitchen entrance. Get it over with, she thought. Find out how long the poor old thing's got, after living here upwards of forty years.

'Mrs Givens?'

The side door stood open, but as before no one answered her knock. She went in, remembering last time, and the bold behaviour that had been so finely rewarded; trespassed into the passage, and went forward. Almost at once she heard the pleasant gossipy rise and fall of conversation coming from Mrs Givens' own little sitting room.

Who was Mrs Givens talking to? Surely that wasn't Rae? It could hardly be poor Minnie. Norah stood still, at a loss. Am I to interrupt some chatty private visit, she asked herself, and *then* hand over the five bob or whatever it is, and tell her she's homeless? Oh, how horrid, what shall I do?

She crept forward again, until she could actually make out what was being said.

'You see our mother with a book like that?'

Norah's heart gave a curious thump, as of fear, in her chest. She saw that though the sitting room's half-glazed door was closed, something had caught at the lace over the glass, and that there was a useful gap one might peep through. Holding her breath for silence, she bent and looked through the gap.

'I don't think so. Put me right off, I can tell you!'

Norah straightened up again, instantly; bent again for another look to make quite sure. There was Mrs Givens, alone in the room, leaning across the table. There was the little looking glass propped in front of her against the teapot.

It was as if, Norah thought later, her ears had noticed and understood something before the rest of her had; that she had trembled with fright peeping in through the lace because in a way she had already known that Mrs Givens, so equable-sounding, so reasonable, was talking only to herself.

Lettie

Opportunity arrived much sooner than she had thought it might. On the way back to her lodgings in the chill February dark she met them in the street, as she had that time before, with Norah: Dr Heyward and his wife, on their way, he said, when he had touched his hat, to the church hall, and the distinguished string quartet performing there that evening.

'D'you care at all for Beethoven, Sister Quick?' This from her, in the same opulent fur, but worn with a cashmere snood this time, in softest dove grey. Her tone could hardly have been more condescending.

'Not really,' said Lettie.

After saying a few more boring things about the weather they made off, and Lettie turned left instead of right and went straight to the surgery. With the key she fancied most for the part ready in her hand she rang the bell, in case Mrs Havers the receptionist was working late, but there was no answer, so she slid her favourite into the lock, and straight away it turned, and she was in.

But Heyward's own room was locked too, and for a full minute she had to stand there in the tiled hallway, every particle of her waiting for Pascoe to come bursting downstairs demanding to know exactly what she thought she was doing.

The third key turned the lock, and she slipped inside, and softly closed the door behind her.

Two keys left.

She dropped her bag by the door and went at once to the wooden filing cabinet beside the window. Three fat drawers. Start at the bottom. One key must fit them all, Lettie told herself. Or how else does he do it? Her hand was trembling, she noticed, as she tried the first key, too big to enter. The second slid home, and the lock turned.

Withers. At the back. There. Withers Stephen, Withers Agnes Elizabeth, Withers Florence Jane.

That one. She pulled the file open, and it was empty.

Well, of course, what do you expect? No point putting Flo Withers' notes back on file, not when she was dead. Forget Flo for now. She should go for the list, the folded square of paper in her pocket: a list of names taken from her own files at the clinic. The names of six women, scarred in ways they could not see for themselves, variously incontinent, troubled with recurrent fistulae, or unable to bear the pain of even the gentlest penetration. Birth injuries that were not so uncommon. Had they gone to Heyward, or to Pascoe? That was one question she could answer. And what would their notes say had happened to them?

Lettie knelt down, smoothed her list on the floor beside her, and began to look for the first name.

Norah

Perhaps she uttered some small sound. She didn't think so; but Mrs Givens turned to the door, and saw her there.

Then she was on her feet and making for the door, and Norah turned without thinking about it and began to walk as fast as she could back down the passage.

'Miss Thornby – please, Miss Thornby, stop!'

Mrs Givens had seldom addressed Norah directly before; and never in such an entreating tone. Norah slowed, stopped, turned round. She could feel herself blushing, as if it had been her caught out doing something crazy. She took another step backwards as Mrs Givens came towards her, and blundered into a coat hook.

'Please – you mustn't mind me, miss,' said Mrs Givens, a little breathlessly, in the same pleading tone as before. 'I don't mean nothing by it.'

There was a silence. 'But you were – you were having a conversation,' said Norah at last. 'With yourself.'

''Tis a private weakness, ma'am,' said Mrs Givens. 'You won't – tell her, will you?'

'Tell who? Oh – you mean Rae – do you?'

'Rae – yes, ma'am, I'd as soon she dint know, please, as I –' She tilted her head back at her room, at the mirror.

'– talk to yourself,' said Norah. 'So you – you do know you're doing it, then?' she asked. Was that reassuring?

Mrs Givens gave a shamed little nod. 'I do, ma'am. I'm

330

sorry if you was frighted, I know it must look . . . won't you come in, ma'am, and sit a while?'

'What, in there?' Ooh no!

''Tis my own sitting room, ma'am. This many a year,' said Mrs Givens. And how very old she looked! At Rosevear upwards of forty years, Norah remembered. 'Come in, ma'am, do. Please.'

It was a tiny room Norah had never entered before, for all the twice-yearly visits. A tiny room full of mirrors, she saw: not only the cheap rectangle propped against the teapot, but a large oval in a painted wooden frame on the chimney breast, and a full-length swivelling glass on a handsome mahogany stand in a corner.

'I ain't mad, ma'am, I don't think. Or, not very.'

'That's not what they say. You know, about talking to yourself,' said Norah briskly, and then all at once she remembered why she was there, and the miserable errand she must soon run.

'I know it, ma'am,' said Mrs Givens. 'But –' She turned, and looked behind her, and Norah, following her glance, saw the photographs there, and remembered the celebrated Mrs Dimond, the dead sister. The twin.

'Do you mean – are you pretending your reflection is your sister?'

'No, Miss Thornby,' said Mrs Givens, a little indignant. 'I ain't doing that. But you ask yourself – who else loses their only sister, and then gets to see her day in day out every time she looks in the mirror? Eh?' She sat down, took the cheap glass in her hands. 'Mostly, I sees myself. I see Bea Givens. But now and then –' she paused, thinking about it, eyeing the wan old face in the mirror – 'I look in, and I sort of see my sister a-looking back at me. And I thinks to her: What I done now, eh? Like, she's come back to tell me off, see. Or she fancies a bit of a chat. I says to her, Bored up there, are you? Got nothing better to do? But – I know it ain't really her, ma'am. It's a comfort to me, see, making out she's come back a while. Like a game we used to play, in the old days. 'Tis a weakness in me. I know that. Please – you won't tell 'er, will you, miss? It'd be such a worry to 'er.'

Norah sat down at the little table. I simply don't know what to do with all this, she thought. It hadn't sounded like a game or a comfort, she told herself; no, it had sounded like a real discussion.

She heaved a great sigh.

'Well, look – let's just forget the whole thing for now, shall we? I won't talk about it. And may I ask you to sit down, please, Mrs Givens? I'm afraid I have some rather bad news from Mr Pender. From Bagnold and Pender, I should say.'

Mrs Givens sat down too, picked up the mirror, laid it down on its face on the embroidered tablecloth. She seemed quite unconcerned now, perfectly at ease. She doesn't care what I think about her, thought Norah. Only what Rae thinks; fair enough, I suppose.

'Old Georgie Porgie Pender,' said Mrs Givens, shaking her head. The laughter lines crowding her eyes deepened as she met Norah's own startled gaze. 'Chucking me out, is he?' she asked.

Lettie

In half an hour she had four of them. All mid to high forceps. All straightforward in the notes. *Keillands applied with good effect*. Four living children. Lettie made some notes of her own on her list. Dolly Wainwright's name on three of them; but the earliest, Elsie Weston, dating from nearly eight years before, had first been attended by one Marion Nesbit.

Well, Nesbit, do you remember Elsie Weston? She's had a lot of trouble since. Back to theatre twice since then. And tell you one thing, she'd rather die than get pregnant again. She told me that herself. Says she's missed three times – she's doing something, see, or letting someone else do it. And she's telling her husband no. Telling him he's done her enough harm as it is.

Is that what you'd call *good effect*? Will you talk to me, Nesbit, if I ask you about Elsie Weston?

Time to go. Lettie stood up, put everything back into place, locked the drawers. Quick rifle through his desk? Why not. She sat in his big revolving chair, spun it round once, tried the top drawer. The third key unlocked it, but there was nothing interesting inside, just assorted stationery, leaflets from drug companies, and oh God, several timetables for liners cruising to hot nasty foreign parts. Ditto the drawer beneath, unlocked with the same key. The third drawer, the lowest one, was empty but for a sheaf of newspaper cuttings. She scooped them up, flicked through them. *The Body on the Beach. Tragic Aspects of the Case of the Body on the Beach.* One or two carried the same studio portrait, Wainwright smiling, gentle or daft, depending on how you felt about her.

As she went to put them back she saw that what she had thought was the bottom of the drawer was really a large manila envelope. She pulled it out. There was no writing on it. She undid the thread holding it closed, opened it, drew out the single photograph inside.

This time she did not even hear her own small exclamation: 'Christ alive!'

Norah

She knocked gently and opened the library door to a sudden burst of muted harmony, and saw several things at once: that the music was coming from a very smart new radio parked beside the window on a tea trolley; that there was already a rather dog-eared copy of that month's *Vogue*, twin to the glossy new version in her bag, lying face down on the library table with several darkened rings on its cover, where someone – well, Rae, thought Norah – had clearly set down a careless cup of tea; and that Rae herself, lying on her back on the sofa, a book still open in her hand, was fast asleep.

Wake up, thought Norah. Please.

I could cough, she thought, looking down at her. I could shift this little table a bit, make its feet squawk, that would do. Or rustle this paper bag. Undecided, she set the grapes down quietly on the low cushioned table where Rae would see them when she awoke, and straightened up.

It was a child's face, she thought. The same touching configuration. The same purity. Perhaps that was what made you want to look after her, shield her.

Why was she here all alone, with only Mrs Givens to look after her? Norah half knew all sorts of things about Mrs Givens, few of them to her credit. Was it true that as a girl she had once tried to throttle her own sister in the street, and later thrown a cabbage at her from a passing wagon?

When she was landlady of the old four-ale Red Lion had she really knocked a belligerent and insulting customer out cold across the bar with his own pewter tankard?

On the other hand, she had certainly run the orphanage here very smoothly for years; and there were persistent rumours that the last surviving Redwood daughter, Miss Daphne as was, now widowed, had travelled all the way down from her grand house in London one summer not long since, and gone out of her way to call in at Rosevear, not so much to see the place as to visit her own old maidservant Bea Givens; because it was she who had altered or perhaps even made the fine gown Miss Daphne had worn all those years before, the very first time she had met her husband.

Even Norah's Mamma had heard that one.

Mrs Givens being a little colourful was all very well, thought Norah. Even quite suitable under the circumstances, given darling Rae's own flamboyant temperament. But I heard her, I saw her, and she wasn't just talking to herself, whatever she says. She was being two people having a chat. Colourful was one thing: mad quite another.

Was Rae safe with her? The book, Norah saw, was a picture book, full of old prints of animals. The thought of Rae looking at it gave her a tight feeling in her chest, made her catch her breath. What was Lettie doing, entrusting such innocent fragility to a crazy old woman in a house in the middle of nowhere, with (as Norah well knew) a highly intermittent electricity supply and faulty drains?

I must talk to Lettie, thought Norah, and she gave up all idea of semi-accidental noises, and crept away as quietly as she could.

Lettie

Her first thought was fierce triumph: *Got him.*

Wherever I want him. Blackmail. Money. For the photograph was of Dolly Wainwright, splayed and naked, her eyes half closed, smiling languidly into the camera. Her back was curiously arched, her arms behind it.

Got him!

Can I take your picture, little girl?

For a puzzled instant Lettie felt the worn handle beneath both hands, the weight of the loaded pram as she tipped it, the better to amuse Ezra; her heart thumped and banged around in her chest as if it was terrified of something, and she realized she was going to be sick, even looked about her for something to be sick into. Then she understood, tipped herself out of the chair on to the carpet, and lay on her side for a while, smelling the dust, the carpet fibres coarse beneath her cheek. Slow breaths, she told herself, and presently was able to take them.

Fine sneak-thief you are, she told herself, as she propped herself up on one elbow. Fainting away red-handed. Rising in stages, she made it back on to the chair and found the photograph where she had dropped it, face down on the desk. This is a bad place for me, she thought again. Silkhampton: I should never have come here.

She turned the photograph over, and looked at it again. Was this what he had meant that day, when he had asked her to pose for him? On account of her perfection, her secret beauty. Was that what he had said to Dolly?

She remembered the nasty old letch of her youth, and his pornographic album; that had been bad enough, she thought, but seeing someone you actually knew in this stretched exposure really turned your stomach.

'Do try one of my cheese scones, Sister Quick!' Dolly Wainwright holding out a plate at Lettie's welcoming do, Dolly in her home-made skirt, in her worn shoes with the leather trim coming off one heel, with her knitting in a faded cotton bag printed with poodles. That had been the real Dolly. Not this dissection.

Carefully Lettie slid the photograph back into the envelope. Her hands still shook, but with something she recognized as strength, with a disgust strong enough to stop her feeling hungry or cold or tired or afraid, maybe for whole weeks at a time.

The envelope fitted nicely into her raincoat. From hidden compartment to hidden pocket, she thought, very neat. She wondered about the negative; she had an idea that these were very small, which meant that dozens of them could be fitted into almost anything, a cigar box, an old wallet; she had a last quick look round to see if anything looked likely. But he had obviously developed the photograph himself, so he must have a darkroom, probably at home. Safe enough there, presumably. Perhaps unlocked by the fourth key on the ring, the one she had not yet used.

Don't any of you dare go into my darkroom! Children, Daddy's darkroom is absolutely forbidden!

Last look round, Lettie told herself. Everything just as

it was? Filing cabinet, desk, chair had been facing more to the left, perhaps . . . yes, like that. Quietly she opened the office door. Dr Pascoe belting down the stairs?

No. No one. The hall in dim silence. Now the only major risk, the front door; overlooked on two sides, anyone might be passing by, and idly note the new nurse, Miss Whatshername, letting herself out of the surgery door well after hours. On the other hand, what was so odd about that anyway? Carefully careless, Lettie pulled the door to behind her, walked lightly down the steps, down the garden path, and through the gate on to the deserted pavement. She started out for home without hurrying, the photograph weightless in the hidden pocket. She could just feel the envelope's edge against her side, as once she had felt the framed picture she had stolen from the cinema.

Freddie Pyncheon, Philip Heyward, local photographers of note.

As a fishing trip, she thought, her expedition could hardly have been more successful; she had hoped for a few sprats or a nice little mackerel, and instead caught something huge and monstrous, with rows of pointed teeth, and for a second almost felt inclined to laugh.

She sobered as she neared her front door. Bringing the monster home. It might turn out to be deadly, she thought. To all concerned. She would certainly need to find it a very good hiding place. It felt so powerfully present in her pocket. A muscular trouble, its teeth so very sharp.

Norah

She gave Lettie fifteen minutes, timed on her wristwatch, and then knocked on the door. 'Lettie – may I have a word with you, please?'

A sound came from within, which Norah took as an invitation, so she turned the handle and went inside, to a strange flurry of bed sheets, Lettie leaning sideways across the bed looking very tense, or even alarmed, thought Norah.

'Is everything alright?'

Lettie slid off the bed, drawing the tumbled sheet up as she did so, smoothing the coverlet into place. 'Fine. You made me jump, that's all.'

'Sorry – I thought you said "come in". I need to talk to you.' How pale Lettie was, she thought, even more so than usual. 'I left some supper for you in the kitchen,' she said, 'but would you like me to make you up a tray?' It was strange to find herself saying those last few words again: Mamma had so loved a cosy supper in her room. This room.

'Oh no, I'm alright,' Lettie said, quite sharply. 'We'll go down, shall we?' Perhaps she had had a difficult day at work, thought Norah. But, of course, I simply cannot let this slide.

'Tea?' she asked, in the kitchen.

'Yeah, alright,' said Lettie. 'Could do with a cuppa,' and

really it was simply impossible, Norah saw, to sense her mood. It was quite a feat, she thought. When she was a girl Mamma had often told her of the absolute imperative of hiding one's everyday moods and petty annoyances; it was what marked one out, she said, from the lower orders, whose coarse outbursts so clearly demonstrated the substandard.

Character lay in concealment, said Mrs Thornby, which had certainly been discouraging for someone as liable to hectic blushing as Norah. Though oddly enough no one in the entire household, Norah remembered, had ever had any trouble divining Mamma's own mood, which had always been as pervasive and changeable as the weather.

How lastingly strange it was that someone whose ways were so entirely familiar could simply disappear! Norah cleared her throat. 'I went to Rosevear House today,' she said aloud.

'Oh yes? Why?'

'Business. Bagnold and Pender – the firm I work for – have given Mrs Givens notice. She's got two months.'

Lettie shrugged.

'No,' said Norah, 'it doesn't matter to – well, there's something I want to talk to you about. Two things, actually. The first is that I took, ah, Miss Grainger – a copy of *Vogue.*' She scalded the teapot.

'Oh yeah?'

'But she already had a copy. So I took it home. I had a look at it on the train. I couldn't take it back, you see. Here it is.'

She took the magazine from the shelf where she had left it earlier, open at the right page. 'I saw this.' She set

Vogue in front of Lettie, spread out like a place setting, and left her to it while she made the tea. Teacups, milk, sugar.

'So?' said Lettie.

'Well – you do see. Don't you?'

It was the picture that had caught Norah's eye first, the gloriously handsome Rod Lacey, Rae's own husband, a smiling Sir Gawaine in a dinner jacket, holding up a little triangular glass. Poor thing, she had thought at once, how worried he must be, really, when his wife is in such delicate health, and so far away.

Then she realized that she must have mistaken Rae's meaning, when they had talked; for the text beneath the picture said that Rod had been attending a party in Mayfair, in London, and barely a fortnight before. Yet Rae had surely implied that Mr Lacey had been offered such a splendid new role in Hollywood that she had persuaded him to go back to America for the sake of his career. So that sadly he had been forced to leave her all alone in the delightful Cornish hideaway where they had planned to enjoy a long break together from the cares of stardom whilst awaiting a certain happy event – this from the article for that ethereal edition of the *Film Lover's Weekly* that Norah was constantly rewriting in her head.

But then she had read the interview on the next page of *Vogue*, and her heart had stood still. The ethereal article had abruptly shut up too. It seemed that the legal proceedings against Rod Lacey, instigated the year before by his wife, the well-known actress and screenwriter Rae Grainger, were at last reaching their conclusion in a procurement of decree *nisi*. He wished his soon-to-be ex-wife well, said Mr Lacey. No, indeed, he certainly did not have further marriage plans, he was happy to be single, foot-loose and fancy-free!

'It's an illegitimate baby, isn't it,' Norah said quietly. All the major teachings of her life informed her that because of this Rae was defiled, a woman without honour. This was not a mere question of manners, like Mamma's strictures on self-control. This was the basis of all morality. A child was legitimate, or it was a dreadful and enduring stain. Norah had shed some painful tears for Rae, on the train, understanding that never again could she be considered straight and clean.

'Got any more sugar?' said Lettie.

'What? Oh. Sorry.' She found the squashed little bag in the larder, refilled the basin. 'That's why she's in hiding, isn't it,' Norah said. 'All on her own.'

'That's about it,' said Lettie, spooning in sugar. She closed *Vogue*. 'Mind if I borrow this?'

'It was quite a shock,' said Norah angrily, for it had stung her further to realize that Lettie must always have been in on the disgusting secret. 'I suppose she's having it adopted.'

'You suppose wrong then,' said Lettie. 'Why shouldn't she keep her own baby? Just 'cause her old man's a git.'

'But – it's not Rod Lacey's child, is it?'

'I dunno. I didn't ask. None a my business. None of yours either. I thought you liked her.'

'Don't be absurd, Lettie! It's not a question of *liking*! One simply cannot – condone – this sort of behaviour.'

'Who asked you to?' said Lettie, sounding bored.

Norah was near to tears; she felt that Lettie was being obtuse on purpose. 'But it's disgusting – a bastard child!'

Lettie gave her a look and got to her feet, *Vogue* tucked under one arm. She picked up her cup and saucer, and said lightly: 'You want to ask yourself, who makes the rules. Are you a bastard, Norah?'

Norah could hardly speak. 'What!'

'Your doing, was it, your mum and dad got married, your choice?'

'No, of course not, but –'

'Mine weren't,' said Lettie from the door. 'Married, I mean. My mum was seventeen when my dad got her pregnant. He was thirty-two. Who was dishonoured?'

'It's different for women.'

'Only if we all *say* it is. It's all made up, see? That stuff. You only think it's real because it's been around longer than you have. It's still junk.'

'This is what *she* says, isn't it, your precious Dr Stopes! That's what your *horrid* job is all about, helping people behave badly, letting them get away with immorality!'

Lettie shook her head. 'Night, Norah!'

'I haven't finished!'

'You have, doll,' said Lettie, and shut the door.

Lettie

She put the tea down on the bedside table and instantly forgot about it. But there was a key in the lock, one she had never bothered with before. She turned it, and then drew back the bedclothes, to reveal again the incalculable weapon she had brought home with her from Heyward's office.

Now she had got used to it enough to carry on looking at it for more than a few seconds there were things about it that were puzzling. Not just disgusting: odd. Dolly's daft or gentle smile was in this case loose, haphazard. Perhaps she had been drunk: that would make sense. Have a little of this, my dear, to help you relax. I'd have had to be flaming plastered, thought Lettie, to agree to a pose like that. Were her arms actually tied behind her back? And what exactly was it she was bent backwards over, was it – could it be – the low waiting-room table, usually stacked with old copies of *Punch* and *Time and Tide*? Had Philip tipped them all off and carried it upstairs, to make secret pornographic use of it? He'd like that the next day, Lettie thought. He'd so enjoy setting out the magazines again.

Enough. She put the picture into its envelope, and stood for a moment tapping her front teeth. The small armchair beside the fireplace was covered in dark-blue velvety stuff, the piping worn with age, not upholstered but fitted, tied on down one side with cleverly hidden tapes. After a certain amount of patient unpicking Lettie pulled two ties free, undid them, slipped the envelope inside, did them up tight again, and poked them back out of sight. Not exactly professional; but it would do for now, she thought.

There was a knock on the door. Norah again, though rather more subdued than last time, by the sound of it. Lettie made no answer. Presently Norah knocked again, and spoke softly through the door:

'Lettie? Um – there really is something else I meant to say, I just forgot about it.'

'Tell me tomorrow,' Lettie called.

'Please, Lettie. I'm sorry. I've been thinking about what you said.'

'What, about me being a bastard?'

'Ah, no. Not about that, actually. Something you said the other day. About – sovereignty.'

Lettie unlocked the door, opened it, and stood leaning against the jamb.

'What about it?'

Norah, she saw at once, had been crying. Her voice still trembled a little: 'I was thinking that I've never tried to have sovereignty myself. In my own life. Except once during the War, when my parents wouldn't let me do nursing, and I – well, I ran away! I jumped on to the London train with my brother. He helped me, he leant out of the carriage and took my hand, and I jumped in.'

'A man,' said Lettie, 'giving you sovereignty.'

'Yes!' said Norah, smiling. 'That's what I thought. But then, he was my brother.'

Lettie stood aside. 'Come on in.'

'I'm sorry, I know it's rather late.'

'Doesn't matter. Want a drink?'

'I could make some more tea,' said Norah, touching the cold full cup on the bedside table.

'Nah. I mean a real drink. Here.' Lettie opened the corner cupboard and took out a cut-glass decanter and two small glasses. Have a little of this, my dear, to help you relax, murmured Philip Heyward in her head.

Norah sat down in the blue velvet chair. 'Is that the decanter from downstairs?' she said.

'Yup.'

'From the drawing-room sideboard?'

'You weren't drinking it.'

'True. So you helped yourself. Is that – sovereignty?'

Lettie shook her head. 'Theft,' she said, taking the other chair. They clinked glasses, and sipped.

'So?'

'I decided I'd been harsh,' said Norah. 'Narrow-minded. I know so little of these things. About as much as your Dr Stopes did. Because I am that most ridiculous thing, a middle-aged virgin. No one's ever – tried to dishonour *me*. Unless I count the builder – he was doing some work on the house when I was twelve, and he kept grabbing me, and kissing me. I didn't know what to do. He didn't hurt me. But it was horrible. He was a big man, about fifty. Just a little kiss, he kept saying. And I would freeze all over with a sort of horror, and let him kiss me, right on my lips! I never even tried to stop him.'

'You were just a kid.'

'But it was so like me, d'you see, to put up with him, pretend I didn't mind. And then – when I met Rae – you know, that day the car had broken down, and I walked all the way back to Rosevear – I volunteered, pretending I didn't mind again. I thought then – it's what women do. It's not just that we let men order us about, and refuse us sovereignty. We connive with them. We call it sparing their feelings, or keeping the peace, or being a good sport.'

Lettie picked up the decanter and splashed a little more whisky into Norah's glass, glancing as she did so at the bottom seam of the blue-covered chair, making sure it was holding. It was actually quite hard to concentrate on anything else, she thought. The photograph seemed to be in on the conversation, as if there had been a faint throb of recognition at Norah's words, as if that splayed and straining image had nodded its carefully lit head, and murmured: I connived with him. I spared his feelings, I kept the peace. I was such a good sport.

'It was so wonderful for me, meeting Rae,' Norah was saying. 'I mean, a real film star – I could hardly think straight! But I can now. And what I think is: that Rae is actually doing something rather splendid. She's trying – despite everything – to hold on to her sovereignty. I was being all Mrs Grundy, but she's *greater* than that.'

'Not sure I follow,' said Lettie.

'I think you do. She's keeping her baby, you said. That's what her sovereignty is. For now. As soon as I thought that, I realized: she's *hiding* at Rosevear, isn't she – it's so no one knows she's pregnant. She's going to pretend she isn't having a baby at all. I don't understand how that helps her keep it, but you're part of that. Aren't you?'

Lettie was at a loss, for once unable to come out with

anything cutting or useful, while in her head the photograph murmured further: What am *I* part of?

As she hesitated, Norah leant forward: 'I may not know much, Lettie, but I know that's illegal.'

Lettie poured herself a top-up, trying to give herself time. 'It's illegal to conceal a birth,' she said at last, 'because the law thinks you only do it 'cause you've killed your baby. Girls used to swing for it. Presumed guilty.' God, I sound tight, she thought.

'Does Mrs Givens know?'

The sudden change of tack threw her completely. 'Who?' Lettie said.

'The housekeeper. Mrs Givens. Because you can't trust her. I'm sorry, but she's crazy – that was what I wanted to tell you. I caught her talking to herself in a looking glass. Today. Honestly – she didn't know I was there, she was chatting to her own reflection. And did you know the electricity fails all the time at Rosevear? It's going to be Rae in labour, and you in the dark, alone with a mad old woman. Unless.'

'Unless what?'

'Unless I come too,' said Norah. 'When – you know, when the baby's coming. I've done some nursing, I'm not completely useless. And I know where the generator is. I can get it going, too. I mean, I've shown Mrs Givens over and over again, but she doesn't like it, she won't do it, any more than she answers the telephone. Rae seems to adore her, of course, well – she has such an affectionate nature. But. Do you really want to have to rely on Mrs Givens, in the middle of nowhere?'

'Suppose I say no. To you coming. What then?'

'Well then, I don't come,' said Norah stiffly. 'I'd like to help, that's all.'

'I'll ask her. Rae, I mean.'

'Oh, but please don't tell her about Mrs Givens,' said Norah at once, 'it would upset her so, and – she begged me not to. Mrs Givens, I mean. Just tell her about – you know, the generator. But if Rae says yes, Lettie, what will you say? May I come?'

Very briefly Lettie allowed herself to remember Flo Withers, and her own choking panic. And then looked further back, to the day she had lost herself at the thought of seeing Frederick Pyncheon, when Norah's kindly voice had brought her back again.

Don't forget *me*, murmured the photograph.

The truth surprised her, but she voiced it: 'Straight up, I'd rather you did.'

Norah breathed out, blushed. 'Oh,' she said, 'good. Well now. Heavens, how late it is! I must be off.' She got up. 'Thank you, this has been so nice.'

Lettie gave a snort of laughter.

Norah smiled too. 'I suppose that did sound rather odd, considering.'

'If we get caught,' said Lettie, standing up too, 'you'll be an accessory. To a criminal conspiracy. They will charge you. You do understand that, don't you?'

'Better not get caught then,' said Norah. 'Oh, apropos – there is one more thing.' She turned in the doorway. 'There's someone else who knows, I think.'

'Who?'

'Well, I'm not certain. Shall we talk about it tomorrow? He's only a boy.'

'What boy?'

'Mrs Givens' grandson. He delivers the bread. He's a very nice child. He's called Barty,' said Norah.

Barty

He swung down the alley to the back of the bakery, stopped dead in a spurt of cinders, and automatically checked his watch. Exactly five to eight; a new Back record. But he felt no triumph at all, and realizing this suddenly made him feel like crying.

He held out against tears, of course, and after a few moments leant the bicycle against the shed wall with all his usual care, took off his bicycle clips, and went to wash his hands in the scullery. Though he went into a sort of dream standing there in front of the sink, the cold water gushing over his wrists.

Years, it felt like. He had adored her for ages and ages. And now!

Now, what?

He didn't know. He knew that he was full of unidentifiable feelings that kept surging around inside him so weightily that he felt he could hardly stand up straight. He knew that something sweet had vanished, gone for good. All that hope and longing had gone too. And after all he had seen so little of her, never had much to go on. It had been enough somehow. He had made it enough.

Several times she had been in the library, bashing away at her typewriter, not ten feet away across the flower bed, but she'd only happened to look up and see him once. She had smiled at him, and waved, and he had felt almost faint with glory, had wheeled the bicycle round the corner and actually had to sit down for a second or two on the damp grass before he could carry on into the house with the bread.

She had never again been in the kitchen though, as she had that first time, when she had looked at him, spoken to him. When like a fool he had made her no reply at all! He'd made hundreds in his head ever since.

He had told her that he had known her straight away, because he had seen her at the Picture Palace, in an old film called *Tell Her Now*. That he didn't mind it being silent, not a bit. That she had been the best thing in it, that he'd remembered her even though he'd seen it ages, months, before she had blown him the kiss that morning in the square – yes, that had been him all along! Did she realize, did she remember?

Oh, because he would remember that moment always, he told her sometimes, in Ivor Novello's voice, though at other times he was Clark Gable. Why, oh why, was she hiding here, at Rosevear, all alone? No – she must not tell him! Her secret was safe with him, he promised her several times in various ways, but usually with a cloak to swirl about him as he strode away into the distance on some manly task he never bothered to go into in any detail: the promise was the main thing, and the way she looked up at him, dewy with gratitude.

Often as he rode his bike as fast as he could up the long hill from Silkhampton Barty had found himself rescuing her from many types of danger. The lake was a constant threat, of course. She fell into it over and over again, and he boated out to her, or waded manfully, or he threw her an inflatable ring (this last a dismally unsatisfactory fantasy, one he tried to shut out whenever he sensed it approaching, but he was a truthful child, and even in imagination knew he could not swim a stroke). She was set upon by dogs, and he wrestled them to the ground. The house began to fall down, and he raced in and carried her unconscious form from the ruins; it caught fire, and he took her in his arms and bore her to safety, despite his own agonizing burns.

Or he did sums in his head working out how long she would have to wait for him. Eighteen would surely be old enough, wouldn't it? Then she would be thirty, which sounded pretty old, but that would mean nothing to him. He would join the RAF and learn to fly and when he had his own Siddeley Jaguar biplane he would land it on the grounds behind the lake, and swing himself out over the wing, the engine still running, and help her in, and then they would fly off together right up into the blue.

It was a great deal to base on so little: the unforgettable kiss blown in the square, the brief one-sided conversation in the kitchen, a wave and a smile through the library window. On one other morning he had seen her walking in the garden at the side of the house, a distant figure with her back to him but unmistakable, of course, in a blue dress that had fluttered behind her in the breeze.

This morning, though, it had seemed at first that some of his prayers had been answered. He'd left early, pedalled hard all the way up the hill, shot along the lanes and hurtled through the Rosevear gateway no more than twenty-two minutes and thirteen seconds later, very close to his There record, and as he trundled more slowly down the weedy gravel of the drive he had seen her straight away in the library wearing the same soft blue dress, not at the table, though, but moving about a little strangely. Then he came close enough to hear the music through the open window, and saw that she was dancing to it.

All by herself in that lovely room full of books, his favourite room, Rae Grainger, the tragic heroine of *Tell Her Now* and *Aren't We Sisters?*, was dancing with her eyes closed, swaying in time to the music, which was something slow, warm, jazzy. He had stopped dead in his tracks, his two hands on the handlebars, watching her, unconsciously holding his breath as she raised her arms and turned, smiling to herself, and then he saw.

Because he had dared to look at her body. He saw: that she was vast. As if she had a cushion stuffed up her frock. Three cushions. She looked like the Michelin Man. She was going to have a baby.

That was when the emotion or emotions took him over. They filled his insides completely and churned around in there so violently that he felt sick. It had been quite hard to say 'Morning' to his Nanna, impossible to eat the toast she had made him. Two sips of tea and he was off, he couldn't wait to fling himself back on to the bicycle and get away, and ride and ride, and now he had broken his Back record and he didn't even care.

It was a sort of revulsion. A hard round lump sticking out in front, like a great boil! She looked as if she might burst at any minute. A lump all tightly full of baby, disgusting! Was that what all women looked like then?

And the great lump of baby had to get out somehow. Tear its way out. Of course, sometimes the woman died. The wonder was that any of them lived at all.

The only clear thought Barty could dredge up from the churning inside him was the fact that he would know his own birth had killed his mother for the rest of his life. He had always understood before that he would somehow grow out of it mattering. Now he knew that he would not.

He hardly knew anything else though. His love was ashes in his heart. But still they burned.

Lettie

Nesbit seemed to be avoiding her. When Lettie knocked on the door of her little terraced house no one came to the door, and twice Nesbit had abruptly crossed the road and disappeared round a corner when sighted in the street. But she would have to turn up to the monthly Friday afternoon meeting at the hospital; I'll get her then, thought Lettie. In the meantime she had remembered something.

'Norah – who's your doctor?'

Norah was chopping onions, and instantly stilled the knife. 'Why – are you not well?'

'I'm fine. But if I weren't – who would you call?'

Norah went back to the chopping board. 'We used to go to this awfully nice chap in London, a cousin of Mamma's actually. But he retired some time ago and anyway – well, I suppose I'd go to Dr Pascoe. Why?'

'Not Dr Heyward?'

'Um – well, he'd be alright, I suppose.'

'You said you didn't like him.'

'Did I? When?'

'On the way to the pictures that time. We met him, with his wife. She had this hat on –'

'Oh yes – that wonderful hat! I wonder where she got it. Nowhere local, of course, you could never –'

'Why don't you? Like him, I mean. Dr Heyward.'

Norah rinsed the knife under the cold tap, and started

on the carrots. 'Well. It's hardly fair of me. But years ago he looked after someone I used to know, someone I'd been at school with, and she died. Grace Gilder. She was – a friend. Well. That's what I like to think she would have been, if she'd lived.'

'What was wrong with her?'

'She died in childbirth, poor thing. Oh, the baby was – it's Barty – the baker's son – remember?'

'The one who was at the Picture Palace?'

'Yes, and goes to Rosevear, Mrs Givens' grandson. Dr Heyward saved him. But he couldn't save Grace.'

'You – think he did something wrong?'

'No – no, of course not. It's just that – well, I tend to think of her whenever I see him. And I don't care for his manner, I suppose. There's something about him I just don't like. Dr Fell, you know. The reason why I cannot tell. D'you like parsnips?'

A pattern, Lettie thought. Or rare things not happening rarely. Had Grace Gilder been the very first bit of a pattern of clumsy mismanagement? Had she died of something rare that was somehow happening often?

At the monthly meeting Lettie moved in smartly, literally cornered Nesbit beforehand.

'I want to talk to you. About Dolly Wainwright,' she said.

'Dolly's dead,' said Nesbit, her normal cool expression unchanged. 'And you're not fit to utter her name. You slut.'

Altogether quite an impressive performance, Lettie thought. She matched it: 'Talk to me,' she said, her own tone as relaxed as Nesbit's, 'or I give this to the police. Your choice, ducky.' Briefly she held open her handbag, tilted so that Nesbit could see the vile photograph inside.

'Afterwards, then?' said Lettie, in the tone of one making cosy social arrangements. 'How about the place in the square – the George and Dragon. I hear they've got a nice little saloon. For ladies.'

Nesbit nodded. Looked sick; but nodded.

There followed the usual dull hour of jawing and hair-splitting, and after it Lettie leant across the table, caught Nesbit's eye, and gaily held up the bag. See you, she mouthed.

Lettie had never been in the George and Dragon before. She was shown into the Ladies' Snug, a small dark cheerless room at the back of the hotel, the least snug Snug Lettie had ever seen, she thought, and of course as it was the Ladies' bar there was no one actually serving behind it.

Still, she was in no hurry. And – hardly a surprise – there were no other customers. Presently someone red-faced and dishevelled peered over the counter, and she ordered two lemonades, though these still had not arrived when Nesbit came in five minutes afterwards. She sat down.

'Well?'

'I just want to talk to you.'

Nesbit looked at her. 'That photograph.'

'Nasty,' said Lettie companionably.

'Did he give it to you?'

Lettie considered this. It was hard to imagine a situation in which one's lover lightly handed over dirty snaps of an earlier mistress; but Nesbit seemed to have come up with one. Tease her by letting her go on thinking this? Or cut her some slack?

Just then the bar door swung open, and the dishevelled barman came back in, wiped the table in front of them with a dirty cloth, unloaded two glasses, and shuffled out again.

'Cheers,' said Lettie. The lemonade was room temperature, and flat. She put the glass down again. 'He didn't give it to me, the photograph. I broke into his office. Stole it.'

'What? Why?'

'I've gone off him.'

'I see,' said Nesbit. She turned, took up her bag. 'D'you mind if I smoke?'

'Go ahead.'

Nesbit took out a tin, and a little rolling device. Lettie watched her small neat fingers, fitting in the paper, pulling free the tobacco strands.

'I have one?'

She waited until Nesbit had rolled another before taking up the first cigarette and putting it to her lips. Nesbit flicked her lighter, held it to Lettie's, lit her own. For a minute they breathed in and out in silence.

'No ashtray,' said Lettie.

'Well, it is the Ladies' Snug,' said Nesbit. She took an empty matchbox out of the pocket of her coat, put it on the table. 'Help yourself.'

'You saw, didn't you,' said Lettie, 'that we were an item, that night. Him and me. All over now,' she added.

'None of my business.'

'Isn't it? Why were you so angry then?'

Nesbit shrugged.

Lettie began again: 'You heard of someone called Grace Gilder?'

Definitely, from the sudden startled glance. 'Why do you ask?'

'Tell me about her.'

Nesbit carefully rolled ash against the edge of the matchbox. 'Before my time. It's all hearsay.'

'What is? Come on, Nesbit, I'm on your side.'

'Hardly,' said Nesbit coldly. 'Well. If I must: a month or so after I started here Joe Gilder came to see me.'

'That's the husband?'

'Yes. The baker, on the square. He said, he'd just heard someone else had died, in childbirth, same as Grace. She was the second since, so that was three of them, he said, in barely a year. Did I think that was normal. And I said yes,' said Nesbit, blowing out a great stream of smoke through her nostrils like a dragon, 'I said yes it was.'

'Was it Heyward attending?'

Nesbit nodded. 'Yes, but it was a retained placenta, the third death – an accreta. He took her straight to theatre, Heyward I mean, but he couldn't save her.'

'Rare, that is. Accreta,' said Lettie, stubbing out her own cigarette half smoked. Too strong.

'Yes. Give me that, I'll reuse it. Anyway I told him – Mr Gilder – I told him it had just been bad luck. A run of bad luck. Very sad and everything, but no one's fault.'

'But all the same . . . ?'

'I asked Dolly, and she said Dr Heyward was the bee's knees. He'd only just taken over from some awful old duffer and he was really getting things done, new wing at the

361

hospital, antenatal care, better surgery hours – he was a real breath of fresh air, Dolly said.'

'She was in love with him.'

Nesbit made a scornful noise. 'If you say so.'

'What do you think?'

'I think Dolly had poor judgement.'

'Was she having an affair with him then, though – that early?'

'I really can't say,' said Nesbit. 'The connection ended years ago. Before his marriage. She told me that much. I didn't ask questions.'

There was a pause. 'Elsie Weston,' said Lettie. 'You looked after her in 1924, first baby, obstructed labour. You called him. Remember?'

Nesbit picked up her glass, took a sip. 'Yes. She tore very badly, a full third degree. I'd never seen one before.'

Interesting, thought Lettie; for she was sure that Dr Heyward's notes had made no mention of any tear at all, let alone a severe one.

'He seemed so unsurprised,' said Nesbit, setting the glass down, pushing it away. 'Not a bit cast down. About the tear – that was the main thing. For me, I mean.'

'Is that when you stopped calling him? He gets a lot of haemorrhages too, doesn't he.'

'He seems unlucky that way.'

'Dr Pascoe's better, then?'

'He was largely trained by Dr Heyward. His methods are similar. But yes. He is. Much better.'

'What did Dolly say? About Heyward, I mean?'

'We disagreed.'

'She wouldn't back you up.'

'No. I think she called him less; but that was as far as she would go. I tried talking to him myself once, a private word. About five years ago. Worked up to it for weeks – I knew he'd be upset – but I thought he'd get over it, see I was doing my best for the patients. That's what I told myself anyway. Like a fool.'

'What happened?'

'He practically threw me out of the office. Did I think he was going to sit there taking insulting drivel from some ignorant interfering bitter old maid. He reported me to the Board. Not for what I'd said to him: about a case – I'd called him to a twin labour, and the second twin died, he said I'd failed to diagnose a malpresentation and hadn't called him soon enough. None of it was true. But there was an enquiry, his word against mine. I was formally reprimanded.'

'Why didn't you leave? Go somewhere else?'

'With that on my record?'

'Alright, then, the inquest. You had him over a barrel then. Illicit relations. And Dolly was dead. Why didn't you shop him?'

'He came to see me,' said Nesbit, dropping her cigarette end on the wooden floor and crushing it underfoot. 'He said that if I named him at the inquest he would lose everything. That the affair had been over for years, that he knew nothing of Dolly's recent troubles. He begged me not to ruin his marriage, his career.'

'I'd've told him to get lost,' said Lettie.

'Oh, I did,' said Nesbit, with a slight smile. 'But then he showed me a photograph.'

'God! What, this one?'

'No. One like that. He had several. He said that if he had nothing to lose, why wouldn't he do what he liked with them. Send them to the press. Her mother's alive, you know. Dolly's mother. And he said, he'd make sure everyone knew that I liked such photographs myself. That I lived with Dolly and liked looking at the pictures, because I am unnatural. Sexually inverted,' added Nesbit, in her usual cool voice.

'Oh!' said Lettie in surprise. And are you? she almost asked. It certainly made sense, she thought. Then was silent for a minute or so. He was so much worse than she had imagined; not just cack-handed, but aware, determined, shameless. He was unfathomable. She remembered the lovely swagger of his overcoat, herself all a-flutter at it, and sighed.

'Of course the suicide makes more sense to me now,' said Nesbit.

'How d'you mean?'

'He'd begun a new affair, with you. Perhaps Dolly found out. Perhaps he told her.'

'Why don't you just report him, you know, to the GMC or something?'

For the first time Nesbit's voice had an edge of anger: 'Just report him – how easy do you think that is? He goes to half a dozen little cottage hospitals and private places and they all think he's wonderful, so big and bold and handsome – people like that, women like it, *you* liked it. His private patients do the worst of all, I think. The richer ones. They get his whole attention. And the injuries – dozens of them – like Elsie Weston – he just cobbles everything together, as if it's *normal*. God knows what it's like afterwards – of course *I* don't know, there aren't any figures, and no one is asking. How could I ever find out who is wetting or soiling herself day and night because that swine thinks a third-degree tear doesn't matter? They go back to him, for the next baby, because they don't know either, they think it's normal. And he doesn't know how awful he is. He gets in there with his forceps and he does his best. His best! He has no idea it's not good enough. He thinks it's normal, and that's the worst thing – the worst thing of all, I think – he's *used* to it.'

There was a long silence. They could hear sounds now from the growing crowd in the public bar, clearly a far more convivial place, voices raised in cheery argument, someone starting to tinker on the piano.

'You been keeping a list,' Lettie said at last. 'Haven't you – things you can prove?'

She turned, saw Nesbit's quick nod.

'Add Flo Withers to it. I'll back you up.'

'And . . . the picture? What are you going to do with it?'

Lettie shrugged. 'Use it,' she said.

Norah

He was working that very evening at the Picture Palace, she knew; all she had to do was take a slightly different route home from work and call in.

'Barty? Hello there!'

He was just leaving, as luck would have it. 'Been giving the place the once-over?' she asked.

He nodded. At once she had a distinct impression of tension, of a heavy unhappiness. Norah was used to ignoring her own senses, however, and told herself she was imagining things.

'You know I work for Bagnold and Pender, so I was at Rosevear the other day,' she went on brightly, as Barty laboriously drew the chain through the gate and locked the padlock. She waited, then began to walk home with him, back towards the square. 'Saw Mrs Givens, looking very well!'

He never had been what you might call a chatty child, she told herself. Then saw how pale he was. 'Are you – alright, Barty?'

'Yes, miss,' he said, looking down, his voice completely flat.

Still, Norah told herself, she was here for a purpose, and must not be diverted.

'I expect you know that your grandmother has a rather special guest, at Rosevear. At the moment. Do you?'

'Yes, miss.'

'And – have you met the guest? Ah, Mrs Wickham?'

He shot her a quick keen glance; she had been right, she thought: he knew exactly who Rae was. But 'Yes, miss,' was all he said, and in the same flat tone as before.

Norah was pleased, with herself, and with him. So far so good, she thought.

'I myself have met Mrs Wickham, Barty. Several times. We are on – quite friendly terms.' He said nothing again, so she went on: 'She asked me to give you a message.'

She saw him blush, and felt for him. 'She asked me to tell you how much she likes getting your father's lovely bread. How it makes the best-ever toast. And that she thinks it's simply marvellous of you to cycle all that way to see your grandmother. Heroic, that was what she said – she hadn't quite grasped how far it is, you see. Heroic, Barty!'

'Yes, miss.' As if that was all he was prepared to say.

'She said your grandmother has been kindness itself to her.'

She paused again, as they waited to cross the road, but he made no reply.

'And she wondered – ah, Mrs Wickham wondered – if she could ask a special kindness of *you*. She doesn't think you've told anyone about her being there – is that so?'

'Yes, miss.'

Norah went on: 'So she asks you – please, as a favour – to go on not saying anything. To anyone.' Norah thought for a moment, then added, 'Well, Barty – do you agree not to tell anyone about Mrs Wickham? Will you do her that kind favour?'

There was a pause. She glanced down at him, saw that he was smiling to himself. He flashed a sly little glance at her, then looked down again. Oh, how like Grace he was!

'Yes, miss,' he said.

Rae

She was wearing the wrong clothes for this sort of thing. No one had told her about the mule-train; as if they'd all expected her to guess. It would have been easier too if she'd been riding side-saddle, but as it was her skirt was far too tight, and kept sliding up and nearly showing the tops of her stockings, and she had to keep hauling it down again, which meant letting go of her hat. I simply can't see where I'm going, she complained more than once, as the fedora tipped over her eyes again, but no one took any notice, and all the while the mule was rocking and bumping her down the steep rocky path, its hooves slipping occasionally and jolting her even more as it tried to catch up with all the other mules. They were far ahead though, out of sight.

The mule kept going faster and faster, stumbling round the hairpin bends inches from the edge of the path and the rocks a thousand feet below. Rae pulled on the reins but they soon came away in her hands, and then she realized that there was no proper saddle either, nothing to hold on to at all, she could only grip the mule with her legs, and the fierce effort quickly gave her a sharp tearing pain that spread all across her stomach, and as she screamed aloud she saw the cracks of light round the curtains.

For a long frightening moment she had no idea where

she was, what country, what side of the world. Then she understood that she was awake in her bed at Rosevear, but the pain of hanging tightly on to her mule was still there, pulling and deepening, as if something inside her was being crushed. It went on and on squeezing until she groaned aloud, and as if the sound had been some sort of signal the pain at once began to lessen, the tightness relaxing all by itself. Then it was gone. Completely over. It felt heavenly, she thought, it was utter bliss, and she lay still for a few minutes.

Need a pee though. Dammit. She sat up, thought a quick prayer, tried the bedside light, thank you God, then sat up and looked about her at the shabby familiar room. Wardrobe closed, everything in order. Nothing to worry about at all, she told herself: that ache had been a sort of early pretend contraction, a thing called a Braxton Hicks. They were alright: they were in *The Mechanics of Birth*. They were normal.

Stay on, lights. Let me trust you, electric. She stood up slowly, waiting for the slight dizziness to pass, and then made her way haltingly along the corridor to the bathroom two doors down. Light still working, thank you thank you. Carefully – she was still unused to the bulk – she manoeuvred her great heft into position and while she peed raised her nightdress to have a quick check on the shingles. They were nearly all dried and shrivelled now, though each blister had left a tiny reddish circle behind it as a memento, spread all across the dome. And who would ever have believed it, that the svelte, the willowy Rae Grainger might one day sit on a lav and look down and see nothing but belly: knees right out of sight behind the bulge!

Human Zeppelin, she thought again as she got up. Airship rising. As she turned to pull the chain she noticed what lay in the toilet bowl. A splash of blood, was that? With difficulty she bent a little and peered more closely. The wad of paper had caught on the side. Not just blood, a smear of jelly-stuff, a tablespoonful of clear nasty goop. Where had that come from? That couldn't be what *The Mechanics of Birth* had called a show, could it?

As she puzzled the mule-ache began again, faint at first, then quickly tightening harder and harder, as if the pain had been practising while it was away, grown more skilful. She leant her hand against the cold tiled wall and waited for it to go away again, and after a while, after it had reached a point where she really didn't know if she could stand a second more of it without screaming, it did.

Those are pretty fancy Braxton Hickses, Rae thought, as she made her way back to bed, a little breathless. What a relief it was to lie down in the warm again! So cosy. Everything would be alright now, she thought. But just as she was drifting off to sleep again the mule-pain came back, stealthily at first. Braxton Hicks, Rae told herself as firmly as she could when it was over, but soon it was quite hard to go on not understanding what was happening to her.

Then impossible.

Lettie

She was fielding calls all morning. Darling. We must talk. When can we meet? This is absurd. You don't mean it. After a while she stopped replying, just let him go on and on. He was angry more than anything, she thought. And incredulous.

At one o' clock she dithered; generally she liked to do herself well at dinner time, something hot, two courses if she felt flush. But today it occurred to her that Philip knew exactly how she divided her working day, and that there were only so many places you could go to in this godforsaken hole. If he felt like it he could visit each one in turn until he found her. Suppose he made some career-destroying scene? Once or twice, over the phone, he'd sounded nuts enough for anything.

So she dined on a glass of water, hardly the first time, then nipped out between patients at four o'clock; the plan was, straight to North Street for one of their fine big pasties, an orange from the greengrocer's beside the chemist's below her rooms, then eat at the safety of her desk.

She was on her way back, the pasty wrapped up warm in her bag, when he fell into step beside her. She was in uniform, her hat on straight, professional, respectable. Still it was daylight, afternoon, in public, and thus unlike every other arrangement they had ever made before. But then this is not an arrangement at all, thought Lettie. Best to confront.

'Dr Heyward. Good afternoon.' She went on walking, noting one or two heads turning already, clocking doctor talking to nurse, wondering perhaps what interesting medical disaster might have struck whom.

'Lettie –' She saw that the seductive brim of his hat, the turn of his lapels, the fine heavy swing of his greatcoat, were all trying to signal to her, as before. But now her insides were unmoved. All they felt in collective reply was *Get lost*.

She addressed his shoulder: 'I have patients to see, Doctor.'

'I will walk with you, Miss Quick, if I may,' he answered, and at least he kept a respectable distance, and spoke low enough: 'You can't keep this up, Lettie.'

She made sure her face was neutral, her eyes lowered, the dutiful nurse considering the patient under discussion. 'I'm sure I can, Doctor,' she said.

All he had to do was raise his voice, she thought, and she and he were undone, it would instantly be all over the place that something fishy was going on. Maddening, when all she wanted now was to stop fishiness altogether, pretend none had ever occurred.

'I think we need some sort of conference, Sister Quick. This matter requires full discussion.' Now there was something purring in his tone; she saw that he had decided they were playing some kind of teasing erotic game. 'I'm afraid I must insist,' he said, licking his lips.

They turned the corner into the street she worked in.

'There's nothing to discuss,' she said, as sharply as she dared. As they reached the chemist's shop she slowed her pace, and they stopped and stood for a moment outside the window, the crowd still flowing round them.

'Usual place then,' he said. 'Usual time.' He took her arm in his hand, gripping it lightly just above the elbow. 'Eh? Eh, Lettie?'

She would not answer. She stood still, looking away, until at last he gave her arm a sharp downward twisting tug, and left her. Immediately she hurried away as if nothing had happened. Had anyone seen?

In her office she pulled off her coat, and rolled up her cotton sleeve. He had left his thumbprint; looking in the mirror beside the door she could make out each separate fingertip of rapidly darkening bruise on the back of her arm.

He didn't mean it, she thought. He surely hadn't *meant* to hurt her. It was just —

Just that he didn't know his own strength. Lettie looked up, met her reflection's eyes. The words had arrived as if by themselves, but they were not her own, they were her mother's.

Rosie had often spoken nostalgically of her early career on the stage. It had not lasted very long, for she had soon met her fate, Mr Bertram Quick, the celebrated London tenor: Bertie. 'We met, we loved, we parted, all too Quickly,' Rosie had said, rather too often for Lettie, whose own scarce memories of her father made her feel that the parting could hardly have come Quickly enough.

'I was the toast of the Alhambra!' Rosie had said, also fairly frequently, especially when she had a glass in her hand. She had been a dancer, wearing filmy costumes and feathers in her headdress, dancing with other lovely young girls while the music played and the gentlemen in the audience cheered and threw flowers. Lettie had been enchanted by this picture as a very little girl. If only her mother had kept one of the filmy dresses or a feather from one of the headdresses for her to see!

'Out a my way,' said Bertie to Lettie's mother, long ago. Rosie had sworn she was broke, but by chance – what could have made him think to look there? – he had come across the rent money hidden in the tea caddy, and expressed his feelings at this duplicity by breaking several of the delicate bones in her face; shoving her aside as he strode away afterwards he made her cut open the side of her head on the mantelpiece. It was a long way from the Alhambra.

'He didn't mean to, lovey,' said Rosie, dabbing at the blood in her hair, when he had gone. 'He don't know his own strength, see?'

It doesn't matter whether he meant to or not, thought Lettie now, rolling her sleeve down, the facts are written in bruises. As she buttoned her cuff the telephone rang again. What now, what did he think he could say to her now, to persuade her?

'Hello?'

'Oh, Lettie!' A woman's voice, urgent, even distraught, sounding somehow very close.

'Rae, is that you? You alright?'

'No! I'm – it's happening, the baby! The baby's – oh God – wait a minute, I've got to, oh bugger –'

'Rae?' A rattle, a series of muffled scraping noises.

'Where's –' But Lettie had forgotten the old woman's name. The pretend nurse. 'Rae. Rae, what's going on? Are you still at Rosevear?'

Rae's voice suddenly loud again, but cheerful now, excited: 'Course I am – sorry, that was an extra one, didn't expect that, gone now. Started this morning, woke me up! Bea wouldn't let me call you. Can you come now, though?'

Lettie's insides had instantly turned over with dread. She tried to soothe herself: It's all perfectly natural, young and healthy, no reason anything should go wrong. And if it does, if it does, I cope. I know what to do. I can manage. I call Pascoe.

But then she remembered Flo Withers, when Heyward had come instead. That was because he knew I was there, she told herself. He wouldn't care to muscle in on Esme Bright. On the other hand, the summons would be to grand old Rosevear House, and a mysterious but obviously moneyed patient. Might that be enough to pique his senior-partner interest?

Rae talking all this time, perhaps a little shrill. Lettie tuned in: '. . . so stern! Soon as I sit down she's on at me again, honestly, all those Rosevear corridors, I've walked *miles*, Lettie –'

Outside on the landing the top step creaked as the next patient arrived. 'Just a minute,' Lettie called, through the closed door. 'I can't come just yet,' she said into the receiver.

'When, then?'

'I'll catch the last train. Be there – what – sevenish.'

'But, darling, that's ages!'

'It'll be fine.' All perfectly natural, no reason anything

should go wrong, Lettie told herself again. Oh, to take the late-night London train instead!

'And Miss Whatshername, Norah? She still coming too?'

'If you don't mind –'

'Oh no,' said Rae, ''cause we've been making the most enormous steak and kidney pie you ever saw. I did the rolling out – in between pains, you know. Oh and we've got drink! We went down the cellars – yesterday – absolutely cobwebby – pre-war burgundy! D'you like burgundy?'

'Prefer champagne.'

'Oh, well in that case I'll nip back down then, and – oh Lord. Here it comes again, a big one – got to – you'll come soon, won't you, Lettie?'

'I'll be there. Rae? Just – everything's going to be fine. I'm coming.'

But Rae had hung up.

Purpose-built mansion flat, thought Lettie, putting the receiver down. Three bedrooms. Balcony, views of the river.

She got up and opened the door to welcome in the new patient, but there was no one there. Nerves, presumably; they often skedaddled, if you kept them waiting more than a minute or two. Then a sudden thought struck her, and she hurried back into her office and looked out of the little window, and there he was below her on the crowded pavement: Dr Heyward striding away in his dashing overcoat and tilted broad-brimmed hat. Had it been him making that quiet creak upon the landing outside her office? Instantly she was sure that it had. Spying on me now, the miserable git!

What had he heard? Nothing much, Lettie thought: me telling Rae I was coming soon. Being all reassuring, obviously to a patient. I didn't say where. Did I?

She thought back, and for a worrying moment was almost certain that she had named the safe house, just carelessly blabbed it. Then decided she wouldn't have; she hadn't needed to say it, so why would she have done so? I just don't do things like that, she told herself.

So that's alright then, thought Lettie, and presently there was more creaking from outside, and it really was the new patient this time. A particularly shy and embarrassed mother of three; requiring all Lettie's best careful attention. Soon she had forgotten Dr Heyward altogether.

Outside Rosevear House

It was a beautiful evening, starry, almost mild; daffodils showed here and there beneath hedges thick with blackthorn blossom.

Norah thought of remarking on its luxuriance, but decided not to; Lettie, she had seen straight away, as soon as she had come home and said in her flattest voice that today was the day, tonight the night, Lettie was not in a good mood. No, as a matter of fact, thought Norah, Lettie was in something of a temper.

'Oh, d'you know – I've never seen a birth before!' Norah had cried, clasping her hands together, and perhaps it was true that she had sounded *gushing*; but really I only meant, she thought now, working it out, that of the serious things there are to witness in this life so far I've only seen suffering, and death. That's what I meant.

'Oh, d'you know – I've never seen a birth before!'

'Well, you ain't gonna see it now,' Lettie had said, and brushed past her up the stairs to fetch her bag. On the landing she had stopped: 'Just the generator.'

'Well, yes –'

'Off in five minutes,' and Lettie marched into her bedroom, the door banging itself shut behind her.

Hoity-toity, said Mamma, materializing at Norah's side as she stood rebuffed on the landing, her hands still clasped.

Understandably anxious, Norah thought back. A great deal is at risk.

A great deal of money, said Mrs Thornby, raising one imaginary eyebrow. For lately it had occurred to Norah that dear Rae must perforce be paying for all the various ways in which she and Lettie intended to break the law. The London doctor Lettie was in league with would surely cost a great deal, signing all those false documents for the Register of Births. And somewhere Rae must be paying a poor woman to pretend that she was having a baby when she wasn't, to give Rae's baby a false name and false parentage; presumably wearing ever-larger cushions stuffed up her frock and complaining how her poor legs ached, a woman able to pretend without forgetting for months on end!

A woman with plenty of children already, Norah imagined. What was she planning on telling her friends, her neighbours, her family? That the baby had been stillborn, perhaps. Then she would have to pretend sorrow. The idea that somewhere in the country there was a woman carrying out this part of the scheme, probably not even knowing who it was she was thus obliging, was enough in itself to make you feel giddy, Norah thought. That there were people like that at all, really. Walking about looking normal, even respectable, perhaps! It made you look at every normal respectable-looking person you saw on the street with new eyes.

Some of them, perhaps even here in Silkhampton, might not be respectable at all; might be utter fakes!

*

380

Slow breaths, slow breaths, Lettie was telling herself as they reached the gates and turned at last into the gravel drive. One thing at a time. First there was this delivery, oh let it be straightforward, please God Almighty. Delivery and then delivery; no reason why any of that should go wrong. Well-laid plans. Very like the ones that had worked perfectly well before. And the money going in.

And soon, in reality at last, the long lease on the new purpose-built mansion flat with restaurant and central heating and uniformed lift attendants and garaging for the motorcar of her choice. Two bedrooms, three, with parquet flooring throughout. And a balcony. And views of the river.

Lettie had carefully cut the advertisement out of the newspaper, but there had been no need to, the words had stuck in her mind like the scraps of poetry some people – men especially, lovelorn ones – came out with now and then, usually in a special soppy poetry-voice. Nothing soppy about a mansion flat, Lettie told herself. Good solid furniture too, all bought at once so it matched. Carpets and curtains to keep out the weather. Her future self in the Vionnet Coat, idly dropping her keys *clang* into a brass bowl. Walking out to snuff the air on the balcony. At night the jewelled lights of London would sparkle all about her.

Then the gravel of the drive crunched underfoot and she remembered again. The mess she was in, the god-awful mess that she wasn't even alone with, not this time. Alone she could've ignored everything, that would have been the safest way. But not now, not like this. Would

Nesbit do as she was told? That was the question she just couldn't answer. I hardly know the woman, do I! Would she keep shtum long enough?

'Miss Quick – Lettie! I must talk to you – it's important!' Nesbit panting on the landing outside Lettie's office earlier that evening, her face white with strain. 'Please!'

'Well – alright then – I got to go really soon, though, got to catch a train –'

'It's the photograph.' Nesbit pushed her way in, shut the door, sat down. 'You know – the one you showed me. Have you still got it?'

'Course I have,' said Lettie sharply, sitting down too, though she was already late leaving, the last patient had taken far too long, and still gone home unconvinced.

'Where? Is it here? I need to see it.'

'Well, you can't,' said Lettie. 'It's not here. I got it – somewhere safe.'

'Can you get it then? Please – I just caught a glimpse, that time. When you had it with you, remember? I knew what it was. I didn't look at it – d'you see?'

'No. What you on about?'

Nesbit's face twisted. 'Her hair,' she said gaspingly. 'Dolly's hairstyle. In the picture. I didn't see it. Not properly. But I've been thinking and thinking about it. The glimpse. In your bag that time. See –' She leant forward, her voice low: 'I thought she stopped – you know, seeing him, seeing Dr Heyward. Years ago. That's what she told me. And the picture he showed me – remember, he showed me a horrible – like the one you – and he said he would –'

'I know, I know,' said Lettie unkindly, 'get on with it.'

Nesbit clearly trying to pull herself together: 'The one

he showed me was old,' she said. 'Dolly had her hair in a bun. But she'd had it shingled. Last summer, it was. So – that's what I can't remember, because I didn't look properly. I just woke up this morning and I didn't know – is the picture you – you came across, is it the same? Is her hair long or short? Because if I could see it I'd know. I could tell from her hair. Whether he took it years ago. Or – or not.'

'Oh. You mean –'

'If it was recent, your photograph, Dolly was lying. She was still his – his mistress. And the person she was meeting – on the cliff – it was him. And he had someone else, didn't he – he had *you*. And then she was dead. D'you see?'

Lettie had seen. She had thought too of his hand on her arm, leaving behind five clear statements of fact.

'Is it? Long or short?'

'I don't know. I'll have to look.'

'When? Now? I'll come with you – we can go straight to the police – I don't care what he says about me if –'

'No, no, not now!' said Lettie in alarm. 'I've – I've got an appointment, honestly, I can't get out of it – I'll check the photograph, I promise –'

'When?'

That was the mess, the new latest godawfulness. Because as soon as she got to her lodgings she had gone straight upstairs to check, ripped apart the laces of the blue armchair, yanked out the envelope, and held the horrible thing to the light: and seen Dolly Wainwright, woozily smiling, trussed like something on a butcher's slab, her neat blonde curls, as Lettie had been almost sure already, just covering her ears.

383

'We turn right here,' said Norah now, making Lettie jump.

'What?'

'We can't get in here, we have to go through the side. It's alright – I've got the key.'

Inside Rosevear House

For a long time the woodland around the lake was known as Rozver. Locals knew that it was an unlucky place where once something bad had happened. It was full of restless spirits, the common-enough notions of lone black dogs, haunted woods, and hooded spectral figures, but there were other more particular tales. On certain nights, for instance, travellers might hear a church bell tolling there, where no church stood; and the lake itself was full of dead people, who on All Hallows' Eve rose streaming from the water and walked hand-in-hand about the banks; anyone unlucky enough to catch sight of them would soon be dead themselves.

The wealthy Bristol merchant who bought the land in 1760 had delighted in these stories, which had so nicely depressed the asking price. The haunted woods spoilt the view so he had them felled. There was a surprising amount of rubbish found during the preliminary excavation work for the fine house he planned: unexpected lines of stone-work got in the way of his foundations, elsewhere the earth turned up by the workmen's spades was strangely stained, as if with rust; they found a great many fragments of tiling, and several indecipherable coins. Roman, said the local antiquary, and took them away, for his private collection.

The wealthy Bristol merchant had lived in his fine new

house for just over a year when he sickened and died. His doctors said it was his heart, but the locals knew better. Since then freehold and lease have changed hands many times; but never, it is claimed, for very long.

Now, at just after half past six in the morning, a car is coming, from a long way off. The faint drone of its engine rises and falls with the curving lanes, deepening as it nears. Now the headlights fleetingly turn the black hedges bright green again, colour travelling with sound, until at last the car rounds the nearest corner, its beams juddering on the lane's uneven surface, and roars up the incline towards the gateposts to pass them in a climax of noise and dazzle, and speed straight past them into the darkness round the next steep bend.

For perhaps another minute the sound of its engine goes on quickly dropping to drone, to distant hum.

A long silence: then, more gradually, the sound begins to return again. In a while the car, travelling much more slowly, reappears, nears the gateposts, slows right down, and stops, the engine still running. Several minutes pass. Then the driver slowly edges the car between the gateposts, steers it off the gravel drive on to the grass, and turns off the ignition. Now the car is not visible from the road at all, behind the high hedgerow.

He opens his door, climbs out, and stands leaning against the flank of his car, looking down the drive to where one corner of Rosevear House is just visible in dim black outline against the sky. The morning is so still that when he holds his breath he can hear the sound of wave meeting rock, at the cliffs two miles away across the fields. The bonnet gently ticks as it cools.

Dr Heyward has been out on a house-call. It was miles away in the opposite direction, but he is pretending to himself that Rosevear is on his way home, that he was just happening by when he passed it. When his foot seemed to press on the brake all by itself and the car slowed down and stopped he had sat still, his gloved hands on the wheel, wondering almost consciously what he was doing there, so far from home in the early morning. Then he told himself: I just felt like a drive. Nice night. I just felt like coming this way.

It could not be true, of course. It was a mistake, something after all only half heard through a closed door. It was certainly strange the way it fitted in with her recent behaviour, though. Not showing up. Putting the phone down on him. Little minx, he had thought, seeing how far she could push him, trying out her little claws, as women must. That had been all, surely?

It was impossible that she was there right now, at Rosevear, with another man. Completely out of the question, he told himself, but it was then that he had carefully backed the car into the gap in front of a five-bar gate, turned it round, and slowly driven back the way he had come, to Rosevear. And parked inside the gateway simply to make sure the lane was fully clear for other traffic. Farm wagons, and so on.

He stood there now in the chilly dark, his hands spread on the ticking bonnet. No lights on, that he could see. But the place was enormous, she – they – might be at the back. He felt curiously shaky inside, hollow, and was reminded of the time so long ago when he had sat waiting with the aeroplane, the Guardian Angel on the bench beside him. He had been brave then, and in reward for his virtue the Angel had saved his life.

He should go home, he thought. Go home, and leave her to it. She was a worthless whore anyway. What did he care? Nothing, he thought. Not a jot. Home, then. As he decided this he locked the car, slipped the keys into his pocket, and began to make his way slowly down the gravel drive, as quietly as he could.

Halfway towards the house he stepped sideways on to the grass. The place was so silent, in complete darkness; but then he saw something odd, a dim light passing all the way across the front ground floor, faintly illuminating first one window, then another, heading towards the service entrance at the side. He came to the central door, hidden in the deeper darkness of the portico. What was going on? As he hesitated he heard something. It seemed to be coming from his right, a sound like a door opening, a possibility of footsteps. Then the silence again.

The sky was a little lighter now. Holding his breath, he passed behind a stand of laurel bushes and came across a flagged path leading to an ordinary door. As he had half expected, it was standing open; someone, clearly, had just come out. Where was that person now? Could it have been Lettie's other man, the one she had spoken so coaxingly to on the telephone? 'I'll be there, Ray!' she had said. No getting away from that, after all.

Beyond the open door all was in darkness. Lettie was in there, he was sure of it now. He had been seeing pictures of her in his head all evening, ever since he had heard her promise this Ray that she would soon be with him. She was in that slippery white evening gown, the one whose satin straps had kept sliding off her shoulder. The thought of the evening dress particularly enraged him, that she should consider wearing it for someone else. She was in for a big surprise now, he thought. He had hunted her out. In her white satin. In flagrante delicto.

He stepped forward into the darkness, and presently his eyes adapted, and he saw he was in a long corridor. There was a faint smell of cooking, something meaty; it made him feel a little sick, even though it was so long since he had eaten. Because after all I am upset, he told himself. This whole miserable business has upset me a great deal.

The corridor reached a corner. Where to go now? He strained his ears for sound, and it seemed to him that for a moment he heard someone talking, a woman's voice, but a long way away, perhaps on another floor. Lettie! Where was she?

As he hesitated there came from somewhere above him a long bursting scream, a woman in extremis.

'Christ!'

Appalled, wildly excited, he ran forward, racing towards the sound as it came again, turning left deeper into the labyrinth along another corridor, the picture in his mind now of her being held against her will. He slid to a panting halt at the foot of a staircase. There was more light here, from windows high above. Where now?

He shouted: 'Lettie! Where are you? Lettie!'

He had so vividly seen her swooningly held captive in her white evening dress that her sudden appearance in uniform and apron on the landing above him, with a foetal stethoscope in one hand, was disconcerting. And deflating. For an instant he imagined that she had somehow gone and got changed, still trying to fool him.

'What the fuck you doing here?' she said.

He remembered everything at once: why he was here, what this paltry little tart had brought him to. He put a hand on the bannister, and began slowly to climb towards her, letting her know clearly enough what she was in for.

'I told you – we're through!'

He smiled at her, kept on coming.

'I know about you and Dolly!'

That startled him, for a moment. How? How did she know? He was aggrieved: 'That was a complete accident,' he said, and went up another step.

Oh delicious: she backed away. She said: 'What, you didn't mean to kill her?'

He looked quickly about him. There was someone else about, of course, the screamer. But not in earshot. And no one had any proof at all.

'It was simply to make her more comfortable,' he said, as he took another step forward. 'A little something so that I could – arrange her in – well, in some quite complicated poses. It was . . . one of the things we did together. I don't expect you to understand. Such specific pleasures. But she really wasn't meant to die. She just stopped breathing.'

'You give her too much!' Another step back.

'By accident. Yes. That may be so.' Another step forward.

'So you chucked her off the cliff – like a bit of ol' rubbish!'

Tiresomely emotive. 'What else could I do?'

The screamer, from somewhere to his left, set up another long wailing screech, and in the second Lettie turned towards the sound he leapt forward, and then he had her, gave her a good hard thump deep into the abdomen, of the kind that usually sorted Mrs Heyward out straight away, when she was having one of her funny turns. Lettie, wouldn't you know it, was made of sterner stuff, and even as she doubled up made – actually – quite a vicious little swipe at his ear with the stethoscope, of all things, but he blocked her wild sweep with ease, pulled the arm behind her back and jerked it upwards, hard; he heard, felt, something give. Most satisfactory: when he let go Lettie dropped flat, moaning, but went quiet after one or two sharp kicks to the back of the head, so nicely in range.

Then the lights all went on.

Sudden, blinding, and disorientating; he jerked aside, seeing someone, a man, Ray even, close beside him; then understood it was his own reflection in the big mirror on the side wall of the landing. He looked down at Lettie at his feet, and it crossed his mind that he might have killed her too.

Really, I simply cannot go through all that again, he thought. He had suffered so much when Dolly died. It had been inexplicable – he was sure he had given her no more than the usual dose. But the sheer practical difficulties of first dressing and then removing the body, stowing it in the boot of his car, driving to the usefully discreet spot where the lane neared the clifftop – the whole business had been such a frightful headache; though of course it had all worked out alright in the end.

On the other hand he was in charge again now, he told himself, Dr Heyward, obviously respectable hard-working everyday hero – good at a party, good in a shipwreck – Dr Heyward, who must of course be very careful now to get out of this particular pickle whatever the practical difficulties involved – when another long bellowing screech came from the closed bedroom door along the corridor, and it came to him at once that he recognized the sound.

It was a woman in labour, a woman about to give birth, near the very edge. He'd always hated the vile animal noise women made and had done everything in his power to shut them up, stop them – well, help them, of course. But he could hardly come to the rescue here. Could he?

What to do! Cloudily he looked about him. He must get out of here, no matter what was happening behind that closed door. It was nothing to do with him, anyway. Lettie Quick, she had been his business, and he had done her. Done for her, perhaps. Suppose she was alright, though? Suppose she came round, and turned spiteful, and went around saying things about him? When like a fool he'd talked about poor old Dolly and their games!

Could he do it cold, though – make sure of her? Decision. Decision *was* courage, most of the time, the War had shown him that. Do or die was true, always had been. Hadn't he successfully managed with Dolly, after all?

He bent over Lettie's body, thinking hopefully that she looked pretty dead already. But when he pulled her on to her back and put his fingers to her throat the pulse beat firmly enough. He had held her slender neck in his hands once before, during love-making; that moment came vividly back to him now, made him understand how unhappy he really felt about this unfortunate turn of events, because of course at heart he was a decent chap, a good man; but needs must, he told himself, and tightened his grip. One of her hands came feebly up, made a pathetic swat at him; she drummed her heels on the landing. He leant all his weight upon her, and the twisted face swiftly changed colour beneath him, white to greyish, blueish, poor little Lettie, he'd been so fond of her after all!

Then something unaccountable happened: there was a sharp gagging pain at the front of his own throat as the collar of his shirt abruptly tightened – all by itself, was his first astounded thought. He let go, put up his hands, encountered someone else's at the back of his neck, and then fell sideways, as the someone hauled him backwards by his own collar.

Ray, attacking him! He fought his way to his feet, Ray hanging on behind him, but squawking in his ear like a woman; he landed a good blow or two over his head and pulled himself free. Christ, it really was a woman! Big and tall, hands like a navvy's, he had time to think, before he thumped her hard in the face; she fell backwards into the corner, but staggered up again straight away, made another hopeless attempt, scrabbling at his shirtfront.

He knew her, he realized, she was local, familiar, not interesting; he dragged her wrists together and held them with one hand, cuffing her about the face with the other as he tried to work out what to do. He needed to check on Lettie, see if he'd dealt with her fully, and meanwhile as if he hadn't got enough to think about the woman in labour began screaming again, God, what a complete nightmare this all was, if only he had just gone home!

He yanked the tall woman forward, then quickly shoved her back again as hard as he could, neatly forcing her off-balance and giving her head a good bash against the mirror. But as she dropped he glimpsed something horrible over her shoulder: a skull-like face grinning with rage and hatred from the mirror's flecked depths, crinkled, malevolent, coming at him fast. He thought instantly of all the evil legends about this place, about the lake full of restless dead, shouted aloud with fear, half turned, felt a great thump on his chest, and remembered that he was right at the top of the stairs.

He should not have tapped Susan there, that had been a mistake, sorry Susie, you know I didn't mean it, lucky she didn't fall, she nearly had, and then she might have been badly hurt, but that was not going to happen to him, oh no, because his Angel was there, his Guardian Angel was there to flicker up a silken ghost and save him, and he was still waiting for it, still counting on it saving him, lifting him, still thinking No, this is wrong, this simply isn't meant to happen, as he began to fall, thinking it once more as he hit his head really hard on the fourth step down as he fell, and then again, on the sixth, and finally, terminally, on the stone floor at the bottom.

For an instant more he opened his eyes and saw. Oaken step. His own hand. A finger moving. Warmth beneath him. For an instant more.

There was a moment of silence then, before Rae began screaming again. The sound seemed to free Norah from something like a trance. She fell forward on to her knees, crawled towards Lettie's body.

'Lettie, darling – speak to me, Lettie, please!' She was shaking almost too much to speak; began weakly to cry from relief, as Lettie was already coming round, gasping, her throat strung purple with bruises. While Bea Givens picked up her skirts and nipped past them both, ran down the stairs as lightly as a girl, bent over the body there, took up the wrist, touched the neck, and looked up in triumph.

'He's a goner!' she said.

'What?'

'Ain't that a wonder, now!' said Mrs Givens. She seemed transfigured, light, glowing with happiness.

'But – you mean – he's *dead*? Oh God – what happened?'

'Fell all the way down,' breathed Mrs Givens. She clapped her hands: 'From the top to the bottom!'

Dizzily Norah turned away. Some part of her was stoutly telling herself not to worry, that none of this was in the least bit real. No, she had not just seen a man die, Lettie was not lying half strangled in her arms, and Mrs Givens had not just gone as mad as a hatter; it was nonsense to suggest that any one of these absurdly melodramatic things had happened, let alone all of them at once.

Lettie opened her eyes, looked at first vaguely and then sharply up at Norah.

'Oh, darling! Are you alright?'

'Christ's sake,' said Lettie, sounding irritated. 'Rae . . . fathead!'

'What?'

'Just go!' She made a weak struggling movement in Norah's arms. There was a short silence in Norah's head,

395

and then the words came to have meaning. Rae. Rae alone. Rae *screaming*.

'Right. Right then,' said Norah, though in someone else's voice, small and wobbly, and she put Lettie down – *Ow fuckit*, said Lettie – stepped past her and went into the strange darkness of Rae's room.

Rae silent now. No, making odd grunting noises.

'Rae?'

Norah had not been in this room before. She had done making tea, playing games of patience in the library, and dozing off. Though she had also done a fair amount of companionable walking up and down the corridors, hours ago, when Rae was still being herself, her gallant funny self.

'I thought you were supposed to lie down,' Norah had timidly said at one point.

'Did you? Why? I mean, what made you think so?'

'Well, I don't quite know.'

'Something you read, perhaps?'

'Maybe. Yes.'

'After all, I'm not ill, am I? Not a bit of it. Entirely natural business.'

'Of course.'

'So I'm much better off – ow. Just a minute. Stop here for a minute – oh –'

More than a minute, much more. Rae leaning against the wall, her eyes closed, while the pain rose, enforced itself, took her over, and slowly, oh, so slowly, retreated.

'Dickens, for instance,' she had said at last, raising her head.

'Oh, yes?'

'Everyone lies down in Dickens.'

'Do they? Shall we turn round now, go back?'

'Not yet. Except Oliver Twist's mum. She walks about. Well, she staggers about. In thunderstorms. Poor old love. I don't think that counts really, do you?' A snuffle of laughter.

But that sort of thing had stopped ages ago.

'Rae?'

In the brilliant light – the generated light, down to her, Norah Thornby, at least useful there for once – Rae lay almost unrecognizable in the wet tangle of the bed, her hair matted dankly to her head, her face white and sweating with effort, her eyes unseeing, her mouth slack. A groan broke from her. She was naked; and unbelievable, horror-film shocking, between her splayed helpless legs Norah saw someone else's sleek wet gummy head, face down, plethoric, dark blue.

'Oh my God!'

Rae's eyes, nearly all white, flickered. Her head turned towards Norah, she murmured: 'Help me.'

Norah fell out of the room, literally fell over on the threshold, scrambled to her feet, shouting for Bea Givens, 'Quick, quick!'

Bea climbing the stairs calmly brushing down her apron as if fresh from rolling pastry rather than committing murder; Norah clutching at her as she reached the landing, holding on to her for dear life.

Then they were both inside the room again, the terrible room with Rae dying in it, Bea on the edge of the bed,

Bea putting out one gnarled hand and feeling right inside Rae, pushing a finger in on top of the wet drowned head (Norah groaned aloud) saying –

'Now then, mother! Don't you push! He can't come out yet – hold her, Norah – you, that's it, hold her hand. Don't you push now, Ruthie my own, my lovely, don't you push!'

Norah kneeling on the other side of the bed.

'Hold my hand! Rae! Don't look, don't look!'

Bea Givens' finger in, two fingers, feeling, pushing, pulling; then something else came. Norah looked down, saw the something, a white jelly ribbon, tightly smearing over the head, a sliding Alice band of flesh, as Bea forced it down with her stiff old fingers; tight and then, suddenly, loose.

'There now!' said Bea. And Rae tensed all over – Norah felt it – and the miracle: the miracle happened right in front of her. The head turned, as if easily, and there was a heave, and then everything slid free at once, a surge of water with each slither of small rounded shoulder, then the back and curled-up legs, the feet, and suddenly another whole person was in the room with them, crying, the poor little thing, in full-throated baby anguish, and Bea was pulling a white cloth from the bodice of her dress, and shaking it into a square, and covering the baby's glistening perfection, the white jelly rope hanging below.

Bea held the child out to Rae who awoke and took it; she swept it in both her arms to her chest, the living sweet curl of it, and it went quiet instantly as if it knew her, as if it was recognizing her voice as she spoke to it, its little wet heavy head on her bosom, *Hello, oh, hello my darling!* Laughing with joy as she spoke to it, *Hello!*

'A fine boy,' said Mrs Givens.

Norah wept.

Norah wept; Bea exulted; Rae laughed, holding her boy; on the landing Lettie hauled herself upright, wincing, cursing under her breath.

None of them heard Barty calling.

It had almost been another record-breaking Out ride, that morning, the lightly frosted dawn so glorious, the golden smell of the two loaves still hot from the ovens, the birds all calling and a weasel slipping like an eel across his path as he turned into the gateposts; then he saw the car – the blue Austin Seven saloon – and stopped in a crunch of gravel.

Dr Heyward's car.

He had come for Rae, he thought at once. Rae Grainger. He had come to help her have her baby, or help her die.

Both.

His heart beating faster, he rode on towards the front of the house, which lay in its usual darkness, but as he drew nearer he thought he heard a door slam. Without clear thought he dismounted, wheeled the bike quietly over the grass towards the great front door, propped it against one of the columns of the portico and peered in through the narrow window to the left of the door.

Darkness. He put up his hands, blocked out the growing light all about him, and then he could see the grand central staircase ascending to the left, and the man,

Dr Heyward, slowly walking up, and the shadowy little figure on the landing at the top, a white apron glimmering in the half-light.

He saw what happened next like a film. Like a silent film, a Picture Palace special, soundless, almost, but for his own heartbeat. The doctor all menace, creepy, he was creeping up the stairs, and the woman – who *was* that? – she was frightened, she was backing away, like the heroine always did, but *no!* he said aloud, no, never in a film, the man never punched the woman or kicked her as she lay at his feet, *no*, said Barty, *no, no –*

Without thought of the bicycle propped against the pillar he ran as fast as he could along the front of the house, giving another cry of alarm as lights leapt into sudden brilliance beside him, tore up the path at the side and hurled himself at the kitchen door. Unlike every other single day in his life the door was locked. He wasted time bashing on it, kicking it, shouting as loudly as he could, *Nanna! Nanna! It's me, Barty, let me in!*

Then heard the distant chugging, and understood that someone must have turned on the generator. Nanna wouldn't touch that; who had, then?

'Nanna, open the door!' No answer. Think, Barty, think, he told himself. Other ways in. Her sitting-room window left open for the cat – could he still get through that one? Or was he too big now? He would have to get over the courtyard wall first. He looked about for something to drag into place to use as a ladder: flowerpot too small, water butt far too heavy –

And remembered: the days when he and his two Nannas had set off all together for Porthkerris with a picnic, locking the kitchen door and taking the big key with them; anyone else needing to get in while they were out always could, if they knew about the other key, the one kept hidden in the special place.

Was it still there, Nanna?

He ran along the uneven cinder path to the wooden water butt clear of the ground on its circle of bricks, and knelt, thrusting a hand between them. His fingertips touched chill steel; and then he was jumping to his feet, ha! the big black key in his hand.

Back to the door; opening it was a struggle, the lock was loose and fought him, until he remembered to pull the door tightly shut first; then at last the key turned, and he was sprinting as fast as he could along the main corridor, biffing the inner doors out of his way, right, left, tore into the hall, and nearly fell over something big stretched out near the bottom of the stairs, just managed not to fall over it by throwing himself sideways, landing hard on the marble.

It was a second or two before he understood what it was. The dead face was inches from his own. The eyes were nearly closed, the mouth drooped a little open. There was a little very dark blood spread out beneath the head.

Giving a yelp, Barty slid away on the marble, quick as he could, far as he could, and screwed himself up small, arms round bent knees. The dead man was Dr Heyward. Who had punched the woman minutes before. Who had saved Barty's life all those years ago. Who had at the same time killed his mother, Grace, if you believed both your Nannas.

Dr Heyward, giving with one hand, taking with the

other, as if he were divine! Dr Heyward, painfully lowering to the spirit if merely glimpsed in passing in the street: if you happened, that is, to be Barty Gilder. But Dr Heyward had been mortal all the time. Now he was dead. Had his Nanna somehow been part of this?

At this thought, so monstrous, so ridiculous, Barty was himself again. Though his legs trembled, he hauled himself upright holding on to the handle of the great door, breathing hard, trying to think. Dr Heyward had been going up these very stairs. It looked as if he had fallen down them; so who was up there now? Was his Nanna there, or Rae? And what had happened to the woman he had seen fall at the doctor's feet? There was no sign of her now.

His legs seemed to be working again so he made them walk upstairs. Past the mirror on the landing, past the box room he knew lay behind the first door. To this one, the best bedroom, in fact, where once long ago he had helped to dust the fat wooden faces of the cherubs carved into the mantelpiece. Rae Grainger's room, he thought now. Door firmly closed.

He made his hands into fists, the thumbs on the outside, banged hard on the door, and shouted in his deepest voice: 'Nanna! Nanna, are you there, are you alright?' Could he hear a faint scuffling within? At once he threw the door open and leapt inside.

Stopped dead, caught up at once in the almost palpable atmosphere of essential activities suspended, business hurriedly broken off. There was his Nanna, unhurt, startled at the bedside; but glorious, queenly, in the great four-poster itself, leaning back on a piled-up bank of pillows with a folded bundle of blanket cradled in her arms, was she. Not wearing much. Dizzily, he saw that. Not much at all. A sheet drawn as if hastily over her. Her white shoulders bare.

His Nanna said: 'Why – Barty!' But Rae Grainger raised her head from the folded blanket, and smiled at him.

'Hello, darling,' she said. Her hair was wild, curling in damp tendrils about her face. She looked utterly relaxed, even abandoned, lying back against her pillows. 'Come and see Baby!'

What? Now? What about Dr Heyward lying dead downstairs? What's going *on* here, have you called for an ambulance, are the police coming?

But as he opened his mouth his Nanna at once shut him up with a look, and he understood. Of course: Rae Grainger didn't know. Yet.

Not a word, said his Nanna's face.

'D'you think he looks like a Henry?' asked Rae Grainger. 'Come and see.'

Nearer the bed there was a funny smell, he thought. Vegetable. Unidentifiable. He saw the pearly glow of her skin; no one else he had ever seen had skin like that. He peered into the folded blanket, and saw the dark sticky head, a bit wet-looking like a glazed currant bun, and a cross fat little face very like the wooden mantelpiece cherubs, except that the real thing had all cheesy stuff smeared round its nose.

He could hardly bear to look at it what with one thing and another but then Rae turned her head and smiled like an angel right up into his eyes, and his heart melted away into dew, into a sweet pure heaviness. 'Isn't he beautiful!' she said.

He saw a blue vein in her breast, and for a second forgot everything, forgot the whole world and everything in it, but her.

'He's got to stay a secret.'

He was able to nod.

'You're the only man in the world who knows.'

His voice came out: 'You can trust me, miss.'

'I know I can.' She smiled up at him, straight into his eyes, and he was so lost in the clear blue of her own that he jumped when his Nanna came up and touched his arm.

'Off you go now. Good lad.'

Rae Grainger said: 'Goodbye then. Dearest Barty.'

Then he couldn't speak at all, only nod, though at the door he turned, and she lifted a hand from the baby and blew him a kiss of farewell; and he was out in the cold dark passage with his Nanna.

'Take the back stairs,' she said. There was something odd about her face, he thought, something distant. He tried to hold her gaze, but she looked away, her familiar hands twisting themselves together in front of her.

'I know about the doctor,' he said. 'I seen him. He's dead, Nanna.'

'He fell,' she said.

'How come?'

She made no answer. 'You should go,' she said. 'I got work to do.'

'You didn't – you didn't push him, did you, Nanna?'

'Me? No!' She spoke lightly, as if he had accused her of some trifle. '*I* dint do it!'

'Who did then?'

She looked about her quickly, then leant closer to whisper. ''Twas my sister.'

'What?'

She nodded, too many times. 'Mind you – I ain't saying I care! Glad to see the back of him, you know that. But my sister, she done it. She come out to help me. Right out of the mirror! And she throwed him down the stairs!'

'Oh,' said Barty.

She looked at him with all her usual kindness. 'You get off home now,' she went on cosily, as if she were the old Nanna. 'Your dad'll be waiting.'

'Alright then. Bye, Nanna.'

'You ain't – what's this? You ain't crying, are you? My lovely?'

'No – just got something in my eye.'

'You sure?'

'I'm fine, Nanna, honest.'

'Well now. You take care on that there bicycle,' she said, and then she went back inside the bedroom, and softly shut the door.

Joe Gilder

The van was a recent venture, cream, with removable shelves inside and JOSEPH GILDER MASTER BAKER painted in green on both sides. It was a risk, he was still paying for it, but it meant expansion, easier supplies, efficient and wider delivery: progress, in a word. Also a bread van was always buzzing about, stood to reason, and there was a nice woman out past Wooton whose husband took less interest in her than her neighbours did. Her name was Judith, and Joe had been drinking a lot less since he and she had come to their discreet but friendly arrangement.

Though he had noticed already how seldom he thought of her, except when he was actually on his way to see her.

Just inside the gateway at Rosevear now he stopped the van, and sat still for a moment in the driver's seat. Then he got out, leaving the engine running, and walked back along the drive. Were those tyre marks on the grass? Following them back, he came to a large rectangle of slightly flattened grass beside the hedge, as if a car had recently been parked there.

He drove on, and stopped the van again at the front of the house to peer into the window beside the great door, but there was nothing to see. He straightened; to his left the end of the lake shone blue in the morning sunshine, flat calm, a heron standing just visible in the shallows. It was very quiet but for birdsong: peaceful, he thought.

At the side entrance the door key stood in the lock, so he took it out and slipped it into his pocket. All seemed normal inside.

'Bea? Hello? Where are you, Bea?'

He could smell toast. He walked along the passage, came to the kitchen, hesitated for a moment, then knocked once and opened it.

'Hello, Joe,' said the strange woman inside. She was tall and nicely buxom; she had wild hair, a cut on her lip and the beginnings of a black eye. She looked a bit familiar, he had time to think, before he realized who she was.

'Miss Thornby – what happened to you?'

'Oh, it's nothing,' she said. 'I went dashing off for a quick look at the generator, fell flat on my face – all my own silly fault – the path's so uneven there. Would you like a cup of tea? There's a fresh pot.'

He stared at her. Of course, he thought, she worked for that mean old git Pender; but not at eight o' clock in the morning. She had to be in on all this too. Whatever it was, exactly.

'No, thanks,' he said. 'I want to talk to Bea – she alright? You seen her?'

'She's very well,' said Miss Thornby, making a move towards him, as if to head him off from the door. 'But she's rather busy at the moment. You know she has a – a special guest?'

He paused, so that she would take his meaning: 'So Barty told me,' he said.

That got to her right enough. 'Really?'

'Some woman having a baby, pretending not to. That right?'

'Ah – did he tell you who it is?'

'I don't care who it is. I care about my lad being mixed up in summat shady.'

'He isn't, Joe! Mixed up in it, I mean – honestly, I just asked him not to talk about it. That's all.' Sounding distressed; but he just couldn't tell whether she was lying or not. It was something to do with her classiness, he thought. He could never quite bring himself to believe the accent was real; her kind always sounded insincere.

'But you're mixed up in it?' he said.

'Yes, I am.' She pushed the hair out of her face with one hand. 'Is that why you're here, Joe? Have you called the police?'

'Why would I do that?'

'Because – well, because we're concealing a birth.'

'Not as bad as concealing a death, though, is it?' said Joe.

She went very still. Then: 'I suppose not,' she said. The black eye gave her a rakish, defiant look, he thought. He couldn't help but admire the cool way she was standing there pretending. Butter wouldn't melt, he thought.

His leg was aching, so he leant back against the door. 'I'll tell you what Bea Givens told my lad Barty this morning, shall I? He come very early with the bread, see. And Bea said that his Nanna Violet had come out of the mirror, and pushed Dr Heyward down the stairs.'

'Well, that's obviously quite mad,' said Miss Thornby briskly. 'In fact, the reason I'm here – apart from being able to start the generator – is because I was a little anxious about leaving our *guest* and Miss Quick, my tenant, she's the midwife making the arrangements – I don't think you've met her, have you? charming woman – I didn't quite like to leave them both here alone with Mrs Givens because, and I'm sorry to have to tell you this, Joe, but I recently came across her – Mrs Givens, I mean – talking to herself in the looking glass. Gossiping with her own reflection. It was rather alarming. Is that sort of behaviour usual, with her? Would you say?'

Joe shook his head, dismissing all this. 'Barty saw the body,' he said. 'The doctor, lying dead in the hall. At the foot of the stairs.'

'Oh. Did he.'

'Was it Bea did it?'

Miss Thornby's eyes shone with tears, but she did not let one fall. 'I believe it may have been all three of us,' she said. 'Lettie inadvertently: she was unconscious, lying at his feet. He'd been trying to strangle her, you see. I pulled him off. Then I think he tripped over her. I pulled on his coat; I was on the floor too, it was all I could reach. I don't know if that did anything. But – I'm sorry, Joe – Bea pushed him: I saw her do it.'

'So – this was at the top of the stairs?'

Miss Thornby nodded. 'And d'you know, she's right, in a way. There *is* a big mirror there, when you get to the top of the stairs, and I think when Bea ran towards us he saw her reflection, and it startled him. Put him off-balance already.'

'This was after the baby, then?'

'Oh, no, not at all, it was at the worst possible moment – poor R–' She stopped herself just in time. 'I mean, poor Mrs Wickham – the guest – was in the most dreadful pain and distress while we were struggling. In – in labour, you know.'

Joe was baffled. 'He hadn't seen her, then?'

'What? Oh, no, we didn't call him for her. We didn't call him at all – it was nothing to do with – Mrs Wickham. He was there because of Lettie. Miss Quick. Because she'd found out that he killed Dolly Wainwright.'

Joe shook his head again. 'You know,' he said, 'I think I'd like that cup of tea now, if you don't mind.' He limped to his usual chair, the one with the cushion, and sat down.

'Joe. Please,' said Miss Thornby. 'Are you going to call the police?'

He stared up at her across the table. 'No,' he said at last.

She drew a deep breath, sat down near him, and began mechanically to take off the tea cosy and fuss with the crockery ready on the table. 'Dolly was his mistress,' she said. 'She met him that night. Lettie said he used to give her drugs.' Her fingers fluttered above the china. 'To make her unconscious.'

'What would he do that for?'

'I really don't know. But he told Lettie it was an accident. That he gave her too much. And she died.'

'It were you that found her, weren't it, The Body on the Beach. It was him then – threw her over the cliff?'

'Apparently.' She pushed the milk jug towards him.

Joe thought for a moment. 'You heard him say all this?'

'No, I wasn't there then. I was doing the generator. That's how he got in, you see, I'd left the door open. But when I came back he was trying to strangle her. I couldn't even see who it was at first! And I thought she was dead –' at this her voice broke, and a tear finally slid from the bruised eye. Impatiently, she brushed it off with her hand. 'I tried to pull him away. He hit me. Then Bea came.

And he fell. I'm so sorry, Joe. That Barty saw – what he saw.'

'He'll get over it,' said Joe, stirring his tea. Though in truth the poor kid had been in a state.

'They'll think she's confessing, Dad. They'll hang her!'

'Of course they won't,' he'd said, trying to calm the child down. 'No chance. She's that old, she don't know what she's saying.'

'They'll take her away then, put her in Sedan!'

Joe had swallowed; the possibility of Sedan Cross had instantly occurred to him as well. It wasn't near anywhere, but everyone knew about it, one of those asylums with high walls all round it, and inhabitants rarely seen though sometimes heard keening or laughing when they were taken out now and then for little outings to the sea.

'Who's to say he didn't just fall?' he had said.

Barty had shed tears: '*Nanna* is!'

That was when he had decided that he had to see it all for himself, work out what to do.

'Bea Givens been taken poorly,' he had told Mrs Bettins, back at work if still pale as death; she'd been only too happy to take over for a while. Making sure he fired her replacement.

'He was worried,' Joe told Miss Thornby now, 'was Barty – about his Nanna being had up.' He stirred in more sugar. 'Why don't you just come clean, about him falling down the stairs? It were self-defence. That's allowed.'

'Far too late for that,' said Miss Thornby. 'Anyway, it was just too risky, you see. Mrs Wickham – she still has no idea what's happened, and if we'd gone to the police – well, she would be ruined, of course, it would all come out about the baby. We would all be questioned, perhaps arrested. And in fact Lettie was particularly anxious to avoid police involvement – I'm afraid she has no faith in the judiciary. There's only her word for it, you see, that Dr Heyward admitted being involved in Dolly's death. Well – there is evidence. A photograph apparently. Ah, an indecent one. It seems. That he took of her.'

'Of Dolly Wainwright?'

Miss Thornby nodded, eyes averted. 'Lettie – came by it. And she really doesn't want to use it. In court or anything: Dolly would be shamed before the world. Because of him.' She looked directly at him now. 'And of course all the time Bea has been insisting that her sister came out of the mirror and killed Dr Heyward on purpose, because – well, I'm sorry, Joe, but because of Grace.'

Before he could frame an answer the door opened, and Bea came in with a tray full of dirty crockery, the remains of someone's breakfast.

'Fast asleep already, both of 'em!' she said happily to Miss Thornby, and then saw Joe. 'Hello – what you doing here, you alright? Barty alright, is he?'

'He's fine. Worried about you, though. Told me you wasn't – quite yourself.'

'Barty said that?'

'He said lots a things.'

'Not like him,' she said, taking the tray to the sink and beginning to unload it. 'That's a lad knows how to keep his mouth shut.'

He stood up, went over to her. 'But do you, Bea?' She looked as old as the hills, he thought; no, she looked older than that. She'd been up all night, he remembered. Been

412

up all night, helped deliver a baby, killed a man, buried him somewhere. Had a right to look worn.

'Perhaps I weren't thinking straight, this morning.' She turned the hot tap on. 'Said some things I dint mean.'

'So – you ain't gonna say 'em again?'

'Tell him, no. Tell him, I'm myself again. Alright?'

'You Joe Gilder?' A voice from the door made him turn round. Another woman leant in the doorway, youngish, skinny and small, sliding her right arm into a makeshift sling. A silken scarf was tied carefully about her throat.

'This is Miss Quick, Joe,' said Norah.

She looked at him, and her pale eyes gave him rather a jolt.

'Barty was here earlier,' said Miss Thornby clearly, as if to the room at large. 'So Joe has come to see how we all are.'

'And how are we?' said Miss Quick, coming closer.

'In the pink,' he said. 'Far as I can see. Though I'm not looking too hard.'

'I'll show you out, Joe, shall I?' said Miss Thornby, after a short silence. 'We have so much to sort out, and Bea really should get some rest – and you, Lettie.'

They went to the side door, and he remembered to take the spare key out of his pocket.

'I'll come back at closing time,' he said, as he handed it over. 'Bring the lad over, see his Nanna.'

'What will you tell him?'

'Not to ask questions, maybe. So he won't get told any lies. I could give you a lift home afterwards, if you like. In the back a the van. Discreet. How'd that be?'

'Thank you, Joe.'

He looked over the van at the end of the lake, glinting in the strengthening sunshine, at the tyre tracks clearly leading towards it in the grass. He wondered how long they would last.

Perhaps she saw the direction of his gaze: 'Lettie said, it made a difference, Dolly being his mistress. Because she wouldn't ever hear a word against him. When, perhaps, she should have.'

'What d'you mean?' he said, though already he had understood her.

'It seems he wasn't nearly as good a doctor as he thought he was. For women anyway.'

He nodded. 'I see. Right. Right.' Then suddenly felt too breathless to speak at all.

'Joe?' Looking anxious.

'He was a hero in the War,' he told her, when he could. 'Heyward. You know that? Got medals for it, saving lives.'

'Some people are good at war,' said Miss Thornby. 'I am myself. As it turns out.' For the first time, she smiled at him. 'Ow,' she added, as the cut lip pained her.

Bea and Violet

When she was in her nightgown later that morning, with her hair brushed and in its plait, she sat for a little while at her table, the curtains drawn against the sunshine, dreaming of the past. So many children, so many babies; sometimes it was as if she could hear their voices still echoing along the corridors, playing outside in the cobbled yard, chanting the half-mad songs of childhood to skipping ropes and games of chase.

All so quiet now. How very weary she was! She ached in every joint. Especially the knees. Too much praying, long ago. Waste of good knee joints; God was there alright, she thought, but He wasn't listening, and never had been, in her opinion. Stiffly she got up and went to the tall cheval mirror on its stand, borrowed long before from the best bedroom.

She stood for a while, waiting. Would her sister still come, after such a night? Perhaps she was wore out too, she thought. What would it take out of you, to force your way through the glass from the other world into this one?

But soon enough she felt her sister's presence. She put out her right hand, and her sister raised her left, just as in the old days, when they had played this game in a different way. Their fingertips touched. Then the palms.

'He's dead and gone,' she said, and her sister echoed

her. Dead and gone! But we saved the little baby, Ruth's baby. Saved Ruth!

Mother would be pleased, said her sister. That we knew just what to do. They smiled into one another's eyes, for once in perfect accord. Good thing, said her sister, that Barty's a lad knows how to keep his mouth shut. He always was a good boy, she agreed.

She raised her other hand, and for a little while longer the two stood palm to palm, Beatrice and Violet, and just as always there was no way to tell them apart.

Norah

For a long time afterwards the events of that spring, that summer, seemed like a dream to Norah, coming back to her in odd snippets, sudden vivid catches, sounds, tastes. There was the final long strange journey with Lettie and the poor darling little baby, all the way to somewhere in London in the back of Joe Gilder's van.

Lettie talking him into it.

'How can I carry a baby with my arm in a sling? Be reasonable!'

Norah had carried him. It had been a painful and exquisite thing, to carry Henry in his soft bundle of blanket, actually hold him for the first and last time. A faint echo, it had occurred to her, of how Rae must have felt, earlier that day.

Bea had brought the big enamel bowl into the bedroom, and Norah had helped fill it with jugs of water from the bathroom, Rae slowly unwrapping the baby on the bed.

Norah had looked at him and seen the white jelly tube-thing draped limply across the stomach tied with string, the blood dried in traces on his head, the clean unused perfection of his body; the round tender little legs and between them the pink balls, with their neatly incised herringbone pattern, the dear little penis on top like a joke, or a toy. She had to smile; was this what had so frightened her, all these years? The power and potency of *this*?

Perhaps the adult article was meant to be a sort of joke too, she thought. One of God's more abstruse japes. He gives us these playthings, and we just get them all wrong.

In the warm water the baby had opened his eyes. It seemed to Norah that he looked up at Rae very intently, and with a certain discreet pleasure, as if he secretly had been hoping it was her all along.

Profoundly asleep, he lay warm in Norah's arms as she walked along beside Lettie to the taxi rank. Veiling pinned to her hat, to hide the black eye. There was an address to give and to forget. There was arriving under cover of darkness at a house standing in its own grounds – the private house also paid for by Rae, Norah had belatedly realized – and a long line of light as the woman – the very woman Norah had so perplexedly imagined, who had been remembering to pretend to be pregnant all this time – opened a door at the back of the house, and welcomed them in.

'Two of you?'

'I'm not here,' Norah had said.

Reporting back afterwards.

'No, she looked really nice. Honestly, Rae – quite pretty, respectable, about your age, but motherly-looking, two other children, sorry, two children. She said to tell you she would look after him as if he were her own. She used to be in an orchestra, she played the violin – that's good, somehow, isn't it? I thought so. We showed her the clothes, you know, the bees and violets, she said she understood. She's going to keep them safe. Her husband plays the 'cello. In the orchestra. But they have fallen on hard times.'

Not as hard as Rae's, perhaps.

'I thought it would be easy! Oh, Norah! What a fool I was!'

That comes back frequently; though not as often as the furious panting despatch of the minutes just after the baby's birth. They come back all the time. Perhaps because the whole desperate enterprise was Norah's idea.

Lettie still dizzy at the top of the stairs saying weakly, *Oh no, please, Norah, not the police, no!*, and herself beside the body making sure that the would-be murderer was murdered, looking up at her and saying – sounding quite cool, too, understanding already some of what lay ahead, thinking perhaps of poor Dolly, thinking perhaps of a sort of justice – *We get rid of him then.*

How we going to shift him? Weighs a ton, Lettie had said. *And what about his fucking car?*

We put him in his fucking car, Norah had said. Asking as if calmly: 'D'you know how to start it?'

Then faster and faster images, the two of them heaving at the body – how very heavy it was, how dead the face! – and finally managing to turn the body over. The jacket tucked up in a wedge underneath him, they had to wrench it free, and that had somehow hit home, made Norah sob with pity, because he had not felt the small everyday human discomfort of it, and never would again.

Groping in his pocket for the car keys. The two of them stumbling half-running up the drive. Lettie swearing in the driver's seat of the Austin Seven, trying to work out which lever to move first, Norah shouting half-remembered instructions through the open door. The tearing noises as Lettie trundled the car slowly down to the front, not daring to mess about with the gearstick. Suppose it stalled! Suppose it behaved like Mr Pender's Humber!

Norah running on ahead to wrestle open the great central door. Dragging him by the shoulders of his fine tweed coat over the smooth marble of the hall.

Lettie shouting: 'Wrap his head, Christ's sake, there's blood!'

Tearing off her own cardigan. The steps were the worst.

Lettie half falling out of the car drawn up as close as she could to the front steps, leaving both doors open so that Norah, by far the stronger of the two, and of course fully able-bodied, could run round and get in and haul the terrible weight of him from inside the car, dragging it across, leaving it half folded. Closing the passenger door on it.

Lettie squeezing herself in beside it to steer one-handed, bumping over the uneven but thank heaven dry grass all the way to the lake and a particular curve of the bank, the place Mr Pender believed to be a species of man-made jetty; the place where after a short shallow stony incline the water was suddenly deep, deeper, deepest.

Getting him upright. Hauling him more or less across, into the driver's seat. Unwinding the smeared cardigan. Opening the windows very slightly.

'Should we let the tyres down?'

'How the hell should I know?'

'Suppose it doesn't sink?'

Lettie saying: 'Then we're fucked.'

That meant, we swing for him; no jury would ever believe self-defence now. Sink or swing, thought Norah then, and goes on thinking it, from time to time, even though like a swan, graceful as a swan, the car rolled gently forward as soon as Norah let off the brake, and given the merest slightest push kept on rolling, slowly, so gallantly, she felt sorry for it, because from where she was standing she could not see him inside it, he had gone already, become a smudge of darkness she could barely glimpse through the little back window; and then the car came to the edge, instantly tipped forward, and in a huge rush of boiling bubbles sank entirely from sight.

Two hundred feet deep, says Mr Pender sometimes, in Norah's head, when the rising bubbles come back to her, vividly, noisily, as if all by themselves. Two hundred feet deep!

And she says back: In the crisis of my life, the Test of Tests, I took sovereignty over events. The bubbles rising is the price I have to pay.

In her dreams the doctor sits in the driver's seat, and turns his head in the water.

Barty

Bea Givens died in her sleep early in the autumn, in the cottage by the harbour wall; Minnie found her the next morning. The funeral was less impressive than Violet's. Far fewer followed the black-plumed horses taking Bea for her last journey through Silkhampton to St George's and the plot where her sister already lay; and the only shop that closed for the occasion was the bakery.

'Thought I'd give you summat,' said Joe, the next day, standing on the threshold of Barty's room with a large brown envelope in his hands. 'I were saving it for when you were grown up. But then I saw you were.'

'What is it?'

'Open it and see.'

The envelope was not sealed. It had slightly furry edges, from being kept so long. Barty looked inside, and then pulled out a thin stack of lined paper, all closely written on, in a small neat flowing script. He recognized the hand straight away. His mother's. His mother's best handwriting. Page after page of it. He looked up at his father.

'It's what she wrote,' said Joe. 'Three stories. That's all she had time for. There's one about – well, it's about being brown. Like she was. Another about the lad you were named for, the boy in the old picture at Rosevear.'

'She wrote stories? My mum did?'

'Is it so odd?'

I don't know, thought Barty. He looked at the pages in his hands. Her writing. Her thoughts. Not private. Not written for him or his dad.

'She used to say' – here his father closed his eyes, a man recalling exact phrasing '– that she wanted to finish something she could bear to show to Katherine Mansfield. You heard of her?'

Barty shook his head.

'She was a writer, died young. Not as young as your mother, of course. She wrote this.' He felt about in the pocket of his jacket, and brought out a small book. 'Here you go.'

Bliss.

'Have you read it?'

Joe nodded.

Really? thought Barty.

'Aye, well, I used to read more than I do now,' said Joe. 'Don't seem to have the time for it.'

You go to the pub instead, thought Barty. Aloud he said: 'What d'you reckon then?' He held up the book.

Joe smiled. 'Reckon your ma would a given her a run for her money.' Barty smiled back.

'Folk were always telling me to marry again when you were a little lad. Oh, find someone new. Just like that. As if you could just marry someone. As if there ever was a woman in the world could hold a candle to her.'

When he had gone, Barty saw a scrap of paper on the floor, which must have fallen unnoticed from the envelope as he pulled out the stories. It seemed to have been carefully torn from a small volume, with one slightly ragged edge, and was folded into four. He opened it, and gently smoothed it flat. At first he was disappointed, thought it was blank. But as he stared at it he saw the faint pencilled writing. His mother's hand, not her best this time, just her normal everyday script. It was a statement. A claim. A boast, he thought. It read:

I am the Silkhampton darkie.

Norah

Sometimes Norah could not sleep for seeing and hearing and feeling that one night's triumphs and calamities. Sometimes she lay awake picturing the agonizing exposures of the trial, the end of everything.

But the police went on not calling.

There was a tidal wave of gossip, of course; a wide variety of theories. Dr Heyward was missing, but who was to say why? He had gone off with another woman, lost his memory, been seen in army uniform taking the train to Exeter. His passport was missing. No, he had carried it with him always. He had mused about starting all over again somewhere new to several friends. He had written to a particular hospital in Salisbury, Southern Rhodesia. He had murdered Dolly Wainwright, and taken his own life out of guilt. He had never been himself since the war.

The only person who came to call was Miss Nesbit, in early June, a week or so after Lettie had worked her notice, handed over the Mothers' Clinic, and quietly left town. She was just passing, Miss Nesbit said. And wondered if Miss Thornby would be so good as to pass on a message to her erstwhile lodger Sister Quick.

'I would, of course,' Norah had said. 'But I'm afraid I have no idea where she is at the moment.' Which was perfectly true; the promised note had not yet arrived, and Norah had already begun to suspect that it never would.

Miss Nesbit ignored her. 'Lettie wanted to wait, you see, until he came back. Before we went to the police. That's what she said, anyway. But tell her, I won't say a word. So long as he never comes back at all. Tell her, that's fine by me.'

'I'm afraid I have no idea what you mean,' said Norah stoutly, and presently Miss Nesbit had nodded, and gone away again.

Eventually it became widely known that Dr Heyward had in fact been called out in the small hours to a respectable address far out on the coast road, and that he had stayed long enough to sign the death certificate, refused all offers of refreshment, and had been seen driving away in the direction of Silkhampton by four family members and a housemaid.

He had driven away, and kept on driving, it seemed, and no one had ever seen him again.

'Think of his wife,' Norah had said, apropos of nothing, as she and Lettie climbed on to the train home at Paddington, Rae's baby left behind at the secret address. 'Think of his poor little children. Awful not to know for sure. Don't you think?'

'Yes,' Lettie had said thoughtfully, 'awful not to know. On the other hand, look at this.' And in the privacy of their compartment she had gingerly rolled up the sleeve of her cardigan, to show Norah the fading fingertip bruises.

'He did that on the street. Because he was angry with me. He does that in public, what d'you think he does in private?'

'But you weren't married to him. Surely he would have more respect for his wife?'

The look Lettie gave her! Norah had almost laughed: 'Good heavens, Lettie – you looked just like Mamma then!'

Lettie ignored this. 'I reckon his missis is lying awake at night dreading him coming back,' she said. 'Maybe someone should send her a note. Unsigned, you know. *Don't you worry. He's a goner.* Or maybe just: *Make sure you clear out his darkroom.* What d'you think?'

Lettie in such pain all the time. The torn ligaments in her arm had not stopped her driving the car, helping lift his deadweight, his dead weight. Norah tearing up a pillowcase to make a sling. Her own black eye and cut lip, her stained cardigan stuffed into the furnace. Lettie flinching as she shone the torch into her eyes to check once more that the pupils were equal and reacting. 'We look as if we've been fighting in ditches,' Lettie had said, and that was when Norah had remembered that the Hon. Daphne Redwood, she who had taken tea with Florence Nightingale, had once described Lettie as a very good type of person, hard-working, used to roughing it, and absolutely above reproach.

'Spot on,' said Lettie, and both of them had burst out laughing, though not for long.

Sink or swing.

The bubbles rising.

A leave-taking. The evening of the day after they had taken the baby away. Rae all packed, waiting for the taxi hired from Exeter to take her to the pleasant hotel in Torquay where she planned to come down with the flu. Only Rae had wept, but then her face was already swollen with weeping. Silently she had embraced them all, one by one. Lettie, Norah, Bea.

A relief, really, when she had gone. Her ignorance of how wildly her best-paid plans had already gone agley had become such a burden; her constant plaintive anxieties about the baby rather hard to bear, given how close they all were to utter ruin.

Lettie turning to Bea Givens as the taxi's noisy engine rumbled slowly away up the drive. 'So. Any doctor been here lately?'

'No, ma'am,' said Bea obediently.

'Not Dr Heyward?'

'No, ma'am.'

'Nobody's sister chucked him down the stairs?'

'I'm sure I don't know what you mean, ma'am.'

'Just keep that up,' said Lettie. 'Hey. Tell you something: your sister. The one that didn't nip out a the mirror – was her name really Violet?'

'That's right. We was the Kitto twins. Her married Ned Dimond. Violet Dimond, she was.'

'I think she delivered me,' said Lettie. 'My mum. She was being discreet. You know. And I was born in Silkhampton. 1903 this was – she doing deliveries then?'

'She was,' said Bea, after some thought.

'There you go then. Must have been her, 'cause I was named after the midwife, see? Because she was so kind, my mum said. And her name was Rose, so we was both flowers.'

'Rose. She living yet, your mother?'

Lettie shook her head. 'No, long gone. Well – there it is. Keep quiet about her now though, alright? Your sister, I mean. And thanks, by the way. About the cord. Good job you were there.'

'Our mother learned us both,' said Bea.

'See you, then.' Lettie held out her good hand, and Bea shook it, but at the same time she put up her other hand and laid it in a delicate caress on Lettie's cheek.

'God bless, Violet,' she said.

The two of them climbing the stairs later that night at last, at home in the square, with the stone soldier outside the window. Rae in Torquay, the baby in another mother's arms, Bea packing her things for Porthkerris and the little cottage she owned there beside the harbour wall. Dr Heyward two hundred feet down at the wheel of his blue saloon.

'Peony Lewin,' said Norah suddenly, on the landing that night. 'I just remembered!'

'Who?'

'She lived at Rosevear. Really – a hundred years ago or thereabouts, and drowned herself in the lake. There were always lots of stories about it. People coming out of it and holding hands all round the banks. How it called you, that was another one: if you lived there long enough you'd start yearning to walk near the edge, and then something in the water would pull you right in.'

'It's just brackish. Makes people imagine things. That's all.'

'Mr Pender says it was the plague. That there was a village there once. Called Rozver. He thinks everyone died.'

Lettie said: 'You help me off with this?'

The sling's knot had tightened. They went into the bedroom so that Norah could use the bedside light to pick at it. She was still pulling it free when she noticed the framed photograph beside the lamp.

'Lettie! *You've* got it!'

'Got what?' said Lettie, wincing as she let the unsupported arm straighten.

'This! You took it from the Picture Palace! Honestly, Lettie – did you think Alice wouldn't notice?'

It was an odd little picture, pleasant enough, Norah thought, of children and a bandstand, and young people all in their best listening to the music. 'You stole it!' she said, exclaiming rather than accusing, but Lettie snatched it from her.

'It's mine,' she said fiercely.

'Alright then. It's yours. Oh, what is it, Lettie?'

Lettie sitting on the bed crying. Lettie who surely never cried. Who took risks and cared for no one. I'm regular army, she had said half seriously to Norah and Rae, as they paced the corridors of Rosevear together in those last sweet hours when Rae was still able to be gallant, when she said that the pain was hard to bear, but that she could bear it: then.

'I hope all this isn't putting you off, Norah,' Rae had said once.

'Well, it hardly matters if it does,' Norah had answered. 'I'm not going to marry anyway.'

'Who says? Mr Right might be just round the corner, or at any rate Mr Perfectly Adequate, we can none of us be too choosy. What about you, Lettie, do you want children yourself one day?'

And Lettie had answered no, that she preferred other women to have the babies, thank you very much, so long as it was as many or as few as they wanted. Because you two – you're like most people, you're just enlisted men, she said, but me – I'm regular army, a professional soldier. And a colonel at least. Or a general. This is in the other war, see? The endless one. The war that starts all wars: the war between men and women.

Rae laughing; until the next pain came.

'What is it, dearest?' said Norah now, as Lettie sat hunched over with the stolen photograph clutched to her chest, her poor thin shoulders shaking with sobs. 'Please – won't you tell me? Why are you crying?'

'It's me,' she had managed at last. 'Me, and my brothers.'

'You mean Freddie took your picture? This is *you*? Oh, Lettie!'

It was about the time our mother died, Lettie had said. Yes, she died in childbirth. I was eleven. And her old man. That git. He looks at me. That builder you told me about, Norah, you was right to be scared. You had your mum and dad and all, he took what he could get, but it wasn't much. My stepdad. That git: no one about at all, see? So I done a bunk. Cracked him one over the head when he was drunk and legged it. Went somewhere else for a bit. Just for a night or two! And when I go back. He's gone. Taken the kids, and gone. He was Irish, one a the neighbours says, he's gone back to Ireland, dunno where. But another one says Canada. And I looked and I looked. Wrote letters. Tried the police! They laughed. 'Cause I don't even know if that was his real name. He hadn't married Mum, he couldn't, he was married already. So I never see them again. My half-brothers. This is Wilf. That one's Joey. And he's Ezra. Their dad wasn't nice, Norah. He wouldn't a been nice to them. Little boys, they were. Mine.'

Barty

Sometimes when he was passing the church Barty dropped in to visit his Nannas. They had the stone up, to have the new name added, so for a while there was only a freshened heap of soil. There was a low stone wall to sit on while you thought about things.

Katherine Mansfield was good. She was in the library, he was racing through her. Stories his mother had not lived to read; he was reading them for her. He told himself he needed to know what his mother had been aiming for, before he could begin to find out if she'd got there. He had not dared try Grace Dimond's work. That was all back in the envelope, safe beneath his pillow.

The thought of reading her filled him for the moment with incoherent fear. Katherine Mansfield wasn't in *Bliss*. She was a voice, she was a sharp pin holding reality still for him to look at. His mother would not be in her stories, even though they had been copied out by her own hand. It was another complicated way of being absent.

He made sense of this by concluding that his dad had just been wrong to give him the stories in the first place. He wasn't grown-up enough at all. Though perhaps, he thought, that was partly because he missed his Nannas so much.

The two of them had been like the earth under his feet, he thought once. They had held him up and he had hardly ever noticed how. Now they were both gone he felt shaky all the time, wobbly. He could fall right through into nothingness any time.

The only consolation was in thinking about how cleverly they had managed things between them. And on their own, sometimes.

He had known straight away. Right from the start, before Nanna Violet's funeral. His dad had taken him to Rosevear to pay his last respects to her; he had not grasped until the last minute what that actually meant, that he would be led into the bedroom the sisters had shared, where now there lay a full coffin on a trestle.

He had been too appalled to understand how appalled he was, in the way of children, he thought now, from the distance of four years. Saying *No thank you* had not even occurred to him. But then before the horror happened and he was made to look into the box and see his own dear Nanna Vi all cold and dead inside, she had got up from the chair set at the narrow end of the coffin, and given him a very particular look, and he had realized that the Nanna in the coffin was his own dear Nanna Bea instead.

It had been a shock but then he had been shocked anyway; in the several days since the death he had suffered a great deal, trying to understand that the two of them could after all be divided. They had been together all his life, it was like having two legs, two eyes, two strong arms. Two Nannas. Even though they had also been one and the same.

For a second, standing beside the coffin, he had told himself that he must be wrong. Everyone knew that

Violet Dimond was dead. She had been Silkhampton's finest handywoman, and her careful hands had long ago brought hundreds of townsfolk into the world, as well as shown almost as many of them out of it. But everyone knew she was dead, leaving her sister Bea Givens to mourn.

But when he looked directly at his living Nanna she had nodded, then raised her hand, and briefly touched her lips with her forefinger. It had to be a secret, he saw, because no one else would understand. She wasn't simply pretending to be her own sister, pretending to be someone else: she was trying to be both of them. Two had been one, but now one must be two. How else could she bear it?

She had needed to tell very few lies; she had just let people assume things. She hadn't even meant to at first, she had told him once. She had gone to the telephone herself that terrible morning, told Dr Pascoe that her sister was dead; as she waited for him she had taken up Bea's own shawl for comfort, held it, folded it at last about her own shoulders. Coming in the doctor had seen it, and called her by her sister's name.

She had answered him in wondering gladness; had seen almost at once that she could in some ways seem to be a living woman called Bea Givens. It had been like bringing her back to life; and sure enough whenever she looked in a mirror it was Violet Dimond who had always looked back.

'Nanna's not herself,' he had told his father that terrible day when struggle and fear had clouded her mind, and made her imagine her twin could come out of the mirror where death had imprisoned her.

Now it almost made him smile.

Norah

In November Miss Pilbeam had a minor stroke, and immediately retired from office work. For a day or two the offices of Bagnold and Pender braced themselves for ruin, for chaos; but everything went on running as smoothly as before.

'Miss Pilbeam,' said Mr Pender to Norah, the following week, 'was irreplaceable. We shall not, therefore, attempt to replace her; but would you consider increasing your hours, Miss Thornby? To a full-time position? There will naturally be some small additional emolument.'

Norah managed not to laugh out loud, though for the rest of the day she and Annie vied with one another to get *small additional emolument* into general conversation. This extended joke somehow turned into a discussion of Annie's current difficulties with her landlady, an overbearing charmless individual who thought egg and bacon meant one rasher.

'The men always get two though!'

'Why don't you come and lodge with me?' Norah said, and there it was: done. Rubicon crossed. An official landlady. But one who would soon be able to afford a new boiler, given the small additional emolument. And a radio.

Her mother's room – Lettie's old room now – needed attention too. It had an exhausted look, Norah thought, looking at it one day near Christmas. It certainly wouldn't do as it was for someone as lively as Annie. How jolly it was that Annie had turned out such a film fan! They often went together now on a Thursday evening, and sometimes called in at the fish and chip shop on the way back, though Annie always had to rush, as the charmless landlady locked the doors at ten o'clock sharp.

I'll give you till ten past, Norah had told her.

How was Lettie, and where? Once there had been a postcard. From Sidmouth, of all places. She was having a nice rest. No forwarding address.

I miss you, Lettie, thought Norah, sitting on Lettie's bed. And have you heard the news? Did you even *see* last week's *Film Lover's Weekly*?

Fresh from an extended European tour, the beautiful Rae Grainger talks exclusively about her forthcoming feature film *The Last Dance*, her hopes for a smart move into studio production, and her plans to adopt a family of her own. Miss Grainger, orphaned herself in childhood, says: 'I know I'm only a single girl, but in this sad world there are so many motherless children just longing for a home of their own – and if I long in turn to give them one – why not?' And we say, why not indeed – carry on, Miss Grainger!!

He is still in the driver's seat. The gallant little car in the darkness at the bottom. Peony Lewin looks through the back window. He turns his head in the water.

Norah was roused from this reversal – for it was weeks now since it had shocked her quite so vividly – by the doorbell. She closed the door of Lettie's old room and went downstairs.

It was the postman, with a parcel. 'Thank you!' Before

the door was shut behind him she recognized Lettie's round childish hand. The parcel was soft. Cloth?

'Oh, Lettie,' said Norah aloud. She pulled at the brown paper. Inside, something folded into tissue, and a note in a rather grubby envelope.

Dear Norah,

The address is on the other side if you dont like it. They got lots of other good stuff your size, you want to go there sometime. Can you thro out that brown tweed thing its godawful its to old for you and Pete's sake get your hair done, tell them shoulder length bob. Yould look great

Lx

After reading the note twice and still failing to understand it, Norah took up the folded tissue parcel, and pulled it apart. It was full of dark-blue material, a soft heavy raw silk. She stood up, holding the stuff out, and it became a dress, full-skirted, plainly cut.

'What? Lettie, what is this?'

She picked up the note again, and this time it made sense. The address on the other side was in London; it was the place round the back of Victoria station, she thought, and with a pang heard Lettie say it, *rahnd the back a Victoria*, the adorable way she had twisted and elongated and made the language her own. As we paced the corridors. Up and down. Rae so gallant, bearing the pain. We foot soldiers, and General Lettie.

Holding up the dress again, she understood that it must be second-hand. Very nice material, of course, but Lettie,

I simply can't. Sorry. I can't bear to. She thought of the church hall after the jumble sales, the stale smell, and her own mother's wizened evening dresses. Cast-offs, ugh . . .

Wincingly she drew the material of the bodice nearer to her face, sniffed hard. Nothing. She tried again, this time holding the bodice directly to her nose. Nothing but the clean faint perfume of the beautiful silk itself. Norah let out a long sigh. It was a gift, and from dearest Lettie, and there was every chance she would never see her friend again: Lettie wouldn't busily keep in touch, she wasn't like that. Lettie shed people, lost them. It was a pattern with her, Norah thought, one that will hurt her, has probably already hurt her. But she won't change now, or perhaps she can't.

Back in Lettie's room Norah pulled off her cardigan, and the jumper beneath it, unhooked and unzipped her skirt – was it this, part of her dear old brown tweed costume, that Lettie meant? *To old for you*. Her blouse was venerable too, one of Miss Harlesden's best tailored efforts.

It's certainly quality, Lettie, Norah thought, as she unzipped the blue silk dress. She saw that the seams in the lining of the bodice were beautifully finished in a stiff complexity of curves. Someone had cut out most of the label sewn inside. She sniffed again, still nothing; and finally flung it into the air over her head, and wrestled it on. The zip was tricky, at the back. A struggle. Then she realized her breasts were not quite in the right place, and bent forward, jiggling herself inside the curving seams. There. Now would the zip pull?

Yes. Well, it certainly felt like a decent fit, was her first thought. That was Miss Harlesden's own formula. 'A very

439

decent fit, Miss Thornby!' Mamma turning away with a sigh from Norah's tall broad reflection in the long mirror, the *stalwart thumper*.

In the blue second-hand dress from the place Lettie knew round the back of Victoria station Norah edged sideways until she could see into that same long mirror.

'Oh!'

A stranger was looking back. The dress was perfectly modest; and yet it somehow made Norah look an entirely different shape. She had a waist, rather a trim one; the slight V of the neck somehow made her throat look milky, and as for her bosom!

'Crikey!' breathed Norah, turning sideways to see if she was imagining things, but no, the woman in the mirror had curves. The full skirt swung as she moved. The whole dress seemed to be saying something about her that no other dress had ever said, or even tried to say. It was saying, *Creamy*. It was saying, *Opulent*. Warmly, confidently, elegantly, it was saying, *Look. Look at me!*

Norah giggled with shock, couldn't help it, and the woman in the mirror laughed too, one broad capable hand raised to her lips. Suppose – quickly Norah turned away from the stranger in the room with her and began pulling at the hairgrips in her hair, three four five, the ties round the plaits, quick quick, she shook her hair out, pulled at it with her fingers, light fluffy colourless stuff it was, *such hopeless hair*, murmured Mamma, but Norah easily flicked her away, and went back again to the woman in blue.

Yes. Shoulder-length, Lettie?

She smoothed the wonderful heavyweight silk with her hands. It was the clever stitching inside, presumably, that held her so firmly, that seemed to push her in and out in various places. What a thing! She thought: Christmas soon. She thought: I must go out, I must go to a party, any party will do, just so that I can wear this dress. This dress has to be seen. This dress. Me.

And right at the back of her mind, as she began to look for a padded hanger to put the precious dress on, was another thought she could not quite look at yet. She would have her hair cut. She would wear this dress and if she had to starve to do it, she would hold off all other pleasures, even the cinema, anything, everything, so that she could take herself to the place round the back a Victoria station and see what else the world there could do for her, say for her.

Because if there was more, if there were other clothes that would do this, one day, fairly soon, perhaps, he would notice. She would try to make sure he noticed.

I wasn't really any sort of soldier in the great unwinnable war between men and women, Lettie; I was hiding behind the lines. I was a conchie. When all the time, as it turns out, I can be pretty good at war. I said so. To him.

Of course she was still her old self in some ways, virginal, shy. If he spoke to her she would blush the same old beetroot. But that wouldn't matter. She would feel all different inside. Anyway, he was a blusher himself, he would understand. Wouldn't you, Joe?

Dressed again, she was gathering up the brown paper to put it on the fire when she caught sight of the corner of a card tucked inside. She pulled it free, read both sides, then had to sit down, shaky with gladness and relief, because she had nearly missed it altogether. When she had read it several times more, she kissed it and slipped it for safe-keeping inside her bodice, and went downstairs humming.

The printed address card put Lettie right in the middle of Knightsbridge; you could practically walk there, thought Norah, from the back of Victoria station. And on the other side of the card, pencilled in Lettie's childish hand, was an invitation.

Norah, come and see me. Aint we sisters?

Acknowledgements

Warm thanks to Sheila McIlwraith, my first reader, for excellent editorial advice; and to my second reader, my dear sister-in-law Sue Sykes, for further advice and reassurance; to Juliet Annan at Penguin; and to Karen Whitlock, virtuoso copy-editor. I took a great deal of information from Ruth Hall's magisterial biography *Marie Stopes* (Virago, 1978) and from *Dear Dr Stopes*, a collection of letters also edited by Ruth Hall (Deutsch, 1978), and managed to read quite a lot of *Married Love* by Marie Stopes (Puttnam's, 1923, 11th edition)

I also used *George Muller and his Orphans* by Nancy Garton (Churchman Publishing, 1987), and several ideas about the early British cinema came from *Distorted Images* by Kenton Bamford (I. B. Tauris, 1999) and *British Film Studios* by Patrick Warren (B. T. Batsford, 1995).

There was a real British silent film called *Ain't We Sisters*, starring Betty Balfour, but my version is entirely imaginary as well as RP.

I paid a very useful visit to the Foundling Museum, London WC1, for information about early orphanages. And my thanks to the V&A Fashion Collection who years ago exhibited a highly desirable suit in dark-red wool by Edward Molyneux. It is presently in storage, but it was unforgettable; Lettie wears a fake version of it.

He just wanted a decent book to read ...

Not too much to ask, is it? It was in 1935 when Allen Lane, Managing Director of Bodley Head Publishers, stood on a platform at Exeter railway station looking for something good to read on his journey back to London. His choice was limited to popular magazines and poor-quality paperbacks – the same choice faced every day by the vast majority of readers, few of whom could afford hardbacks. Lane's disappointment and subsequent anger at the range of books generally available led him to found a company – and change the world.

'We believed in the existence in this country of a vast reading public for intelligent books at a low price, and staked everything on it'
Sir Allen Lane, 1902–1970, founder of Penguin Books

The quality paperback had arrived – and not just in bookshops. Lane was adamant that his Penguins should appear in chain stores and tobacconists, and should cost no more than a packet of cigarettes.

Reading habits (and cigarette prices) have changed since 1935, but Penguin still believes in publishing the best books for everybody to enjoy. We still believe that good design costs no more than bad design, and we still believe that quality books published passionately and responsibly make the world a better place.

So wherever you see the little bird – whether it's on a piece of prize-winning literary fiction or a celebrity autobiography, political tour de force or historical masterpiece, a serial-killer thriller, reference book, world classic or a piece of pure escapism – you can bet that it represents the very best that the genre has to offer.

Whatever you like to read – trust Penguin.

"Chelsea Cain's *One Kick* has all the bones of a great thriller—a high-octane story that will never let you catch your breath, non-stop action, and twists galore. But it's Kick Lannigan that really gives this stellar read its heart and soul. Kick is a total badass, armed and dangerous. But you'll cheer for her, worry about her—and you'll pray that, if you ever meet anyone like her, she'll be on your side. Chelsea Cain has outdone herself—and that's no small feat."

Lisa Unger, *New York Times* bestselling author of *In the Blood*

"Author Cain has done it again. *One Kick* is superb! From its breathtaking opening sequence, through scenes of wrenching evil and heart-clutching emotion to its roller coaster finale, this novel will stay with you for a long time. And what a heroine ... Here's hoping for more Kick Lannigan soon!"

Jeffery Deaver, *New York Times* bestselling author of *The Skin Collector*

"Prepare to read *One Kick* with your heart in your throat. Chelsea Cain has created a world that's both utterly exhilarating and emotionally rich. With Kick Lannigan as our protagonist—resilient yet broken, conflicted yet righteous—we find ourselves willing to go anywhere, even to the darkest places, knowing she'll protect us, surprise us, move us."

Megan Abbott, author of *The Fever* and *Dare Me*

"Kick Lannigan is my kind of heroine, brave and honorable, with a big gun and a sharp tongue. Chelsea Cain is at the top of her game here with crisp prose, rich characters, and breakneck pacing. Read the first chapter, and you'll be hooked."

Alafair Burke, author of *All Day and a Night* and *If You Were Here*

Also by Chelsea Cain

Let Me Go
Kill You Twice
The Night Season
Evil at Heart
Sweetheart
Heartsick